The Secret

G·K
Hall
&Cº.

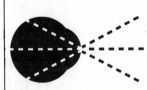

This Large Print Book carries the
Seal of Approval of N.A.V.H.

The Secret

Kat Martin

G.K. Hall & Co. • Waterville, Maine

Published in 2001 by arrangement with Zebra Books, an imprint of Kensington Publishing Corp.

G.K. Hall Large Print Romance Series.

The text of this Large Print edition is unabridged.
Other aspects of the book may vary from the original edition.

Set in 16 pt. Plantin by Myrna S. Raven.

Printed in the United States on permanent paper.

Library of Congress Cataloging-in-Publication Data

Martin, Kat.
    The secret / Kat Martin.
      p. cm.
    ISBN 0-7838-9534-8 (lg. print : hc : alk. paper)
    1. Single mothers — Fiction.   2. Montana — Fiction.
   3. Large type books.   I. Title.
   PS3563.A7246 S43 2001
    83′.54—dc21   2001026377

The Secret

Chapter One

Kate Rollins cast a nervous glance at the glowing red numbers on the digital clock on her desk. Ten P.M. She should have been home by six.

She darted a look at the tall corner windows of her seventh floor office. It was black as sin outside, no sign of a moon, any stars obliterated by the bleak gray overcast and the downtown LA smog. She didn't like working so late, being one of the last people to leave the building, didn't like the eerie sound of her own footsteps echoing down the empty marble-floored halls.

She didn't like walking out onto the dark, deserted sidewalk, especially not tonight. Not when she had promised her twelve-year-old son, David, she would take him to the new Schwarzenegger movie that was playing at the cinema. But her boss had called just before five and insisted on a change in the ad campaign she was presenting to Quaker Oats, one of her biggest clients, first thing in the morning.

Finished at last, Kate slid her ballpoint pen back in the top drawer of her desk and rolled back her chair. Determined to say goodnight to David before he fell asleep, she collected her leather briefcase, slung the strap of her Bally handbag over her shoulder, and headed for the bank of elevators waiting down the hall.

In the lobby, she waved to the deskman, said a quick goodnight to the security guard next to the revolving door, and walked out onto the sidewalk. The night was damp and still, the March air cold and sticky, heavy with the smell of car exhausts and throbbing with the distant blare of horns. Knowing the area could be dangerous this late, Kate nervously hoisted the strap of her bag a little higher on her shoulder and started walking down the sidewalk to the parking garage around the corner where her Lexus was waiting.

As she made the turn, she spotted the entrance down the block that descended into the garage. She had almost reached it when she heard a sound behind her, someone running down the sidewalk. More than one person, she realized, her pulse kicking up, beginning a worried beat inside her chest. Two young men, both wearing bomber-style leather jackets, Hispanic, perhaps, with their black hair and olive skin.

At the high-pitched squeal of tires, one of them glanced back over his shoulder, and she saw a low-slung, iridescent-green, '62 Chevy sliding on two wheels around the corner. The men caught up with her at the same instant the car roared up beside them.

A hand swung out the open window.

The stubby, blue-metal barrel of a pistol appeared.

Kate never heard the shot. Instead, as she started to run, she felt only a searing, white-hot pain in the side of her head, saw the ground rushing up to meet her, then her eyes rolled back and the world fell into darkness.

Chapter Two

The wail of the siren awakened her for an instant in the ambulance. Fifteen minutes later, Kate woke up on a fast-moving gurney, her head pounding in agony, the metallic smell of blood in her nostrils. Two green-gowned orderlies, shouting orders as they rushed her down a narrow white corridor, shoved the gurney through swinging double doors marked in bold red letters, SURGERY.

She couldn't guess how many hours had actually passed before she awakened what must have at least a full day later. She heard the steady beeping first, a comforting rhythm she latched onto, fixing her senses there, using it to ground herself.

She was lying on a narrow bed, chrome railings protectively locking her in, a plastic tube down her throat, a needle stuck into her arm, wires attached to her chest and forehead. She wore a white cotton nightgown that bunched around her legs, trapping them uncomfortably. She couldn't muster the strength to free them.

A faint hum entered her consciousness, and the whoosh of air rushing in and out of some machine. The pounding in her skull began again, swelling until it was nearly unbearable. A nurse arrived, plunged a syringe into the shunt in her vein and the pain began to recede. She slept for a while then awakened to the muted sound of voices, and distant, muzzy fragments of conversation.

". . . drive-by shooting . . ."

". . . still looking for the guys . . ."

". . . miracle she's still alive . . ."

Male and female voices, fading in and out, leaving snatches of conversation that began to fit together like the pieces of a puzzle. Eventually she heard enough, remembered enough, to know what had happened. To know that a shooting had occurred and a bullet had ripped into her head.

Technically, one of the doctors said, she'd been dead on the operating table for almost ten minutes. Her heart had completely stopped. Her breathing continued only by the mercy of a respirator. For a few brief moments, she was no longer a living human being.

Kate had no doubt it was true.

Lying in her narrow bed in the intensive care unit of Cedars-Sinai Hospital, with monitors beeping and needles stuck into her arms, Kate knew deep down inside, where her heart pounded erratically and the blood pumped with sluggish rhythm through her veins, that during those vital moments in surgery, everything in her existence, everything she had ever believed had drastically changed.

She concentrated on the hum of a nearby machine, the repetitive sound soothing in some way. She had read about such occurrences, when people died and were brought back to life. A *near-death experience,* it was called.

It had certainly been that and a whole lot more. Whatever it was called, it was something so profound, something so utterly amazing she would never, for the rest of her life, be able to forget it.

Kate closed her eyes and let the memory return, as crystal clear as it was during the time it had occurred. Lying on the operating table, she had heard the distant, muffled urgency in the voices of the doctors and nurses, felt the last few, erratic beats of her heart. Then her body suddenly shifted and she started drifting upward, floating away from the commotion below, toward the ceiling above her head. For a moment, she hovered there, confused, disoriented, looking down on the five green-gowned doctors and nurses working over the still form on the table. She could hear them very plainly.

"She's going into vee-fib!" someone shouted, the bleeping from the machine beside her changing to a steady hum.

"We're losing her!" one of the nurses called out.

"Get those paddles over here!"

She watched them a moment more, feeling so light, so completely unfettered.

Realizing that the person on the operating table must be she and if it were true, that she must be dead.

Then she started drifting upward again, right through the roof of the hospital, up above the city. The view was spectacular, like looking out the window of an airplane, seeing all the sparkling lights below.

If I'm dead, she remembered thinking, how can I possibly see? She started moving faster, faster, out into the darkness. It should have been cold, but it wasn't. A pleasant, warm nothingness surrounded her, comforted her, kept her from being afraid. The thick, penetrating blackness took the shape of a tunnel and she was drawn into it, carried upward through the darkness toward the tiny white pin-dot of light she could see at the end.

The light grew bigger, brighter, more pervading, until she was swallowed by it, became part of it. A soft, yellowish glow at first, it grew to the purest hue of sparkling white that she had ever seen.

My eyes should be hurting, she thought, but then she remembered that she had no eyes, had no real body. Looking down at herself, she could see the light streaming through her transparent form, glowing in every molecule of her being. She reached the end of the tunnel, came fully into the light, and a magnificent landscape appeared. Plants and flowers, shrubs and trees, in scarlet and emerald and purple, the purest, most vibrant colors that she had ever seen.

Shapes began to appear. They were people, she realized, recognizing her mother first among the others, looking younger than she had at thirty-four when she had been killed in the auto accident. Beautiful and vital and glowing with the same bright light that enveloped them all. She didn't see her father, but she hadn't seen him since she was two years old, and though she'd occasionally wondered if he might have passed away, she supposed he probably hadn't.

Other familiar faces appeared, her fourth grade teacher, Mrs. Reynolds, looking radiantly healthy and content; a young man who had worked with her at the office and died unexpectedly of a heart attack.

Another face appeared, a woman with the first hint of gray in the long, dark brown hair she wore pulled back in a bun, an attractive woman she had never seen but somehow looked familiar.

Her mother was smiling and though she didn't speak, Kate somehow knew her thoughts. *I love you. I miss you. I'm sorry I left you.*

More thoughts intruded, thoughts that compelled her to think about her life, about what was really important and what wasn't. About how the years sped past and you had to make the most of them.

One thought overrode all of the others. *It isn't time for you to be here. Someday you'll return, but not yet. Not yet.*

But she didn't want to leave, not now, not

when the light was pouring through her, filling her with joy, with a complete and utter rapture unlike anything she had ever known before. Not when every cell in her body sang with it, pulsed with it.

No! she thought, *I want to stay!* She reached toward her mother, tried to resist the pull, the feeling of being drawn backward, but she was powerless to stop it.

A last thought reached her, a disturbing thought that came from the lady who looked familiar but wasn't. She was trying to tell her something. It was important. Urgent. It was a dark thought about pain and fear, nothing like the warm, pleasant thoughts she had received from the others. Kate struggled to decipher what it was, but it was too late.

She was plummeting backward away from the light, hurtling through the tunnel, spinning through space, moving even faster than before. With a sharp wrenching pain, she slammed back into physical awareness. For an instant, she lay there stunned, feeling the steady pumping of her heart, the tingling of her skin. She was alive and breathing, her mind whirling with thoughts of what had just occurred.

Then the black void of unconsciousness engulfed her once again.

Days passed. Kate drifted in and out of consciousness. She stirred in her narrow bed in the ICU, the sound of a woman's voice pulling her from slumber. When she opened her eyes, she saw her best friend, Sally Peterson, standing next to the bed.

"You look like hell, kiddo. But then, I doubt anyone who gets shot in the head is going to look much better."

Kate felt the faint pull of a smile. Her throat felt scratchy when she tried to speak. "How long . . . how long have I been in here?"

"Four days. I came to see you yesterday. Do you remember?"

She thought for a moment and the memory surfaced. She smiled with a measure of relief. "Yes . . . I do."

"Good girl." Sally moved closer to the bed. She was taller than Kate, who stood just a little over five-foot-two. She had straight blond hair while Kate's was thick and curly and a deep dark red. A thirty-three-year-old divorcee who ate compulsively when she suffered from stress, Sally had put on twenty pounds in the five years they had been working together at Menger and Menger, the advertising agency where they were both employed. But she was bright and hard working, and the best friend Kate had ever had.

"They're going to move you into a regular room tomorrow," Sally told her. "The doctor says you're responding to the surgery very well. They say you're going to be as good as new and out of here sooner than you think."

"Yes . . . Dr. Carmichael . . . told me." Kate

moistened her dry lips. "Is David . . . ?"

"Your son is fine." Sally poured water into a paper cup and held it to her lips so she could drink. "Your husband is bringing him in to see you a little bit later this afternoon."

She rolled her eyes upward, toward the bandages covering all but her face. "Did they . . . shave my head?"

Sally laughed. "Ah — a note of vanity. She must be feeling better. Just a small circle above your left ear. They have such great techniques these days. Not like the old days."

Kate relaxed back against the pillow. It was silly to worry over something as trivial as the way she looked, but somehow she felt better knowing her appearance hadn't changed. It was perhaps the only thing about her that hadn't.

"Is there anything you need?" Sally asked. "Anything I can get for you?"

"Nothing I can . . . think of. But thanks for . . . coming."

Sally set the cup back down on the tray beside the bed, reached over and squeezed her hand. "I'll be back again tomorrow. That old bat, Mrs. Gibbons, will have my head if she thinks I'm tiring you too much."

Kate worked up a smile. Her eyes felt heavy. She let them slide closed. Her head ached and the bandages around it felt thick and uncomfortable. She heard Sally slip out of the room and the door softly close. As she drifted back to sleep, her mind returned to what had happened to her during the surgery, to the glorious place she had been, a place filled with light and joy. Kate wondered if the place might be heaven.

She thought of the familiar/unfamiliar lady and wondered who it might be. *What was she trying to tell me? What had she so desperately wanted me to know?*

Then she wondered if any of it had even really happened. Or if it were all some sort of fantastic dream. It didn't feel like a dream. Nothing she had ever experienced had ever felt more real.

As she drifted into a fitful sleep, Kate knew she wouldn't rest until she knew the truth.

Chapter Three

The April rains came. Not much as storms went, just a light spattering that barely moistened the earth, a little wind, then the sun popped out again. Kate heard the knock she had been expecting and hurried to the front door of her condo. She opened the door for Sally Peterson, who stood out in the hall.

"You ready to go?" Sally asked.

"Almost. Are you sure you don't mind driving me? I know it's a lot to ask."

"Don't be silly. I needed an excuse to get out of the office, anyway. If I had to sit there and listen to that obnoxious Bob Wilson bragging about another one of his conquests I would have put a gun to my head." Sally's eyes flashed toward Kate. "Sorry. I didn't mean —"

"It's all right," Kate said. "Hopefully, I'll be able to joke about it myself before too long." It was Friday, three weeks since the shooting. Sally was driving her to Westwood, to see a doctor named William Murray. Murray was renown for his work on NDE — the medical term for near-death experience.

"I hope I'm doing the right thing," Kate said, leading Sally into the kitchen where she had left her purse.

"You told me this has been bothering you.

You haven't been sleeping like you should. I have a feeling it's even worse than you're saying."

Kate sighed. "I can't get it out of my head. I dream about it at night. I think about the shooting, but mostly I think about the light and the people I saw. I need to understand what happened to me. I need to find out if it was real."

"Then you're doing exactly the right thing."

"What if this guy turns out to be some kind of quack?"

"You said he had a very good reputation. You got his name from the psychology department at UCLA, for heaven's sake. He can hardly be a quack."

"I suppose you're right. It's just that . . . This is really hard for me, Sally."

"I know it is. But maybe this guy will able to help you make some kind of sense of all this."

"God, I hope so." Kate walked into the kitchen. Like the rest of the condo, it was ultramodern in style, with stark white walls, black granite countertops, and expensive brushed-chrome appliances. It wasn't really her taste, but the location was one of the best in downtown LA and the price had been right. She had always meant to remodel. "Before we go, there's something I want to show you."

Sally sat down on one of the stools around the circular granite-topped breakfast table. "What is it?"

"Remember when I first told you about my experience? How I described the light and told you about seeing my mother and the others?"

"Telling me you saw your dead mother isn't something I'm inclined to forget."

Kate smiled. "Then you remember the other woman I mentioned, the one I didn't recognize but who somehow looked familiar."

"Yeah, what about her?"

"I was up in the attic the other day looking for some of my old high school yearbooks and I ran across a box of my mother's things I had stored up there. I forgot I even had them. I was only eighteen when she died. At the time, it was simply too painful for me to look at them. When I found them, I got to thinking . . . the woman I saw must be someone I know or am somehow connected with, since the others were all people I remembered. I thought maybe I'd find something in the box that would help me figure it out."

Sally stared at the yellowed, dog-eared photo Kate held in one hand. "Don't tell me you found a picture of the woman you saw in the light?"

Kate sat down at the table across from her, slid the faded, black and white photo in Sally's direction. "I know it's hard to believe. I found this in the driver's license compartment of my mother's wallet, wedged behind her license. I should have guessed who the woman was when I saw her, but I'd never met her, never seen even a picture of her, and I just didn't put it together."

Sally studied the faded photo. A woman and a young girl stood side by side. The younger woman, dressed in bell-bottom jeans and a long-sleeved turtleneck sweater, looked a lot like Kate, but she was more slenderly built. Her breasts were small and pointed, while Kate's were round and full, Kate's hips more curvy than slim. The woman's nose was straighter and not turned up at the end like Kate's.

"I assume the younger one is your mother," Sally said.

"That's right and the other woman — that's my grandmother, Nell Hart." In the photo, Nell looked about the same age as she was when she had appeared in the light, an attractive woman with a few streaks of gray in her thick, dark brown hair. "They look a lot alike, don't you think? That's the reason she seemed so familiar. When she died she would have been much older, but all the people appeared much younger there."

Sally glanced up from the photo, her expression full of disbelief. "You're telling me this is the woman you saw the night you were shot?"

"I remember her face as clearly as if she were standing here with us right now."

"And before that, you never knew what she looked like? You'd never even seen a photograph of her?"

Kate shook her head. "She and my mother

had a falling out when Mama was only sixteen. My mother rarely talked about her. She told me once that Nell kicked her out of the house when she found out Mama was pregnant. Apparently Nell didn't like my father. She said he was no good and forbade my mother to see him. My mother, of course, being my mother, immediately ran off and married him. Jack Lambert took off two years later, so in a way my grandmother was right. But Mama never went back to Montana, and she and my grandmother never saw each other again."

"Your mother lived in Montana?"

"She was born there, but I gather she couldn't wait to leave. Mama hated the country. She was a city girl through and through. She loved the nightlife . . . and the men. I guess that's why she ran away."

Sally stared down at the photo. "Your grandmother hasn't been dead all that long, has she? It seems like you mentioned something about an inheritance of some kind."

"She died about two months before the shooting. I didn't hear about it until three weeks after her death. I got a letter from a lawyer named Clifton Boggs. Boggs said Nell had left her property to me, since I was her only living relative. I have no idea how he knew where to find me. As far as I knew, Nell and my mother never made contact. At any rate, the estate isn't much. A farmhouse on eighty acres and a small cafe."

"Where exactly is it?"

"A little town called Lost Peak."

Sally grimaced as if Lost Peak, Montana must be the end of the earth. She set the photo back down on the table. "You said the woman in the light was trying to tell you something."

Kate nodded. "That's right. I think it was really important. I wish I knew what it was."

"I hate to say it, Kate, but odds are, you're never going to find out." The corners of her mouth tipped up. "At least not in this lifetime."

Kate flashed a smile of amusement. "Maybe not. At any rate, I need to talk to someone about it."

"And that's exactly what you're going to do." Shoving back her chair, Sally hauled herself to her feet. "Which means we'd better get going. You don't want to be late for your appointment."

As it was, even with the traffic, they arrived exactly on time. Sally parked her dark gray Mercury Sable at the curb, and they walked up Gayley Street to the doctor's office.

When they pushed through the door, Kate was pleasantly surprised to find the place had been decorated in the best possible taste. If Murray was a quack, he was a very successful one. Comfortable, gray leather sofas rested on plush burgundy carpet. A granite-topped coffee table sat in front of the sofa, a sign that read NO SMOKING perched next to a stack of carefully chosen magazines.

To Kate's relief, she only had to wait ten minutes before the nurse called her in.

"Kate Rollins?" She nodded.

"I'll be right out here if you need me," Sally said as Kate walked past her into the wood-paneled office and closed the door.

"Thank you for seeing me on such short notice, Dr. Murray."

"I'm glad we found a way to fit you in." He was a slender man in his mid-forties with short, dark brown hair and hazel eyes. His smile seemed sincere as he poured her a cup of coffee and seated her in an overstuffed chair in front of his desk.

"All right, Mrs. Rollins, why don't we just begin? I read about the shooting several weeks back. Anyone who watched the news was aware of it — and that it was a miracle you survived. I also saw a recent article in the *Times*."

Kate inwardly grimaced at the reminder of the article that had been written about her "trip to The Other Side."

"Since my specialty is the study of NDEs," the doctor went on, "I presume that's why you're here. If that is the case, the easiest way to start is simply for you to tell me about it."

Kate took a steadying breath, her fingers wrapped securely around the coffee mug she held in her lap. For the next half hour, she told Dr. Murray what had happened the night she was shot.

"It isn't something I can simply put behind

25

me," she said when she was finished. "It changed me, Dr. Murray. It changed everything I believed. The doctors at the hospital say it was only an hallucination, but I don't think that's true."

She told him about the photo she had found and that her grandmother had turned out to be the woman in the light.

"Surely what happened must be real. There's no way I could have known her, yet I recognized her immediately as the woman I had seen."

The doctor sat forward in his chair, his elbows propped on his desk. "Believe it or not, your story is fairly typical — and during the course of my research, I've heard nearly five hundred of them. Most people don't realize how often this phenomenon occurs. The Gallup Poll reported thirteen million people claim to have had a near-death experience."

Kate's eyes widened. "Thirteen million?"

"That's right. And I know what happened to you after you told people about it. There were those who looked at you as their last, desperate hope while others saw you as the nearest thing to Satan. The truth is you are simply one of millions who have taken some sort of unfathomable journey. I like to think of it as kind of an enlightenment, if you would."

Kate ran a finger around the rim of her cup as she considered the doctor's words. "I've been reading everything I can find on the subject. From what I gather, the medical community isn't convinced it's real. They've come up with a number of theories to explain it. I read one that proposed it was simply the result of a dying brain."

He nodded. "There are those who are convinced that in an NDE, the dying person isn't traveling toward a beautiful afterlife; they believe the neurotransmitters in the brain are simply shutting down, creating a lovely illusion. The pattern, they believe, is the same for anyone facing death. The question is, if that is so, why would the brain be programmed that way in the first place? And it doesn't explain the small percentage of people who have a negative experience."

"I gather there are some who do."

"That's right. Mostly people carrying some sort of guilt, or are, perhaps, attempting suicide. What happens to them is almost exactly the opposite of the joyous emotions you felt."

"I've read other explanations."

"The temporal lobe theory, perhaps?"

She nodded.

"It's true that some features of a typical NDE can occur in certain forms of epilepsy associated with damage to the temporal lobe of the brain. Proponents of the theory believe the stress of being near death can stimulate the lobe. But the usual results are sadness, fear, and feelings of aloneness. Not what you've described at all."

27

"What about lack of oxygen? That's what my doctor told me it was."

"Yes, well, did your doctor happen to mention that the hallucinations produced by an oxygen-starved brain are extremely chaotic, more like psychotic delusions? They're completely different from the tranquility, peace, and calm you encountered."

"So you believe what happened to me was real."

"It doesn't matter what I believe. What matters is what you believe."

"It felt real. It still does. I wish I knew for sure." Kate looked off toward the window. The clouds were all gone. Another sunny day in California. She wondered what the weather was like in Lost Peak, Montana. "I keep thinking about the people I saw . . . thinking about my grandmother. If it really happened, whatever she wanted me to know seemed crucial in some way."

"People have returned from The Other Side with all sorts of messages — everything from warnings of impending global disaster to personal communications from loved ones. Perhaps she wanted you to do something for her. Perhaps she wanted to warn you."

"Warn me?" A little shiver ran down Kate's spine. "Ever since this happened, I've been trying to recall the details of those last few moments. The feeling I got from her seemed so cryptic, and somehow very frightening, out of synch with everything else that was happening. This may sound crazy, Dr. Murray, but I keep thinking it had something to do with her death. I don't exactly know why I feel that way, but I do."

The doctor drummed his fingers on the desk. "It's possible, I suppose. As I said, I've encountered any number of different occurrences."

Kate sighed and shook her head. "I never wanted any of this. I wish I could just forget it, but I can't."

"In time, the memory will begin to fade. I can't promise you it will completely disappear. Occurrences such as these are often life-changing. People come away with a completely new perspective. They see things more clearly, understand what is important in life. If you're lucky, perhaps that will happen to you."

Kate mulled that over, thinking that in a number of ways it already had.

She stood up from her chair. "Thank you, Dr. Murray. You've been extremely helpful. I'm glad I came."

"If you ever need me . . . if there's anything else I can do, don't hesitate to call."

"I won't." But she didn't think it would happen. Speaking to the doctor had helped to clarify her jumbled, uncertain thoughts.

Now that she had a better understanding of what she had experienced, Kate had other, more important things to do.

Chapter Four

Two months passed. Two months, and not a day went by that Kate didn't think about the night she had died. As Dr. Murray had said, in those few brief moments, she had seen herself, seen her life in a way she never had before. She had discovered what was important, and been given a second chance to do something about it.

Standing in the entry of her condominium, Kate pulled a soft gray cashmere cardigan over her suit, and eased her curly, shoulder-length dark red hair out from under the collar.

"You're leaving?" She couldn't miss the anger in her husband Tommy's voice. "I don't believe it. I thought last Sunday was a fluke."

"I told you I was taking David. I asked you to come with us, but you said that you were too busy."

"I *am* too busy. Too damned busy to waste half the day sitting on a pew in some damnable church." At the age of thirty-two, three years older than Kate, Tommy Rollins was tall and thin, with angular features and straight brown hair that nearly reached his shoulders. They'd been married since she was seventeen, when Tommy was the lead singer in the Marauders, a local rock band, and Kate was head cheerleader, pregnant after the second time they made love in the back seat of Tommy's old Ford coupe.

She'd thought then that she loved him. Now, she wondered how she ever could have been that stupid.

"I tell you, Kate, I think that bullet did more to your brain than punch a hole in it. You've been acting half crazy ever since the shooting."

"I don't see how taking my son to church on a Sunday morning is acting half crazy."

"Oh yeah? Well, it isn't just church and you know it. You used to like to party. Man, when we were first married, you could outdrink half the guys in the band. Now you hardly even drink a glass of wine. You're really turning into a bore, Kate. You know that?"

"You're right, Tommy — I don't drink like I did when I was twenty. I have an important job with a ton of responsibilities — something you couldn't begin to understand — and I have a twelve-year-old son to take care of."

"Yeah, well, what about those crazy books you've been reading?" Tommy sauntered past his electric guitar case, open and sitting on the camelback sofa she had saved for months to buy after they'd moved into the condo. A rush of air scattered the pages of the latest song he'd been trying to write. He stopped at the pile of books neatly stacked on the small, antique French writing desk in the corner.

"Look at this crap." He held up the leather-bound volume that sat on the top. *"Beyond the*

Light: Finding the Spirit Within." He grabbed another. "*Life After Life.* Here's a hot one — *Return from Tomorrow: Is There Life After Dying?* What a load of bullshit!" With an angry grunt, he swept his arm across the desk, sending the whole stack crashing to the floor.

Kate bristled but made no move. The books might not have the answers to all of her questions, and she might not find the comfort she sought in church, which up until now she had rarely attended, but she had to explore every possibility. Considering what she had experienced, she was doing the best she could.

"I don't like it, Kate. I didn't marry some religious fanatic and I don't want to be married to one now."

Kate glanced down the hall, checking to be sure that David was still in his room. "I'm hardly a religious fanatic. But I have to admit you have a point. Maybe you haven't changed all that much in the past twelve years, but I'm a different woman than I was at seventeen. Our marriage was a mistake from the beginning and both of us know it. For David's sake, I've stayed when I should have gone. I've put up with your infidelity. I've ignored the tantrums you call your artistic temperament. I've supported you, hoping you would finally grow up and make something out of yourself. But as of this minute, Tommy, I'm through with all that."

She drew in a steadying breath and plunged ahead, determined to take the course of action she should have embarked on long before this. "I didn't mean to do it this way, but the fact is, I want a divorce. I should have gotten one years ago, but I wanted David to have a father. Since you've never really been there for him anyway, I don't really see that it matters anymore."

Tommy's face turned the shade of a pickled beet. He opened his mouth to argue, but the sound of his son's voice cut him off.

"Mom?" David stepped out into the hallway. Seeing the worried expression on his face, Kate's chest tightened. She hadn't meant for him to hear. She would call back the words if she could, but it was too late.

She forced herself to smile. "It's all right, honey. Your father and I have some things to work out, that's all."

"Yeah," her husband said snidely, "like getting a divorce — which, by the way, is fine with me."

David's thin face turned pale. "What are you guys talking about? You aren't really getting divorced, are you?"

The worry in his eyes made her throat close up. With his slender build, hazel eyes, and straight brown hair, David was a smaller version of his father. But unlike Tommy, her son was sensitive and vulnerable. He had always been shy and a little withdrawn, exactly the opposite of Tommy, who was at his best when he was belting out a hard rock tune in front of a hundred people. Kate didn't want to see David hurt and yet, now that she had finally taken the first step, she knew she had done the right thing.

She walked toward her son and leaned over to hug him, but David turned away. Kate's heart squeezed painfully. Lately, he'd been growing more and more distant, arguing all the time, getting bad marks in school. Last week he had even been sent to the principal's office. Kate prayed the divorce would make things better not worse.

"We'll talk about all this after church, okay?" Pulling his navy-blue jacket off a hanger on the back of a chair, she held it out for him to put on. "We'd better get going. We're going to be late if we don't hurry."

David didn't budge. "I'm not going to some stupid ol' church. I'm staying here with Dad."

Tommy flashed a look of triumph. "That's right, kid." He turned a mocking glare on Kate. "You go on to your damnable church, Kate. David and I are staying right here. There's a ball game on. That's better than listening to some stupid preacher yapping about hell and damnation."

Anger made her cheeks go hot, but Kate knew better than to argue. She had already crossed one line — a very important one — and she didn't intend to go back. The next step would take careful thought and planning, but she was determined.

Everything had changed the day of the shooting. For the last few years, she had simply existed, trapped in a rotten marriage, catering to a husband she merely tolerated, working twelve hours a day in a job that left no time for her son.

In a single instant of clarity, she had seen the years of her life slipping away, seen the damage she was doing to the child who needed her so badly — and found the courage to do something about it.

Tomorrow she would start the divorce proceedings.

The day after that, she would begin the rest of the changes she planned to make.

It would take a little time to prepare, to make the necessary arrangements, but Kate believed she owed it to herself — owed it to her son — to make something out of the life that had been returned to her the night that she had died.

The days seemed to drag, but a month had passed since his mom had filed for divorce and they had moved out of the condo into a small apartment. Tonight it was clear and cool, the Monday night traffic lighter than usual.

David Rollins' jeans made a faint brushing sound as he eased the stairwell door closed and crept toward the pillar in the lobby. His tennis shoes squeaked on the polished floor and he stopped dead-still, praying the security guard hadn't heard.

His heart was pumping, his palms felt clammy. He plastered himself against the pillar and waited for the guard to get up and make his rounds as he did each night, David had discovered, around ten P.M.

As soon as the man was out of his chair and starting down the hall, David made a break for the door, shoving it open and racing out onto the Hill Street sidewalk. It was a school night, past time he should be getting ready for bed, but his friends, Tobias Piero and Artie Gabrielli, were waiting. Artie had his hands stuffed into the back pockets of his baggy jeans. Toby had his bill cap on backward.

"Hey, man," Toby said, "we thought you might not get out of the house. You know how your old lady is about stayin' home on a school night."

"Yeah, well, she thinks I'm asleep in my room. I figure what she doesn't know won't hurt her."

Artie just laughed. "I knew you wouldn't let us down. Toby's scored some weed, man. Tonight we're gonna howl."

David had only smoked marijuana a couple of times, and all it had done was make him dizzy. But Toby and Artie thought it was cool, so he guessed he would try it again. It was a warm, dark night, with only a sliver of moon, but it was too smoggy to see any stars.

The three of them started off down the block, talking about Mr. Brimmer, the history teacher who had kept Toby after school for writing the F-word on the blackboard in big chalk letters, but they hadn't gotten more than a couple of feet when a fat guy in a windbreaker, jeans, and Reeboks walked up.

He slowed his pace to match David's. "Hey, you're Kate Rollins' kid, aren't you?"

David looked up at him warily. "Who wants to know?"

"Listen, kid, I'm Chet Munson with the *National Monitor*. We'd like to do a story on your mom. If you'd be willing to cooperate, it would make you a nice chunk of change."

"Hey, man, cool!" Toby said.

"Bullshit," said David. "You leave my mother alone." He set his jaw, hoping he looked tough, but inside he was feeling a little bit sick. He'd read the story about his mom in the newspaper, her trip to "The Other Side." A small column hidden on a back page of the *Times*, but that was bad enough. The *National Monitor* — jeez — that would be awful. He could just imagine his mother's picture plastered all over the cover of one of those stupid magazines they put beside the checkout stands in the grocery stores. The kind with headlines like HALF MAN, HALF ALLIGATOR FOUND IN FLORIDA SWAMP. OR WOMAN ABDUCTED BY ALIENS — GIVES BIRTH TO THREE-HEADED BABY. David shuddered to think what the kids at school would say if they read about his mother in a paper like that.

The reporter still walked beside him. "All right, then, just tell me a little about heaven. Your mom's been there, right? What'd she say about it? Did she see any angels? What did they look like?"

"I don't know anything about it," David said, which was more or less the truth, "and even if I did, I wouldn't tell a scumbag like you."

Artie punched him in the shoulder. "Don't be a chump, man. So your mom's a little spooky. What of it? If you can make some cash —"

"Forget it," David said. He turned to the reporter. "Get the hell outta here, man. And don't come around here bothering me or my mother again, you hear?"

The fat man shrugged his shoulders. "Okay, kid, but sooner or later, I'm gonna get the story anyway. When I do, you're the one who'll be the loser." The guy in the windbreaker jammed a card into the pocket of David's jeans. "Call me if you change your mind." With a glance at the other two kids, he turned and jogged back toward the blue Chevy van that was parked at the curb.

"What an asshole," David mumbled.

"I think you shoulda done it." Toby lifted his baseball cap then settled it back down on his head, hiding most of his dirty brown hair. "We coulda bought some great weed with that kinda cash."

David didn't answer. He was still thinking what would happen if the *National Monitor* really did do a story about his mother. His friends had teased him ruthlessly after the article in the *Times*. Most of them thought it was a load of bull.

"Hey, I got an idea," Artie said. "Let's go down to the parking lot on Fifth Street. Sometimes somebody leaves a car in there after the attendant's gone home. If they do, sometimes the keys are still in it."

"Cool!" Toby said. "Let's go."

David bit his lip. "I don't know if that's such a good idea. What if we get caught?"

"We ain't gonna get caught," Artie promised. "I've done it a couple of times already. We'll just go for a little ride then bring it right back."

He didn't really want to. He didn't even know if Artie could drive. Still, he didn't want to go home yet. If he did, he'd just lay there thinking about his mom on the front page of the *Monitor*, imagining all kinds of horrible stuff.

"All right," he finally agreed. "Let's go." It was something to do, better than worrying about the newspapers or missing his dad. The truth was he missed his mom, too, since she always worked so much. Yesterday she had quit her job the way she'd promised. Maybe things would be different now, but he wasn't really sure. And he hated the weird stuff she'd been doing lately — getting divorced, saying they had to move.

God, he'd like to kill the sonofabitch who shot her in the head.

"So . . . I guess you had a pretty exciting night last night." Sitting in the kitchen of Kate's small apartment, Sally accepted the mug of coffee Kate set in front of her on the inexpensive oak table Kate had recently purchased. She had moved in the day escrow had opened on her condo, the sale part of the preliminary divorce settlement that she had made with Tommy.

She sighed as she poured the last of the coffee into her cup and walked over to brew a fresh pot. She had told Sally about David's joy ride in a stolen car and that he had spent the night in juvenile hall.

"It was awful, Sally. The place was unbelievably cold and sterile. And the kids . . . they all seemed so hopeless. The matron treated me like I was Ma Barker and David was a member of the gang." She shook her head. "I still can't believe it . . . not my David. But it happened. And I'm afraid it could happen again."

"Maybe it's good they were hard on him. Seeing what it's like when you commit a crime might be exactly what he needs. Maybe it'll straighten him out."

"I hope so. I don't think I can take something like that again."

Sally took a drink of coffee. "What about Tommy? How are things going with him?"

"You know, at first I actually believed he was going to be decent about all of this. Then he hired some fancy lawyer. Yesterday he threatened to sue me for custody of David — not that Tommy really wants him. I reminded him he had no means of supporting a child. I mentioned the times he'd been arrested for possession of marijuana when he was younger. All it did was make him mad. The only way I could convince him to leave us alone was to agree to pay him alimony."

"Alimony! Are you kidding?"

"In a bizarre way, I suppose it makes sense. Tommy hasn't earned a nickel in years. He'll need time to get back on his feet."

Sally made a rude sound in her throat. "Like he isn't coming out of this whole thing smelling like a rose? He gets half the money from the sale of the condo, doesn't he? The property you bought with the money you earned working sixty hours a week? The one you've been making all the payments on?"

Kate refilled Sally's mug with the freshly brewed coffee, refilled her own, and returned the pot to the burner. "Doesn't seem right, does it? But you know what, Sally? I don't really care. All I want is to finally be rid of him."

"I don't blame you. He's been a pain in the ass for years. Besides, you've got to do what's best for David."

Kate's heart twisted. *David.* She could hardly believe the troubled, sullen youth her son had become. Part of it was the divorce and losing his father — not that Tommy had ever really been much of a one. Part of it was her job and the demanding hours it required. Some of it was the way her life had changed since the shooting.

Kate shook her head. "A lot of what's happened with David is my fault."

"A lot of people work long hours, Kate. With Tommy unemployed you really had no choice."

"It isn't just work. It's all the changes I've made. Getting a divorce, moving out of the condo, quitting my job." She smiled. "I'm finished with the last of the projects I started. I've already given them my notice."

"I figured you had. I can't say I'm happy about it but I really don't blame you."

Kate reached for the copy of the *LA Times* that lay open on the table. "On top of all that, take a look at this." She shoved it over to Sally.

"What? Not another one of those horrible stories?" Sally smoothed the newsprint and began to scan the columns in search of the article Kate referred to. Halfway down the page, she spotted it. " '*Woman Tells Tale of Life After Death. Gives Dying Man Hope.*' Oh, God." Sally blew out a breath and started to read. For several long moments, she said nothing, then she muttered a curse at the reporter who had been so malicious.

"I can't believe it. This is the second time in the past three weeks your name's been in the paper. The last one made you sound like some kind of saint. This one makes you sound like a certified nut case." She tossed Kate a disappointed glance. "I thought you weren't going to say any more about your experience."

"Mr. Langley was so afraid of dying," Kate said. "He was such a dear little man. You remember him, don't you? The grocer who owned the store down the block from the office? I heard he was sick and I stopped by the hospital to see him. When I saw him lying there, I thought maybe if I told him what I saw the night I was shot it might make things easier for him."

"You're such a pushover, Kate. If someone asks for your help, you can't ever seem to say no."

Kate glanced away. "I know."

"So what happened to poor Mr. Langley?"

A chill swept through her. She curled her fingers around the mug, trying to absorb the warmth. "He died two days later. I hope what I said helped to comfort him in some way."

Sally sighed. "I hope so, too."

Kate stared off toward the window looking down on the small grassy park where David played basketball after school. "God knows what the kids in junior high will say to David when they see it. Kids can be so cruel."

She set her nearly untouched mug of coffee on the table in front of her. "I've got something to tell you, Sally."

"Oh, oh. I don't like that look."

Kate just smiled, thinking how much she was

going to miss her friend. "You remember the day you drove me to Westwood to see Dr. Murray? We talked about the property my grandmother left me."

"I remember. I presumed you were going to sell it."

"I was. I've never even been to Montana. I thought, what in God's name would I do with a business out in the middle of nowhere?"

"Has my hearing gone bad, or is there a ring of past tense to that?"

"I'm not selling it, Sally. Not now. Not with everything that's happened and my worries about David. I've decided I'm going to move there. A lady named Whittaker has been running the place since my grandmother decided to retire, but apparently the woman is getting too old for the job. My timing couldn't be better."

Sally's blond brows pinched together. "I don't know, Kate. Lost Peak, Montana? Good Lord, it *snows* there. It doesn't sound exactly like a trip to Newport Beach."

"No, it doesn't, thank God. It sounds like a place with good old-fashioned values, a place where the late news isn't filled with rape and murder, where innocent people don't get shot in the head just walking down the street. I won't be making anywhere near as much money, but my hours will be my own, and I'll have a lot more time to spend with David."

Sally sighed. "I suppose, when you get down

to it, that's all that matters."

Kate agreed wholeheartedly. David needed her. He needed a place with families who cared about each other. He needed to get as far from gang wars and juvenile delinquency as he possibly could.

The more Kate thought about it, the more eager she was to leave. She had no relatives; she was an only child. And Tommy's parents were a lot like Tommy, spoiled and self-centered, with little time for David. The school year would soon be over. Except for her friends, there was nothing to keep her in LA.

Kate tried to imagine what she might encounter in Montana. She had never really thought of herself as a country girl, but recalling the eye-burning LA smog, the frustrating traffic snarls, her concrete and asphalt existence, the idea was more than appealing.

It would mean a drastic change of lifestyle for both of them. It wouldn't be easy, yet Kate found herself looking forward to the challenge.

Sally took a drink of her coffee. "That day we went to see Dr. Murray . . . you said your grandmother was trying to tell you something. That isn't the real reason you're going, is it? You're not on some sort of mission to discover what Nell was trying to say?"

"I'm going because it's the right thing to do. I've got a chance to start over, to give David and me both a new life. If I happen to learn a little about my grandmother while I'm there, what could it hurt?"

Sally scowled, knowing Kate's curious nature only too well.

"Look on the bright side — now you'll have an excuse to visit Montana. You always said you wanted to learn to ski."

Sally rolled her eyes. "Skiing's one thing. Grizzly bears are another."

Kate just laughed. Still, she couldn't help wondering what she might learn about Nell Hart, once she got to Lost Peak.

And she thought that faraway Montana might just be the answer to her prayers.

Chapter Five

There were a lot of places a guy could be in the world, but as Chance McLain stood on the banks of Beaver Creek at the base of the snow-capped Mission Mountains, he watched the frothy water rushing over the slick, mossy rocks and thought that Montana had to be the best of them.

Which is why it made him half crazy to see the dead fish floating on the surface of the stream, to know that Consolidated Metals was up to its old tricks, and arsenic waste from its gold mining operation was pouring into the creek.

Damn, why couldn't anybody stop them? Probably because Beaver Creek ran mostly across the Salish-Kootenai Indian Reservation and no one really cared. No one but the Salish, that is.

Maybe being part Indian on his mother's side was the reason Chance felt so strongly about it, but he didn't think so. He believed any man worth his salt who knew the damage Consolidated Metals was doing to the environment would be damn mad about it. Unfortunately, knowing it and proving it to the people who mattered weren't the same thing.

The sound of heavy, rubber-soled boots

crunching on the rocks along the bank drew his attention. "I saw a nice white-tail buck up on the side of the mountain, but I couldn't get a shot." His best friend, Jeremy Spotted Horse, stopped at the edge of the creek beside him. They were hunting elk on the reservation, meat for Jeremy's freezer, since he had a wife and two kids to feed and his job at the lumber mill didn't pay all that much. They hadn't seen any elk, or even much sign, but a nice fat deer would do almost as well.

"You seen anything?" Jeremy asked.

"Yeah, I saw something, all right." Chance squatted on his haunches beside the creek. "Take a look at this."

Jeremy stared down at the water, caught the glint of silver that had once been a beautiful rainbow trout. Now its mouth stood open and its eyes were cloudy, staring up at the clear Montana sky but never seeing it again.

"Damn! Those rotten bastards are at it again."

"Somebody's got to stop them before they wind up killing half the fish in Montana — and God only knows what else."

"Easier said than done." Jeremy sighed and scratched his head. "We've had half a dozen meetings about it, talked to them till we're blue in the face. You can see how much good it's done."

"Every time I see that sonofabitch Barton, it's all I can do not to punch him out."

"You do, you'll wind up in jail for assault. Lon Barton's one of the richest men in the state and his father's richer than that. He's got the best lawyers money can buy, and you aren't one of his favorite people."

Chance grinned. "That, my friend, is my one claim to fame."

Jeremy slapped him on the back. "Well, you had better leave Barton alone, ol' buddy. And on an equally important subject, I'm getting hungry. We can try our luck again in the morning. In the meantime, let's go get something to eat."

"You got it, Kemosabe."

Jeremy laughed, enjoying the joke they had shared since they were kids. Chance the Lone Ranger. An only child whose mother had died when he was three and a father who mostly ignored him. Jeremy his faithful Indian sidekick.

They headed down the mountain to the place where Chance had parked his silver Dodge pickup, opened the doors, and slid onto the sheepskin-covered seats. Chance stuck the key into the ignition and fired up the powerful V-10 engine. "The Lost Peak Cafe is the closest place around."

"Perfect. I can already taste a piece of Myra's apple pie."

Chance drove the pickup onto the gravel road leading down from the mountain. He passed the open field at the edge of town where a hundred years ago the assayer's office had been, splashed through a couple of mud puddles, and pulled up in front of a low-roofed, batten-board building that sat on the only street in town. Climbing out of the truck, they stepped up on the wooden sidewalk in front of the Lost Peak Cafe.

Chance halted in front of the door, staring at the Gone Out of Business sign that hung on the screen as if it were a venomous snake. He shoved back his black felt hat, hardly able to believe it.

From a few feet away, Jeremy softly cursed. "Well, that damned well puts a thorn in our plans," he grumbled.

Chance just scowled. He'd been coming to the Lost Peak Cafe since he was a boy, driving into town with Ed Fontaine, the owner of the ranch next door to his father's place, or occasionally with the old man himself, though as bad as he and his dad got along, he'd tried to forget most of those times.

"I can't believe it." Jeremy looked into the darkened interior of the cafe. "The place was practically an institution. Mrs. Whittaker didn't say anything about closing it down the last time we were in."

"I guess once Nell was gone, some of the fun went out of it for her." The two old women had been best friends since they were girls. When Nell had wanted to retire, Aida Whittaker had taken over running the place.

"I guess that's probably it." Jeremy thumped

a finger against the offensive sign. "We'll have to drive twenty miles more just to find a place that's open."

"Yeah, and so will everyone else in Lost Peak." Which wasn't saying much since there weren't that many people who lived in a place most folks saw as little more than a grease spot in the road.

"Damned shame about Nell," Jeremy said. "She was a good ol' gal. With her dead and buried, I guess I should have figured Aida would eventually close the place down. Somehow I just never really believed it would happen." Jeremy was shorter than Chance, his complexion even darker, but both of them were broad-shouldered and black-haired, though Jeremy's hair was long and straight while Chance's was shorter and slightly wavy.

"Times change, Jeremy. Besides, you never know. Maybe somebody will buy it. There are worse places to live than Lost Peak."

Jeremy laughed. "Maybe for people like you and me. We look out there and see the snow on those mountains, see the whitest clouds God ever put on this earth, and think we've cornered a little bit of heaven, but the average guy only sees the ice in the winter and the bugs in the summer."

"Maybe so. I guess we'll just have to wait and see."

"So, what do you think? Shall we head on into Arlee or skip breakfast altogether? I know

51

you probably got a lot to do at the ranch."

"We've got things pretty well under control right now. Besides, now that you got me thinking about it, I'm damned hungry. The Lone Eagle's the next closest spot. The food isn't all that good but it's better than nothing."

"I'm sure gonna miss Myra's apple pie," Jeremy groused, speaking of the cafe's long time cook.

"You can say that again," Chance agreed as they turned and headed back to his pickup.

But more than that he would miss the two old women he'd been so fond of. He didn't get into Lost Peak all that often, but whenever he did, he tried to stop by and see Nell and Aida. After Nell's death, Aida had started talking about moving to Oregon to live with her daughter and son-in-law. Apparently, she'd finally done it. He hoped she would be happy there.

"As long as we're heading north," Chance said, rounding the truck and jerking open the driver-side door, "we might as well stop by and see that lawyer, Frank Mills, up in Polson. See what progress he's making with Consolidated Metals. We can tell him what we ran across today and give him a little nudge in the right direction."

"Yeah," Jeremy agreed, sliding into the passenger seat. "I suppose we oughta go see him . . . even if it probably won't do a lick of good."

Chance clenched his jaw. "We'll find a way to

stop them. If this lawyer can't do it, we'll hire one who can."

But Jeremy didn't look convinced, and deep down, neither was Chance. With a last disappointed glance at the locked door of the Lost Peak Cafe, he shoved the Dodge into reverse and backed out onto the street.

Chapter Six

Lost Peak, Montana. Population 400. When the lawyer had called it rustic and out of the way, he'd made the year's biggest understatement.

A gas station with an out-of-date pump that also sold hunting and fishing gear sat next to a grocery store with an old-fashioned Coca-Cola sign in the window and sagging plank floors. There was a beer bar with eight barstools and a slightly uneven pool table; Dillon's Mercantile, a store that held an astonishing assortment of nearly obsolete merchandise; and Kate's own little slice of paradise, the newly refurbished Lost Peak Cafe.

No, Lost Peak wasn't much of a place in the overall scheme of things, not when you'd once lived in a deluxe condominium in downtown LA, but Kate was convinced it was also quite possibly one of the most glorious, most scenic spots on the face of the earth. In fact, sometimes when she looked out the restaurant windows at the snow-capped mountains across the valley, she thought that the problems that had brought her to Lost Peak were an odd sort of blessing.

"Mornin', Kate. Didn't hear ya come in." Myra Hennings, the cook and the woman for whom Kate still thanked God every day since arriving a little over a month ago, stood behind the gleaming stainless steel griddle, waving a greasy metal spatula like a band leader's baton.

"Sorry I'm late, Myra." Standing behind the long Formica counter on the other side of the pass-through from the kitchen, Kate shrugged out of her nylon jacket and stuffed it behind a stack of napkins on one of the shelves underneath. "The power went out and the well wouldn't work. David didn't have any water for a shower. We finally realized we'd only tripped a breaker. I'm afraid we're still pretty new at this country-living thing."

"Don't worry — you'll get used to it."

"At any rate, David missed his ride and I had to drive him to school." They had decided to enroll him in summer school. With the turmoil of the past few months, he had gotten behind in his studies, and taking a remedial math course might help him meet some of the kids in the area.

Myra grinned, showing a row of crooked teeth. "Don't worry about it — we did just fine without you. I figured you'd be here as soon as you could or you woulda called. Besides, we just got busy a few minutes ago."

A woman in her late fifties, Myra Hennings was broad-hipped and stoutly built, with hair God had lightened to gray and Myra had turned a brassy shade of blond. She was a widow with three grown kids scattered around the country and an army of grandkids. She was a hard worker and she really knew the restaurant business, but it was her warm, unflappable disposition that made her invaluable to Kate.

"Well, I'm here now and ready to go to work." Kate refastened a button that had popped loose on the front of her pink nylon uniform, tied a matching pink apron around her waist, and shoved a pin into the bun at the back of her head that held a wad of her thick dark red hair. "Just tell me which orders go where and I'll get them on the tables."

But Myra wasn't listening. She was staring through the pass-through, across the Formica counter into the dining room. "God, if I was only twenty years younger . . ." A wistful smile lifted the sagging skin along her neck. "Isn't that the most gorgeous hunk of man you've ever seen?"

There wasn't the slightest doubt whom Myra meant. Kate watched the tall, black-haired man return from the pay phone and slide into one of the pink vinyl booths in front of the window. She hadn't been out on a date in years, hadn't been the least bit interested in a man, hadn't even noticed one. After Tommy, she wasn't sure she ever would again. But this man, dressed like a cowboy but looking more like an Indian, was impossible to miss.

"Who is he?"

Myra's pale eyebrows shot up. "Are you kidding? That's the owner of the Running Moon

Ranch, one of the biggest spreads in the county. His name's Chance McLain."

Of course it was. It seemed like every guy in Montana had a name like Rex or Chase or Cody. "Who's the guy with him?" Six inches shorter, even darker-skinned but not as athletically built, with black hair hanging down in a single long braid, the man was obviously a Native American. Living so close to the Salish-Kootenai Reservation, Kate had seen a number of them around.

"That's Jeremy Spotted Horse. Chance is part Indian on his mother's side. He's got lots of friends on the rez. Tries to help them as much as he can." Myra slid a platter of steak and eggs, a side of biscuits, and a tall stack of pancakes heaped with crisp fried bacon across the stainless steel shelf. "As a matter of fact, this is their order. You might as well take it on over."

Kate didn't miss the sparkle in Myra's eyes. The woman was the town's resident matchmaker. What she didn't know was that Kate wasn't in the market for romance — not anymore. Her single bout with love had been a disaster. She wasn't interested in men, now or any time in the future. She had a son to raise and a business to run. She had left her past in LA, found a place where she and David could start over, and she hoped her troubles were behind her.

One look at Chance McLain, with his hard

good looks and lean, rangy build, and it was clear the man was nothing *but* trouble.

Still, he was a customer and she had a job to do. Balancing the plates in one hand as she had learned to do working her way through college, she grabbed the coffeepot and started across the room.

Chance leaned back in the padded booth and stretched his long legs out beneath the gray Formica table. The restaurant wasn't fancy, not by a long shot, but the pink ruffled curtains at the windows and the wood-framed samplers Nell Hart had stitched gave it a certain homey charm. And the food was always good. He'd been damned glad when the place had reopened.

His mind slid back to the times he had come to the cafe as a kid and Nell always managed to save him that last piece of hot apple pie. Smiling at the memory, he jumped when Jeremy nudged his leg, signaling that the food had arrived and reminding him to get his elbows off the table to make room for the plates.

He looked over at the steaming platter of buckwheat pancakes the waitress was setting in front of Jeremy, and his eyes fixed on a pair of size D breasts straining against the front of a pink nylon uniform. One of the buttons popped open just then and he caught a glimpse of pale skin and frilly white lace.

Chance sat up a little straighter in his seat. He knew he was staring; he could feel his face heating up. His body tightened, and under the table, he felt the first stirrings of an arousal.

Damn!

Maybe it was the fact that the woman he'd been seeing for the past three years was a model, slender and fashionably small in the bosom department. Or maybe it was just that she'd been away in New York for the last three months and he hadn't slept with anyone else, as he usually did on occasion.

Whatever it was, he found himself tipping his head back to see what the woman in front of him looked like, curious in a way he rarely was.

Soft was his first impression. Soft eyes. Soft mouth. Soft curves. She wasn't very big, maybe five-foot-two, but there seemed to be a lot of woman packed into that petite body. Her hair was a pretty shade of dark red. A curl had come loose from her otherwise tidy bun and brushed against a cheek that looked as soft as the rest of her.

This time he did go hard and he straightened in his seat, trying to get comfortable. It wasn't like him to react this way, not at all. Still, his palms itched to cup those heavy, feminine breasts, and his jeans went tighter still.

When the platter of steak and eggs slammed down in front of him so hard some of the juice spilled over the edge, Chance inwardly groaned. It was only too obvious what he had been thinking. He silently thanked God she couldn't see the heavy bulge hidden beneath the table.

Instead, she set her jaw, gave him a cool look the length of her lightly freckled nose, and walked away, disappearing back inside the kitchen.

Jeremy's soft laughter drew a muttered curse. "So . . . you like that, do you?"

Chance just grunted. "Apparently, I do. Who the hell is she?"

"Her name is Kaitlin Rollins. Old Ironstone says she's Nell Hart's granddaughter." Harold "Chief" Ironstone was the town's oldest citizen. "She and her son, David, moved into the old Hart house about a month ago and reopened the cafe. I know you don't get out much, but I figured you'd have heard by now."

"I've been busy. I was in once since the place opened back up, but I didn't see her."

"She's a pretty little thing. Ironstone says she's a real nice lady. Her kid's kind of a troublemaker, though. Got that LA-tough chip on his shoulder."

Chance cut into his steak. He liked it cooked well-done and Myra had managed her usual good job. Then again, why shouldn't she? She'd been cooking at the Lost Peak Cafe for the past twenty years. He was glad the new owner was smart enough to know a good thing. "How old is the boy?"

"About twelve, I think. I've seen him once or twice. He's working part-time over at Marshall's Grocery."

Chance dug into his eggs, also cooked just

right. The biscuits were buttery and golden. "She married?" He hadn't meant to ask, but the words seemed to slide past his lips.

"Was, I guess. Divorced now."

"You say they're from LA?"

"Yeah, so I heard."

"I didn't even know Nell Hart had a grand-daughter."

"Neither did I. I'm surprised she never mentioned it."

Chance downed another bite of eggs. "Even if Kate Rollins inherited the place, I'm surprised she didn't sell it. I can't imagine a young, single, city gal moving way out here."

Jeremy shrugged. "Ironstone says she's kinda secretive about it. Might be interesting to find out why."

It might be at that, Chance couldn't help thinking. It might be even more interesting to unbutton that row of buttons down the front of her uniform and see what the lady had hidden inside all that pretty white lace. It was an astonishing thought, considering. It occurred to him he hadn't felt such an instant attraction to a woman in years, maybe never.

"I thought you and Rachael were getting pretty thick," Jeremy said, jerking Chance's gaze back from where it had wandered toward the kitchen and reading his mind so clearly he felt the heat rise at the back of his neck.

"We are, I guess. We've always had an understanding. We figured we'd get married sooner or later. In the meantime, Rachael has her freedom and I have mine. She's been pressing me lately, though."

"I figured she would, sooner or later."

Chance shrugged. "It's what her dad's always wanted, and marrying her would certainly be in my best interest."

"You can say that again. Once Ed's gone, the Circle Bar F will belong to Rachael. That would double the size of your spread."

"So I guess when she comes back home, we'll probably set the date."

Jeremy swallowed a mouthful of pancakes. "If that's the case, then my advice is to stay away from the pretty little redhead."

Chance glanced up, saw her bent over a table across the way, her hips wriggling as she wiped up a spill, and felt the same shot of lust he had felt before.

"You're right, Jeremy. That's damned good advice." And Chance meant to take it. But even as he finished the last of his eggs, tossed down money for the check, and added a hefty tip, he found himself thinking that surely it wouldn't hurt if he happened to stop by again in a couple of days.

Ever since the cafe had reopened, he'd been craving a piece of Myra's homemade apple pie.

"I'm sorry to have to do this, David, but for the next two weeks, you're grounded."

"Grounded? Aw, Mom."

"You deserve it, David, and you know it." They were standing in the entry of the white wood-frame house they lived in on the hill behind the cafe. It was part of the eighty-acre parcel of property, including the cafe, Kate had inherited. With its incredible views of the mountains, and surrounded by tall ponderosa pines, it was the very best part to Kate.

"I hate this place," David grumbled. "It's the pits. There's nothin' to do and the kids are all geeks. I want to go back to LA."

Kate looked over at her son, saw the stubborn way his mouth was set, saw the tension in his shoulders. She knew he wasn't happy in Lost Peak. She had known it would take time for him to adjust to such a drastically different lifestyle, but she hadn't expected him to get into trouble even out here.

"Mr. Marshall caught you stealing a package of gum. Now you've lost your afterschool job. I thought you liked working at the market."

He shifted from one foot to the other, dragging the toe of his sneaker back and forth across the polished oak floor. "It was okay, I guess."

"Then why did you steal the gum?"

His thin shoulders went up in a shrug. "I didn't think I'd get caught."

"Oh, David."

"Come on, Mom, it's no big deal. At home everybody takes stuff. The stores are used to it. It's right in their yearly budget."

She walked over to the narrow window beside the front door, stared out at the mountains for a moment, then turned and walked back to her son. "God, I can't believe this. You actually think it's all right to steal?"

"I'd never take anything big."

Kate gripped his shoulders. He was already taller than she was. She had to tip her head back to look him in the face. "Stealing is about character, David. It's like lying. There are people who lie, people who cheat, and people who steal. They're all the same kind of person. They aren't the kind other people respect. They aren't the kind other people trust. Is that the kind of person you want to be?"

"In the city, they —"

"I don't care what they do in the city! We don't live in the city anymore and we aren't going back there again. The people who live here have good old-fashioned values. They don't lie, they don't cheat, and they certainly don't steal. That is the way I've tried to raise you. You've always been a good boy, David. Once people get to know you, they're going to like you. But you have to earn their respect, and stealing from them isn't the way to do it."

His fist slammed hard against the wall. "You don't get it, do you? I don't care if these hillbillies like me or not. I want to go home! If you won't leave this place, I'm gonna call my dad. I can go back and live with him."

A wave of nausea swept through her. David

returning to his delinquent friends in LA. David being raised by a father who would indulge him all the way to a jail cell in some dismal prison.

"Is that what you really want — to live with your dad? In your heart, you know what he's like. He can hardly take care of himself, let alone you. He doesn't even know anything about you. You pretend he's the perfect father, but deep down you know it isn't the truth."

David didn't argue, just stared down at the toes of his dirty sneakers.

"I love you, David. I only want what's best for you. You know that, don't you?"

"I suppose so," he muttered without looking up.

"We've got a chance to make a new life here. We can do it, if you'll only give it a try."

David said nothing.

"I want you to go over to Mr. Marshall's store. I want you to take some of the money out of your savings bank and pay for the gum you stole. And I want you to apologize. If your apology is sincere, Mr. Marshall will know it, and maybe in time, he'll decide to forgive you."

David's shoulders slumped. "I already told him I was sorry."

"Did you mean it?" Kate found herself holding her breath.

"I know I shouldn't have taken it." Embarrassment formed small pink circles in David's cheeks. "I've only done it a couple of times.

The other guys thought it was cool, but it always made me feel kind of funny."

Kate wrapped her arms around her son and gave him a hug. "That's because, in your heart, you knew it was wrong. Everything's gonna work out, honey — you'll see. Just give it a little more time."

David just nodded. When she let him go, he went up to his room and came down with a handful of change. He left the house, heading for the store, and when he came back, his shoulders looked a little bit straighter.

"I paid him for the gum. I told him I'd never steal anything from him again. He wouldn't give me my job back, though. I guess I really don't blame him." Walking past her, he slowly climbed the stairs and disappeared inside his room.

Kate sighed. It was a hard lesson, but one she hoped he'd learned. She shuddered to think what would happen if he hadn't.

Or if he was serious about going back to live with his father.

Kate despised the thought of returning; she liked it here in Lost Peak. The people she had met had been friendly and helpful, more so once they learned she was Nell Hart's granddaughter. Nell had been well liked, Kate was surprised to discover. On the rare occasion her mother had ever mentioned her, she had described Nell as a heartless, emotionless sort of woman, the sort who would toss her pregnant, unwed daughter out in the street.

But the house Nell lived in from the day she married Zachary Hart was warm and cozy, filled with a charming feeling of home. The place was in far better repair than Kate had imagined it would be. With a new coat of paint on the walls, the old carpet pulled up and the hardwood floors refinished and covered with colorful throw rugs, it was the sort of place she might have chosen over her high-rise condo if she had been given the choice.

When she had lifted the dust covers off the furniture, she was thrilled to find dozens of lovely antiques. Mixing them in with the furniture she had brought with her from LA kept the charm of the house intact, while her overstuffed sofa and chairs gave it a comfortable, slightly more modern feel.

She wondered if Nell Hart would approve. She didn't have the slightest idea what Nell was really like, but she intended to find out. Now that they were settled, Kate meant to begin her search.

Chance wheeled his pickup into a parking space in front of the Lost Peak Cafe, turned off the engine, and cracked open the door. He knew he shouldn't be there. He had commitments, even if they were more or less unspoken. The last thing he needed was to get involved with a woman.

I only want a goddamn piece of pie, he told

himself. But he knew it wasn't the truth. The sexy little redhead had been on his mind since he'd seen her that day at the cafe.

"Hey, Chance!" Harold "Chief" Ironstone sat on a rickety wooden bench beside the front door. He was there more times than not, wrapped in a blanket, wearing his moccasins and a high-crowned hat with a feather stuck in the top, looking exactly like the wooden Indians they had for sale to the tourists down at the trading post on Highway 93.

"Hey, Chief, how's it goin'?" Chance shook the old man's hand, felt the strength that remained there in spite of his more than eighty years.

He gave Chance a grin. Amazing how many teeth were still left in the old man's head. "Good day. Nice weather. You meet the new owner?"

His glance swung toward the door. "Yeah, sort of."

"Good woman. Nice boy." Chief wasn't really a chief — the Salish had tribal leaders, which wasn't at all the same — but everyone called him that and had for years and he didn't seem to mind.

Chance nodded. "I haven't met the kid. Ms. Rollins seems all right. Food's still good."

Chief patted his protruding stomach. "Yeah, especially the pie."

Chance grinned. He touched the brim of his hat. "Good to see you, Chief."

"You, too, Chance."

He pulled open the screen door, turned the handle on the front door, and walked in.

The place never changed. He was glad about that. Oh, there was a bright new sign on the roof and one out on the road that hadn't been there before. Both of them had the cafe's new logo — a picture of distant, snow-capped Lost Peak inside a forest-green circle. Aside from that, the new owner seemed to like the homey charm of the place and left things pretty much the way they were. It was cleaner, he saw, the curtains freshly washed, the wooden floor waxed to a high sheen. He liked the fact Kate Rollins hadn't made things different, just better.

He saw her as he slid into a chair at one of the Formica-topped tables in the center of the room, took his hat off and rested it on the chair next to his. He ran a hand through his hair, erasing the creases and shoving it back from his forehead.

For a few short minutes, he watched her work. She was efficient, he saw, never forgetting an order, careful to see that none of her customers were ignored. Which, he supposed, was why she walked over to him, though the look on her face said she didn't really want to.

"Coffee?" she asked, standing several feet back from the table as if she couldn't trust what he might do. Damn, he'd certainly got off on the wrong foot with the lady.

"That'd be great." He gave her what he hoped was a charming smile and turned over his cup, waited while she poured it. "You're Kate Rollins, the new owner."

"That's right. And you're Chance McLain. You own the Running Moon Ranch."

Chance's smile deepened. At least she'd asked his name. "I guess when you live in a place this size, everyone pretty much knows everyone."

"I suppose. Until I moved here, I'd never lived in a town this small."

He wanted to ask why she'd come, but he didn't think she'd tell him. Maybe the house she'd inherited was the only place she could afford to live. "We were all disappointed when Mrs. Whittaker closed the cafe. The place was sort of an institution around here. Considering the job you've done since you reopened, I think I can safely say most of the folks hereabouts are darned glad to have you."

Some of the stiffness left her shoulders. "Thank you. When I came here, I hoped the people in Lost Peak would be friendly. So far, they've all been great." She handed him a plastic-coated menu. It was new, he saw, with the same dark green, mountain-in-a-circle logo that was on the sign, but most of the items listed were still the same. As his eyes ran down the page, his mouth curved faintly at the small red hearts beside the heart-smart, low-fat items. He didn't imagine they'd be hot sellers here in Lost Peak.

"Mrs. Whittaker ran the cafe for my grand-mother — Nell Hart. Did you know Nell, too?" she asked.

He nodded. "For as long as I can remember. She was even more of an institution than the cafe. We were neighbors, in a manner of speaking. Part of her property — your property now, I guess — borders a portion of mine."

She looked like she wanted to ask something else, but another customer walked in. "Take your time," she said. "I'll be back in a minute to take your order."

Chance just nodded. He watched her make her way across the floor, liking the uncon-sciously sexy way she moved. He had to admit he was curious about her. What was she doing in a place like Lost Peak? Even if Nell had left her the cafe, why hadn't she sold it and taken the money? Mostly he was trying to figure out what there was about Kate Rollins that made him think of taking her to bed. He only knew that he wanted to.

She came back and took his order, then con-tinued busily serving the rest of her customers. She returned a few minutes later with a plate heaped with warm apple pie and just slightly melted vanilla ice cream and set it on the table in front of him. He could feel his mouth begin to water.

"Man, this looks great."

Kate smiled. "Myra's a wonderful cook. I'm lucky to have her."

"You're right about that." He took a big bite of pie, swallowed most of it and talked around the rest. "Nobody but nobody makes better apple pie."

The lunch hour was nearly over and the place had begun to clear out, as Chance had been hoping it would. Kate went up to the cash register at the front of the restaurant to take the money from the last of her customers. A few minutes later, she returned to his table, armed with a fresh pot of coffee.

"Warmup?"

"You bet." She leaned over to refill his cup and he tried not to stare at those magnificent breasts. "You're new to Montana," he said, swallowing another bite of pie. "Have you had much chance to see it?"

"Not really. Mostly my son David and I have just been getting settled in."

"I heard you had a boy. How's he adjusting so far?"

Kate hesitated and for a moment he thought she might not answer. Then she sighed. "Not very well, I'm afraid. He misses his friends — though believe me, I don't. He feels out of place here, I suppose. He knows how to play basketball, but he doesn't have a clue how to fish. I imagine it's hard for a twelve-year-old who's always lived in the city."

"Yeah, I imagine it would be." Worse than that, he thought. He couldn't imagine not knowing how to toss a line in the water. Or hunt, for that matter, or pack horseback into the mountains. He couldn't help wondering what kind of man the boy's father was. Maybe a lot like his own. He felt a shot of sympathy for Kate Rollins' son.

"You still closing the place on Sundays?" he asked.

She nodded. "We open at six and close at eight on weekdays. We're open till nine on Friday and Saturday nights."

"Pretty long hours."

"Not for me. I set my own schedule. One of the reasons I came here was to spend more time with my son."

He liked hearing that. He was too young when his mother died even to remember her, but he thought that he would have liked it if she had wanted to spend time with him.

"There's some mighty pretty country hereabouts. Since you haven't had a chance to see it, I'd be happy to show you around."

Her expression subtly shifted, began to close up. "As I said, my son and I are just beginning to settle in. Thanks for the offer, but I'm afraid I'll have to pass."

He fiddled with his pie, kept his eyes on the ice cream melting on his plate. "Maybe some other time."

But her lack of response said it wasn't going to happen. As he watched her walk away, he was amazed at the degree of his disappointment. Chance leaned back against his chair with a sigh, the pie getting cold though the coffee was still steaming, his appetite suddenly gone. It galled him a little that she had so flatly refused him. In his wilder days, half the women in the county had tried to get him to take them to bed and half of them had succeeded.

But obviously Kate Rollins wasn't interested. Chance found himself wondering what he might do to change that.

He left his pie unfinished, tossed a handful of money down for a tip, picked up the check, and had almost reached the cash register up front when the bell rang above the door. Randy Wiggins and Ed Fontaine, two of his best friends, appeared in the opening. Randy was a male nurse of sorts — though Ed never referred to him that way — a caregiver for a man with too much pride to admit he needed one. Holding the door, Randy waited while Ed rolled his shiny chrome wheelchair inside the cafe and let the door swing closed behind them.

Chance strode toward the slim, gray-haired man who had been more of a father than his own ever was. "I thought you'd gone to Denver," he said to Ed with a smile.

"I'd planned to. My meeting with the Cattle Association was cancelled." Ed shook the hand Chance offered. "I was on my way back from Missoula when I saw your pickup parked out front. I've got some news I thought you'd want to hear."

"Oh yeah? What's that?"

"Consolidated Metals just filed a permit to construct a new mining operation on Silver Fox Creek — right here in Lost Peak."

"Damn!"

"I knew that'd make you happy. Those bastards don't know when to quit. That lawyer, Frank Mills, the Indians hired hasn't done a blasted thing. The guy's probably on Lon Barton's payroll, just like half the judges in the county." Ed was lean and hard, wiry and tough as boot leather. He ran a ranch the size of Chance's and he did it from a wheelchair. There wasn't a man alive Chance admired more than Ed Fontaine.

"Mills is trying to get an injunction," Chance told him. "But he says we need more evidence. Jeremy wants to get some pictures of the leaks in the tail pond, but we'd have to get inside their compound to do it. We were hoping the sworn testimony of some of the tribal leaders, along with the lab results on the water would be enough."

"It probably will be. Unfortunately, that isn't going to stop them from building a new mine here in Lost Peak."

Chance heard a noise behind him. He turned to see Kate Rollins walking toward them. God, she was a pretty little thing. Not that Rachael wasn't. Rachael went light years beyond pretty. With her elegant cheekbones and silver-blond hair, Rachael Fontaine had graced magazine covers all over the country. She was model-thin, with a set of legs that went all the way up to her neck. She was stylish and sophisticated in a way Kate Rollins never would be. He wondered how he could be attracted to two such opposite women.

"I'm sorry to interrupt," Kate said, "but I couldn't help overhearing. Now that I live here, I consider myself a member of the community. From now on, what happens here in Lost Peak affects me, too."

"Ed Fontaine and Randy Wiggins, meet Kaitlin Rollins, the new owner of the cafe."

"A pleasure, Ms. Rollins," Ed said, extending a gnarled, weathered hand that had seen fifty years of hard work. Kate gave him a warm smile and shook it, a firm, confident handshake, Chance noticed, that made Ed look at her a little differently than he had before.

"Ma'am." Randy tipped his hat in her direction.

Kate smiled a greeting then returned her attention to Ed. "I gather this mining operation wouldn't be the best thing that could happen to Lost Peak."

"From your standpoint it might not be too bad. It would probably bring in more business, if that's what you're after. Families would start moving in; the town would probably grow."

Chance could have sworn her face went a little bit pale. "I like the town just the way it is,"

76

she said in a voice as firm as her handshake. "I wouldn't be living here if I didn't."

He smiled at that. He liked it the way it was, too. As far as he was concerned, Montana was the last best place. He wanted it to stay that way.

"Consolidated Metals isn't known for its environmental consciousness," Chance told her. "Their mine on Beaver Creek has had more than twenty-four water quality violations, including half a dozen cyanide spills and acid mine drainage problems. They can't put in another heap-leach mine here now — thanks to a recent change in the law — but they're trying for an appeal even as we speak, and knowing them as I do, if they start an operation in Lost Peak, sooner or later, they'll pollute Silver Fox Creek, one of the prettiest little fly fishing streams in the country."

"What can we do to stop them?" Kate asked. Her eyes seemed greener than they had before, and he thought they held a spark of determination.

"I suggest we hire an attorney of our own," Ed said, "preferably one who can't be bought."

"Good idea," Chance agreed. "Got any idea who might be the best man for the job?" Pulling his wallet from the back pocket of his jeans, he tossed down enough bills to pay for the pie. Kate punched the amount into the register and handed him the change.

Ed scratched the back of his head. "We could talk to Max Darby, or maybe Bruce Turnbull. I've had dealings with them before."

"All right, and while we're at it, a private investigator might not be a bad idea. Maybe he can uncover something about Consolidated that might be useful."

"If there's anything I can do to help," Kate said, "I hope you'll let me know."

Chance smiled down at her. "Thanks for the offer. We're going to need plenty of help getting the word out, letting people know what the company's trying to do. We might just take you up on it."

"Getting the word out is my specialty. I was in advertising before I came here."

"You sold advertising?"

She gave him the same tight smile she had given him the last time he'd come in. Chance cursed himself for the ground he'd just lost.

"You might say that. I was vice president of Menger and Menger, a big ad agency in LA. We worked on everything from political campaigns to breaking out new food products for companies like Quaker Oats. In comparison, I don't imagine getting the word out on Consolidated Metals to the people in Silver County would be too tough a job."

Chance inwardly groaned. If there was one thing Ed had taught him it was not to make snap judgments. When he glanced at his mentor, the older man's eyes were twinkling, saying, *See what happens when you do?*

"Sorry. I guess I just didn't expect a corporate bigwig to be running a cafe in Lost Peak."

"*Retired* corporate bigwig," Kate corrected, and he could see that she was enjoying herself. "And to tell you the truth, I like my change of occupation. It feels darned good not to have to answer to anyone but myself."

"Well, we're happy to have you on our team," Ed said. "We'll keep you posted. And you can be sure we'll take you up on that offer to help."

While Randy held the door, Chance wheeled Ed out to his Chevy van. Randy pushed a button and the lift gate at the rear hummed as the metal platform dropped down.

"We've got to keep on this thing," Ed said, referring to Consolidated's project.

"No one knows that better than I do." Chance rolled Ed's wheelchair onto the lift gate then waited as it hoisted the older man up.

"Have you heard from Rachael lately?" Ed called down to him from the back of the van.

"Not for a couple of weeks. She's busy with that new modeling contract. They've been shooting on location all over the country. I imagine she'll call when she can."

"I imagine she will." Ed sighed. "What that girl needs is a husband and babies. Think about it, Chance."

Chance only nodded. He rarely thought of Rachael, Ed's daughter, when she wasn't

79

around and she hadn't been around much lately. He ought to feel guilty, and maybe he did, a little.

But the hard truth was, the only real guilt he ever felt came from putting Ed Fontaine in that chair.

Chapter Seven

It was five minutes till closing. The late July sun had succumbed to clouds and rain, and the cafe had been empty for nearly half an hour. While Myra finished up in the kitchen, Kate sat down in one of the empty booths, took out her notepad, pulled out the pencil stuck behind her ear, and began to list the information she intended to gather about Nell Hart.

Now that the restaurant was running smoothly and the house was in order, she was determined to get underway. Unfortunately, she wasn't exactly sure where to begin. The best way, she figured, was simply to amass as much data about the woman as she could get her hands on.

Birth Certificate, she wrote. She'd get a copy of both Nell's and her mother's at the Silver County courthouse in Polson.

Death Certificate. While she got the certificate on her grandmother, she might as well obtain a copy of Zachary Hart's, as well. Kate's long-dead grandfather had died when Kate's mother, Celeste, was only six. Since her mother could barely remember him, Kate knew nothing about him, either.

Copy of the will. She'd been notified by mail of her inheritance. It hadn't occurred to her to ask the lawyer for a copy of the document. She would try the Recorder's Office first, since one of her customers had told her wills were often a matter of public record. If not, she could write to Clifton Boggs. Either way, a copy should be easy enough to get.

Boxes in the attic. There was a ton of old stuff up there she had noticed when she had moved in. She had picked out a few of the smaller antiques to use as accents throughout the house, but she hadn't gone through the stacks of papers and boxes of clothes that were still up there. It would be interesting to see what she found.

Call Aida Whittaker. Nell's longtime friend might have general information that could be useful. She underlined the words, having meant to phone the woman long before this.

The bell above the door jingled. She looked up just in time to see Chance McLain walk in. He peeled off his rain slicker, slapped his low-crowned black Stetson against the leg of his jeans, and started walking toward her. Kate's stomach fluttered. She felt the oddest urge to run.

"I know you're closed," he said before she could say what she was thinking. "I've been on the road most of the day. I thought you might still have the coffeepot on. I could sure use a cup before I head the rest of the way up the hill."

Kate nodded. "No problem." She could

hardly ask him to leave, as wet and tired as he looked. And wet and tired as he looked, he still looked unbelievably good.

He stood at the table till she returned a few minutes later, a steaming Styrofoam cup in her hand and a lid to go with it.

"It's thick enough to cut," she said. "With the storm, business has been slow. We haven't made a fresh pot for a while."

"I'm used to it that way. Long as it's hot, it'll do me just fine." He reached into his pocket for the money to pay her, but Kate raised a hand to stop him.

"This one's on the house."

He smiled. "Thanks." He reached down for the cup, saw her list sitting next to it, and his straight black brows arched up in silent question.

"I'm trying to gather some information on my grandmother," she explained, though it was hardly any of his business.

"You ever meet her?"

Kate shook her head. "She and my mother . . . didn't get along."

He blew across the top of the coffee, carefully took a sip. "I'm surprised to hear it. Everyone liked Nell."

"So I've been told." But Kate wasn't convinced. From what her mother had said, Nell Hart was cold and selfish, more concerned about what the neighbors might think about her unwed daughter being pregnant than she was about her daughter's welfare.

"Half the county showed up at the funeral," Chance was saying as he set the cup back down. "We all felt bad about the accident. The old gal had plenty of life left in her. She died way before she should have."

She died way before she should have. The words echoed through her head and Kate's legs started shaking. She must have swayed toward the Styrofoam cup because it suddenly tipped over and red hot coffee splashed across the table. Chance leaped out of the way just in time.

"Oh my God! I'm so sorry!" Kate turned and raced for a towel then rushed back to sop up the mess she had made. "Thank heavens you moved so quickly. I nearly scalded you."

"It's all right — no harm done." He stared down at her with those intense blue eyes of his. "Was it what I said about Nell?"

Kate finished wiping up the coffee then sank down in one of the captain's chairs around the table. "It just came as such a surprise. It never occurred to me that her death had been anything other than natural causes. Nell was seventy-two. Mr. Boggs, her attorney, mentioned her sudden death. I just assumed Nell died of a heart attack." She looked up at him. "What sort of accident did she have?"

Chance sat down across from her, looking uncomfortable in his role as the bearer of bad news. "Nell slipped and fell, that's all. She hit

84

her head on a corner of the sideboard in the dining room of her house. It could have happened to anyone."

But it didn't. It had happened to Nell Hart. She had died before she should have. Did her premature death have something to do with the mystery Kate was determined to solve?

If there really was a mystery.

If any of what had happened the night of the shooting was real.

"Are they . . . are they sure it was an accident?"

Chance eyed her strangely. "Everyone assumed it was. There wasn't any evidence of foul play. No one broke into the house or anything — at least not that I heard anything about."

Kate bit her lip. She was probably being ridiculous. Probably. "I'm sure you're right. It's just that . . ." *That I saw her after I died and I think she was trying to tell me something. Get real, Kate.*

"Just that what, Kate? Do you have some reason to think it might have happened otherwise?"

She summoned a nervous smile. "No, of course not." She got up from the chair, picked the Styrofoam cup up off the floor, and started for the kitchen. "I'll get you another cup. You're probably more than ready to get home."

Chance said nothing, just stood up from his chair and waited for her to return with another cup of coffee. This time the lid was already on.

"Thanks, Kate." She watched him walk to the door and pull it open. He paused and turned to face her. "That offer's still open. I'd love to show you around."

Kate shook her head. She didn't want to go. Chance McLain was trouble and she already had her share of that. Man-shy, she guessed. Her mother had definitely had bad luck with men. After Jack Lambert and her own husband, Tommy, Kate figured she and Celeste were pretty much alike. And Chance McLain was just too damned attractive.

"Thanks, anyway," she added as he settled his hat back on his head, grabbed his wet slicker off the coat rack, and headed out into the storm.

The bell rang as he left. The rain picked up. Heavy sheets pounded against the window-panes as she sat back down at the table, shoved Chance McLain's tall image out of her mind, and returned to her list.

Sheriff's office, she wrote, though she wouldn't have thought of that before.

Coroner's report. She wasn't sure she could get a copy, but she could try. She might have started into this thing a little slower than she had intended, but with Chance's innocent revelation, she was ready to move a lot faster now. And perhaps in a more specific direction.

She had an odd hunch about all of this. A feeling she was right, that the darkness and fear she had sensed in Nell Hart's presence had something to do with her death.

Kate meant to find out what it was.

Kate shoved open the glass door leading out of the County Recorder's Office in Polson, the Silver County seat. She was armed with a copy of her grandmother's will, a copy of the deed to the property she had inherited, as well as the document by which Zachary Hart had first acquired the eighty acres back in 1949.

A deed recorded in 1975 showed Nell's purchase of the Lost Peak Cafe from a man named Jedediah Wheeler thirteen years after Zach had died.

Kate paused on the sidewalk, shuffled through the papers to the copy of Nell's birth certificate. A quick calculation said her grandmother had been forty-six when she bought the cafe — three years after she had tossed her daughter out in the street.

At a cursory glance, none of it looked particularly useful, but she had to start somewhere. She was reading the first page of the will, trying to decipher the legalese, wondering who else might have received an inheritance and thereby benefited from her grandmother's death when she stepped off the curb onto busy First Street. A horn blared. At the same instant a big hand shot out and gripped her arm, jerking her out of the path of a speeding black Toyota.

"Jesus, Mary, and Joseph! What the hell were

you thinking? You damn near got yourself killed!" Fierce blue eyes bored into her. Chance McLain still gripped her arm.

"Sorry." The heat of embarrassment washed into her cheeks. "I guess I should have been paying more attention."

He let her go, but made no move to leave. "You've gotta be more careful. This time of year, the place is crawling with tourists. Most of them are so busy gawking at the mountains around the lake they haven't got a clue what's going on."

Right now she didn't have much of a clue herself.

"So . . . what are you doing in Polson?" he asked, both of them still standing on the corner. He was more than a foot taller than she was. Counting his hat and boots, taller than that. She had been trying to ignore him since the first time she had met him. Every time she saw him, it was a little bit harder to do.

"I'm gathering some of the information I told you about. I'm on my way to First American Title. The recorder said I could get plat maps of the land I inherited. After that I'm going back to the sheriff's office."

"The sheriff? What for?"

"I've asked them for a copy of the accident report that was turned in the day Nell died. The clerk says I'm not allowed to see it. I'm hoping the sheriff will be a little more coopera- tive. Unfortunately, he isn't in."

Chance studied her with those discerning blue eyes that had a way of making her stomach flutter like a feather in the wind. "I get the feeling there's more to this than simple curiosity."

"That's ridiculous," Kate countered a little too quickly. "I just feel like . . . well, like I'd like to know something about her. We are, after all, related." Before he could raise another question, she changed the subject. "What about you? Polson's a long way from Lost Peak."

A corner of his mouth tipped up. "Everything's a long way from everything up here. You get used to it after a while. I came to see a lawyer named Mills. He's supposed to be getting an injunction to halt Consolidated's mining operation on Beaver Creek, but so far he hasn't done squat."

"Why not?"

"That's exactly what I'd like to know."

"How's the campaign to stop the new mine coming along?"

"Actually, I've been meaning to stop by and talk to you about that. Ed asked me to find out if you'd be available some night next week. He thought you might be willing to give us some suggestions how to get this whole thing off the ground."

"I'd be more than happy to do that."

"Great." They had reached the door to the title company. Chance held it open while Kate walked in. "There's a great Mexican restaurant over on the river — the El Rio? After you're finished, maybe I could buy you some lunch."

Lunch with Chance McLain. Oh God, did she dare? *It's only lunch,* a little voice said. But her stomach was still misbehaving every time he looked at her, and she found herself shaking her head. "I'd love to, Chance, but I've just got too much to do."

Something moved over his features, disappointment, or maybe determination. "All right, then I guess I'll give you a call, see when we can set up that meeting."

Kate just nodded. Her heart was beating a little faster than it should have been. Her palms had begun to sweat. God, she couldn't remember meeting a man who could do that to her. Had Tommy ever had that kind of effect on her? She didn't think so. If he had, surely she'd be able to recall.

Kate waited for the copies of the plat maps, and returned to the sheriff's office. Since he still wasn't in, she would have to come back to Polson another day. The sheriff was also the coroner, so she would have to pursue that topic later as well.

It was late afternoon by the time she returned to her car, tired but only a little discouraged. She had yet to go over the information she had gathered, and next time she would call for an appointment with the sheriff before she drove all the way into town.

She had just pulled out of her parking space,

her mind on the drive back home, when she spotted a big silver Dodge pickup turning onto the road behind her. Chance waved when he saw who it was.

Kate waved back and kept on driving.

Chance slammed his palm against the steering wheel of his truck. Damn! The woman was beginning to drive him crazy. He had come to Polson to order some feed and see Frank Mills. The tribal council had asked him to stop by on their behalf, to inform Mills they would be holding a special meeting in regard to the problems on Beaver Creek. If he didn't get that injunction in the next few weeks, they'd be looking to hire another lawyer.

He hadn't expected to see Kate Rollins. He certainly hadn't expected to find her about to commit suicide on the corner of the street! He almost smiled. He was damned glad he'd shown up when he did. He only wished she'd been a little more grateful.

Chance gave up a frustrated sigh. There was something about Kate Rollins. Something that intrigued him. He wasn't sure what it was, but he wanted to find out. Driving down Highway 93 back toward the ranch, he could see her shiny white Lexus on the road a couple of cars ahead of him. He couldn't believe she'd said no to him again. He couldn't seem to charm her, no matter what he did. Hell, maybe she just didn't like him.

He chewed on the thought for a while, but somehow it didn't seem to fit. He wasn't fifteen anymore, mooning over the head cheerleader. He wasn't imagining things. He could feel the pull of attraction between them. He was sure Kate felt it, too.

Why then, did she go to such lengths to avoid him?

Both of them were unattached adults. They were responsible people who knew their own minds. Why not let nature take its course? If that meant winding up in bed, what was wrong with that? It was obvious Kate wasn't looking for a permanent relationship and neither was he, but a little physical enjoyment never hurt anyone.

As tense as she sometimes seemed, it would probably be good for her.

Thinking of her softly feminine figure and those round, voluptuous breasts, Chance had no doubt that it would be good for him.

Chapter Eight

The weather remained clear, just a few puffy clouds floating over the pine-covered peaks. Kate tucked in the clean sheet she had just put on David's bed and plumped the feather pillows.

Fortunately for her, he had always been fairly neat. Not perfect, but he kept his CDs carefully stacked so he could find the one he wanted, and his "treasures," as Kate secretly called them — Sammy Sosa's home run baseball caught at Anaheim Stadium, the plaque he'd gotten for winning the fourth grade spelling bee, the shells he'd collected on Malibu beach, and half a dozen other objects — sat evenly spaced on the top shelf of his bookcase.

He wasn't that great about picking up his dirty clothes, but he usually made his bed in the mornings and Kate was happy with that.

Carrying the load of dirty sheets, she stepped out of the room into the hallway, heard the phone ringing, and hurried downstairs to answer it.

"Hello, is this Kate Rollins?" a familiar voice asked.

"Dr. Murray?"

"Kate. I had a bit of trouble getting your new number. Apparently the one you left with my secretary was only temporary. Then I remembered you had also left your friend, Sally Peterson's number. I called and she gave me this one. I hope that was all right."

"Of course it was. It took a while to get the phone hooked back up at the house. It's good to hear your voice, Dr. Murray."

"I wish I was calling just to chat, but unfortunately a problem's arisen, and I thought you'd want to know."

A chill swept through her, a premonition of something she wasn't going to like. "A problem? What sort of problem?"

"A reporter came to see me . . . a man named Chet Munson. He's with that sleazy tabloid, the *National Monitor*."

"Yes . . . I know the one. Munson tried to get information from my son, but that was before we left LA. I thought by now he would have forgotten all about me."

"Apparently, he hasn't. From what he said, he's been talking to Margaret Langley." *Mrs. Langley — the grocer's wife.* "With *Embraced by the Light* and a number of other books on NDE hitting the bestseller lists, I guess he figures your story might turn into something."

"That's all in the past," Kate said. "I'm not talking to anyone else about what happened. Can't you tell Chet Munson that?"

"I tried to, Kate. I'm just not sure he's going to give up."

Her fingers tightened around the phone. "Do

94

you think he'll be able to find me?"

"Hopefully not, but those tabloid guys are pretty good bloodhounds. So far, he just seemed to be nosing around. If nothing new surfaces, maybe he'll decide you're old news."

"Maybe . . ." But she was thinking how much she was coming to like Lost Peak. And what her neighbors would say if an article appeared in the *Monitor* about what the newspapers called "her trip to The Other Side." "Thanks for the call, Dr. Murray."

"No problem, Kate. I hope you'll stay in touch."

She nodded and said, "I will," just as the front door swung open and David rushed in. He was carrying his school books close against his chest, his head turned away from her in a way that instantly made her suspicious.

"David!" She hung up the receiver as he bolted up the stairs. "Come down here. I want to talk to you."

He paused halfway to the top, but he didn't turn.

"Honey, I know something's wrong. You're shaking all over. Come down and tell me what's happened."

A sigh of resignation whispered past his lips. When he turned around, she saw one of his eyes was black and his lip was cut and swollen. "Oh, baby, what happened?" She drew him toward her and wrapped him in her arms, pressing his head against her shoulder. Fine, silky brown hair that hadn't changed since he was a child slipped through her fingers. David clung to her for an instant, then pulled away.

"It was that Jimmy Stevens kid, Mom. He called me a wimp because I wouldn't ride his stupid ol' horse."

She wanted to reach out and hug him again, but she knew it would be a mistake. "Names can't hurt you, honey. You ought to know that by now. You have to learn to walk away from people like that."

"I hit him and I'm glad."

She brushed a piece of grass from his jacket just to have an excuse to touch him. "You were right in refusing to ride. Horses can be dangerous if you don't know how to handle them."

"You know how to ride. You said you took lessons at Griffith Park."

Though she'd been raised in Culver City, on the fringes of LA, she had always loved horses. When David was six, after she'd finished college and started to work, one of her friends had suggested they take lessons down at the stables in Griffith Park. She'd done it for a while and she had loved it. But Tommy thought it was crazy, and her job had started taking more and more time. Eventually she'd been forced to quit.

"I never rode enough to be very good, but at least I learned the basics. We rode English, though, not Western, like everyone does around here."

"Horses are stupid, anyway — I don't care what that hick Jimmy Stevens says." With that he turned and raced up the stairs only to come back down a little bit later with his old jeans on and a blue nylon windbreaker slung over one shoulder. "I'll be back in a while."

"What about your eye? Don't you want me to put some ointment on it?"

"I'll put some on when I get home."

She wanted to argue but she didn't. His dignity had already suffered enough. "Be back before supper, okay? And be careful if you're going off by yourself. This is pretty wild country, you know."

David made no reply, just headed for the back door and jerked it open, let it slam closed behind him.

Kate watched him through the window, heading down toward the stream that ran across the back of the property, her insides still churning. She wasn't sure what she should worry about the most: Chet Munson and the *National Monitor*, the mystery that still plagued her, or the continuing problems with her son.

David sat down on a rock at the edge of the stream, just out of sight of the house. It was pretty here, he had to admit. Nothing at all like LA. He had never seen a sky so blue, or one that looked so big. He had never seen clouds as white and fluffy as these, never seen mountains that stretched so high they seemed to go on forever.

Still, it wasn't home and he was lonesome. He missed Artie and Toby and the rest of the kids. If it wasn't for his mom, he'd do what he'd threatened and go back and live with his dad. But he couldn't leave his mother all the way out here alone and he knew she didn't like the city. And he hadn't forgotten the newspaper article or that fat creep, Chet Munson.

With a weary sigh, David reached down beside the rock he sat on and picked up the long, thin aspen branch he had fashioned into a makeshift fishing rod. Using the pocketknife Artie had given him for his birthday, a present he figured his friend had probably stolen, David had neatly sliced off the branches and smoothed the sides. He'd tied a length of twine to one end and bought a couple of fish hooks from over in the fishing gear section of the gas station to tie on the other end of the twine.

Every day this week after school, he'd come down here to the creek to try his hand at fishing.

So far he hadn't caught a thing.

He knew there were fish in the water — he could see them swimming in the shadows beneath the rocks. He baited the hook with one of the pine beetles he'd caught in the windowsill of his room and tossed in the line, dragging it beneath the boulders along the edge of the creek and hoping he could at least get a nibble.

An hour later, he was still trying, but he wasn't having any luck. He was concentrating so hard he almost didn't hear the stranger approaching. He glanced up at the sound of splashing water and the click of hooves against rock as horse and rider crossed the stream, the man's tall shadow falling over the rock where he sat.

"You must be David Rollins."

David hauled the line up out of the water and set the pole on the ground beside him, embarrassed for some dumb reason that the man had caught him trying to fish. "Yeah, so what if I am?"

The cowboy swung down from his horse, a pretty brown and white spotted one. He had never seen a horse like that except on TV. "I'm Chance McLain. I'm your neighbor over on the east . . . the Running Moon Ranch."

"I've heard of it," David said. He'd overheard Jimmy Stevens talking about the big cattle ranch that ran for miles along the road and all the way up into the mountains.

"My house is a couple of miles from here, but my property line touches yours, at least in this spot along the creek. I've got a crew out mending fences in this section today." He smiled and little lines crinkled in the dust at the corners of his eyes. They were the bluest eyes David had ever seen.

"Your grandmother always let us ride across her property," the man said. "It's a shortcut into town. I hope you and your mom don't mind." He must have assumed they wouldn't because he just turned around and started un-tying one of the leather thongs behind his saddle.

He looked even taller standing on the ground, lean and tough looking, not the kind of guy you'd want to mess with. His black felt hat was so dusty it looked gray. It occurred to David, if he'd ever imagined what a cowboy ought to look like, it would be Chance McLain.

"Hard to fish without a good rod," McLain said. "I carry one with me wherever I go." He took the lid off the silver tube he'd untied and drew out what looked like a broken fishing pole. In minutes, he had the parts assembled and a fly tied onto the end of the line.

"Ever cast one of these?"

David just shook his head. He watched as Chance McLain waded out into the water in his boots, not even worried about getting them wet, and drew out a long length of line.

It was really something to see, the way the fly waved and floated, then snapped out into the stream. He made it look so easy, like anyone could do it.

"Want to try it?"

He shook his head. He'd probably get the damned thing caught in a tree.

"I'll show you how, if you want. It takes a little practice, but once you get the hang of it, it isn't so hard."

He wanted to. His hands itched to get hold of that long, pretty rod.

100

"Come on. You can't hurt it. If you get it caught, I can get it undone."

There it was. His fear out in the open and the guy said it wouldn't be a problem. Chance McLain was back on David's side of the creek, putting the rod in his hands and David was letting him. It was lighter than he thought, yet it felt good in his palm, balanced just right.

"The trick is not to rush. Get the feel of the rod. Drag the line out easy and slow. Whip it over your head as if you've got all the time in the world. When the line's right at the top, make just the slightest hesitation, then let go. Throw it like you'd throw a baseball. Just let it sail right on out there. We'll try it on the grass a couple of times, then you can try it in the water."

His heart was pounding. His fingertips tingled, he wanted to do this so badly. The rod felt warm, curved just right against his hand. He whipped it, watched the line sail out and land not nearly far enough away.

"You started off smooth, but you snapped it a little too much at the end. Try it again."

He did it again, then again. Two times then three, he started to lose track. When he looked up, Chance McLain was smiling.

"You're a natural, David. Nice hands and an easy stroke. Want to try it out in the water?"

His mother would kill him for getting his shoes and pant legs wet, but David didn't care. He walked past Chance McLain out into the middle of the stream and it felt so darned good to be there. The water was running past his feet, icy cold yet it didn't really matter.

"Do it just like you did on the grass, nice and easy."

He took a deep breath, closed his eyes and tossed out the line. It didn't go too well at first, but after a while he relaxed a little and it got easier. Then the line snagged on a rock beneath the surface of the water.

"No problem. It'll come loose." McLain waded out and showed him how to untangle it by tugging it the opposite way, then he waded back to the bank. David kept waiting for him to ask for his rod back or tell him he was ready to leave, but he didn't seem to be in a hurry.

David knew he was taking advantage, that he ought to give the rod back and let the guy be on his way, but he couldn't seem to make himself quit. There was something about being out in the middle of that stream, about tossing out that fly and making it land just right on the top of the water, about the easy rhythm that was almost hypnotic. When something snagged the end of his line, nearly jerking the rod from his hands, and a big silver fish leaped out of the water, David felt a rush of excitement unlike anything he could remember.

"A fish!" he yelled at the top of his lungs. Already McLain was sloshing through the water at a run, wrapping one of his big hands around David's and helping him hold the rod steady.

"You've got to set the hook, then we'll reel him in." It seemed like hours. It seemed like seconds. One minute the fish was there, then in an instant it was gone.

McLain just laughed. It was deep and husky, kind of sandpaper rough. "Damn, almost had him." McLain grinned and so did David. "They're slippery little suckers. That's what makes them so much fun to catch."

David just nodded. It didn't matter that the fish had gotten away. It only mattered that he'd caught one.

"He was a dandy, too," McLain said. "A big German brown."

His heart was still thundering. He didn't want to quit. "It's early yet. Maybe there's time to catch another."

Chance looked up at the house. "What time's supper? Your mom'll be wantin' you home by then."

It was nearly six. Time to go in. "Yeah, I guess you're right."

"Tell you what. I got a couple more rods at home. Since we're neighbors, why don't I loan you this one? You can practice your technique after school and try again tomorrow."

David wondered if his grin looked as stupid as it felt. "You sure it's all right?"

"No problem. Just remember, you gotta release 'em if they're less than eight inches. And if you keep 'em you gotta eat 'em. You ever cleaned a fish?"

He only shook his head.

"I'll stop by tomorrow and show you how." He smiled. "Assuming between us we can catch one."

David just nodded. He felt funny inside his chest, as if something important had just happened, but he didn't know what it was. It was crazy, but that was the way he felt.

"Thanks, Mr. McLain."

"Chance," McLain said. "Just call me Chance like everyone else."

David nodded. Picking up the fishing rod, he started up the hill toward the house. Halfway there, he saw his mother. She was standing in the shadows beneath a pine tree and he realized that she had been watching.

She brushed at something in her eye and smiled as he walked past, but she didn't say anything. He waved at her but didn't stop to talk. He was thinking about the fish and how it had felt to have something so wild and beautiful dancing on the end of his line. How tomorrow, he'd be back at the stream, practicing with Chance McLain's rod and trying his luck again.

If that dumb punk Jimmy Stevens could ride a horse, surely he could learn to fish.

Kate strolled down the grassy slope toward the creek, where Chance McLain stood beside his pinto horse. "That was very nice . . . what you did for my son."

"Every kid ought to know how to fish."

"He doesn't have many friends here. You acted like a friend today. You'll never know how much I appreciate that."

He looked down at the braided reins he held in his hands. They were strong hands, dark and long-fingered, with nicks and scars across the back, hard working hands, she thought.

"It was nothing. The boy wants to learn — I'll teach him." He glanced up, smiled. "He's got a natural knack."

His hat was dusty, his face covered with a fine sheen of dust. Still he was handsome. "It was a great kindness. I wish there was a way I could repay you."

His eyes fixed on her face, intent now, the easy, slightly embarrassed expression gone. "Maybe there is."

She stiffened. She should have known there would be a catch. In this world, you never got something for nothing. "And that would be . . . ?"

Chance McLain grinned. "Let me show you around. I know this country as well as anyone, better than most. I'm proud of it. Let me show you the place you've come to live."

"That's it? You just want to show me around?"

His easy smile faded. "What did you think? That if I taught your son to fish, I'd expect to take you to bed? This isn't LA, Kate. People help each other out here. They have to. You'll learn that if you stay."

She felt like a fool. Of course he hadn't meant anything like that. "If I stay? Why wouldn't I stay?"

"You haven't been through a winter out here. You haven't walked through a field a million grasshoppers call home. You haven't had your sweet little housecat eaten by a coyote, or been chased by a grizzly bear. Life's hard out here, Kate. But I promise you, it's worth it. Let me show you this country and you'll see what I mean."

What could it hurt? He wasn't asking her for a date. Dating a man like Chance McLain was a whole different thing and far too dangerous for someone like her. Forgodsake, her divorce wasn't even final. And the way Tommy had been acting lately — making threats, refusing to sign the settlement papers — she had to be even more careful.

She couldn't risk getting involved with a man, didn't even want to. But McLain wasn't interested in anything but building a friendship. So what if he was good looking? So what if she felt flushed and warm whenever he looked at her the way he had just then. The man was her neighbor. She couldn't simply ignore him. And the truth was, she needed friends just as much as David did.

"All right, you've convinced me. I'd love to see my new home."

"How about Sunday? You can bring David along if you like."

She relaxed even more. He wouldn't be asking David to come along if he had any sort of designs on her. "I'm sure he'd like that."

"Good, then I'll pick you up at six on Sunday morning. The earlier start we get, the better chance we'll have of seeing some animals."

"Animals? I thought we were going sight-seeing."

"The animals in Montana are part of the sights. If we're lucky, on Sunday you'll see what I mean."

And so she finished working through the week, growing more and more nervous about the weekend. She should have said no. She shouldn't take the chance of spending time with a man like McLain. She knew his reputa-tion — Myra said he had any number of women at his beck and call. As handsome as he was, it was easy to believe. But surely a single day with him wasn't going to throw her into a tailspin.

Then she remembered the effortless, graceful way he swung up on his horse, how rugged he looked in his long black duster, the way he had winked at her and grinned.

She remembered how her stomach had floated up with that grin and neatly turned over, and Kate began wishing she hadn't agreed.

Chance stood up in his stirrups, stretching the long muscles in his legs after so many hours in the saddle. They were mending fences in the northern pastures, where the graze was good and a number of cattle collected during the summer months.

He lifted his hat and let the breeze blow through his hair, then settled the hat back on and pulled the brim low across his forehead. He'd been riding for most of the day. They'd gotten a lot of work done, but again and again his mind had strayed. He kept thinking of Kaitlin Rollins, remembering the way she had looked, yesterday down by the stream.

All that dark red hair curling down to her shoulders. Big green eyes shiny with a hint of tears at the joy she had seen on her son's face because he was learning to fish. *Soft* was the word that always came to mind when he thought of her. Soft lips, soft skin. Thinking of yesterday, he mentally added, *soft heart.*

She had finally agreed to go out with him. He didn't mind that she'd only done it because of the boy. The attraction was there. Chance knew it. Kate knew it. It was only a matter of time until something came of it.

He had a feeling Kate would be worth the wait.

One of his men whistled at one of the steers and his attention returned to the task at hand. Across the way, his foreman, Roddy Darnell, picked his way through a cluster of white-faced Herefords and rode up beside him.

"We got a problem, boss. You better come

take a look." Roddy had been working at the Running Moon since before Hollis McLain had died and the spread had gone to his son. He was bone-thin and sun-browned, a good man that Chance felt lucky to have.

He reined his paint horse, Skates, up the trail behind Roddy, wondering what lay ahead. It was always something in the cattle business. Too much snow. Not enough rain. Beef prices down. And there was nothing in the world he would rather be doing.

They stayed on the trail, winding slowly upward, the country here more open than it was farther east. There the Mission Mountains ran along the border of the ranch, a nearly impenetrable string of high, forested peaks that shot up nine thousand feet.

But here, the grass grew thick and sweet, grama and bunch grass, buffalo grass farther down on the plains.

They stopped beside a small, meandering creek and Roddy swung down from the saddle. Chance followed him up onto a knoll where a side stream had formed a pond, and both men stopped beside it.

"Jesus, Mary, and Joseph." Six dead steers lay around the pond, their eyes glazed over, their tongues hanging out. "Looks like it's the water."

Roddy just nodded. "The creek crosses the fence line onto reservation land 'bout half a mile up. We followed it till we found what we were looking for. Someone dumped a load of mining sludge into a canyon up there. It was probably done some time back . . . a couple of years, maybe. Must have finally seeped into the ground water and somehow made its way into the creek."

"Long as it was flowing, it was partially diluted. In the pond, the pollution had time to build up." Chance swore foully. "No way to prove it was Consolidated, I don't suppose."

"Probably not. There were a couple of other mines in operation a few years back. Could have been any one of them."

"Could have been, but we both know it wasn't."

"What do you want me to do?"

"Fence off the pond. Move the cattle into that pasture east of here. The graze isn't as good but at least they won't die."

"What about the waste?"

"I'll call the county. And whoever needs to know on the rez."

"Maybe now we'll get some action."

"Maybe," Chance said. But he didn't really believe it. Silently, he wished Lon Barton straight to hell.

Chapter Nine

Kate always looked forward to Sunday mornings. It was the one day of the week that she could sleep in. She'd never really been an early riser, though she had done it all her life. First with a baby and working to put herself through college, later with a high-paying job that demanded hours of overtime, she'd never had any other choice.

She groaned as she slapped the alarm clock into silence at five A.M. and pulled herself out of bed, trying to imagine how she could have let Chance McLain talk her into giving up her precious Sunday sleep. Yawning, she padded into the bathroom, turned on the shower, and stepped beneath the hot water, letting the warm spray wash over her.

She felt better by the time she had dressed and headed downstairs. David was dressed as well and waiting in the kitchen. An empty cereal bowl and the crumbs from his toast sat on the counter. The fishing rod he had borrowed from Chance McLain leaned up against the back door.

"I was thinking . . ." he said. "Wondering if maybe you wouldn't mind if I didn't go with you. I thought . . . since I still got Chance's . . . Mr. McLain's fishing rod, today might be a good day to really give it a try."

An image of the hard-edged cowboy appeared, and a thread of uneasiness washed through her. As long as David was coming along, she'd felt safe. Now wariness settled over her at the thought being alone with McLain.

"I know how much this means to you, David, but I don't like the idea of you going off on your own. What if something happened to you out there?" The stream behind the house, Little Sandy Creek, was shallow and according to the locals, not dangerous. All fishermen went off by themselves, they said. It was part of the sport's appeal.

Still, it made her nervous to think of her son out there by himself.

"I'm not going off by myself. Chief is coming over. He said he'd go with me."

Old Chief Ironstone, David's only real friend. They made an odd pair, one so old, the other so young, yet knowing how lonely David had been, Kate was grateful for the old man's friendship.

"Well, he certainly knows his way around the forest. I suppose if he's going along, you'll be all right. I'm sure Mr. McLain will be disappointed, but I imagine he'll get over it."

David tossed her a look that said, *Come on, Mom, get a grip.*

"All right then, *I'll* be disappointed. At any rate, if that's what you want to do with your Sunday, it's all right with me — as long as you're careful and don't go too far from the house."

David leaned over and hugged her. "Cool, Mom. Thanks a million."

She gave him a tenuous smile. She had come to Montana determined that they would make a life here. That meant learning to live the way country people lived, doing the things they did.

She watched David escape out the back door as the doorbell rang out front. Taking a deep breath, she went to greet Chance McLain.

Wearing jeans, a sweatshirt, and tennis shoes, she pulled open the door, hoping it was the proper attire for their little adventure. The look of approval on his face said it was, and a warm feeling slid into her stomach.

"I see you're ready." Chance glanced toward the kitchen. "Where's David?"

She smiled. "My son went fishing. Ever since you lent him that rod, that's all he wants to do."

A corner of his mouth curved up. The most sensuous mouth she'd ever seen. "I guess that means I'm stuck with just you."

"I guess you are."

"Grab your jacket and let's get going. We're burnin' daylight here."

"My jacket? It isn't that cold outside. Surely I don't need —"

"First rule of living in the mountains, Ms. Rollins. Never go anywhere without a coat. The weather's unpredictable up here. The temperature's been known to drop fifty degrees in a single afternoon. Believe it or not, the record's closer to a hundred."

"Oh my God."

He grinned. "No big deal — as long as you're prepared."

Kate rolled her eyes. "No big deal," she said beneath her breath, wondering, as she had more than once, if in coming here she'd gotten in way over her head.

Chance led her out to his pickup, one with an extended cab, mud flaps, and a toolbox in the back. He opened the door and helped her climb in, not an easy task, since she was so short and the truck sat so high off the ground.

She set her purse on the floor and leaned back against the seat. "I guess I'm just not built for a truck this big."

At the mention of her body, his eyes shifted down to her breasts, then he jerked them back up to her face. "I suppose I oughta get a running board," he said, sounding a little embarrassed and staring straight ahead. "That makes it a whole lot easier."

"Where are we going?" Ignoring his momentary indiscretion, Kate clasped the seat belt around her, noting with approval that Chance did the same.

"There's a logging road up through the mountains behind the ranch. There's some incredible views from up there."

Kate sat back in the comfortable sheepskin-covered seat, enjoying the ride along the forested road and the opportunity to study the man at the wheel without being seen. He drove with the confidence of someone who had done this sort of thing every day of his thirty-odd years, taking the steep turns as if they weren't there, gently braking when he needed without really thinking about it.

Pine trees lined both sides of the road, tall ponderosas, lodge poles, and cedars; birch trees and cottonwoods along the banks of the stream. White-barked aspens ran up the draws and she thought how pretty they must be when their leaves turned golden in the fall.

With July nearly over, the trees were fully leafed out and the snow had melted in the valleys. A blanket of white still capped a few of the tall, forbidding mountains that surrounded the town of Lost Peak. In the sunlight, the glistening snow appeared almost fluorescent.

They turned off the main, black-topped road and drove onto one of gravel, passing through a gate fashioned from two huge pine logs standing upright, a third forming a bar across the top. A weathered sign hung down — RUN-NING MOON RANCH — burned into a thick slab of wood.

"My father was born on this ranch," Chance said. "Of course it was a lot smaller then."

"How big is it now?"

"Twenty thousand acres." He said it matter-of-factly, as if it were nothing out of the ordinary to own thirty-odd square miles of land.

"My father built it up from practically nothing. Spent most of his life doing it. He died about eight years ago."

There was something in his words, something he wasn't saying. "Were the two of you close?"

He gave a sarcastic snort in answer. "I would hardly say that. I rarely saw him and that was just fine by me."

She wanted to ask him why, but she was afraid to. She didn't like the hard look that had come into his eyes.

"What about your mother?" She hoped it was a more pleasant topic.

"She died when I was three."

"I'm sorry."

Those brilliant blue eyes swung to her face. "Why? You didn't even know her."

"I'm sorry for you, Chance. You and your father didn't get along. You must have been terribly lonely as a boy."

He stared at her a moment longer than he should have, considering he was driving. Then he glanced back to the road. "You're right, I had a pretty rotten childhood. David's lucky to have a mother who cares about him the way you do."

"I'm not sure exactly what you mean."

"As near as I can figure, David is one of the reasons you came to Montana. You were worried about him getting into trouble. You figured he'd have a better chance of making it out here."

He was right on every score. She wondered how he knew. "He's a good boy. He just got a little mixed up."

Chance covered her hand where it rested on the seat. "You did the right thing, Kate. Montana's a good place to raise a child."

Kate stared down at those long dark fingers. "For David's sake I hope you're right." She could feel their strength, their warmth. It seemed to flow into her like the light that night at the end of the tunnel. It occurred to her she had never known the comfort of having a strong man in her life. Not a husband or a father. She couldn't imagine what it must be like to have a man a woman could really lean on.

Just then the brakes slammed on and his hand came up protectively in front of her, holding her in place though the seat belt worked perfectly fine. "Hang on!" he said rather belatedly.

"What is it? What's wrong?"

McLain just grinned in that appealing way of his. "Moose," he said.

"Moose? Moose what?"

"That moose there." He pointed toward the side of the road.

Kate shot upright in her seat. "Oh my God!" It was huge and nearly black, with legs that seemed eight feet tall. It lifted its massive head and stared at the pickup, the long stringy whiskers on its chin moving up and down as it chewed, then it lowered its head back to the grass and just kept on munching as if they weren't there.

"He's incredible. I've never seen anything so magnificent."

Chance seemed pleased, his eyes warming, little lines appearing at the corners. "There's a cow over there."

"A cow?" They'd passed a thousand head of cattle. Why, she wondered was this one more special than the rest?

"A female moose."

"A female," she repeated again, beginning to hate herself for it. "Yes, I see. A female moose is a cow."

"So is a female elk." He flashed another of those endearing grins. "It won't take you long to get the hang of it."

Kate sighed, her eyes still fixed on the two massive beasts on the side of the road. "I could sit here and watch them all day."

Chance laughed, and even his laughter sounded strong. "Not a chance, lady. I've got lots more to show you."

And so he did, amazing her with one incredible sight after another. Towering waterfalls that soared over the edge of cliffs, then crashed into a foamy white spray on the rocks below. Deer, elk, snowshoe rabbits. Even a coyote. They left the ranch by a back road leading even higher into the mountains and wound up at the headwaters of Silver Fox Creek.

When Chance stopped the truck at a wide

spot in the road, she could see for miles out into the mountain-lined valley.

"You were right, Chance. This was well worth getting up early for."

"I'm glad you like it." He leaned back in the seat, stretching those long legs out in front of him. "Now just imagine what will happen to all of this if Consolidated Metals gets that mining permit."

Her eyes swung to his face, but most of it was shaded by the brim of his hat. "You're saying the pollution will affect not only the stream but all of the wild life around here."

"That's right. The fish and insects are food for larger game. And the heavy metals can sink into the ground water. Yesterday up in the northwest pasture, we found six dead steers that had stumbled across a pond fouled by mining waste."

"Oh, Chance, no."

The lines of his face looked grim. "Unfortunately, it's happened more than once."

"I meant what I said. I'll do anything I can to help."

"Thanks, Kate. We need people who care. Ed's been pressing me about that meeting. How about some night this week?"

She usually worked till two Monday through Thursday, so she could spend time with David. The evenings were pretty much open. "Just let me know which evening works best for you."

"Like I said before, we're glad to have you

here in Lost Peak." He turned just a little and those incredible blue eyes fixed on her face. *I'm glad you're here,* they seemed to say.

Kate shifted beneath his close regard, trying to ignore the warm, buttery sensation working its way out through her limbs. It was ridiculous. The man was simply being polite.

"Are you hungry?" he asked, dragging his gaze away and breaking the mood.

"I was too busy watching the scenery to think about food, but now that you mention it, I'm starved. Unfortunately, I don't see a deli on the corner."

Chance smiled. Reaching behind the seat, he dragged out a thermos of coffee and a bulging paper bag. "BLTs. Sort of a cross between breakfast and lunch, since it's still pretty early. These aren't as good as the ones from your place, but they're the best my cook could do on short notice."

"You've got a cook?"

Chance settled the bag in the crook of his arm, grabbed a blanket, and cracked open the driver-side door. "You'll need your jacket," he said. "This early, it's still pretty chilly up this high."

She grabbed the nylon jacket he'd insisted she bring and reached for the handle on the door.

"Just sit tight. I'll come around and get you. And yeah, I've got a cook. Pretty much a necessity with half a dozen full-time hands to feed."

She hadn't thought about what it must take to run a ranch the size of his. She was pondering the notion when the door opened up and Chance's big hands clamped around her waist. He lifted her down with an ease that was almost scary and lowered her slowly to her feet.

Her body brushed his along the way, and she could feel the lean hardness, the strength she had felt before. She was standing way too close and this time when she looked up into his face, there was no doubt what he was thinking.

Something passed between them, something hot and turbulent, something she hadn't expected to feel and didn't want to.

"Kate," he said, the single word deep and slightly rough. Her stomach did a flip and slowly collapsed in a heap. Kate moistened her lips, determined to say something that would end the moment, but no words came out. Instead, Chance lowered his head and kissed her, a hot, wet kiss she felt all the way to her toes.

Unconsciously, her hands crept up and her fingers spread over the front of his sheepskin vest. Chance cupped her face between his hands and kissed her again, slowly and very thoroughly. She was shaking when she finally broke away.

The world fell silent around them. Her breath came out in soft, quick little puffs. Chance dragged in a long, calming breath and slowly released it. He glanced down at the scuffed toes of his boots then out across the valley.

121

"Sorry. I didn't bring you here for that. It just sort of happened."

Kate didn't answer. Her heart was still hammering, her body tingling. One thing was certain. Chance McLain knew how to kiss.

"I'm still hungry," he said, trying to return the light mood they had shared before, then having the grace to flush at the underlying meaning in the words. "The sandwiches, I mean. We wouldn't want them to go to waste."

Inwardly, she smiled at the subtle hint of shyness. There was a hard, rough edge to Chance McLain but there was a softness there, too, an unmistakable vulnerability. She had seen it in her son, the attempt to retreat behind a tough facade. Chance was older. He'd had a lot more practice. But if you looked hard, you could see the gentleness was still there inside him.

"We need to find a place to spread the blanket," she said, and he visibly relaxed. "How about over there?" She pointed to a big flat boulder that overlooked the valley.

"Perfect." Chance smiled. God, he had the straightest, whitest teeth. He spread out the blanket, opened the bag, and handed her a sandwich, then poured coffee into a couple of Styrofoam cups.

"I bet you use cream," he said. "I didn't think to bring any."

"I imagine I can tough it just this once."

He smiled his approval and handed her a cup. "So tell me a little about you. I know you worked for an ad agency. How'd you happen to get into that line of work?"

Kate shifted on the rock, the bite she had taken suddenly feeling a little too big. This was one of the reasons she hadn't wanted to come. Talking about the past wasn't something she was ready to do. "I was a business major in college. UCLA. I was solicited by Menger and Menger during my senior year. What about you?" she asked, hoping to get him talking instead. "Did you go off to school or just start working on the ranch?"

"I went to the U of M — University of Montana — down in Missoula. My father passed away two months before graduation. I dropped out to take over running the ranch."

"Two months and you didn't go back and finish?" It seemed impossible after the struggle she'd gone through to get her degree.

Chance just shrugged his shoulders. "I always knew what I wanted to do. The Running Moon was all I ever thought of. I didn't need a diploma to run it." He took a bite of his sandwich, chewed and swallowed. "So why'd you come to Lost Peak? I know you were worried about your son, but you could have sold the cafe and the land, taken the money and gone somewhere else. There are lots of other places, slightly bigger towns that could have offered more of a life for a single woman."

Kate carefully wiped her mouth with the napkin he had pulled from his brown paper lunch sack. She thought of the shooting and the experience she'd had, of Chet Munson and the articles in the newspaper; of Tommy and the divorce, of her mother and Nell Hart and the mystery that had compelled her to come to Lost Peak.

But none of those were things that she could risk telling Chance.

Her hand faintly trembled and she was no longer hungry. "I wanted to get away from the city. When Nell died and left me the cafe it seemed like the perfect solution."

"I would have thought you'd have picked a town that at least had a theater and —"

"Well, I didn't," Kate snapped, setting her unfinished sandwich back down on the piece of wax paper it had been wrapped in and rising to her feet. "Listen, Chance, I really appreciate the tour, but I've got a lot to do when I get home, and I need to be getting on back."

Chance said nothing for the longest time. "All right, Kate. Whatever you say." Wordlessly, he tossed the last of his sandwich into the sack along with hers, cleaned up the mess they had made, and screwed the lid back on the thermos of coffee.

Kate felt a little guilty for ruining such a perfect morning, but maybe it was better this way. She shouldn't have weakened, shouldn't have come with him in the first place. With Tommy stirring up trouble, Chet Munson sniffing around, and David to think of, she didn't have time to get involved with a man.

Especially not this one.

She knew what kind of man Chance was. It was written in every line of his handsome face. Just yesterday she had overheard Bonnie Delaney, one of the waitresses who worked part time for her. "Chance's a real heartbreaker," Bonnie had said to one of the female customers. "He's left a string of broken hearts all over Silver County."

One look at the heat in those sultry blue eyes and she was certain it was the truth.

When they pulled up in front of the house, he turned off the engine and Kate cracked open the door, ready to jump and run like the little black snowshoe rabbit they had seen.

Chance caught her arm before she could leave. "Listen, Kate. Whatever your reasons for coming to Lost Peak, it's your business, not mine. I won't pry into your affairs again, but I'm not letting you run from me any longer. I want to see you again."

She shook her head a little too fiercely, stirring the curly hair around her face. "It's not a good idea."

"Why not?"

"Because I've got a son to think about and a cafe to run."

"Sorry — not good enough."

"Because we have nothing in common. I'm from the city. You're a country boy."

He only shook his head. "Try again."

"Because I'm just plain not attracted to you."

"Bullshit." Grabbing a fistful of her sweatshirt, he hauled her halfway across the car seat and captured her mouth in a scalding, mind-numbing kiss. She struggled for an instant, but the heat was too much, the fire too unbearably hot. She'd never felt anything like it.

Chance kissed the corners of her mouth, kissed her lips again, and she opened for him, letting his tongue slide in, feeling the hot, wet silkiness, desperately wanting the kiss to continue. She was trembling all over, damp in places that hadn't been damp in years. She heard herself whimper when Chance pulled away.

A long dark finger smoothed along her jaw. "Listen to me, Kate. I don't have the foggiest idea what's going on between us, but something damned well is. I didn't plan for it to happen. I know you didn't either, but I mean to find out what it is. I'll be in town on Thursday night. Don't eat before you close. We're going out to dinner."

He didn't give her time to argue, just climbed down from his side of the truck, rounded the front, jerked open her door, and lifted her down. He walked her to the door and waited while she unlocked and shoved it open.

"I'll see you Thursday," he said and then he was gone, leaving her staring dumbly after him.

Kate watched his pickup pull out of the driveway, feeling as if her world had somehow shifted. All she could think was *Oh my God, what have I done?*

Chapter Ten

For the balance of the day, Kate worried about the date she had made with Chance McLain — or more correctly, the date *he* had made that she had never really agreed to.

It was silly, she finally decided, ridiculous to let it upset her so much. Chance was only a man, after all. She had worked with men for years. At the ad agency, most of her clients were men. She knew how to handle them, knew how to say no without bruising their fragile egos. Of course, she'd been married back then.

Still, Chance was no different than the rest. Better looking, maybe. But a man, nonetheless. As long as she remembered that, she'd be all right. So he was taking her out to dinner. So what? She might even wind up enjoying herself.

With that thought in mind, she set to work on other, more important endeavors.

She had been meaning to call Aida Whittaker, Nell's best friend, just to see where the conversation might lead. Myra had given her the woman's number in Eugene, Oregon, where she was living with her daughter. As soon as David headed upstairs to play one of his computer games, Kate dialed her up.

"Mrs. Whittaker?"

"Yes . . . ?"

"I'm Kaitlin Rollins — Nell Hart's grand-daughter? I've been meaning to call you for some time." They spoke for a while, just small talk, getting to know each other a little. Aida seemed genuinely glad to hear from her. She wanted to know how the cafe was doing since Kate had taken over and any new happenings in Lost Peak.

"I'm afraid I don't have much news. I haven't really been here long enough to get in on the gossip. I know they're trying to put a mine in on Silver Fox Creek, but a few of us are getting together to see what we can do to stop them."

"Good for you," Aida said, her voice filled with approval. "Maybe you're more like your grandmother than you know."

"What do you mean?"

"Nell was dead-set against mining up in those hills. She thought it was a shame what it did to the land and the animals. She told Lon Barton so, too — on more than one occasion."

Perhaps they felt the same about some things, but thinking of her mother, Kate knew she would never have treated her own child as Nell had treated her daughter.

"Who's Lon Barton?" she asked.

"You'll meet him. Sooner or later. His father, William Barton, is the major shareholder of Consolidated Metals. Lon runs the company for him. Both of them have more money than they know what to do with."

"Was there anyone else Nell didn't get along

129

with? What I mean is . . . did Nell have any enemies?"

"Enemies? Good Lord, no. At least none that I know of. She and your mother had a terrible falling out, but that was years ago. I imagine you know all about it."

Only what her mother had told her, and it wasn't a pretty picture. Kate remembered her mother crying every year on her birthday.

"I wonder if she ever even thinks of me," Celeste had once said. But it was water under the bridge now, and nothing anyone could do to change things.

They talked a little longer, then Kate said goodbye, promising to call every few weeks with news of what was happening in town. The conversation had been a pleasant one. Though she had never met Aida Whittaker, she felt a certain connection to the woman on the other end of the phone. It was obvious what good friends Nell and Aida had been. Perhaps their next conversation would prove a little more fruitful.

A few minutes after she hung up the phone it rang again. It was the voice of Ed Fontaine.

"I hope I'm not calling at a bad time."

"No, not at all."

"Chance said he mentioned getting together to discuss the campaign against the mine."

"As a matter of fact, he did."

"I know it's short notice, but any chance you'd be ready by tomorrow night?"

Mondays were always slow. She only kept the place open because there was nowhere else for the locals to go. "Tomorrow would be fine. We can use the meeting room in the back of the cafe, if that works all right for you."

"That'd be great. We'd like to ask anyone who's interested to join us. Would that be a problem?"

"I think it's a good idea."

"All right, then. We'll see you tomorrow night."

Kate wondered if the *we* included Chance, then shoved the unwelcome thought away. Why was it just thinking about him always made her nervous? It was ridiculous. This was business. The sort she was extremely good at. Whether Chance was there or not was unimportant. She could help these people who had so graciously accepted her into their community. Kate intended to do just that.

The meeting began at seven o'clock in the back room of the Lost Peak Cafe, an extension, according to Myra, that Nell had added fifteen years ago. It was used for large parties, special occasions, or just about anything where more than ten people needed to get together in a town of four hundred.

The group that showed up was an interesting mix of locals: Ed Fontaine, owner of the Circle Bar F; his male nurse, Randy Wiggins; Silas Marshall, the old rock hound who owned the grocery store; Maddie and Tom Webster, owners of the local beer bar, the Antlers, down the street; and Jake Dillon, a recently widowed man in his fifties who owned Dillon's Mercantile.

Jeremy Spotted Horse was there, arriving just as Chief Ironstone walked in. Half a dozen people she'd never met showed up as well. The last one through the door was Chance McLain.

Kate ignored the sudden Ferris wheel drop in her stomach and gave him a smile. Chance smiled back, but this was a business meeting and his manner said he respected that.

Leading the group toward the room at the back, she waited while everyone took a seat. She'd arranged the banquet tables in a U, putting Ed, Chance, and Jeremy beside her at the front of the room.

Ed began by thanking everyone who had taken the time to come and filling them in on the latest news about the gold mine Consolidated intended to develop on Silver Fox Creek.

"They're convinced they can overturn the ban on any new heap-leach mining, and if we don't do something to stop them they just might succeed. It won't be easy, but with all of us working together we can keep them from destroying Silver Fox Creek."

A mumble of uncertainty floated around the room. Going up against a huge company like Consolidated Metals wasn't going to be easy and they knew it. A few people voiced their reservations. Both Tom Webster and Silas Marshall were worried about waste pollution, but they thought the advantages the mine would bring might be worth it.

"A mine that size requires a great deal of labor," Tom said. "They'd be creating a lot of new jobs. Our businesses would grow. Hell, the whole town would prosper."

Jeremy Spotted Horse countered. "The biggest thing we have to sell around here is the land itself — the mountains, the forests, and the animals. That's what people come to see. A mine is hardly scenic — not when it creates a heap of tailings as high as a four-story building. And if they poison the streams, they'll kill the wildlife. You might get a few more families moving in, but you'll lose the tourist business and the quality of life will turn to sh— . Well, you get my drift. The place won't be fit to live in."

Silas Marshall looked worried. "Consolidated Metals is a big corporation. I don't see how a handful of us has the power to stop them, even if we wanted to." A man in his seventies, Silas was tall and thin with a neatly trimmed beard that covered a long chin. Every time Kate looked at him, she thought of an aging Abraham Lincoln.

Chance stood up in reply to Silas's doubts. "Consolidated has a damned good political machine and the best lawyers money can buy. As Ed said, it won't be easy. That's where Ms.

Rollins comes in. She's had experience with this sort of thing and she's going to help us figure out what to do."

This time he looked directly at her. She could feel those sky-blue eyes moving over her face and the air seemed too heavy to push out of her lungs. Hoping no one noticed the warm flush in her cheeks, she took a moment to study her notes and compose herself.

"As Silas pointed out, taking on a company the size of Consolidated Metals is a difficult task. But it isn't impossible either. The first thing we need to do is inform the public about the company's efforts to overturn the ban and remind them of the mine's potential dangers."

"How do we do that?" a man in the back row asked.

"To begin with, we'll go after the media, involve them on a local, regional, and national level. We'll need newspaper and magazine articles, and television coverage as well. We can print educational brochures, which we'll use when we hold public meetings. Ultimately, we'll need a website, and —"

"Hold it, Kate." Jeremy Spotted Horse held up one big hand. "How in blazes are we supposed to pay for all this?"

"Good question, Jeremy. We'll have to have a sponsor to help us — at least in the beginning. But as soon as we get organized, we can start raising money to fund our efforts."

Chance cleared his throat. "I imagine Ed and

I can come up with enough cash to get things rolling." He tossed a glance at Ed and received a confirming nod from the older man.

"We can sell bumper stickers and T-shirts," Kate went on. "We can also hold fund-raising events." She started to add something more, but the discouraged look of the crowd held her back.

"Maybe Silas is right," Jake Dillon said glumly. "There's no way in hell we can do all of that."

Kate just smiled. "That's the best part — we don't have to." She handed out a printed sheet she'd typed up on her computer and copied on the Xerox machine in the upstairs bedroom she'd converted to an office. She might have moved to the country, but there were some things a city girl just couldn't live without. To Kate's mind, a modern, efficient office was one of them.

"You're suggesting we contact each of these agencies?" Ed asked.

"That's right. All of them are dedicated to improving the environment. They worked on getting the cyanide ban on the ballot in the first place. They'll be more than happy to help us, once they understand what Consolidated is attempting to do."

Chance read the list out loud. "Five Valleys Trust, Sierra Club, Trout Unlimited, John Muir Chapter, Montana Environmental Information Center, Montana Wilderness Association." He looked up from the list that went on for half a page and grinned. "With these guys on our side, Consolidated is in for one helluva battle."

"And it's a battle they aren't going to win," Kate said firmly.

Silas still looked worried. "Those guys aren't gonna like this."

"That's putting it mildly," Jeremy grumbled.

"Silas and Jeremy are right," Tom Webster said. "Not everyone is gonna be happy you're trying to stop them. Over near Yellowstone, environmentalists tried to stop the World Gold Mine from going in and things got really nasty. A couple of people got hurt pretty bad."

"Some things are worth fighting for," Chance said.

Kate silently agreed. She hadn't lived in Montana all that long, but already she had fallen in love with the place. The thought of ruining one of the country's last wilderness frontiers was simply unthinkable.

"All right, then. How does the Silver Fox Creek Anti-Mining Coalition sound?"

Several heads nodded and smiled. "Sounds good to me," Chance said, getting a rumble of agreement from the crowd.

"I think it would be best if Ed made the initial phone calls to the organizations on the list, since he's so well known in the community. I'm the logical person, I guess, to lay out the brochure. I'll need photographs, though. Is there anyone here who can help me with that?"

"I can," Jeremy said. "Wildlife photography is sort of a hobby of mine. And I've got pictures of some of the pollution problems caused by the Beavertail Mine over on Beaver Creek."

"Perfect. Does anybody here know any of the local newspeople? We can start with the problem of Chance's dead cattle. That ought to be of interest to the people who live around here."

Jeremy's eyes swung to Chance. "What dead cattle?"

The room turned strangely silent as Chance explained the grisly sight he had found by his high-meadow pond. "Now you understand why this is so important. Instead of cows, that could have happened to somebody's kids."

They went on assigning tasks and before they left, Kate asked them to sign a volunteer form, giving their names, phone numbers, and addresses. They were off to a very good start, she thought as the last of them disappeared out the door.

All but Chance, who stayed behind to help her pick up the empty coffee cups and dirty napkins and set them on a plastic tray. The cafe was just closing. She could hear the sound of Bonnie in the kitchen cleaning up.

"You were great tonight," Chance said once they were finished, one wide shoulder propped against the doorframe.

"I know it was a little overwhelming. Getting

137

something like this started isn't easy."

His eyes moved over her, lingered on her breasts. "Nothing worthwhile ever is," he said, looking back into her face. "The best things take a little effort." He wasn't talking about the campaign anymore, and a little shiver tingled up her spine.

"I wish it was Thursday," he said. "If I were bringing you home after supper, I'd have an excuse to kiss you."

Kate couldn't move. Her heart was zinging, flying against the walls of her chest. He was standing so close she could smell his aftershave, Old Spice, she thought. Nothing fancy for a man like Chance, but boy, did he smell good.

"Then again," he said softly, "maybe I don't need an excuse." He moved with purpose, lowering his head until his mouth softly settled over hers. Her eyes slid closed and the world seemed to tilt on its axis. Their lips melded, sank warmly together, and her palms flattened out on his chest. It was as hard as steel, as solid as the wall behind her, wide bands of muscle that tightened as his arms came around her, pressing her against his long lean frame.

The kiss went on and on, nibbling, tasting, gentle, then deep and incredibly erotic. She knew she should end it, but his mouth was so warm, his lips so soft, she simply refused.

A loud noise sounded through the walls, Bonnie dropping a pan on the kitchen floor. Both of them broke away.

Chance smiled faintly. He reached down and ran a finger along her jaw. "I'll see you on Thursday," he said. She thought he might kiss her again, but he didn't. He must have realized she wouldn't have let him.

Even so, he seemed satisfied at the progress he had made, and that drew her stomach into a knot. Lifting his hat off the rack by the door, he settled it low on his forehead, touched the brim in farewell, and he was gone.

Kate's heart finally started to slow.

Sitting in his wheelchair next to Randy outside the cafe, Ed Fontaine spotted Chance walking toward him and wheeled himself in that direction. "I wondered if you were coming out — or if maybe you planned to spend the night in the cafe." He had wanted a word with Chance before he left for home. It hadn't occurred to him the boy might not be ready to leave, though thinking of the way he'd looked at Kate Rollins, maybe it should have.

"Sorry," Chance said, "I didn't realize you wanted to see me."

"Meeting went well, didn't you think?"

"Kate knows what she's doing. No doubt about it."

No there wasn't, Ed thought. The girl had done a masterful job of communicating her plans and getting the campaign off the ground. "There's a lot to do, but at least now we have some idea how to go about it."

"We're lucky to have her."

"Damned lucky," Ed said. He just didn't like the way Chance had kept looking at her at the meeting, or the way she kept looking at him. Not that they both weren't trying their damnedest not to. That's what worried him the most.

Oh, he knew Chance had an occasional affair. He figured maybe his little girl, Rachael, might have done the same thing, living in a big city like New York, but he tried not to think about that. In a way, it was probably good for them to get their wild oats sown before they settled down and got married. He just didn't like the notion of Chance getting in over his head.

Especially not now.

He had just received a letter from Rachael today. In another thirty days, his daughter would be finished with the modeling assignments she'd contracted for. She was going to take some time off, come back to the ranch for a couple of weeks. *I can't wait to see you, Daddy,* she'd said. *And of course Chance, too.* She'd talked about her career, but said she was getting a little tired of all the travel. *Maybe it's time I started thinking about the future.*

Ed looked up at Chance, saw him staring off toward the cafe. Inside he caught a glimpse of Kate Rollins in the light of the kitchen window.

Maybe it was time? As far as Ed was concerned it was high time indeed.

Kate got up early Thursday morning, worked on some ideas she had for the layout of the brochure, then headed over to the restaurant. Breakfast was busy, lunch was pretty much average. She'd started into the kitchen with the last tray of dirty dishes just as Myra walked out and the two of them nearly collided.

"You been doin' that all day," Myra said with a sparkle in her eye. "Wouldn't have nothin' to do with that date you got tonight with Chance McLain?"

Actually, it had everything to do with it. Ever since he had kissed her after the meeting, she couldn't get him out of her head. Now he was even interfering in her work!

"I shouldn't be going out with him," Kate said with a sigh, moving past Myra into the kitchen. "It's obvious the kind of man he is. If he has all the women you say he does —"

"I said the women all chase after him — there's a big difference. Oh, he's got his lady friends, all right — the man's only human, after all. And it gets darned lonely way out here. But Chance is a good man. From what I know, he's gone out of his way to be honest with the women he sees. He just hasn't met the right gal yet."

Kate set the tray of dishes down on the counter. "It doesn't really matter. I'm not ready to get involved in any sort of relationship. I don't think Chance is, either."

Myra cocked her head. "Sometimes whether you're ready or not don't make a damn." Hanging her apron on the peg beside the door, she turned and strolled out of the kitchen.

Kate followed her out, trying not to think about what Myra had said. "I've got a couple of calls to make. If you need me, I'll be over in my office."

"You're supposed to be off after lunch during the week or have you already forgot?"

Kate grinned. She was basically a workaholic, but she was trying hard to reform. With a wave at Myra, she left the cafe and started up the gravel road that led up the hill to the big white, two-story, wood-frame house. Upstairs in her office, she flipped open the file she had started on Nell Hart and called the sheriff's number written inside. This time she reached him.

The conversation was brief and completely one-sided.

"But surely just looking at the report wouldn't hurt anything. I'm her granddaughter. I just want to know what happened. If this happened to someone in your family, surely you'd want to know."

"I'm sorry, Ms. Rollins. The accident report is confidential."

"What about the coroner's report? Can't I at least take a look at that?"

"I'm afraid what you're asking is impossible." Sheriff Conrad patiently explained the rules, which seemed ridiculous to Kate. Since it was obvious no amount of arguing would convince the man to change his mind, she forced a little politeness into her voice, thanked him for his patience, and hung up the phone, wondering what new tack she might take.

The August day was warm. A soft breeze blew in through the screen door. As she turned and headed back downstairs, she noticed a tall figure climbing the front porch stairs — Chance McLain. Her stomach did its usual barrel roll, but Kate ignored it. Their supper date wasn't until later tonight.

A hopeful thought struck. Maybe something had come up and he had come to cancel.

Wishing she'd at least had a chance to comb her hair and change out of her pink nylon uniform, she pulled open the door. Hat in hand, he stood in front of her, dressed in a white, long-sleeved shirt with pearl snaps, black lizard boots, and the jeans he always wore, though these were newer, not yet faded, obviously worn for a special occasion.

Her heart skipped. She told herself it wasn't because she was glad to see him.

"Has my memory failed," she asked, "or aren't you here about four hours early?"

Chance just smiled, opened the screen door, and stepped into the entry. He took a quick look around, assessing the newly refinished hardwood floors, the overstuffed sofa, and freshly lemon-oiled antiques.

"The place looks terrific. I think Nell would have approved."

She didn't really care whether Nell Hart liked it or not, but she didn't say so. Like everyone else, Chance was convinced Nell was a paragon of virtue. Kate saw her more from her mother's point of view.

"If you've come about our date — I mean if something more important's come up —"

Chance grinned. "I can't think of anything more important than taking you to dinner."

Kate wet her lips. "If you're here about the campaign, I can show you what I've done so far with the layout on the brochures."

"Actually, I'm on my way to Polson. I remembered you were usually free in the afternoons. I know you wanted to go back and talk to the sheriff. I thought if you could get someone to cover for you later, you might want to come along."

Kate sighed. "I did talk to the sheriff. In fact, I just hung up the phone. Unfortunately, he won't let me see the accident report or the autopsy. I suppose I'll have to get a lawyer. Maybe there's some legal avenue I can use."

"It's that important?" He studied her face, trying to read her motives.

Kate kept her expression carefully blank. "I want to know what happened. Is that really so hard to understand?"

Chance's gaze held hers a moment more, making her want to squirm. "Maybe not. Tell you what. The sheriff — Barney Conrad — is a friend of mine. He owes me a couple of favors. If you want to come along, I can probably get him to let you read that report."

Her heart took a leap. "Do you really think he would?"

"Like I said, he owes me a couple of favors."

Kate wondered what sort of favors but didn't ask. Chance McLain was one of the wealthiest land owners in the county. That gave him a certain amount of power. He just might be able to help her.

"All right, I'd love to come along."

"What about David? Do you think he might want to come with us?"

She smiled just because he'd been kind enough to ask. Most men wouldn't have wanted to be bothered with a twelve-year-old boy. But summer school was over and since David hadn't made any new friends, he was more lonely than ever. He would probably have jumped at the opportunity to go if he had been home.

"David's off fishing with Chief. I think you've made a convert. Until you taught him how to fly fish, he was always talking about going back to LA. He hasn't said a word about it lately."

"I'm glad to hear it. I like your son." He smiled. "Almost as much as I like his mother."

Kate flushed a little, wondering if he meant it. She left him and hurried upstairs, phoned Bonnie to cover her evening shift, then changed into a clean pair of jeans, a cream silk blouse, and a brown tweed sport coat with leather patches on the elbows. She didn't want to look like a city girl, but she didn't want to look like a hayseed, either. She wrote David a quick note, pinned it on the message board in the kitchen, then returned to where Chance stood waiting in the living room.

She flashed him a sunny smile. "I'm ready when you are."

"If you're waitin' for me, darlin', you're backin' up. Let's go."

Kate grabbed her purse and walked past him out the door, her chest oddly full at his endearment. She couldn't help wondering if he called every woman that. It was a Western-man kind of thing. Undoubtedly he did. It was ridiculous to wish he had meant the word especially for her.

Chapter Eleven

Sitting on the comfortable seat, Kate watched Chance drive the busy, two-lane road to Polson with the same confident nonchalance he had shown before, handling the big Dodge as if it were a sports car instead of a truck she could barely climb into.

They made casual conversation along the way, Chance asking about David, how he was adjusting, whether or not he had begun to make friends.

Kate sighed. "He spends most of his time with Chief, which is fine, of course, certainly better than the kids he hung around with in LA. I just wish he had a few friends his own age. Now that summer school is out there's even less hope of that happening."

Chance seemed to mull that over. "He's a good boy. In time the other kids will figure that out. In the meantime, at least he's staying out of trouble."

True, thank God, but lately he seemed to be withdrawing again, spending more and more time up in his room. Still, her son was hardly Chance's problem. "What about you? You haven't lost any more cattle?"

Chance shook his head. "We've been keeping a close watch lately. No more problems so far."

They turned down the main street of Polson. Chance drove into a parking area behind a wood frame building and backed the truck up to a big metal roll-up door.

"While they load the feed I ordered last time I was in town, we can go over and the see the sheriff."

Kate waited for Chance to come around and open the door. She was usually too liberated for that sort of thing, but the truck was so high she didn't have much choice. And in truth, it felt kind of good being with a man who had old-fashioned manners.

They started walking the two blocks to the courthouse, Kate hurrying to keep up with those long legs of his. When he realized he was walking too fast, he slowed down.

"Sorry. I guess I'm not used to someone so small."

Her lips tightened. "I'm not that small."

One of his eyebrows quirked up. He looked like he was fighting a grin. "My mistake," he said with only a slight twitch of his lips.

They rounded the corner and walked up the long cement sidewalk leading to the three-story brick building that housed the sheriff's office. Chance pushed open the heavy glass doors out in front and they continued on into the lobby.

"Give me a minute," he said. "This won't take long."

Kate wandered while he spoke to the sheriff, filling the time by reading the community posters taped on the walls: The Silver County Fair and Rodeo, coming up in two weeks, the 103rd Annual Arlee Powwow, scheduled for next Sunday; the 4-H Horse Show at the Polson fairgrounds the end of the month. She smiled to think how different life was up here.

"Kate?"

She turned at the sound of Chance's voice and he motioned for her to join him.

"You talked him into it?" she whispered when she reached him, only a little surprised.

"He didn't much like it, but he grudgingly agreed." Chance grinned. "I told him he owed me for keeping quiet about what happened at his bachelor party the night before he got re-married last year."

Kate laughed. "So now I suppose I'm the one who's in your debt."

Chance's blue eyes seemed to dance. "Maybe. If you are, I'm sure I can think of a way for you to repay me."

Kate made no reply but her legs felt suddenly shaky. What would Chance McLain want in re-turn? Images of his tall, sinewy body, naked and lying on top of her, made perspiration bead between her breasts. Kate walked through the door with her shoulders a little straighter, forcing her mind to the meeting ahead.

Sheriff Barney Conrad stood waiting. He was almost as tall as Chance, spare and fit, with brown hair and hazel eyes. He was a man in his forties whose smile showed a few too many teeth, but they were white and even, his lips curved up in a friendly manner. Still, she couldn't help thinking it was the smile of a consummate politician.

"Ms. Rollins. It's a pleasure to meet you. Chance says you're new to Montana. Welcome to Silver County."

"Thank you, Sheriff."

He led them into his private office and closed the frosted-glass door. Reaching down, he picked up the manila folder lying on his desk and handed it over. "You realize these files are confidential. We don't usually share the information outside the office. However, since there are mitigating circumstances in this case, I suppose we can bend the rules just this once."

The mitigating circumstances being his behavior at the bachelor party? Kate just smiled. "Thank you, Sheriff. Since I never had the chance to know my grandmother, I'd like to find out as much about her as I can. Even the way she died is of interest." *Especially the way she died,* she silently amended, opening the file.

She had never read a sheriff's report, but it looked fairly straightforward. Case number. Date of occurrence. Name of the parties involved. Next came a description of the deceased, Nell Mary Beth Hart. *Mary Beth.* It was her mother's real name. She had changed it from Mary Beth Hart Lambert to Celeste Heart because she thought it sounded more glamorous.

It was a surprise to find Nell had shared her

name with her daughter, an ironic sort of bond, since in life they had been so far apart.

She continued to read the report. The deputy, an officer named Greer, described the scene, that he had come upon a woman in her seventies, approximately five feet in height, weighing 95 to 105 pounds on the floor of the dining room of the house at 48 Sandy Creek Road in Lost Peak. It went on to give details of the accident scene and what the officer believed had occurred.

In response to a 911 call from a Mrs. Aida Whittaker, a close friend of the deceased who had arrived for a visit, I pulled up in front of the house at approximately 3:12 PM. On entering the house, I discovered the body of a female Caucasian personally known to me for more than ten years to be Nell Hart. The deceased appeared to have been dead for at least several hours. An examination of the scene indicated she had tripped over a throw rug that was found entangled between her feet. The subsequent fall had apparently caused her to hit the back of her head on a corner of the sideboard. There was trauma to the head that resulted in a large amount of bleeding.

No other marks were evident on the body. There were no signs of forced entry and no signs of a struggle.

Kate read on, trying not to be moved by the

picture of the old woman dying alone on the floor of her home.

She cast a look at Chance. "It says there was no forced entry. Would you know if Nell kept her doors locked?"

"I doubt it. Nobody around here does."

Kate went over the report one last time, memorizing the details, but seeing nothing that seemed significant. She handed back the file.

"Thank you, Sheriff Conrad. I believe I understand what happened. Now if I could just see the autopsy report, I'll be —"

"I'm sorry. I thought you understood. Silver County is small and far from wealthy. In instances such as these, where the manner of death is so completely clear-cut, an autopsy is not performed. It saves the family a certain amount of grief and the county a considerable sum of money."

"But surely —"

"This is Montana, Kate," Chance gently put in. "Your grandmother was seventy-two years old. When people reach that age, sometimes unfortunate things happen. We've learned to accept that out here."

Kate held her tongue. Chance was probably right. Even in the city, people had accidents all the time, some of them fatal. It wasn't unusual. It was just part of living.

So why did she feel so strongly that in this case everyone was wrong?

She gave the sheriff the politest smile she

could muster. "I appreciate your help, Sheriff Conrad. I'm sorry for any trouble I might have caused."

His politician's smile slid back in place. "No trouble at all, Ms. Rollins. That's what we're here for — to serve those in need."

Chance settled a hand at the small of her back and they started toward the door.

"Thanks, Barney," he called back over his shoulder. Outside the building, they walked in silence back to the feed store. The pickup was loaded and ready when they got there. Chance paid for the feed, helped her climb into the cab, then slid into the driver's seat and closed the door.

He eyed her with a long scrutiny. "You're awfully quiet. I thought once you saw the report you'd feel better."

She tried for a smile, but it faltered. "Thanks for helping."

"What is it, Kate? Why is this so important? What is it you're not telling me?"

She stared down at her lap, remembering the gunshot that had very nearly killed her, the anguish she had seen that night in her grandmother's face; thinking of Chet Munson and the terrible newspaper stories; wishing she could tell him the truth.

Knowing he would think she was out of her mind.

"I don't know, Chance. Something about it just keeps nagging me. I can't seem to let it go."

He reached over and caught her hand, laced her fingers with his. "It's natural, I suppose, to wonder what happened when you lose someone in your family. I gather yours is pretty small. That probably makes it worse."

Kate didn't answer. She didn't really have a family, only she and David and a couple of distant cousins.

"It's almost five o'clock," Chance said with a glance at his big chrome wristwatch. "Why don't we go over to the El Rio and I'll buy you a margarita? You're a California girl. You gotta like margaritas."

She did, though she hadn't had one in as long as she could remember. She worked up a smile. "Sounds like a winner to me."

Chance fired up the pickup. They skirted the bottom of Flathead Lake, where Polson was situated, and arrived at a restaurant that overlooked the river. The parking lot wasn't full this early, but a few cars were lined up out front. A white Jeep Cherokee pulled up just as Chance opened her door and helped her down. She couldn't miss the scowl on his face.

"What is it?" She followed his gaze to the men getting out of the Cherokee.

"Lon Barton and some of his cronies. Just my luck I'd run into them tonight." His hard look said he had plans that didn't include anyone but the two of them, and Kate felt a soft, unexpected quiver of desire.

"Come on," he said. "We were here first and

154

those margaritas still sound good." She let him take her hand and tug her toward the front door of the restaurant, beating Lon Barton and his men by several seconds. The place was surprisingly sophisticated, by Montana standards, done in bright blue and lemon yellow with light wood floors, ceiling fans, and pretty mosaic tiles, more like a restaurant she might have encountered at Newport Beach.

Chance led her into the bar off to the right, which was also done Santa Fe-style. They sat down at one of the tables along the side and he ordered a pitcher of margaritas.

"A pitcher?" Kate eyed him warily. "You aren't trying to get me drunk and take advantage of me, are you?"

His mouth edged up at the corners. God, such a sexy mouth. "No, but it isn't a bad idea. It'd be interesting to see what you're like once you let your guard down."

Kate took a sip of her drink, suddenly needing the calming effect. It was cold and frosty, not exactly like the ones she used to get back home, but not bad either. "I don't let my guard down often."

"You're telling me?" He took a sip of his drink. "The question is, why not?"

Kate glanced away, nonchalantly shrugging her shoulders. "Too much at stake, I guess."

"Like what? Or am I getting too personal again?"

She took another sip of her margarita. "You

are. But in this case, I suppose you have a right to know."

"I'm listening." He took another drink, licking the salt off with his tongue. It was long and wet and slick. For a minute Kate forgot what she was going to say.

She drank a little more of her margarita. "The truth is, my divorce isn't final. Technically, you're out with a married woman."

One of his eyebrows inched up. "I don't make a habit of it. In your case I suppose I can make an exception. Since I've got you in the mood to be candid, what's the problem?"

Kate sighed. "My ex-husband. Tommy's been a problem since the day I met him. He wanted a bigger settlement, which dragged things out. He threatened to sue for custody of David unless he got it. I wound up having to pay him alimony for the next five years just to get him to cooperate."

"You're kidding."

"I wish I were."

"Not exactly my kinda guy."

"No, I don't suppose he would be. He hasn't been my kinda guy for at least the last ten years."

"So why did you stay?"

"Mostly because of David. Because I didn't want what happened to me to happen to my son. I was raised without a father and I didn't want that to happen to David. Eventually I realized having a father like Tommy wasn't much better than having no father at all."

"I always wanted a mother, but my father never remarried. He thought women were only good for one thing. Fortunately, he wasn't around all that often and I never believed much of what he said when he was."

"Then you don't believe women are only good for one thing?"

His mouth edged up. "Women are good for a lot of things. I won't deny, however, sex ranks high on the list."

She couldn't help a smile. Sex had never been high on her list. With Tommy it was simply an obligation. After she discovered his endless infidelities, it dwindled to nothing at all.

She glanced over at Chance. He was watching her in that intense way of his, and her insides melted like a warm cube of butter. What would sex be like with a man like Chance? And, God above, did she dare risk finding out?

They finished their drinks, then went in to supper. Kate hadn't eaten Mexican food since she'd left LA. Considering they were 1,500 miles from the border, the enchiladas were surprisingly good, and the chile verde that Chance ordered was downright delicious. As a side benefit, the meat and cheese soaked up the margaritas they had drunk earlier.

It wasn't quite eight o'clock when they left the restaurant, but both of them started work with the sun, and everyone in Montana seemed to live on an early-morning schedule. They had just walked out in the parking lot when she spotted the man Chance had said was Lon Barton.

He was tall and blond, maybe a couple of years older than Chance, but instead of the corporate image she had expected, Barton wore his curly yellow hair a little bit long and sported a thick blond mustache. He was dressed in a red plaid shirt and jeans, looking more like a logger than the wealthy mine owner he was.

"That you, McLain?" Barton started walking in their direction, and beneath his breath, Chance swore softly. "I thought I saw you earlier," Barton went on. "How are things going over on the Running Moon?"

Chance's dark look returned. "They could be better. I could still have six more live cows instead of six dead ones if they hadn't drunk some of that water you polluted up on the rez."

Barton stiffened. "I didn't pollute anything. If your cattle are dead, that's your problem, McLain. It's got nothing to do with me." He turned his attention to Kate, whipping a red bill cap off his head that said LIFE IS SOLID GOLD.

"I don't think we've met." He extended a hand to Kate. It was smooth and pale, she noticed as she grudgingly shook it, not work-roughened, a contrast to the blue-collar look that marked the rest of his appearance. "I'm Lon Barton. It's a pleasure to meet you, Ms. . . . ?"

"Rollins. Kate Rollins."

"Of course. You're the new owner of the Lost Peak Cafe. I've heard a great deal about you."

"I've heard about you, too, Mr. Barton."

"Lon. Please. Over the next few months we'll be seeing a lot of each other. We might as well dispense with formalities now."

Chance eased her a little behind him. "I don't think she'll be seeing all that much of you, Barton. If you're counting on opening that mine on Silver Fox Creek, it isn't going to happen."

All three of Barton's companions moved in a little closer, the tallest of the bunch edging in front of the rest. "Oh, it's gonna happen, McLain," he said. "Whether you like it or not."

"Easy, Duke," Barton warned, but the man didn't yield an inch. He was taller than Lon, about the same height as Chance, but heavier through the chest and shoulders, his fleshy face slightly ruddy. As the old saying went, he looked like he ate nails for breakfast.

"You better keep your guard dogs on a leash," Chance warned Barton. "If you don't they might wind up hurting someone."

"Yeah," Duke said, stepping forward, "and tonight that someone's gonna be you!" He swung a heavy fist, and Kate bit back a gasp of alarm, but Chance anticipated the blow and ducked it easily.

"I'm glad you did that, Mullens. I've been looking for an excuse to clean your plow for the last two years." Throwing a quick hard punch that came straight from the shoulder, Chance's long reach connected solidly with Duke Mullens's chin. The man reeled backward and nearly went down. When he regained his balance, there was bloodlust on his face and murder in his small black eyes.

Worry for Chance rose up. She didn't want him getting hurt and Duke Mullens looked more than capable of doing just that.

Bouncing once or twice on the balls of his feet, Mullens spat in the dirt and charged back toward Chance. A couple of swift left jabs took Chance by surprise. A hard right to the jaw sent him spinning into the dirt.

"Chance!" Kate started toward him, but Barton caught her arm.

"Stay out of this, Kate. You'll only get hurt."

"We can't just let them fight. Can't you do something?"

Beneath the thick mustache, his mouth curved up. "Let 'em have their fun. They've been itching for this for the last two years."

"Why?"

"Bad blood, you might say. Duke stole one of Chance's women a couple years back. I guess he doesn't cotton much to that."

Duke stole one of Chance's women. The words made her feel slightly sick. Was that what this was all about? Jealousy over one of his past

160

lovers? Kate made no reply, just stood trembling, watching in growing horror as the two men continued to battle back and forth in the parking lot.

By now, blood was running freely from Duke Mullens's nose. Chance had a cut near the corner of his mouth and blood streamed from above his left eye down his cheek, staining his white shirt crimson. Muttering a curse at his opponent, he swung a powerful blow that would have done any normal man in. Instead, Mullens lowered his head, rammed Chance like a bull, and both men crashed to the ground.

Chance rolled on top, getting in a few good blows before Mullens shoved him away and staggered back to his feet. Chance was ready and waiting. Ignoring the blood leaking into his eye, he shot a hard left to Mullens's stomach, followed by a blow to the bigger man's jaw. A hard final blow, and Mullens sailed backward, landing hard in the dirt. This time he didn't get up.

"That was for Sherry," Chance said, wiping the blood from his mouth with the back of his hand. He bent and grabbed his Stetson up from where it had landed on the ground, slammed it on his head, and strode toward her. Wordlessly, he gripped her arm, nearly lifting her off of her feet as he tugged her toward the truck.

One quick jerk and the door flew open. Chance swung her up on the seat. In minutes they were tearing out of the parking lot, gravel flying out behind the wheels as they pulled onto the street, headed back to Highway 93 and Lost Peak.

Kate's heart still pounded. But now that she was over the shock and fear, her trembling came mostly from anger. Even the dark red blood trailing down Chance's lean cheek couldn't cool her temper.

"All right, now that you've had your fun, the next fight you're having is with me." She turned a fierce look on the man with the tight jaw staring down the road ahead of them. "Was all of that really necessary? You had to brawl like an animal because some woman you were dating dumped you for another man?"

For an instant, his long brown fingers tightened around the wheel, then he sighed. "Sherry is only a friend. We dated years ago in high school. Since then, she's been more like a sister."

"Go on."

"Duke and I played football together on the varsity squad. He was a jerk then. He's an even bigger jerk now."

"That's hardly an excuse for battering each other all over the parking lot."

His mouth tightened. "Two years ago Sherry made the unfortunate mistake of going out with him. Before the evening was over, Mullens raped her."

The air seemed to stick in Kate's lungs. Date

rape. It happened all the time. "If that's true, why isn't he in jail?"

"Because Sherry wouldn't press charges. She didn't think anyone would believe her. She'd known Duke for years. She'd been divorced for a while and I guess she got lonely. That night when Duke took her home, she invited him up to her apartment. It was two in the morning and both of them had been drinking. She wanted to make him some coffee before he drove back to his apartment. Instead, once he got inside, he slapped her around, dragged her down on the sofa, and raped her."

Kate stared at the muscle flexing in his jaw. The headlights of passing cars blinked past, one after another, throwing his prominent cheekbones into shadow.

"Even if that happened," she said a little more gently, "it wasn't your fault. You had nothing to do with it."

"Like I said, Sherry's a friend. Mullens is also the SOB who does most of Barton's dirty work. Which means he's most likely the guy in charge of the dumping that killed my six cows."

Whatever argument she had left slowly faded. She lived in Montana now. Apparently people here still handled their troubles with their fists. Opening her purse, she pulled out a Kleenex, leaned over, and dabbed at the blood at the corner of Chance's mouth.

She could feel his lips edging up. "Thanks."

"You're welcome." She blotted the blood

163

over his eye, wiped it off his cheek, then tucked the Kleenex back in her purse.

Chance cast her a sidelong glance. "You know this wasn't exactly the evening I had planned."

"It wasn't? And here I thought you set the whole thing up just to impress me."

"If I had, I'd have left out the part where Mullens knocked the hell out of me." He worked his jaw back and forth a couple of times. "Duke throws a punch like a mule. Good thing he's clumsy."

"From the looks of you, I'd say it's a very good thing."

He chuckled and relaxed back against the seat. They rode the rest of the way home in silence. When they reached her house, he walked her up to the door.

"I don't suppose you're gonna invite me in."

"I don't suppose."

"Next time I promise I'll be a paragon of gentlemanly conduct."

"Next time? After what happened tonight? Who says there's going to be a next time?"

His expression turned intense, his eyes so blue they looked neon. "I do, Kate." Bending forward, he kissed her, the softest, sweetest kiss she'd ever had. Then he groaned and the softness fled.

His mouth took hers with utter abandon, hot and restless, possessive now, telling her what he wanted. His tongue slid in and heat flooded into her stomach, sank like liquid into her core. Her legs were trembling, her heart racing madly. She could feel the jagged cut on his lip; caught the faint, coppery taste of his blood. She found herself swaying toward him, going up on her toes, pressing herself more closely against his solid length.

His hands slid down, wrapped around her bottom and lifted her a little more, pressing her softness into his groin. He was iron-hard and pulsing, bigger than she thought a man could be, and straining against the zipper of his jeans. A wildfire flamed inside her. Any minute she'd go up in a puff of smoke.

Chance kissed the side of her neck, then cupped a breast, massaging her nipple until it grew stiff and tight.

"I wish I hadn't screwed things up tonight," he whispered, easing back, though she no longer wanted him to, pressing a last soft kiss on her mouth. "I had plans for you that didn't include Duke Mullens. I'll make it up to you, I promise."

Kate just stood there. After watching him brawl in the dirt like a cave man, she had every reason to refuse to see him again. Instead, the fact he had been fighting for a woman he considered a friend only made him more appealing. She had never known a man like him.

"How about Saturday night?" he asked, taking a step down off the porch. "You run the place. You can take the evening off if you want.

I'd like to show you the ranch. We could have supper there."

She'd love to see it. But her common sense was screaming at her to say no. At the rate they were going, sooner or later, she would wind up in Chance's bed. She wasn't ready for that to happen. She wasn't sure she ever would be. And what about the consequences? Chance was far more experienced with women than she was with men. What if all she meant to him was a simple one-night stand?

Worse than that, what if her ex-husband found out? He might start trouble with David again.

Kate looked away. "I don't think that's a good idea."

"Why not?"

"The divorce, for one thing."

"My cook is extremely discreet. And the hands know better than to gossip. No one will ever know you were there."

"Chance, I don't know . . ."

He stepped back up on the porch, framed her face between his hands. "Yes, you do, Kate. You know what's going to happen and so do I." He kissed her, very deeply, very thoroughly, then he backed away. "But I won't press you. You can have all the time you need." He stepped down off the porch. "I'll pick you up at six. I want to show you around a little before we eat."

Kate said nothing, just watched him walk

away, his long-legged strides carrying him over to his pickup.

I won't press you. You can have all the time you need. The words had a calming effect. The pressure was off. They could simply be together and have a good time.

Kate sighed as she walked back into the house. And even if he meant to seduce her it wouldn't change her mind. No matter how many times between now and then she tried to talk herself out of it, in the long run, she knew she would go.

She wanted to see him. She wanted to be with him. Dear God, she wanted him to make love to her. It was the most insane thing she could possibly do.

Chapter Twelve

Chance drove back to the ranch a little slower than he usually did, mentally hashing over the night's events. His knuckles were scraped and raw, burning as his fingers wrapped around the leather-covered steering wheel.

The cut over his eye was turning a purplish blue. His lip was cut and swollen — a fact he seemed to have forgotten when he had been kissing Kate.

He thought of her and silently cursed. Damn, he'd behaved like a fool tonight, letting his temper get the best of him. He'd had a premonition of trouble the minute he'd spotted Lon Barton and Duke Mullens. He should have climbed back in his truck and driven like a bat out of hell the other way, as soon as he'd seen Barton's car.

But the truth was, he wasn't a damn bit sorry. Mullens had deserved a beating for what he'd done. The bastard ought to be in jail.

Chance sighed. At least the first part of the evening had gone fairly well. He liked Kate Rollins. Liked her intelligence and the grit it had taken for her to move from the city to a place like Lost Peak. He even liked the fact she kept saying no to him. Not many women did. Especially not the ones he pursued the way he had Kate.

Kate had principles, something too many people lacked these days. On top of that, she had the sexiest, most desirable little body he'd ever seen. Kate wasn't tall and svelte like Rachael. She didn't have the almost unreal beauty the haughty, I'm-the-hottest-thing-in-town manner, that had attracted him to Rachael. Kate was a down-to-earth, no-nonsense kind of female, yet she was soft and feminine, voluptuous in a way that really turned him on. He could imagine all of that thick red hair spread out across his pillow. His jeans went tight every time he thought of filling his hands with those magnificent breasts.

Chance slowed the pickup and turned off the road, pulling through the big pine gate that led to the Running Moon. He'd brought a lot of women up to see the ranch, but only a few had ever been invited into his house. It was his private refuge, his place of escape from the problems he faced every time he walked out the door. Still, for some odd reason, he looked forward to showing the place to Kate.

Chance drove up the long gravel driveway that led to the big two-story log house, pressed the garage door opener on the visor above his head, and drove into the three-car garage.

Stepping out of the truck, he paused for a moment to look out into the darkness. The night was unbelievably crisp and clear, so black you could see every star, and there was a whole diamond spray of them. He loved nights like these. If he hadn't been bruised and battered from head to foot, his clothes torn and smeared with blood — some his, most of it Duke's — he'd have driven Kate up to the top of Lookout Mountain and they could have watched the stars together.

Somehow he knew she would have liked that. And he would have liked just being with her.

Chance frowned, for the first time uneasy at the train of his thoughts. He hadn't been this attracted to a woman in years, maybe never. For nearly as long as he could remember, it had been clear that Rachael was the woman he would marry. He had known her since she was a child, had been attracted to her since the day she'd come home from her fancy Eastern college all grown up and looking like she'd just stepped off the cover of *Vogue* magazine — which was exactly what she hoped to do.

They had dated all that summer. By the time she was ready to leave for the modeling job she had landed in New York City, they had reached an unspoken agreement. Eventually, when both of them were ready to settle down, they would marry.

In time Rachael would inherit the Circle Bar F. Their children's legacy would be a spread twice the size of the Running Moon.

Even more important, the marriage was what Ed wanted, and Chance owed everything to Ed.

Marrying Rachael was the best thing for all

of them, probably even Rachael. Trotting around the world as a famous cover model could only last so long. The fashion industry was all about youth and beauty, and it didn't take long before a woman was simply too old. Way before that happened, Rachael would be ready to settle down.

And he would take good care of her. Ed could count on him for that.

Chance thought of her exquisitely beautiful face, her pale blond hair, and slim, boyish figure. He tried to picture himself married to Rachael, coming home to her dusty and tired after a hard day of working on the ranch.

Instead of a tall, sleek blond, the woman who came to mind was way more petite, with clouds of thick dark red hair, and soft, voluptuous curves. A man could get lost in those curves. He could imagine their softness easing his fatigue.

Chance shook his head, uncomfortable with the image. He couldn't afford to get involved with Kate, not on a serious level. Nothing could ever come of it. He was already committed to somebody else.

Then again, marriage to Rachael was still months away, maybe even years.

Chance pressed the button, lowering the garage door, and went inside the house. He was worrying for nothing. Kate wasn't looking for a permanent relationship. She wasn't even divorced from the last guy she had married. She didn't want any more from him than he wanted from her. In the meantime, they could simply enjoy each other.

A knock on the front door interrupted his thoughts. He paused halfway up the pine staircase on the way to his room.

His foreman, Roddy Darnell, stuck his head inside the door. "Sorry to bother you, Chance. Ed Fontaine stopped by earlier. Said to tell you the court's finally granted that injunction against Consolidated for the spill up on Beaver Creek."

"So old Frank Mills finally came through." They'd had a helluva time collecting enough evidence to convince a judge, but apparently it had finally happened. "It was damned sure time."

"That's what Ed said. He thought you'd want to know."

Hoping maybe this time the judge would squeeze enough money out of Consolidated to actually pay for the spill and make them think twice about letting it happen again, Chance started back up the stairs. "Thanks, Roddy."

The man didn't budge, just continued to stand in the doorway. "You all right, Chance?"

He glanced down at the blood on the front of his shirt. "Had a little misunderstanding with Duke Mullens. We got it straightened out."

Roddy cracked a smile, which he rarely did. "Mullens could use a little straightenin' out."

Chance just smiled and continued up the

stairs, his mind on Consolidated Metals. He just hoped whichever judge they drew wasn't on Lon Barton's payroll.

Turning into the parking lot, Lon Barton pulled up in front of the Consolidated Metals headquarters building at the mine on Beaver Creek. All four doors on the Cherokee swung open and the men stepped out. With a wave in Lon's direction, they set off toward their cars.

"See you tomorrow, boss." Duke Mullens started after them, heading for his Chevy pickup.

"Wait a minute, Duke. There's something I need to talk to you about." Mullens turned away from the others. He looked like hell, both eyes swollen nearly closed and turning black and blue, his nose broken, and his lip puffed up. Duke had lost to McLain tonight, and he didn't like it. Lon wondered how long it would take before he evened the score.

Mullens walked toward him, joining him next to the car. "Yeah, boss, what's up?" A note of interest rang in his husky voice.

Duke was always eager to do Lon's bidding and it wasn't just the pay. The jobs he did were often dangerous and risky. Sometimes they even called for a bit of rough stuff. That was the part Duke liked best. Undoubtedly he was hoping whatever it was had something to do with Chance McLain.

In a way, maybe it did.

"The Rollins woman. From what I gather, she's the one heading the campaign to stop us from overturning that cyanide ban. I want to know everything you can find out about her."

Duke's interest piqued even more. "She's a hot little number. All that fiery red hair and those big round tits. I'd like to have a taste of that myself."

"I hear she's from LA. Give Sid Battistone a call. See what he can dig up." Battistone was a private investigator Lon had used on the West Coast a couple of times before. "And while you're at it, do a little local snooping. See if you can find out why she moved to a godforsaken hole like Lost Peak."

"You got it, boss. Anything else?"

"Not at the moment. First, let's see what we find out. Might turn out to be interesting."

Duke waved as he crossed to his pickup and climbed in. Mullens was well paid. And aside from the mess he'd made of things tonight, he was good at his job. It wouldn't be long before Lon knew everything there was to know about Kate Rollins.

He wondered what secrets she kept. And what he might be able to do with them once he found out.

Kate dreamed that night. It was a dream she'd had before, disturbing thoughts about the night of the shooting. In the dream, she was floating upward, hovering above the operating table, drifting away from her body. She rose through the darkness into a long black tunnel, heading for the beautiful light at the end. When she finally reached it, she saw the warm familiar faces of people she once knew. The smiling face of her mother, the faces of lost friends.

Nell Hart was among them, in the simple blue-print housedress she had been wearing in the photo. She was trying to speak, but Kate couldn't hear her. She was pleading, reaching out to her, trying to tell her something. It was important. Urgent.

Kate tried to touch her, tried desperately to understand. *What is it?* she silently pleaded. *Tell me what it is you want me to know!* But like the dreams that had come before, it was too late.

Kate moved restlessly on the pillow, trying to escape the disturbing images, struggling to awaken. On the edge of consciousness, a single thought formed in the back of her mind, hazy at first, concentrating slowly, until it was crystal clear.

Murder.

Kate slammed wide awake. She was trembling all over, her body bathed in icy perspiration. Her mouth felt dry and her muscles were taut as a shoestring. Her hair was a damp, tangled mass that clung to her neck and shoulders. As soon as she was lucid the dream began to fade, but this time she remembered it long enough to register her last single thought.

"Murder," she whispered into the darkness of her bedroom, shivering, though the room wasn't cold. Could it possibly be true? Was that the message her grandmother had wanted to give her? Or was it only some morbid trick of her imagination?

Kate sat up in bed, her back propped uncomfortably against the antique carved wooden headboard. Maybe none of it ever happened. No brilliant white light. No faces from the past. Maybe the whole thing was just a bizarre hoax conjured in her mind. Kate rubbed her eyes, feeling limp and drained. She glanced at the digital clock beside the bed. Only four A.M. She didn't want to get up, but she was wide-awake now and there was no way she could possibly go back to sleep.

Reaching over, she snapped on the bedside lamp, tossed back the pretty blue quilt she had found on Nell's bed when she'd first moved into the house, grabbed her yellow terry cloth robe, and padded into the bathroom.

She came out feeling a little better. Not wanting to awaken David, she picked up the flashlight she kept beside the bed for emergencies, stepped out into the hall, and flipped it on. It was dark in the house. The floorboards squeaked as she climbed the narrow staircase leading up to the third floor attic.

She'd been meaning to go through her grandmother's things since she'd moved into the house. There was simply so much to do that time had slipped away. Then yesterday a copy of the will had arrived in the mail, sent as requested from Nell's attorney in Missoula, Clifton Boggs. Kate was almost disappointed to discover no other bequests in the will except the ones to her. No one had benefited from her grandmother's death, as she had secretly thought might have occurred.

She sighed to think of it. Left with another dead end, she was almost ready to give up the search. But the dream had prodded her, refused to let her quit. She was forced to begin again and at least take this last, final step.

It was dusty up in the attic. Kate sneezed a couple of times as her robe flapped open, sending a fine, silty spray of dust into the air. She picked her way past a stack of old chairs, a shadeless lamp, a pair of outdated cross-country skis, and finally reached the towering stack of boxes.

After Nell had died, Aida Whittaker had taken charge of her things, storing clothes, costume jewelry, and all of Nell's bills and correspondence up in the attic.

Kate dug around until she located the boxes marked TAX RECORDS, PERSONAL AND BUSINESS FILES, then she pulled up a little maple rocker she hadn't had the heart to throw away and started digging through the first box in the stack.

Given the assumption Nell was actually murdered — which was a very big stretch, since she didn't have a single shred of evidence to that effect — there had to be a reason. Who would want to murder a harmless old woman? What could anyone possibly have to gain? And if it was murder, how had the murderer managed to make it look like an accident?

Random murders happened, of course. Serial killers often tortured and killed victims they came upon merely by chance. Considering there were no signs of a struggle, it didn't seem likely. Nell Hart appeared to be a strong, self-possessed woman. She wouldn't have gone down without a fight. No, she had to have known her assailant, probably even trusted him.

Motive was the key. If she could discover the why, she could begin to work on the how.

The sun was coming up by the time she was halfway through the next to last box of aging yellow papers, and so far her search had been no more fruitful than any other of her endeavors. Shoving a mass of heavy red curls out of her face, rubbing the ache in her back that zinged clear up into her neck, Kate started through the last manila folder in the box.

There were documents inside, some of them dating back a number of years: the deed to the house, the deed and chattel mortgage — paid in full — for the cafe, a bill of sale for some cattle Zach Hart had purchased. Neither Nell nor her husband ever seemed to throw anything away.

Kate pulled out another envelope, this one tattered but not looking quite so old. There was another deed inside. It was dated April 18, 1972, ten years after Zach Hart had died and three years before her grandmother had purchased the Lost Peak Cafe. Kate did a quick mental calculation. Nell had been forty-three years old.

She took a closer look at the document. Unlike the other property her grandmother had owned over the years, this piece was held jointly with someone else. She recognized the name. Silas Marshall. Silas owned the grocery store across the street. He was the man who had been kind enough to give David a part-time job when they'd first arrived in Lost Peak. Two days ago, Silas had stopped by to see her. Apparently, he'd forgiven David for stealing the package of gum. Silas offered him his old job back and, eager for the extra spending money, David had agreed.

She liked Silas Marshall.

Kate tapped the document thoughtfully against her knee, then looked down at the printing on the front. Joint Tenancy Grant Deed. It was the kind of deed married couples often used, the sort that granted the right of survivorship. If one of the parties died, all rights went to the other party.

She wondered why her grandmother would have used that kind of deed with Silas Marshall. And why he had never mentioned anything about it. Surely it was simple coincidence that Silas was the only other person Kate had discovered who had benefited from Nell Hart's death.

She studied the legal description, saw that the land was somewhere in Silver County. She wondered where it was and whether or not it had any real value. She refused to let her mind go further. Maybe they had sold the piece years ago. Maybe the property was nothing but a worthless hunk of dirt.

Still, as soon as she finished working the breakfast shift, she'd go upstairs to her office and call First American Title. She'd find out if the property was owned by Nell and Silas at the time Nell died. If it was, she'd ask for a map showing the property's location and get the tax collector's assessed evaluation of its worth.

Wondering if she had just found the first real clue to the mystery, Kate took the document and headed downstairs.

Two days passed before Kate had a chance to learn more. She was refilling the last lunch customer's coffee cup and contemplating what she'd found out from First American Title when the screen door swung open and Chief walked in.

Kate smiled and carried the coffee pot over to the booth where he sat down.

"Want a cup?" she asked.

Chief just nodded and turned over his heavy

white china mug. Kate filled it up, but made no move to leave. "Have you got a minute, Chief? There's something I'd like to ask you about."

"Plenty of time," Chief said, motioning her toward the pink padded vinyl seat on the opposite side of the booth. Kate set the pot on the table and sat down.

"I know you knew my grandmother."

Chief nodded. His domed hat rested on the seat beside him, revealing his two long silver brands. He was the absolute cliche of a wooden Indian. Inwardly, Kate smiled to think that he probably dressed that way on purpose, laughing all the while at the reaction of the tourists.

"Did you know Nell and Silas Marshall owed a piece of property together?"

He looked pensive for a moment, then the light of remembrance came into his dark eyes. "Silas wanted to buy land next to his ranch, but he needed money. He and Nell were friends. Nell offered to loan it to him. Silas refused. Said they could be partners, that the land would make a good investment."

"Why? What was so special about it?"

"Big water. Deep well. People always need water. Made Silas's property more valuable."

"I see." But she didn't really, of course. Or maybe she just didn't want to. She was beginning to think her single clue wasn't a clue at all. Nobody would kill someone for a well — would they?

"Thanks, Chief."

"Your son. He's going to be a very good fish-erman."

Kate smiled with pleasure. "Is he?"

"Caught a big brown yesterday. Catch and release, though. He had to let it go."

"That's all right. I'm sure he had fun just catching it."

"He's a good boy."

"Yes, he is." Kate took the coffeepot back to the kitchen, thinking of David, wishing some of the boys his own age would give him a chance.

Myra stood just inside the door. She grabbed a dishrag off the counter as Kate walked in. " 'Bout time for you to take off for the after-noon, ain't it?"

Kate looked over at the clock. "I suppose so. I've got those brochures almost done, but I need to finish the layout for the T-shirts. Da-vid's been helping me with them. We've de-cided to use the slogan, 'Silver Fox Creek — More Precious Than Gold.' "

Myra smiled. "That sounds real good."

"You're sure you'll be okay without me to-night? Saturday's the busiest night of the week. Maybe I should call Chance and —"

"Bonnie's a hard worker and the customers really like her. We'll be just fine." Myra eyed her over the top of her spatula. "How 'bout you? You gonna be all right? You ain't gettin' cold feet, are you?"

If anything, the problem was exactly the op-posite. Just thinking about Chance made her hot, and in far more dangerous places than her feet. "Are you kidding? If I had any brains at all, I'd run like a scared rabbit as far away from Chance McLain as I could get."

"But you don't really want to. And I think Chance would be real disappointed if you did."

"I feel like I'm getting in too deep, Myra. I don't have time for this sort of thing. I've got a business to run and a son to think about. I didn't come here to get involved with a man."

"Chance ain't just any man, honey. I think you already figured that out."

Kate didn't argue. Chance was different from the typical, LA, pseudosensitive types she had known before. He was stronger, more sure of himself. More passionate about things that were important to him.

Perhaps that was what she liked best about him. That he cared so much. A lot of men were handsome, though rarely in such a hard-edged, virile way. But few men were as passionate about life as Chance.

Kate took off her apron and hung it by the door. She'd said she would go with him, and so far she hadn't been able to convince herself not to. Besides, when she talked to Chance, she could ask him about the land Silas Marshall had owned with her grandmother. She needed to understand what sort of well was on the property, and exactly how valuable it really was. She was sure it was another dead end, and if it were, perhaps she could convince herself to let the whole thing drop.

If she did, she would also have to live with the knowledge that very likely nothing that happened the night of the shooting was real. She hadn't caught even a small glimpse of life in the Hereafter. There was nothing after you died but the end.

The real truth was, Kate wanted to believe there was a beautiful place waiting for us after we died. She wanted to believe she would see her mother and her friends again. Solving the mystery, if there was one, would prove — at least to her — that such a place was real.

Kate couldn't bring herself to give up until she'd exhausted every effort.

Chapter Thirteen

Chance pulled up in front of the house a little before six P.M. He figured Kate would keep him waiting. It was a woman kind of thing, but he didn't really mind. He'd always felt at home in Nell's old house, even more so with the comfortable overstuffed furniture and colorful accents Kate had added since she had moved in.

He knocked on the door, heard galloping footsteps racing down the stairs.

David jerked open the door. "Hi, Chance. Mom said you were taking her out tonight."

"Sure am." He stepped inside, sweeping his wide-brimmed hat off. "That is . . . if you don't mind."

He shrugged. "It's good for her to get out once in a while."

"What about you, Davy? You gettin' out much these days?"

"Me and Chief's been fishin' some. Tonight I'm spending the night at Myra's. One of her grandkids is in town. His name is Ritchie. He's my age, I guess. We're gonna watch the football game on cable."

"That sounds like fun."

"I got my job back at the grocery store. Soon as I get enough saved, I'm gonna buy myself a rod. Hope you don't mind my keepin' yours till then."

"Like I said, I've got a couple of spares. Say, I've got an idea. Tomorrow's Sunday, right?"

"So?"

"You aren't working are you?"

"I don't start till next Wednesday."

"Well, how'd you like to go horseback into the hills? Jeremy Spotted Horse and his son, Chris, are coming along. We're heading up to Moose Lake. The place has got some really great fishing."

David's expression filled with the sort of yearning Chance had seen the day he had been trying so hard to fish. It was obvious he wanted to go. Then the yearning disappeared behind a mask of indifference, and David shook his head. "No thanks. I hate horses. They're ugly and smelly. I like cars."

Inwardly Chance cursed himself. If the boy couldn't fish, it was a sure bet he couldn't ride. "Well now, that's too bad. We got a whole string of remuda up on the ranch. Some of them need exercising pretty bad. I figured you'd be perfect for the job . . . once you learned to ride."

David set his jaw. "I don't think so. I'm not interested in horses." Turning, he started back up the stairs. "I'll tell my mom you're here." Sneakers untied, baggy jeans barely hanging on his slim hips, he pounded on up to the second floor and disappeared down the hall. Chance

186

heard him shouting for his mother, and a few minutes later, Kate stood at the top of the staircase.

"You're early," she called down.

"Just a little. I'll wait in the living room if you aren't ready yet."

"I'll only be a minute. I just have to get my purse."

Chance nodded, not really surprised. Kate wasn't the sort to play the usual female games. It was one of the things he liked about her. She returned a few minutes later, carrying a sweater, since the weather had turned cool, a small white leather purse draped over her shoulder. She looked especially pretty tonight, in a pale blue silk blouse and matching pale blue jeans. She was wearing ankle-high English riding boots, her dark red hair tied back with a light blue ribbon.

As she came down the stairs, he watched the way her breasts bobbed up and down, rubbing against the sheer blue silk, making his groin feel suddenly heavy. Kate must have noticed the look on his face, for a faint flush rose in her cheeks. By the time she reached the bottom stair, her nipples were firm little nubs and it was all he could do not to reach out and curl his fingers around one.

Damn, he was hard already and they hadn't even left the house. He had promised he wouldn't rush her, and he meant it. But tonight was gonna be one helluva damned long night.

Clamping his jaw, he mentally formed a picture of a bald-faced Hereford, the way he used to when he was in high school, anything to take his mind off sex. It was ridiculous. He'd been with more women than he could count, but none of them affected him like Kate. Fortunately, his desperate ploy worked and he began to relax a little.

"Ready?"

She nodded and he settled a hand at her waist. Guiding her out the door and down the front steps, he led her over to the pickup.

"What's this?" Kate stared down at the gleaming length of chrome below the door.

"It's a running board." He glanced away, trying to act as if he hadn't bought the damned thing just so she could climb in and out a little easier. "I needed a set of them anyway. Thought I might as well go ahead and get them."

Kate smiled up at him. "They're great." She got in with a lot less effort than she usually did, and he couldn't help feeling pleased with himself. So she was shorter than any other women he'd ever dated. So what. With a little ingenuity, it didn't make a lick of difference.

He couldn't help wondering what it would be like to take her to bed. Interesting. Definitely interesting. He groaned to think he probably wouldn't be finding out tonight.

Kate sat on the seat of the pickup, trying to

calm her jittery nerves. So he was taking her up to see his ranch. It was only natural that he would be proud of it. Having supper at his house was no big deal. He had a cook, so they wouldn't be alone. Besides, Chance had old-fashioned values and she didn't believe they included pressing an unwilling woman for something she wasn't ready to give.

The question was, how unready was she?

Very unready, she told herself. Maybe she would never be ready. Her nerves relaxed a little and they drove to the ranch making easy conversation. Chance told her the latest on Consolidated Metals, mentioning the injunction the court had granted. They talked about David, Chance telling Kate about the fishing trip he'd invited David to go on and the dislike the boy had for horses.

"He doesn't really dislike them," she said. "At least I don't think he does. Jimmy Stevens, one of the boys he met in summer school, gave him a hard time about not being able to ride. His pride was stung pretty badly. Now he won't admit that he'd really like to learn."

"How about you? You ever ridden?"

"I took lessons when I was a few years younger. I rode English, though, and I was never all that good. But I loved every minute of it. I missed it when I had to give it up."

"Why did you?"

"My job, mostly. I was working more and more hours. Whenever I did get time off, I wanted to be with my son."

"What about your husband?"

"Tommy was always too busy, too wrapped up in his band. The only mistake I made with Tommy was in not leaving him a whole lot sooner."

Chance tossed her a look, but didn't say more. He drove the pickup through the big pine gate leading into the ranch, and a few minutes later they parked in front of a huge log house. The place stood two stories high, with dormer windows in the rooms upstairs and a long covered porch out in front.

"It's a lot bigger than I imagined," Kate said. "I had you pictured in a quaint little cabin."

Chance chuckled softly. "Actually I added on to the house my father built, the place I lived in as a boy. It was much smaller. But I like room to move around in. Besides, I figured someday I'd want to have kids."

Kate said nothing to that, but a funny little quiver moved through her stomach. She had always wanted more children. She just didn't want them with Tommy. What would it be like to have a family with Chance? Kate shook her head, dismissing the image. Chance had any number of women. If he were looking for a wife, he'd have found one long before this.

And she certainly wasn't in the market for a husband. Been there, done that, thank you very much.

Still, it was fun being with him. She felt comfortable with Chance in a way she rarely did with men.

"Come on," he said, "I'll show you around." For more than an hour, they walked the grounds of the ranch, which nestled at the base of the towering Mission Mountains. Chance took her into the barn, where his foreman, a man he introduced as Roddy, was busy shoeing horses.

"We don't shoe them all," Chance said. "The boys have been working some pretty rocky country east of here so we're shoeing this bunch to use in the rough terrain."

He showed her the equipment shed, which was a big metal building that looked more like an airplane hangar. A hay baler stood at one end, along with a couple of John Deere tractors, endless miscellaneous ranch machinery and equipment, and some sleds that were used to haul hay in the winter. They walked through what he told her was the birthing barn and Kate paused to look around.

"What's that?" She pointed to a long, metal, pole-like object fitted with several feet of chain.

"Calf puller. Sometimes the calves are too big to come normally. The chains increase the leverage. It takes a couple of men to use it, but it helps the cow deliver her calf safely and in good health."

He explained how most of the calves were delivered in the spring. "That way they have a better chance of survival. That's also when we do the branding, spraying, vaccinating, and de-horning."

They walked outside the barn and over to one of the corrals where a group of cowhands perched on the fence, watching the men in the arena.

"Some of the hands are competing in the Polson rodeo. Team roping, mostly, a few of them are calf-ropers. That big guy sitting on the fence over there, that's Billy Two Feathers. He's Lakota Sioux. He's entered in the steer wrestling."

It was all so different from anything she was used to. It was like stepping back in time, into the frames of an old Western movie, and she found it completely enchanting. "Are you going to compete?"

"Are you kidding? After I nearly got my head kicked in a couple of times riding bulls, I finally got some sense."

Kate looked out to where the men practiced team roping, now that their day's work was through. Big, rawboned steers shot out of a long, narrow shoot, then two mounted riders charged out behind them, whirling stiff nylon ropes above their heads. "I've never been to a rodeo."

Chance's astonished gaze swung to her face. "You're kidding." For a moment she lost track of the conversation. It was amazing what those brilliant blue eyes could do.

"I'm a city girl, remember?"

"They have rodeos in LA. Even Madison Square Garden in New York."

"I suppose they do. I guess I just never thought about going to one."

Chance grinned. "I'll take you, then. The Polson fair starts in two weeks. The rodeo's the first weekend. Mark your calendar. We've got a date."

Kate smiled, thinking how much fun it would be to go to a rodeo with a real, bonafide cowboy. Even a year ago, if someone had told her she'd be running a cafe in rural Montana, having dinner at a ranch, and going to an actual rodeo, she'd have thought he was out of his head.

Chance finished his tour of the ranch and led her up to the house, making a point to take her in through the heavy, carved front doors.

Kate stopped in the slate-floored entry, tilting her head back to take it all in. "It's beautiful, Chance." Constructed of big pine logs, the walls were a soft, golden yellow. The ceiling rose two stories above wide plank floors that were covered by brightly woven rugs. A massive stone fireplace dominated the room, surrounded by comfortable leather sofas.

"The original house now serves as the kitchen and guest wing," Chance said. "I built this section — the living room, dining room, and master suite."

"From what I can see, you did a fabulous job."

"Come on, I'll show you the rest." He led her down the hall to the bedrooms in the guest wing, each decorated in a Western motif, accented with Indian-woven rugs and bedspreads, antique furniture, and leather chairs. The dining room, lit by a massive antler chandelier, had a long, carved wooden table big enough to seat a dozen people. They went into a study warmed by a smaller stone fireplace that matched the one in the living room.

Kate paused beside his big oak desk, which was topped by a state-of-the-art computer. "I suppose I shouldn't be surprised, but I am. Your good-ol'-boy image is shattered forever."

Chance laughed. "Frankly, I'm glad to hear it." He walked over to the computer and flipped it on, sat down in the brown leather chair in front of it, and logged on to the Internet. "Believe it or not, we have our own website — *www.runningmoon.com*. The page shows some of our prize-winning Herefords as well as a list of quarter horse stallions that are currently standing at stud. It's a good way for our clients to stay in touch, and it brings in new buyers. It's just good business."

"Yes, it is."

He logged off the Net and turned off the computer. "Don't tell me you're on the Net."

"The cafe hardly needs a website, but I'd be lost without my computer, and of course I have an e-mail address. It's a great way to stay in touch with friends."

Chance smiled. "A lady of the twenty-first century."

"I guess I am." She wandered around the study, admiring the Western art on the walls and some very good wildlife photography. "Is this Jeremy Spotted Horse's work?"

Chance walked up beside her. "Some of his earlier photography. I've got some of his more recent stuff upstairs in my bedroom."

Kate tossed him a playful glance. "And I was expecting you to say something about seeing your etchings."

Chance just laughed. Kate moved slowly around the study, looking at each of the photos. She particularly admired one of a huge grizzly bear lying on its paws in a field of yellow mountain daisies.

"He's really talented, isn't he?"

"He's definitely got a knack. Lately, he's been getting a little of the recognition he deserves, but it hasn't been easy."

"Nothing's ever easy, remember?"

Those incredible blue eyes swung to her face, turning hot as she recalled too late, the subtle inference had been about making love. He was standing so close she could feel the heat of his body, smell his Old Spice cologne.

"I'd really like to kiss you," he said softly.

Her insides curled, rolled up in a neat little ball. She had no idea what she would reply until she opened her mouth and said, "Then why don't you?"

Chance didn't wait another heartbeat. He simply leaned forward, tilted his head, and pressed his lips over hers. They were firm, yet incredibly soft, and a jolt of electricity shot through her, zigzagging out through her limbs. She found herself leaning toward him, her breasts flattening out against his chest.

Chance deepened the kiss, tasting her softly, then coaxing her lips apart and taking her with his tongue. He framed her face between his hands and kissed her more deeply, tilting his head first one way and then the other. She could feel the tension in his body, the faint tremor that ran the length of his tall lean frame. Then he drew away, ending the kiss before she was ready.

One of her hands still rested on his chest, but she had no idea how it got there. Beneath her fingers, his heart beat way too fast, and the dark skin over his high cheekbones looked slightly flushed.

Chance cleared his throat. "Why don't you make yourself comfortable while I tell Hannah we're ready to eat?"

"Hannah? That's your cook?"

He nodded. "She lives in the cabin you saw out behind the barn. She'll get dinner on the table, then she's off for the rest of the night."

Kate felt suddenly uneasy. She had thought there would be someone in the house, but it would only be the two of them. She managed to bolster a smile. "Sounds good. I'm starved."

196

The heat in his eyes said he was hungry, too, but not for food. And the real truth was, she would rather have had another of his intoxicating kisses than a platter of filet mignon.

As it was, they sat down to a meal of roast beef, potatoes, green beans, and salad. It was a hearty meal, a man's sort of meal, and it was delicious.

"Your Hannah is a very good cook."

Chance nodded and swallowed the bite he'd been chewing. "She's been working for us since before my father died. I guess Hannah Evert's the closest thing to a mother I've ever had."

She appeared in the dining room a few minutes later, a matronly woman in her sixties, broad-hipped and gray-haired, a walking Aunt Bea, Kate thought.

Chance shoved back his chair and came to his feet. "Hannah, this is a friend of mine, Kate Rollins. She's the new owner of the Lost Peak Cafe."

Hannah eyed her sharply. "Yeah?"

Kate politely nodded. "Hello, Hannah." The older woman continued to size her up in a way that made her want to fidget. It was obvious she was protective of the man she had raised from a boy. Kate wondered what it took to pass Hannah's inspection.

"It's a pleasure meetin' you," the woman finally said. "I hear the food's still good down to the cafe — 'specially the apple pie."

Kate smiled. "I'm lucky Myra agreed to

come back. I don't know what I'd have done without her."

Hannah nodded as if she approved Kate's candor, and swung her attention back to Chance. "Dessert's on the stove — apricot cobbler. Coffee's made, too. If you need anything else, just give me a holler."

"We'll be fine," Chance said. "Thanks, Hannah." The older woman disappeared back into the kitchen and a few minutes later, Kate heard the door slam closed.

"I guess we're on our own," Chance said, looking a little uncomfortable. Endearingly so, Kate thought, and the fact it was true made her own nervousness fade.

"You don't bring women here often, do you?"

"No," was all he said. Chance refilled her wine glass with a surprisingly sophisticated Napa Valley cabernet, and she took another drink.

"Why me?"

Both of them had finished their meal. Chance relaxed in his high-backed leather chair. "To tell you the truth, I'm not sure. I respect what you've done. It took a lot of guts to give up a high-paying job and move to a place like Lost Peak. But you did the right thing — for both you and your son. I guess I wanted to share a little of what I've accomplished. Maybe I was hoping you'd approve."

Kate felt a rush of pleasure. *I respect what*

198

you've done. How many men would ever say something like that? "You have a beautiful place here, Chance. The house. The ranch. All of it. You have every right to be proud of what you've done."

Chance seemed pleased at the words. He shoved back his chair. "Come on. There's a storm coming in. Why don't I build us a fire? We can have coffee and dessert in the living room."

"Sounds wonderful. I haven't had a fire since we moved here. I've been dying to try out Nell's wood-burning stove."

"I can tell you from personal experience, it works like a charm." So saying, he disappeared outside through a door beside the fireplace and returned a few minutes later with an armload of wood. Another trip and he seemed satisfied that he had enough. Squatting in front of the big stone hearth, he had a roaring blaze going in minutes.

Kate walked over as he came to his feet. "It's obvious you've had a lot of practice at this." For a moment, they stood there staring at the flames, then Kate felt his eyes on her and slowly turned to face him.

"I've had a lot of practice at a lot of things," he said softly, roughly. Something shifted in his features, turned turbulent and hot. The kiss he claimed wasn't the soft, gentle, tender kiss she expected. It was a fierce, taking kiss that left her breathless and yearning, a wild, reckless kiss that made her legs begin to quiver and her heart beat like a drum. His mouth moved over hers as if this moment was more important than drawing his next breath, and suddenly she found herself feeling the same insane sensation.

She kissed him back with a recklessness foreign to her until now, her nails digging into his shoulders, her breasts aching, her nipples swelling. They strained toward the front of his denim shirt, rubbing, moving, the friction exquisite, drawing a moan from her throat.

"Kate," he whispered, kissing her even more deeply, his hands sliding into her hair. The pale blue ribbon fell free and the heavy curls tumbled loose, wrapping themselves around his fingers. She could feel his barely controlled desire and it set the blood pounding in her ears, made her burn as she never had before.

"We can't do this," she whispered as he pulled her down beside him on the big bearskin rug and angled his body over hers.

He kissed the side of her neck, the hollow of her throat above the buttons on her blouse. "Tell me why not." His mouth moved lower, dampening the pale blue silk, his breath hot where it fanned over a nipple. "Tell me, and I'll stop."

Her eyes slid closed, the pleasure so intense she felt as if she were melting. "I don't . . . don't want you to stop."

Every muscle in his body tightened. She could feel the strength of him, the power.

"God, Katie, you'll never know how much I've wanted to hear you say that." Chance kissed her again, tasting the inside of her mouth, stroking her deeply with his tongue. With unsteady hands, he began to unbutton her blouse, the buttons popping free one by one.

Kate didn't stop him. What she'd said was the truth. She wanted him to make love to her. Just this once, she wanted to know the touch of a man she desired, a man who could make her feel things she wasn't even sure existed, things she had only imagined in secret, forbidden dreams.

Chance slid the blouse off her shoulders, a whisper of silk that made her skin start to tingle. A pretty white lace bra pushed her heavy breasts up into soft pale hills. Chance looked at them as if they were a sacred offering.

"Incredible," he whispered, pressing his mouth to the narrow line of cleavage between them, kissing the rounded tops, sliding his tongue inside a lacy cup to circle a nipple. A sliver of heat rose up, forming a hot, damp curl in her stomach, and Kate bit back a sob of pure pleasure. The warmth slid downward, settled in the place between her legs, and unconsciously, she arched upward, giving Chance access to her throat and shoulders. He kissed her there, unsnapped the clasp on her bra, and tossed it away.

His gaze moved downward, fastened on her naked breasts, and the blue of his eyes seemed to glow. "God, you're lovely." Reaching out, he cupped one, lightly stroked his thumb over a nipple, watched it pucker and tighten. "And so damned sexy."

He lifted the fullness into his palm, bent his head, and his teeth closed over the stiff peak at the crest. A firm little tug sent a ripple of heat to her toes. His tongue darted out, swirled around the tip, and Kate bit back a soft moan of pleasure. Then he opened his mouth, took as much of her as he could, and hot, wet, heat enveloped her.

Kate closed her eyes and tried to stop the trembling that had taken control of her body. Chance eased back down on the rug and came up over her, kissing her deeply again. She wanted to touch him, to know the contours of his body, the texture of his skin. With shaking hands, she unbuttoned his denim shirt and shoved it away from his shoulders. They were wide and hard, with thick bands of muscle across the top. His chest was broad and muscled, and covered with a fine mat of curly black hair that arrowed down between the ridges of sinew across his stomach.

Kate pressed her mouth against his warm, dark skin and felt his muscles bunch. She ringed a flat copper nipple with her tongue and heard him groan.

Chance cupped her face in his hand. "I can't remember wanting a woman so badly." He kissed her deeply, thoroughly, his fingers moving down to caress a breast. He took her mouth in another searing kiss and in minutes both of them were naked. In the light of the blazing fire, he was all dark skin and hard male muscle, his sex jutting forward, slightly intimidating in its size and length.

Lightning flashed outside the window. The echo of thunder followed, but Kate barely heard it. His hand found the soft red curls between her legs, and he gently began to stroke her. He seemed to know exactly where to touch her, *how* to touch her, and pleasure slammed through her with the force of a class five storm. Chance spread her thighs with his knee and settled himself between them. She could feel his arousal pulsing against her, big and hot and hard.

"Chance . . . ?"

"It's all right, darlin'." He smoothed back her hair. "I'm not gonna hurt you." A soft, nibbling, tender kiss followed, then one of raging passion as he slid himself fully inside.

He was huge and throbbing, stretching her to the limit, but the fullness only heightened her pleasure. Clinging to his neck, she began to move even before he did, straining upward to take more of him. The rhythm increased, Chance moving faster, deeper, harder, his control beginning to slip, continuing as if he moved on instinct alone.

Her body tingled, tightened, her muscles as taut as a bowstring. Two more pounding thrusts and the tension inside her snapped, hurling her into a powerful climax, her body shuddering as wave after wave of pleasure washed over her. Chance followed close behind, muscles rigid, head falling back, a low growl erupting from his throat.

He held himself above her for long, pleasure-filled seconds, then the tension in his muscles began to fade. He eased himself down beside her and pulled her firmly against his side, one arm forming a pillow beneath her head.

"You all right?" He turned and brushed his lips against her temple.

Kate nodded and smiled. Drowsiness was beginning to settle in, and a wonderful, lazy contentment. The heat of the fire kept her warm and the thick bear rug felt soft against her bare skin. Her eyelids drooped closed. Snuggling closer to Chance, she drifted into a peaceful sleep.

The rhythm of his heart finally slowed to normal, no longer tried to hammer its way through his chest. In the silence of the living room, the wind blew hard through the trees and distant lightning flashed, but the fire crackled pleasantly, casting golden shadows over the woman lying on the rug beside him.

Chance let his gaze roam over her in a way he hadn't had time to do before. The urgency, the burning need to have her, had simply been too great.

Now he noticed how smooth her skin was, how soft and womanly her body looked all over. Her breasts were large, the nipples round and plump in slumber. The dark red curls between her thighs still glistened with dampness in the light of the fire, though he'd had sense enough to use a condom.

He hadn't wanted to. He'd fought the notion of a barrier between them. He'd wanted to feel her softness, to mesh with her, be part of her in a way that had never been important to him before. He wanted to absorb her into his very skin, and the fact that he did scared the living hell out of him.

He'd thought, once he made love to her, some of his attraction to her would fade. Once he had seen those luscious breasts, once he had satisfied himself with her small, womanly body, he would regain his objectivity, his control. When it came to Kate Rollins, he somehow seemed to have lost it.

He watched her sleeping, thought how lovely she looked with all that glorious red hair in a tangle around her shoulders, and his body began to stir. Reaching out, he ran a finger over her breast, lightly circled a nipple, and watched it tighten.

She was a passionate woman, incredibly responsive, though he didn't think she realized it quite yet. He drew his finger lightly down her ribcage, circled her navel, moved lower, gently stroked the flesh partially hidden beneath the damp red curls. His arousal strengthened until it grew almost painful.

He wanted her again, wanted to take her slowly this time, had, almost from the moment they had finished making love. He moved above her, bent to nibble the side of her neck, and eased himself slowly inside her. She was warm and wet and he slid in easily, impaling himself to the limit. Her eyes sprang open on a soft moan of pleasure that made him smile. He had hoped she wouldn't be angry at his method of rousing her. When she arched her back, pressing herself against him like a lazy cat, he knew that she wasn't. Chance kissed her softly and started to move.

Chapter Fourteen

Kate awakened as the first gray light of dawn filtered into the room. The wind blew outside and a light rain pattered against the window-panes. She listened to the sounds, for a moment disoriented, not quite certain where she was. She glanced at her surroundings: a king-sized bed made of hand-hewn logs; an antique coat rack near the door that held a heavy sheepskin coat, a dusty black Stetson, and a pair of spurs. Several beautifully framed wild-life photos hung on the walls.

Vaguely she remembered Chance carrying her up to his room.

Kate bolted upright. Good grief, she was still in Chance's bed! She should have been home hours ago. What would David think when she didn't come back until dawn? Grabbing the blue terry cloth robe hanging from a hook on the bathroom door, she jammed her arms into sleeves at least eight inches too long and quickly belted the sash. She was frantically searching for her clothes when the door swung open and Chance walked in.

"You don't have to panic. David spent the night at Myra's, remember?"

The breath she had been holding rushed out of her lungs. She sighed. "That's right, I forgot." She looked up at him with suspicion. "How did you know?"

He was carrying a breakfast tray, she noticed, spotting the covered dishes and the yellow mountain daisy in the bud vase.

"David told me. And before you get your jeans in an uproar, that didn't have a damned thing to do with you ending up in my bed. I didn't plan it. In fact, I tried my best to put the notion out of my head. Then I kissed you and, well . . . it just sort of happened." He walked to where she stood, set the tray down on top of an antique steamer trunk that sat beneath the window.

"I figured you'd want to get home before David did. I knew you'd be tired. I thought I'd let you sleep a little while longer."

A flush rose into her cheeks. *He knew she'd be tired?* Of course she was tired! They'd made love most of the night. She was also pleasantly battered and deliciously sated. Making love with Chance McLain was unlike anything she had ever experienced.

Still, it was a stupid, idiotic thing to do. Chance was the kind of man women dreamed about. Strong, handsome, virile — fabulous in bed. The kind who made you fall madly in love with them.

The kind who broke your heart.

He dragged over a chair for her to sit on and crouched down on a little footstool he brought over for himself. "I hope you like bacon and eggs. I'm a pretty fair cook, as long as it's nothing too complicated."

She gave him an uneasy smile. "Bacon and eggs sound fine, but . . ."

Her cup was being filled with his great-smelling coffee when he paused. "But what? But you wish you were home instead of still in my bed? You wish you didn't have to face me after what we did last night?"

She turned away, hugging the huge robe more tightly around her. "I guess that about sums it up." She sighed, feeling embarrassed, yet wanting him to understand. "I've only been with one other man in my life, Chance. After I found out he was cheating, even that ended. And to tell you the truth, Tommy's idea of sex was a whole lot different from yours."

His gaze held hers and it was relentless. "Are you telling me your husband couldn't satisfy you?"

Her flush deepened to the color of a ripe to-mato. "I don't think it ever occurred to him to try."

Chance's lips edged up at the corners. "I'll take that as a compliment."

Kate couldn't help remembering how soft and warm those lips had felt moving over her body. A little shiver she couldn't quite control slid through her body. She glanced away, wishing again she were anywhere but there, dis-cussing her outrageous behavior of the night before. Last night she'd seen a side of herself she had never seen before. She wasn't sure she liked it.

"Why don't we eat?" Chance said gently, tuning in, as he seemed to have a way of doing, to the sensitive nature of her mood. "Then I'll take you home."

Kate just nodded. The sooner she finished and dressed, the sooner she could escape. She needed time to think, to sort out what she'd done. She needed to make some decisions.

They finished the meal in record time and Chance showed her where he had hung up her clothes. They left the house a few minutes later, sneaking quietly out the front door while Hannah hummed away in the kitchen.

It was silent in the truck on the ride back down the hill. Searching for a topic that had nothing to do with sex, her mind grabbed onto the question she had meant to ask Chance the night before. Somehow, once he kissed her, the subject had flown right out of her head.

"Last night . . . earlier in the evening, I mean, before . . ." Her face turned warm, and a corner of Chance's mouth edged up. Kate ignored it and plunged ahead. "I meant to ask if you might happen to know anything about the twenty-acre parcel of land Silas Marshall owned with my grandmother. Chief was telling me there's some sort of well on it."

"Chief was telling you that?"

She bit back a smile. "Actually, what he said was, 'Big water. Deep well.' I thought you

210

might be able to elaborate a bit more on the subject."

Chance grunted, his expression turning grim. "I know the piece. Everyone around these parts does. I wish my father had bought the property when it was for sale years ago. Unfortunately, he didn't."

"What sort of well is it?"

"Artesian. Believe it or not, that well puts out more than seven hundred gallons a minute. More important, it comes out of a rocky strata that runs for miles in an area where it's nearly impossible to find any water."

"Chief said the well was next to Silas's property, but I don't know where that is."

"A couple of miles up the mountain on the north side of Silver Fox Creek. It's right next to the section of ground that Consolidated Metals wants to develop. That's why they wanted to buy it so badly."

"Consolidated Metals wanted to buy the property?"

Chance nodded as he steered the truck around a corner. "Yeah. They'd dug half a dozen wells up there and come up dry every time. They offered Nell and Silas a small fortune for the piece, but your grandma refused to sell. She knew what it would mean to the surrounding land and animals if Consolidated put in that mine."

"What about Silas?"

"Silas wanted to sell. He said it was only

good business, considering the profit they would make. Two weeks after your grandmother died, he made a deal with Consolidated. We might not be worrying about that mine going in if he hadn't. Without water, the company had some really big problems ahead of it. Once they owned the well, one of their biggest problems was solved."

Hearing Chance's last words, the air she had been breathing froze like a block of ice in her chest. She hadn't bothered to ask the title company if Silas still owned the property. She simply assumed he did. But Silas had sold the land just weeks after her grandmother's death. He'd made a huge profit in the bargain.

"Kate . . . ?"

She looked up at him, the blood draining out of her face. She felt oddly light-headed, like she might actually keel over in a faint.

Chance pulled the truck to the side of the road. "What is it, Kate? Dammit, you're white as a sheet."

"I'll be all right in a minute. It's just that . . ." *That I've finally found a motive for Nell's murder.* Silas Marshall had gained a small fortune because of Nell Hart's death. Was it possible that he could have killed her?

"This has something to do with Nell, doesn't it?"

She barely heard him. "I'm . . . I'm all right now. I need to get home though, if you don't mind."

"Dammit, Kate. I know every beautiful inch of your body. I've touched you, been inside you. Can't you trust me enough to tell me what's going on?"

The heat of embarrassment washed through her, yet his words struck a chord of truth it was hard to ignore. "Even if I told you, you wouldn't believe me."

"Try me. I might surprise you." It was said with such earnestness she had to take the chance.

She dragged in a deep breath of air, hoping to bolster her courage. "All right then. I think my grandmother may have been murdered. This morning, I think you might have helped me figure out why."

Chance's gaze was so intense she had to look away. He took off his Stetson, tossed it up on the dashboard, and raked a hand through his hair. "Christ." He turned toward her. "All right, you've gone this far. Why don't you tell me the rest?"

"There isn't anything else to tell." At least nothing he would remotely accept. "I had this . . . this hunch . . . that something wasn't right about my grandmother's death. I've been digging, trying to see if I might uncover something that proves I'm right."

"Just because a man makes a profit out of an unfortunate accident doesn't mean he's capable of murder."

"I know that. But as you pointed out, there

was a great deal to gain. A piece of property 'worth a small fortune' — those were your words. And the chance to build a major gold mine."

"Nell's death was an accident," Chance said firmly. "There was no forced entry, no sign of a struggle, no reason to think it was murder. Your grandmother fell and hit her head."

"Yes, she did. I don't have any doubt about that." She looked him straight in the face. "What I'm wondering is if someone might have pushed her."

Chance sat unmoving on the car seat while the silence stretched uncomfortably thin. Reaching toward the key, he started the engine, then drove the rest of the way to Kate's house. It was obvious she was still upset, but there was nothing he could say that would soothe her. As he walked her to the door, she thanked him rather absently for showing her the ranch, dismissing their hours of lovemaking as if they had never occurred.

Chance ignored a thread of irritation. "I'll call you later," he said, trying to sound as matter-of-fact as she had. As he started back to the truck, he couldn't help thinking about their earlier conversation. She had a hunch, she'd said. Even before she came to Lost Peak. It made not the least amount of sense, yet over the years, he often followed his own gut instincts and they rarely led him astray.

Still, murder was a very long stretch. Especially when the chief suspect was Silas Marshall. Silas was seventy years old himself. For as long as Chance could remember, Silas and Nell had been friends. There was even talk that some years after Zach had died, they'd had a brief affair.

It was all just speculation, of course. Still, it was obvious that Silas had a soft spot in his heart for Nell and equally apparent the old woman cared a great deal for him. It was highly unlikely Silas would kill her, no matter how much money was involved.

Wishing the subject had never come up, he jerked open the door to his pickup and started to climb in just as Myra's old beat-up Suburban turned down the gravel lane, returning David home. Chance silently thanked God he had gotten Kate home first or she never would have forgiven him.

The car parked behind the restaurant. Myra went inside to begin her duties in the kitchen and David started jogging down the road toward home. Before he could reach his destination, another car turned down the drive, a white Ford Taurus with rental plates on the front, passing him on the drive and stopping next to where Chance's pickup was parked. Curious who it might be, he watched the door crack open and an overweight man step out at the same moment David jogged past.

The boy took one look at the man, and even

from a distance, Chance could see his face turn pale. Ignoring Chance as if he weren't there, David raced up the front walk, shot up the porch steps, and jerked open the door.

"It's him, Mom!" His thin voice sounded even higher that it usually did. "That fat guy from LA. You better come quick!"

Chance sat there for several long moments, knowing he should start the engine and head back to the ranch, telling himself that whatever was going on, Kate wouldn't appreciate his interference. The guy, about five-foot-eight, wearing jeans and a Dodgers' baseball cap, climbed the front porch stairs, and Chance told himself it was none of his business.

Then he saw the look of fear on Kate's face as she yanked open the screen door, and thought, *The hell it isn't.*

Before he could change his mind, he was out of the truck and moving toward the fat man standing in front of her door.

Kate stared at the man in the jeans and sneakers standing on the porch. She saw Chance striding toward him, thought of what was about to happen, and felt her world tip precariously toward disaster.

"This is private property, Mr. Munson," she said, praying she could get him to leave before Chance could reach them. "I didn't invite you here and I want you to leave."

"I just came by to talk to you. I've had a

heckuva time finding you, Ms. Rollins. I think the least you could do is give me a couple of minutes."

"And I think you should leave."

"Just a few questions, that's all I ask."

Chance reached the porch and stepped between them, pulling her a little behind him. "Who the hell are you?"

Munson's face drained of color, but he didn't back away. "My name is Chet Munson. I'm a reporter for the *National Monitor.* And you would be . . . ?"

"None of your damned business. What are you doing here? What's a sleazy tabloid like the *Monitor* want with Kate?"

Oh dear God, she didn't want him to find out. "It isn't important, Chance. I just want him to leave."

A sly look came over Munson's face, his newspaperman's instinct kicking in as he sensed a new method of getting the information he wanted. He turned his attention to Chance. "I'm here to do a followup story on the shooting."

"What shooting?"

"It doesn't matter, Chance. I just want him —"

"Last March in LA, Kate Rollins was the victim of a drive-by shooting. She nearly died. Actually, she did die. She was dead for nearly ten minutes before the doctors were able to bring her back. It was in all the papers. That's the reason I'm here."

Chance's questioning gaze swung to her. "Why didn't you tell me?"

"It wasn't important. It —"

Munson broke in before she could finish, his expression entirely too smug. "You mean she hasn't mentioned her journey to 'The Other Side'? Why, Kate caught a glimpse of heaven — or so she claims. She talked to her mother while she was there, and of course, all of her other dead friends — even her grandmother. From what I gather, the old lady gave her some sort of message. Isn't that right, Ms. Rollins?"

Kate stared at Munson, a chill creeping over her skin. "How did you know that?"

Munson smiled wolfishly. "I've got ways of finding things out. Uncovering a story is what I'm paid for."

But she hadn't told anyone about Nell. Well, almost not anyone. Just Sally and Dr. Murray, and one of the girls at the office who had read a number of books on NDE and begged to know what had happened. Kate inwardly groaned. God, why hadn't she just kept quiet?

"Kate . . . ?" She could hear the uncertainty in Chance's voice, a slightly raspy note, like a file running over stone. Her chest constricted, making the air burn in her lungs.

"I want you to leave," she said to Munson. "Now. This minute. If you don't, I'm calling the sheriff."

"Now, don't be so hasty, Kate. The *National*

Monitor is willing to pay you a very hefty sum of money. Everyone wants to know what it's like in heaven."

She was starting to shake. If she didn't get him out of there soon she was going to make a fool of herself. She released a breath but it sounded more like a sob. The instant Chance heard it, he grabbed Chet Munson by the front of his coat and lifted him up on his toes.

"Ms. Rollins told you to leave. Now I'm telling you. Get the hell off her property and don't come back. If you do, you'll answer to me."

Munson's face looked pasty white. "All right, all right, I'm going."

Chance set him back on his feet, released his hold on Munson's jacket, and brushed at the wrinkles he had squeezed in the man's lapels. "Lost Peak is a very small town. You aren't welcome in it. Not now nor any time in the future. Do I make myself clear?"

Munson staggered backward a couple of paces. "Yes, yes, perfectly clear."

"Then don't let your shirttail hit your ass on your way out of here."

Munson nodded vigorously, turned, and nearly ran to his car. The tires spun and gravel flew into the air as he shoved it into reverse, then jammed on the gas and flew down the driveway to the road leading back to Highway 93.

For an instant, Kate wished she could join

him, wished the boards under her feet would open up and she could drop out of sight beneath the porch.

"Mom?" David's voice, sounding reedy and thin, floated toward her from the entry.

"It's all right, David. He's gone and I don't think he'll be coming back anytime soon. Go on up to your room."

For once, David didn't argue, just pounded on up the stairs. She thought that perhaps he didn't want to face Chance.

The truth was Kate didn't either.

He stood right in front of her, so near she could feel the tension still pulsing through his body. "You gonna tell me what the hell's going on?"

How could she? What could she possibly say? She swallowed against the thickness building in her throat and forced herself to look up at him. "Nothing is going on. That awful man left and that is the end of it. Hopefully, he won't be coming back."

"That's it? That's all you've got to say?"

She swallowed, but her throat was so tight it wasn't easy. "I . . . I really appreciate your help in getting him to leave."

Those fierce blue eyes cut into her like laser beams. "What about the shooting? What about your trip to 'The Other Side'? What about Nell?"

"What . . . what about her?"

"Come on, Kate. That's what this whole

murder thing is about, isn't it? That's why you've been looking into her death. Because you think she gave you some sort of message."

Her chest refused to expand for her next breath of air. She was sure she wouldn't be able to force out her next sentence. "What happened to me has nothing to do with you. I'd appreciate it if you would just let it drop. If not for my sake then for David's."

"Just let it drop," he repeated darkly, as if she had lost her wits.

"That's what I said. Besides, it really isn't any of your business."

A muscle leapt in his jaw. "You made it my business when you stayed with me last night. Or have you forgotten about that already?"

Forgotten? How in God's name could she forget the most wonderful night of her life? But one thing had nothing to do with the other, and it was obvious if she told him the truth, he wouldn't believe her.

She simply shook her head. "I think it would be better if you left now, Chance."

"Dammit, Kate."

Her lips were starting to tremble. She didn't want him to see. "Please . . ."

Chance swore softly, foully. "All right, fine, I'll leave, if that's what you want." Muttering something about hard-headed women, Chance stormed off toward his pickup. Kate stood trembling as he climbed in and fired up the engine, jammed the truck in gear, and tore down the long gravel drive. She watched until the truck disappeared around a bend in the road, then she turned and went back inside the house.

David came down the stairs as Kate started up.

"I can't believe that guy found us," he said. "You really don't think he'll be back?"

She could see the worry in his face and a thread of guilt filtered through her. David would be starting school in just two more weeks. If the kids found out about her trip to 'The Other Side,' they would give him nothing but grief.

"I really don't think so. Munson is a coward. He isn't going to want any more trouble with Chance."

"I hope you're right," David mumbled. He paused at the bottom of the stairs. "He isn't mad, is he? Chance I mean."

Her fingers tightened around the banister. "No, honey, of course not. He just had to get back to the ranch."

David nodded as if he accepted the tale, but she wasn't sure he believed her. "Do you care if Ritchie and I go fishing? He doesn't know how yet, but he says he'd really like to learn."

Ritchie's, Myra's grandson. She worked up a fairly good smile. "I think that's a terrific idea. I gather you two got along all right last night."

"Ritchie's way cool, Mom. He's from San Francisco, but he really likes the mountains. He says he loves to come here and visit. He even said maybe I could come and visit him in San Francisco."

"Oh, honey, that's wonderful. Why don't you see if Ritchie can stay for supper? I don't think Myra will mind."

"Great, Mom, thanks." In a flash, he was out the door and on his way to the cafe, where he was meeting his new friend. Silently, Kate thanked Myra Hennings for bringing the two boys together. Kate only wished he lived somewhere near, instead of in the city.

Continuing up the stairs, she went into her bedroom, kicked off her riding boots, and tossed her sweater on the bed. Desperate for the comfort of a good, hot bath, she headed into the bathroom, threw the blouse and jeans she had worn last night into the hamper, bent and turned the taps on the old claw-foot tub.

As she stepped out of her lacy white panties, she could smell the sticky-sweet odor of sex, and a rush of heated memories flooded through her.

God above, she had slept with Chance McLain. They had made wildly erotic, incredibly passionate love. It was the most thrilling, most exciting night of her life.

How could it have turned into such a disaster?

Feeling the heavy weight of depression, Kate forced her legs to carry her over to the tub. She tested the water and found it scalding hot, the way she liked it. She climbed in and sank down. If she closed her eyes, she could still see Chet Munson standing on her doorstep, ranting and raving about her trip to heaven, shooting off his big mouth. Now Chance undoubtedly thought she was some kind of refugee from the nut ward and she would never see him again.

Leaning back against the tub, Kate sighed into the silence of the steamy room. She had warned herself time and again not to get involved with him. Instead she had gone out with him, even gone to bed with him.

The truth was she cared about Chance McLain. More than she ever intended. She wanted to see him again. She wanted to be with him.

Chet Munson's words had undoubtedly killed any possibility of that.

Closing her eyes, Kate tried not to think of Chance. She tried not to see the disbelief stamped on his face as he had listened to Chet Munson's words, or imagine what he must be thinking about her right now.

She tried, but she failed miserably.

Chapter Fifteen

Chance slammed through the door of the Antlers Saloon, an old, batten-board building across and down the street from the Lost Peak Cafe. The place was smoky, the floor littered with peanut shells, but it had a sort of old-fashioned charm, which was why the place was still open after more than fifty years.

He sat down on one of the red vinyl bar stools in front of the long oak bar and propped a boot on the tarnished brass rail.

"Chance! Kinda early to be seein' you in here, ain't it?" Maddie Webster smiled as she wiped off the bartop in front of him. "What can I get you?"

Two or three straight shots of tequila might help, but he doubted it. And Maddie was right, it was way too early. "How about a red beer? You've got Moose Drool on tap, don't you?"

She nodded. "Comin' right up." While Maddie went to get it, Chance sat staring at the old-fashioned back bar, but not really seeing it. He didn't notice Jeremy Spotted Horse till the big Indian stood over his right shoulder.

"You look like a freight train that just got derailed."

Chance sighed. "Thanks. That's just about the way I feel."

"You're not usually an early-morning drinker. Something must be stuck real tight in your craw. Want to tell me about it?"

Chance blew out a breath, knowing he should keep silent. That it wouldn't be fair to Kate. Not that he really gave a rat's ass at the moment. "Just a little woman trouble. Nothing you can do to help."

"Yeah, well, don't feel bad. Willow got pissed off about the money I spent for a new Nikon lens. She was yelling the house down, so I left."

"She'll cool down in an hour or two. She always does."

Jeremy grinned. "Yeah, that's one of the things I love about her. She doesn't hold a grudge."

Chance thought about Kate and couldn't help feeling a twinge of bitterness that she had refused to confide in him. He took a sip of his beer, looked over at Jeremy, who had climbed up on the stool beside him. "You ever thought about what it would be like to die?"

Jeremy just grunted. "Painful."

"I don't mean the dying part. I mean the after. You know, what you might find on the other side, once you pass away. You ever try to imagine what might be waiting out there?"

"I don't have to imagine it. I've seen it. A lot of us have."

"What do you mean?"

"I'm talking about a vision quest. When an Indian seeks a vision, he travels to *Schi-mas-ket*

— the land of the Great Spirit. That's where our visions come from."

"I remember when we were boys, you talked about it. Three days on the mountain. No food, barely any water. I'd forgotten all about it."

"It isn't something I'll ever forget. By the end of the third day, I was thirsty, cold, and hungry enough to eat a buffalo — raw. But the hours finally paid off."

"What happened?"

"My vision finally came. I saw my great-grandfather, Many Feathers. He talked to me for a while, then he transformed into an eagle right in front of my eyes. The two of us soared into the sky above the mountains. I remember how much we could see from up there — deer, moose, bear, huge pine forests, beautiful lakes, roaring rivers. I wanted to be like the eagle, to see everything as clearly as I saw it then, and I wanted to be able to remember. That was my quest. That's the reason I learned to take pictures."

Chance felt the oddest sensation. He took a sip of his beer and tomato juice, the only thing his stomach could handle this early in the day. "Kate says she's been to the other side. She says she saw her dead friends there. She claims she spoke to Nell Hart. She thinks Nell may have been murdered."

Jeremy blew on the cup of coffee Maddie had poured and set in front of him. "Interesting."

"You could say that."

"That's the trouble you were talking about?"

He nodded and Jeremy shrugged. "So Kate's had a vision — what's the big deal? The Salish would think that makes her a very special woman."

Elbows propped on the bar, Chance raked both hands through his hair. "She didn't want to talk about it. She didn't think I'd believe what she had to say."

"Would you?"

"I don't know, probably not at the time. She doesn't want anyone in Lost Peak to know. I think that's one of the reasons she came here. Apparently, something was printed in the newspapers about it. It was probably hard on her son."

"Having a vision is nothing to be ashamed of."

Some of the tension eased from his body. For the first time that morning, Chance drew an easy breath. "No, I guess it isn't." He was glad he had spoken to Jeremy. He trusted him, and he knew that Kate could trust him, too.

"Maybe you should tell her that."

Chance mulled that over, feeling a little like a fool. He never questioned Jeremy's beliefs, or those of his other Indian friends. Why was it so hard to believe the same sort of thing had happened to Kate?

"I'll give it some thought." Pulling a couple of dollars out of his pocket, he tossed them onto the bar. "Weather's beginning to clear. We still going fishing today?"

Jeremy nodded. "Your place at noon. Chris has been looking forward to this all week."

Leaving his barely touched beer on the bar, Chance got up from his stool and headed for the door. "I'll have the horses saddled and ready," he called over his shoulder. "See you at noon."

By the time Kate finished her bath, she was feeling a little bit better. Telling herself she had more important things to do than mope over Chance McLain, she headed down the hall to her office and turned on her computer. She wanted to track down information, and the Internet was the fastest way she knew.

Assuming Nell had actually been murdered — still a very shaky assumption — the house was most likely the murder scene. If that was the case, there might be clues right under her nose. The police would use forensic techniques in this sort of investigation, but so far, she had nothing to take to them, only her unconfirmed suspicions. If she were going to find any clues, she would have to dig them up herself.

"All right," she muttered, "let's see what we can find out." Logging onto Yahoo, she typed in "forensic science," and let the search engine go to work.

The list that came up was lengthy. She began exploring each site one at a time, starting with *www.tncrimlaw.com/forensic* Carpenter's Forensic Science Resources. The site had its own list of suggested links: forensic medicine and pathology; forensic chemistry and toxicology; forensic DNA analysis; criminalistic and trace evidence — the sources went on and on.

She started with general forensic homepages and set to work.

Three hours later, the phone rang, and Kate had to rouse herself out of her computer trance to answer it. She recognized the whining tone of her ex-husband's voice and drew in a steadying breath.

"Hello, Tommy."

"Kaitlin — it's good to hear your voice." Kaitlin. He never called her that unless he wanted something. Kate pressed her fingers against the bridge of her nose, trying to stop the headache that had suddenly begun to throb.

"I've been wanting to talk to you," Tommy said. "I just got the final divorce settlement papers."

Now that *was* good news.

"I've been thinking, Kate. We were married nearly thirteen years. That's a lot to throw away. Maybe we got too hasty, you know what I mean? We have to think of David. For his sake, maybe we ought to call this whole thing off. Give it another try."

Her shoulders went tense. Anger bubbled like hot oil in her throat. Who was he kidding? Tommy couldn't care less about their marriage, or even about his own son.

"What's the matter, Tommy? Now that you're having to pay your own way, you just figured out how much it costs to live?"

She could hear his teeth grinding over the phone. "Always a smart ass, aren't you, Kate."

"I'm a lot smarter than I used to be, that's for sure. Smart enough to know when you're trying to con me."

"You love to put me down — you always have. I must have been crazy to think you might have changed."

Her fingers tightened around the phone. "You're crazy, all right — if you believe for an instant I'd ever consider going back to you."

"You bitch."

Kate sighed into the receiver. "Just sign the papers, Tommy. Let's get this whole thing over with once and for all."

"I'll sign the fucking papers. You can bet on that. But one of these days you're gonna be sorry." The phone clicked loudly in her ear and Kate set the receiver gently back down in its cradle. He'd mentioned David, but only because he'd wanted something. He hadn't asked about his son's welfare, hadn't asked to speak to him. She shouldn't have been surprised but somehow she was.

The final settlement papers hadn't reached her yet. Mail took forever in Montana, but they were on their way. Soon the divorce would be final and she could put that part of her life behind her.

Returning her attention to the computer, she reached for the stack of information she had printed off the Web, then glanced at the notes she had made.

By the time she finished reviewing it all and read the books she had ordered, she would at least have some idea how the whole thing worked. She wasn't ready to tackle the job of actually searching for evidence, but sooner or later, she'd know enough to give it a try.

In the meantime, she intended to speak to the undertaker. According to one of the sites she had visited, morticians had, on occasions when no autopsy was performed, stumbled upon something out of the ordinary that they reported to police. As far as she knew, that hadn't happened in Nell's case, but it was worth a try.

She was usually off in the afternoons. A quick trip to the Dorfman Funeral Home in Polson, where Nell's body had been taken after the accident, wouldn't be much trouble. It was one more item on her list and at least worth a try.

Kate took her pile of research material, headed back to her bedroom, and settled in to read.

After a pleasant trip into the hills, Chance, Jeremy, and Chris arrived back at the ranch late in the afternoon. Though the fishing had been good and the weather had turned clear, Chance had wished a dozen times that he could go back and see Kate. He couldn't. Not yet. He was afraid she still wouldn't talk to him.

Instead, on Monday afternoon, he saddled Skates and a couple of other horses, gauging his arrival about the time he figured the lunch shift would be over and Kate would be back at the house.

Leading a couple of gentle mares, he headed cross-country, taking the trail that led to the fence line behind her house. He hoped by now Kate would be more amenable to hearing what he had to say, and bringing a horse for David was a little added insurance. Kate might refuse to go with him, but she wouldn't be able to refuse her son . . . assuming he could convince the boy to join them.

Unwiring the makeshift gate in the fence between their properties, he rode onto her eighty-acre parcel, forded Little Sandy Creek, and led the mares up in her back yard. The old hitching rail, a fixture on the property for over eighty years, still remained standing. He tied the horses up at the rail, walked over, and knocked on Kate's back door.

A few minutes later, she pulled it open. "Chance . . . ? What . . . what are you doing here?" She was obviously surprised to see him and he couldn't blame her, after the way he'd acted the last time he was there.

His eyes ran the length of her, which didn't take all that long, as short as she was, and he thought that she looked even prettier than she had the last time he had seen her. She was dressed in a tight-fitting pair of jeans that cupped her bottom the way he suddenly itched to do, and a red plaid shirt that pulled a little across her bosom when she moved. Her cheeks were bright with color, her eyes as green as the grass outside her door.

He cleared his throat and kept his eyes on her face. "I was hoping you might have time to talk. I remembered what you said about liking to ride. I thought maybe we could take off up in the hills for a couple of hours. I figured we might convince David to come with us."

She eyed him with a hint of suspicion. She might have said no if the boy hadn't slammed out the door at that very moment, looking even more surprised to see him than his mother had. Apparently, they both thought Munson's revelation had ended their newly formed friendship. Chance inwardly cursed.

"Hi, Davy."

"Hi, Chance." The boy's wary glance slid over to the horses.

"I know you haven't started working at the store yet. I thought you and your mom might want to go for a ride."

"I told you, I hate horses."

"Yeah, well, sometimes, I do, too. Especially when one of 'em's acting like a bonehead. But other times, they can sure be a lot of fun." Ignoring Kate's steady gaze, he went over and untied the little white-stockinged sorrel he had brought for David. She was fifteen years old and so gentle just about anyone could ride her.

"This is Mandy. She's got a real pleasant nature. I thought maybe you might want to give her a try."

David shook his head. "No thanks."

Damn, this wasn't going to be as easy as he had planned. Chance ran a hand along the mare's smooth neck. "She needs exercising real bad. I was hoping you would do it . . . you know, sort of as a favor."

"A favor? What do you mean? Are you asking me for help?"

"Yeah, I guess I am. Mandy's kind of a favorite of mine. I don't let just anyone ride her. I figured I could trust her with you."

David seemed to waver. Chance could read the indecision on his face. He wanted to go, but he didn't want to look like a fool. "You let me borrow your fishing rod. I suppose I owe you for that."

"Like I said, I hate to ask."

"I never learned to ride, you know." David moved closer, till he stood next to the stirrup.

"It just takes a little getting used to. With a little practice, I bet you could be really good."

David looked up. "You really think so?"

"I know potential when I see it. Here, just slide your foot in the stirrup, grab hold of the saddle horn, and you can pull yourself up." With a little boost from Chance, David found himself in the saddle. He slid his foot into the stirrup on the opposite side.

"I had to guess how long to make them," Chance said. "How do they feel? About the right length?"

"I guess so."

"Stand up. If you can stick two fingers between you and the seat, they're just about right." David did and it was.

"Good. Now here's how you rein." For the next half hour, Chance showed the boy how to make the animal turn, how to stop, and how to go. All the while, Kate stood watching, an uneasy look on her face.

"You're doin' great, Davy. If your mom says it's okay, the three of us can go for a ride."

"I don't know, Chance," she said. "Jeremy brought over some slides this morning. Some of them show that spill up on Beaver Creek. I wanted to work on the slide show we're putting together for some of the environmental groups."

Chance strode over to where she stood warily on the back porch. "Come with us, Kate, please?"

"Come on, Mom. I'm not going if you don't."

As Chance had hoped, the boy's insistence persuaded her. "All right, but I can't stay away too long."

Taking her hand, he led her over to the little mare, Tulip, an extremely manageable twelve-year-old quarter horse with a comfortable gait. He helped Kate swing up in the saddle and adjusted the stirrups a little shorter.

"Ready?" he asked. Kate nodded, but she didn't look all that pleased. Walking the animals back across the river, he led them single file through the gate leading onto his property, and up into the hills, hoping the next couple of hours would go better than the one that had passed so far.

Riding single file, Kate's little mare followed David's sorrel and Chance's paint along the narrow trail. She had to admit it felt good to be riding again, different in the heavy Western saddle, but just as exhilarating as she remembered.

They rode through dense forests and out into wide-open pastures, passing herds of white-faced steers and an occasional deer or rabbit.

An hour into the ride, Chance reined the paint up beneath a pine tree at the edge of a stream. "Cedar Creek is usually pretty good fishing." He swung down from his horse, walked over and helped David down. "I brought a fly rod. I thought you might want to try your hand while I talk to your mom."

David studied his face and a look passed between them. Her son was no fool and Chance didn't treat him like one. He took the rod Chance held out, along with a small box of flies, and walked off toward the stream.

As David waded into the shallow creek bed and began to cast his line, Chance turned his attention to Kate. She could feel his gentle blue gaze as if he reached out and touched her.

"I'm glad you came," he said.

She was holding the reins, letting the little mare graze. "You tricked me into coming and you know it. You used my son as bait. You knew I couldn't refuse him."

His faint smile was unrepentant. "Guilty as charged. I don't think David minded, do you?"

She couldn't help smiling in return. "I think it was wonderful the way you convinced him to give it a try."

"Now all I have to do is convince his mom."

Kate waited while Chance pulled a blanket from his saddlebag and spread it out on the ground beneath the tree. He tied the horses up to graze a little way away and returned to where she sat on the blanket, her legs curled up beneath her.

"You've been awfully quiet today." He sat down cross-legged beside her, plucked a piece of long-stemmed grass, and twirled it in his hands. His fingers were long and dark and she couldn't help remembering how they had felt moving over her body.

"I didn't expect to see you again."

"Did you really think something some idiot like Chet Munson said could keep me away?"

She looked up at him. "Actually, I did."

"Because you figure if you were to tell me

what happened in LA I'd think you were crazy."

"I know how bad it sounds. That's why I didn't tell you in the first place. Everyone else thinks I'm crazy, why shouldn't you?" For a moment, Kate closed her eyes, fighting the urge to climb back on the mare and ride as fast as she could back to the house.

"I want to hear your version of what happened. Then it's up to me to decide what I will and won't believe."

Kate smoothed a wrinkle in the blanket. Maybe it was time he knew. By now he knew most of it anyway. "All right, but don't say I didn't warn you."

For the next twenty minutes, she explained about the shooting, and what had happened to her the night she had died. She left nothing out, not even the part about her grandmother and the message she had only partially received.

"I realize it sounds completely nuts. But I believe it really happened." She told him about the photograph of Nell she had found. "That's how I knew who the woman was. Until I found the photo, I had never seen her face."

Chance twirled the black hat resting on one bent knee. "And you think she was trying to tell you she was murdered."

"I'm not sure. I think it was something about her death, or the way she died. I've had dreams about it since then. In the dreams, she's trying

239

to tell me that she was murdered."

She watched his expression, waiting for the condemnation to appear. Instead, when he finally looked at her, a faint smile softened the lines of his face.

"My grandmother was a full-blooded Blackfoot Indian. She believed in the land of the Great Spirit. She talked to me about it when I was a boy. I hadn't thought about it in years. Jeremy Spotted Horse and a lot of the men on the rez have experienced visions. Sometimes it tells them things about the past or the future. A vision quest, they call it. I don't suppose it's fair to accept what they believe is real and not believe what you say."

Her throat went tight. Tears welled up in her eyes. Until that moment, she hadn't realized how badly she had wanted him to believe her. She fumbled in the pocket of her jeans for a Kleenex, but came up empty. Chance pulled a faded red bandana from his back pocket and mopped at the wetness on her cheeks.

"It's all right, darlin'. I didn't mean to make you cry."

She took the bandana out of his hands, wiped away the rest of the moisture, then handed it back. "I need to know if it's true, Chance. If it is, then everything that happened to me that night was real. I was actually there. Such a place really exists."

"I guess I can see why it would be so important. I'd like to believe there's such a place, too." He tucked the bandana back into his hip pocket. "I won't sit here and say I'm convinced Nell Hart was murdered. But if you want to dig a little deeper, I don't see anything wrong with that. And I'll help you in any way I can."

She wanted to throw her arms around his neck. She wanted to kiss him, right there under the pine tree. "Thank you, Chance. You don't know how much that means to me."

He came to his feet and hauled her up beside him. "Next time, don't be afraid to trust me. I won't let you down, Kate."

She only nodded. Chance glanced toward the river, saw David engrossed in fishing a ways upstream, and pulled her into his arms. "I keep remembering Saturday night. God, I think about making love to you every damned minute." Softly at first, then more deeply, he kissed her. Her knees were shaking by the time he was done.

"When can I see you again?" A note of urgency rang in his voice as he kissed the side of her neck.

"I don't know, I —"

"How about Saturday night? We'll go dancing. Every other weekend, they have a Country-Western band at the Antlers. It's really a lot of fun."

She laughed. "I haven't the foggiest notion how to dance Country-Western, but I'd love to give it a try."

"Great. Wonderful." He bent his head and

lightly brushed her lips. "Terrific." He glanced to where David had just hooked onto a big silver fish. Chance cocked his head in the boy's direction and grinned. "I think he's getting the hang of country life."

Kate followed his gaze and her heart squeezed a little. "So it seems."

"We'll give him time to show off his fish and release it, then we ought to be getting on back. The first time out, you'll be sore if you ride too long."

Gathering their horses and belongings and finally rounding up David, Chance led them back to the house a little over an hour later, David now grousing that it was far too early in the day to quit.

"You won't be saying that tonight," Chance warned with a chuckle. "It takes a little while for your muscles to adjust to the saddle. If you want, we can ride again on Wednesday, after you get home from work."

"Yes!" David shot his fist into the air, and Kate laughed. Chance smiled at her and the look on his face made her skin go tingly and warm. They reined up in front of the hitching rail. David jumped down and Chance helped Kate alight.

"What time on Wednesday?" David asked.

"What time do you get home from work?"

"Five o'clock. That isn't too late, is it?"

"It doesn't get dark this time of year till ten. We can get in a couple of hours before that."

"Great! See you Wednesday, then." David rushed off, slamming into the house and leaving them alone.

"This has been wonderful, Chance. You'll never know how much I appreciate what you're doing for David."

He glanced away, looking a little embarrassed. "I like your boy. I hope I can help him learn to fit in." Holding the horse's reins in one hand, he swung up into the saddle. Beneath the worn, soft jeans, that molded to his body, muscles tightened in his thighs, and Kate felt suddenly too warm.

"Well, I guess I'd better be going," he said with what she hoped was a hint of reluctance. "I have work to do and I imagine you do, too."

She certainly did. The slide presentation she was working on, and her other, even more important project. Tomorrow she was heading into Polson. She was hoping for a miracle, she knew, something that might help in her search.

But Kate wasn't discouraged. She knew better than anyone that miracles really did happen.

Chapter Sixteen

Leaning back in his tufted leather chair, Lon Barton skimmed the file Duke Mullens had just brought in.

"I can't believe this. The damned woman was vice president of one of the biggest ad agencies in the country."

"Yeah. And from what this says, she was making big bucks in LA."

"Sid's note says she was one of the best ad execs in the business. She would have been pretty financially set if it weren't for her divorce. The guy held her up like a bandit."

"Yeah, well, it's usually the guy who gets stuck," Duke grumbled.

Lon read on down the page. Sid Battistone was thorough, no doubt about it. Then again, for what he was being paid, he'd better be. The file told him about Kate's fatherless childhood and that her mother had died in a car wreck when Kate was eighteen. The file held a wealth of information on her no-good, worthless husband, including the drug charges Tommy Rollins had been brought up on six years ago, and the fact he had been sponging off Kate practically since the day they were married.

He read another paragraph on down the page. "What the hell is this?"

Duke moved around till he could read the file over Lon's shoulder. "Crazy, ain't it? I guess that's the reason she moved up here — to get away from the newspaper reporters and stuff, after the shooting."

Lon reached down and picked up an article that had been clipped out of the LA *Times*. WOMAN TELLS TALE OF LIFE AFTER DEATH. Lon scanned the article, more dumbfounded by the moment.

"Jesus — it says here Kate Rollins barely survived a drive-by shooting, that she died for nearly ten minutes before they revived her. During that time, she claims to have had a near-death experience. The article quotes her as saying she talked to her dead relatives on 'The Other Side.' Do you believe that? The woman must be out of her skull."

"Yeah, and guess what? She's been nosing around ever since she got here, asking questions about her grandmother. A couple of weeks ago, she went to Polson and asked to see the sheriff's report on Nell Hart's death. She's asked half a dozen customers about her. I looked up her phone records. She's even called old Aida Whittaker."

"I wonder what the hell she's trying to find out."

"I don't know, but on Sunday, a guy from LA was in Lost Peak looking for her. Tom Webster said he came into the bar, said he was a reporter for the *National Monitor*."

"The *National Monitor*? Isn't that one of those goofy tabloids you find in the grocery stores?"

"Sure is."

"Find this guy — whoever he is. Find out what he knows about Kate Rollins. A person with her background, someone who really knows how to run this anti-mining campaign, could give us big-time trouble. I want that cyanide ban overturned and I'm not about to let some big-titted redhead get in my way."

"Don't worry, boss — I'll take care of it."

Duke Mullens's smile looked downright wolfish as he headed out the door.

On Wednesday evening, as promised, Chance arrived to take David riding. Kate had traded nights off, so she could go dancing at the Antlers on Saturday, which meant she was working when Chance came over, but according to David, he had brought Chris Spotted Horse with him.

"He's an Indian, Mom," David said with a far too serious face when she got home from the cafe that night, "but he's really okay. He goes to that Indian school — Two Eagle River? But he doesn't live very far from town. Chris says he likes to fish, so we're gonna go after I get home from work on Saturday."

"Honey, that's wonderful." Kate could have hugged Chance McLain. Then again, just thinking about him made her want to do a lot more than that. Her insides vaguely quivered. She pushed the erotic, highly inappropriate thoughts away.

On Thursday, Chance and Jeremy Spotted Horse showed up at the cafe for lunch. Kate served them her secret recipe special meatloaf. Myra was great at apple pie, but Kate had a few talents of her own.

"This is phenomenal," Chance said, mopping up the gravy with some of the cafe's homemade bread. "How do you make it?"

Kate grinned. "I could tell you, but then I'd have to kill you."

Chance laughed, a deep, entirely too masculine sound. She turned her attention to Jeremy before wicked thoughts started building in her head. "Those slides you brought over were wonderful, Jeremy. I've got the entire presentation laid out. Ed's going to have copies made and take them to the various environmental agencies next week."

"That's great, Kate." The big Salish Indian wolfed down another bite of meatloaf, the special of the day. "I've got a lot more landscape stuff, if you need it."

"I might just take you up on that." She glanced at the clock on the wall over one of the booths. "You two need anything else? I'm taking off a little early. I've got something to do in Polson and I —"

"How'd you like some company?" Chance wiped his mouth with a paper napkin. "I've got a couple of errands I need to run. It would save me making a special trip." His eyes fixed on her face and her stomach did its usual little flip.

"That'd be great."

Chance stood up and tossed down money for the check. "I'll see you on the flipside, partner," he said to Jeremy, who shot him a look Kate couldn't read.

"Don't take any wooden nickels, Kemosabe."

Chance grinned and Kate laughed. It was obvious the men were extremely close friends. Kate liked Jeremy. She was eager to meet his son, Chris, and Chance promised she would meet his wife, Willow, at the dance on Saturday night.

Leaving them in the cafe, she went up to the house, changed into jeans and a yellow cotton shirt, then returned. Chance volunteered to drive and they set off down the road to Highway 93.

They pulled into Polson less than an hour later. Chance didn't seem surprised when she asked him to stop at Dorfman's Funeral Home. He just pulled up in front as if it were an everyday occurrence and ushered her inside.

"Hello there. May I help you?"

Kate turned at the sound of a soft male voice.

"I'm Marvin Dorfman. How may I be of assistance?" He was a short, slightly pudgy man with pale, lightly freckled skin and thinning sandy hair. His smile seemed a permanent fixture on his face.

"It's nice to meet you. I'm Kate Rollins and this is Chance McLain. We came to talk to you about a woman named Nell Hart. Mrs. Hart was my grandmother. She died in January of last year."

"Mrs. Hart . . ." he repeated, his sandy brows pulling together. "Let me check my records." He disappeared into his office, and she and Chance followed through the open door. The funeral home was small, done in light woods, the walls painted a soothing shade of blue. Through another doorway, she could see a family viewing room with several rows of padded chairs and gauzy curtains in front of the area designed to display the coffin.

Kate returned her attention to Marvin Dorfman, who pulled a manila folder out of a metal file cabinet, slid a pair of those little half reading glasses onto his nose, flipped open the folder, and began to read.

"Ah, yes, Mrs. Hart. I would have remembered — I always remember the departed ones we've cared for — but that week I had come down with a terrible case of the flu. I had to leave early the day Mrs. Hart arrived. I was there in the beginning, though, to see that she was comfortably settled in."

Comfortably settled in. Kate wondered what that particular euphemism meant. "Then you did see the body?"

"Why, yes. As I said, I was there when they brought her in."

"I'm interested in knowing whether you might have noticed anything unusual about her? Was there anything you observed about the injuries she suffered that might have been inconsistent with the sort of fall that was the cause of her death?"

He frowned. "Inconsistent? You're asking if there were any additional injuries other than those caused by the trauma to the head?"

"That's exactly what she's asking," Chance answered for her.

Dorfman looked down at the file, then raised his head. "If we'd noticed anything unusual it would have been reported to the sheriff's office." He looked down again and Kate realized he was studying something in the file.

"May I see that?"

"We would prefer that you didn't. It is often painful for family members to see —"

"Let the lady have the file," Chance said, and Dorfman gingerly handed it over.

Kate looked down and sucked in a breath of air. What Dorfman hadn't wanted her to see were photographs of her grandmother's naked body, her modesty protected only by a very small towel. They must have been taken when Nell first arrived at the mortuary.

"I hope you don't find the picture too upsetting," Mr. Dorfman said consolingly. He had a soothing, reassuring way about him that made him perfect for the job he had chosen. And strangely enough, he did seem sincere. "We like

250

to document each case. The information is strictly confidential and just for our records."

There were photos of Nell lying on her back, sides, and stomach. In one picture, Kate could see dark blood congealed on the back of her head. In another, Nell's ribs were showing, as well as her hipbones. She was a frail little woman. A stiff breeze would have been enough to blow her over.

Kate started to hand back the file when she noticed a slight darkening of the skin on both of Nell's upper arms.

"What's this?" She pointed out the area on the photo.

"The first stages of bruising, perhaps. It's a little hard to say simply by looking at the picture."

"Why didn't the sheriff's report mention this?"

"Possibly because they were beneath Mrs. Hart's clothing when the deputy first saw her. Her dress wasn't removed until she got here. The deputy would normally be in attendance at this point, but if I recall correctly, that was the afternoon the school bus ran off an icy embankment and the deputy was called away to assist before he could get here."

"If these are bruises, is it possible they occurred during the process of moving the body?"

"Absolutely not. We're extremely careful when making a removal. Besides, once the heart stops beating, it's impossible for a bruise to form."

Kate felt a chill slide through her. Whatever had happened to cause the marks had occurred before Nell's death. "Why weren't these reported?"

"Older people often bruise easily. And there was no reason to suspect foul play."

"So no one called it in."

"I don't think so. As I told you, I was extremely ill that day. I left Mrs. Hart's care in the hands of one of my assistants."

"And his name is . . . ?" Chance asked.

"Walter Hobbs."

"Is Mr. Hobbs in?" Kate asked.

"I'm afraid not. He's retired. He only comes in when we're very short-handed. That afternoon, my regular assistant was also out with the flu. There was nearly an epidemic at the time."

"Do you have a phone number for Mr. Hobbs?" Chance asked. Dorfman nodded and politely wrote the name, address, and phone number on the back of one of his personal cards. He really did seem like a very nice man.

"Is there any chance you could lend me those photos for a while?" Kate paused. "I promise I'll return them."

He hesitated only a moment. "Of course. I would appreciate getting them back, though. We like to keep our records complete."

"Thank you, Mr. Dorfman. You've been extremely helpful."

"We're always glad to assist members of the family. That's what we're here for."

They left the funeral parlor and made their way back to Chance's truck. Kate was silent along the way, her mind racing with possibilities.

"Dorfman's right, you know," Chance said gently as he started the truck and they drove off down the street. "Even if those marks are bruises, older people bruise fairly easily. Nell could have done damned near anything to get them."

"Or someone could have grabbed her by the arms and pushed her into that sideboard."

"Think about it, Kate. What are the chances your grandmother would hit her head hard enough to kill her? If someone wanted her dead, that's hardly a reliable way to go about it."

Kate mulled that over, said nothing for the longest time. Then she sighed. "You're right, I suppose. Still, it bothers me. Something just isn't right about this, Chance."

"We'll keep after it, then. I've got to see Frank Mills. We'll call this guy, Hobbs, from Frank's office."

They did, but Walter Hobbs wasn't in. Since he didn't have an answering machine, Kate made a mental note to call him again when she got home.

Waiting in the reception area of Mills' office, she stood up when Chance walked back into the room. "I don't believe it," he said.

"What is it?"

"Consolidated Metals pled no contest to the charges of environmental pollution."

"That's good news, isn't it?"

"Not in this case. They offered to pay what they considered reasonable damages, in this case twenty-five thousand dollars. A measly twenty-five thousand — and the judge agreed. That kind of money won't touch the damage to the environment that arsenic spill caused. And it isn't enough to stop them from doing it again."

"Oh, Chance, I'm sorry."

He didn't say anything, but a muscle knotted in his cheek. All the way home, he stared broodingly down the road, saying very little, answering her questions mostly in monosyllables.

When they finally reached her house, he walked her absently up to the door.

"Sorry I wasn't better company."

"I wasn't a whole lot of fun either."

"Saturday night we'll do better. Let's make a vow to forget all this crap — at least for one night."

Kate smiled. "You got it."

He bent his head and pressed a quick hard kiss on her mouth. "That'll have to do until then." He cocked his head toward the window, where David peered through the starched criss-cross curtains.

"I see what you mean." A long, silent glance passed between them.

"Damn. How the hell am I going to make it till Saturday night?" Kate caught her breath as he leaned forward and kissed her again. She could feel the heavy bulge straining against his Levi's just before he turned and walked away.

Saturday seemed to drag. As soon as the lunch shift ended, Kate went upstairs to her office to call Walter Hobbs but he still wasn't home. She tried to work on some storyboard displays but couldn't seem to concentrate. Instead she made some calls to her list of volunteers and got them set up to begin a postcard-writing campaign to local politicians.

Eventually, the day slipped into late afternoon and Jeremy arrived with Chris, who was almost as tall as David but more filled out in the chest and shoulders. His eyes were the same obsidian black as his father's and so was his hair, but Chris wore his cut short beneath his battered cowboy hat. He had high cheekbones and smooth, dark skin. Kate figured he must be the terror of the female population at the Two Eagle River School.

"It's really nice to meet you, Ms. Rollins," he said without a trace of the self-importance a lot of really attractive young boys had.

"It's nice to meet you, too, Chris."

Jeremy spoke up from beside him. "I thought I'd take them up to a spot I know where the fishing's real good. Since we probably won't get

255

back till dark, I was thinking . . . maybe you wouldn't mind if David stayed overnight. My daughter Shannon is nearly sixteen. She's very responsible. She'll be there while her mother and I are over at the dance."

"Can I, Mom, please?"

Kate bit her lip. She didn't like the idea of the two boys staying with only a high school girl for supervision, but she wanted David to make friends, and Jeremy and his son seemed like good ones.

She looked at David, saw the hope in his eyes. He hated babysitters. He thought he was too old and maybe he was. She glanced over at Jeremy, saw something in his expression that made her think that Chance might have had something to do with this, but decided not to press it.

"Myra said she'd stay at the house till I got home, but I suppose I could tell her David is spending the night with Chris."

"Thanks, Mom, you're the best!"

"Like I said, Shannon is real reliable. And Willow and I won't be out that late. She worries about the kids if we don't get back at a fairly respectable hour."

Kate smiled. "I guess it's settled, then." David collected his fishing gear and the little group left the house, leaving Kate to wander aimlessly, trying to pass the hours until the dance.

Chapter Seventeen

Late afternoon turned into evening. At eight o'clock sharp, Chance arrived on her doorstep dressed in his special-occasion blue jeans and a pale blue Western shirt with silver collar tabs.

"I hope you're in the mood for chicken and frozen pizza," he said. "That's about all they've got at the Antlers, but it really isn't too bad."

"Are you kidding? I'm so sick of my own cooking, frozen pizza sounds like a treat."

Chance caught her hand as she walked out the door and turned her around to face him. "You look terrific."

Kate smiled, ridiculously pleased at the compliment. "Thanks." She was wearing an outfit she had bought on a whim one day in Missoula, a navy-blue broomstick skirt and matching Indian-patterned vest, cream-colored cotton blouse, and silver concho belt. Since she didn't have cowboy boots, she was wearing her ankle-high English riding boots.

The Antlers Saloon was already packed. A weekend dance was a major occasion in a town the size of Lost Peak. The band, Rocky Mountain Mist, a mother, father, and two sons, was assembling on a makeshift stage, but hadn't started to play. A jukebox punched out Western tunes and several couples already circled the dance floor.

Kate listened to Garth Brooks singing "The Beaches of Cheyenne" and thought with amazement how much she had come to like country tunes. Myra had told her they had played Country-Western in the cafe for as long as she could remember. Somehow it seemed so right for the place Kate hadn't had the heart to change it. In the months that followed — rock and roll devotee that she was — she had actually begun to enjoy it.

Now, although she liked all kinds of music, she found herself most often tuning into EAGLE 94.5, the country station on the radio.

"Over here, Kate." Chance waved her over to a table he had commandeered in the corner away from the loudspeakers. They sat down and ordered pizza and beer.

"Now that we're settled in," he said, "there's something I've been wanting to do."

She arched a brow. "What's that?"

He leaned over and kissed her very softly on the lips. "Just that. I want you to think about that when we're dancing . . . and what I'm gonna do to you after we're through."

She couldn't seem to breathe. Her stomach did a quiet little roll and heat floated out through her limbs. She knew exactly what Chance intended to do. If she closed her eyes, she could almost feel him moving inside her. She could feel his mouth against her skin, his hands caressing . . . Her eyes snapped open. Color washed into her cheeks.

Chance chuckled softly. "You see? It's working already."

Kate tossed him a playfully indignant glance. "Don't be too sure of yourself, cowboy."

Chance just smiled. He looked like a man who knew exactly what he wanted and tonight he meant to get it. The way he kept staring first at her mouth and then at her breasts, she was surprised he didn't drag her down on the dance floor and make love to her right there.

She was growing flushed and beginning to perspire when the band began to play, firing out a Texas two-step. Chance grabbed her hand and hauled her to her feet.

"Come on, darlin'. I'll show you how it's done in Montana."

She thought that he already had, but she didn't say so. He pulled her snug against him, pressed his cheek to hers, and kind of wrapped himself around her.

God, he felt so good.

"Just follow me. I promise it isn't that tough." Oddly enough, it wasn't. He showed her the steps a couple of times, until her feet had accepted the memory. In her earlier years, she had been a very good dancer. It didn't take long to remember how to follow his lead, how to relax into the rhythm of the music and let him guide her through the movements. He moved like he did everything else, with a natural, easy grace that seemed rooted in his very bones.

By the end of the hour, she was dancing Country-Western as if she had been doing it for years. She was even able to make some of the difficult back and forth turns while they moved clockwise around the floor.

"You didn't tell me how good you'd be at this," he said, obviously pleased.

"I told you I liked to dance. Besides, I didn't know how good you were, either."

A thick black brow arched up. "Didn't you? I was kind of hoping I'd made that clear."

A flush rose into her cheeks. She knew how good he was. Damned good. And those hot blue eyes said he meant to prove it again tonight.

They took a break from the dancing when Jeremy Spotted Horse walked in. "Come on. I want you to meet Willow." As Chance started leading her back through the crowd, Kate recognized the woman as a customer who had been in the cafe a couple of times for lunch. Willow was beautiful, tall and reed-slim, with big dark eyes and ebony hair bobbed at the shoulder. She was wearing a pair of red jeans, a red-checked cowboy shirt, and boots. Beneath her thick black hair, long silver earrings dangled from her ears.

Introductions were made and the four of them sat down at the table.

"I like your son," Willow said, endearing herself to Kate in an instant. "He seems so intelligent. Like his mother, I think."

"That's a very nice thing to say. David's always been good in school, at least he was until he started running around with the wrong sort of crowd. I'm happy he's found a friend like Chris."

"Perhaps they'll be good for each other. Your David and his computers. My Chris and his love of the outdoors."

Kate smiled, liking Willow more and more. "I think that's a very good combination." Both couples danced for a while, then the music slowed and the band played a country waltz.

"I bet you've danced this way before," Chance teased, leading her back on the floor.

She thought she had — till she slow-danced with Chance McLain. He pulled her close and she could feel him all around her, feel the brush of his jeans, the silkiness of his hair where it curled over her fingers. She could smell his aftershave and the faint, salty tang of his skin.

He pulled her even closer, flattening her breasts out against his chest. "God, Katie . . ." He nuzzled the side of her neck and little prickles of heat rippled over her skin. One of his thighs moved intimately between her legs and she could feel his growing arousal. He was hard as a stone by the time the music ended and she heard him softly curse.

"I'm not sure this was such a good idea," he

grumbled, walking close behind her as they headed back toward the table. Kate hid a pleased, secret smile that she'd been able to have that effect on him. Then, just before they reached the table, she spotted Silas Marshall walking in.

He headed toward the rear of the bar, so tall he had to bend his head to avoid a rafter where the roof sloped down. He still made her think of Abraham Lincoln, but now she wondered if he was a whole lot stronger than he looked.

And just how badly he had wanted that piece of property he had owned with Nell Hart.

"I'll be right back," she said to Chance. "I've got to make a pit stop." Knowing she shouldn't, Kate meandered in Silas's direction, weaving her way through the crowd and stopping right in front of him.

"Silas — it's nice to see you."

He smiled. "It's good to see you, too, Kate."

"How's David working out? No problems this time, I hope."

"He just got a little mixed up, living in the city and all. I think he's learned his lesson."

"I think so, too."

"Too bad Nell never got the chance to meet him. I think she would have been proud of you both."

"Thank you, Silas." It was a very nice thing to say and the perfect opening. She simply couldn't resist. "Speaking of Nell, I was cleaning out some boxes in the attic and I happened to run across the deed to some property the two of you owned together."

In the light of the neon beer sign, she saw his Adam's apple bob up and down. "We owned that piece for more than twenty years."

"After Nell died, I guess you sold it."

He looked away. "My son wanted to borrow some money to buy a house. It's hard for kids to make the down payment with prices so high these days."

"Yes, I imagine it is. I gather Nell didn't want to sell."

He cleared his throat. His eyes began darting around as if he wished he could escape. "No, she didn't."

"You two were friends. I'm surprised you couldn't talk her into it."

"I tried to. It was a really good deal — a big profit for both of us — but Nell wouldn't listen. She could really be hardheaded sometimes."

Kate forced a smile. "Well, in the end, I guess it didn't matter. Once Nell was dead, you got the land, sold it, and got the money for your son."

His long face paled. He looked like he wanted to run. "I have to go. I'm supposed to meet some friends."

"Nice to see you, Silas."

"Uh-huh." He left as if he couldn't get away fast enough and Kate returned to the table, thinking of his reaction.

"I saw you talking to Silas," Chance said,

eyeing her over the top of his beer.

"I asked him how David was doing."

He cocked a knowing black eyebrow. "Did you?"

"Yes, I did," she replied a bit defensively.

"Exactly what else did you ask him?"

Kate plopped down in her chair. "All right, I asked him about the property he and Nell owned together. So sue me."

"I thought we agreed we weren't going to worry about any of that tonight."

"I know but . . . Dammit, the opportunity just came up and I couldn't resist."

"Leave it alone, Kate, please. At least for tonight."

She felt like a spoilsport. He had brought her here to have fun, not look for clues to a possible murder. "You're right. I'm sorry." She took a sip of her beer. It was icy cold and a little foamy. It went great with frozen pizza. "I've already forgotten all about it."

He gave her one his sexy smiles. "Good girl."

"Come on, you guys." Willow stood up at the table. "They're playing a line dance."

"Not me," Chance said, shaking his head. "I draw the line at herd dancing. Besides, I've got to hit the head."

"That leaves you, Kate. Jeremy and I will show you the steps. It's easy, once you get the hang of it."

It did look like fun. Kate followed them out on the dance floor where no one danced with partners and half the bar lined up facing the band. She took a place between Willow and a tall, good-looking cowboy she had noticed when they first walked in. Chance had said hello to him. She remembered he'd called the guy Ned.

"They're playing 'Boot-Skootin' Boogie'," Willow said, practically hopping up and down in her bright red cowboy boots. "It's one of my favorites." It seemed to take forever to memorize the steps of the dance, but eventually Kate began to catch on and it really was a lot of fun.

Willow laughed. "You're a natural at this, Kate. It took me weeks to learn all of the steps."

Feeling pretty smug that she was catching on so quickly, Kate turned the wrong direction just then and bumped squarely into the cowboy named Ned.

"It's all right, sweet thing." He grinned. "You can bump into me anytime you like."

He really was good looking, tall and barrel-chested, wearing boots and a white straw hat. They say every woman loves a cowboy — or will. She already had one of her own, but this one was staring at her as if he'd like to eat her up and it felt darned good.

Kate laughed at something Ned said, bending a little closer so she could hear him over the music. Then she looked back toward the table and saw Chance glaring at her with a look as black as the sky outside the windows.

The music ended, but as she turned to go back to the table, Ned caught her arm. "How about a dance, sweet thing?"

She should have said no. Any other time, any other place, she would have. But from the corner of her eye, she could see Chance leaning against the wall, his arms crossed over his chest, and some little demon just wouldn't let her.

"All right." It was a two-step, thank God. And he didn't hold her overly close. Still, by the time the tune was over and she was heading back to the table, she could see she had made a grave mistake.

"Fun's over," Chance said, "we're leaving."

Kate moistened her suddenly dry lips. "But I thought —"

"I said we're leaving. Now."

Kate didn't argue, just said goodnight to Jeremy and Willow and let Chance tug her out the door. Wordlessly, he helped her climb into his pickup, cranked up the engine, and drove out of the parking lot.

He took the curvy mountain road a little faster than he should have. Kate knew better than to ask him to slow down.

"Where are we going?" she finally got up the nerve to ask.

"Lookout Mountain."

"Where's that?"

Chance turned off the narrow road into an open area surrounded by trees on three sides

266

and looking out over the valley on the other. He slammed on his brakes and turned off the engine. "Right here."

Kate fell silent. Her nerves were hopping, her heart pounding. When Chance jumped out of the car and slammed the door, she leaped as if a pistol had been fired.

He came around to her side of the truck, jerked open the door, and swung her down to the ground.

"All right. What the hell was that all about?"

She plucked at a piece of lint on her sleeve. "I don't know what you mean."

"The hell you don't. You did that on purpose. You were trying to make me jealous."

She tilted her head back to look up at him. "Were you jealous?"

"Hell, yes."

She guiltily glanced away. "I'm sorry. I didn't realize —"

"Bullshit. You knew exactly what you were doing. What I want to know is why?"

Kate sighed. The jig was up, so to speak. She might as well confess to the crime and get it over with. "You want the truth? All right, here it is. I've never had a man jealous over me in my life. I married Tommy when I was seventeen. He didn't have a jealous bone in his body. He couldn't care less if another man was attracted to me. I thought . . . I thought that maybe you would. I wanted to know what it felt like."

"You wanted to know what it . . . ?" He swung away from her, tore off his hat, slammed it up on the hood of the truck.

"Just once," she said. "Just once, I wanted to know."

He raked a hand through his wavy black hair. "Fine, now you know. Since you're having this learning experience at my expense, you want to know what it felt like to me?"

She opened her mouth, but he didn't wait for her to answer.

"It felt like I wanted to wipe up the floor with Ned Cummings. Ned is a friend and I wanted to knock him flat. I saw the way you smiled at him and I wanted to drag you out of there by your gorgeous red hair and put my brand on you. I wanted to make sure none of those guys ever touched you again."

He looked down at her and something hot and hungry moved in his eyes. "I wanted to tear your clothes off. I wanted to drive myself inside you. I wanted to do this."

Sliding his hand behind her neck, he dragged her mouth up to his for a hard, punishing kiss. For an instant, she tried to pull back, frightened by the violence she had unleashed, then the bruising kiss gentled, turned coaxing, and his tongue swept in. Heat roared through her, sank into every particle of her flesh. She felt dizzy, disoriented, as if she were falling off a cliff. He kissed her endlessly and she found herself clinging to his shoulders,

268

fighting just to stay on her feet.

"It made me want you, Katie," he whispered as his mouth moved along her throat. "Even more than I did already." His hands found her breasts and he massaged them through her clothes. He shoved the vest off her shoulders, popped a button as he struggled to unfasten her blouse.

Her head fell back. He kissed her throat, her collarbone, unhooked her bra and filled his hands with her breasts. His lips, soft and hot, so very, very hot, slid over her skin, moved lower, and he took the heavy fullness into his mouth. He suckled her, used his teeth to caress a nipple, and Kate heard herself moan.

She was shaking all over, her legs rubbery, her insides throbbing with heat. Another passionate kiss and he tugged her narrow skirt down over her hips. The elastic band made it easy. Vaguely, she wondered if perhaps this was the reason she had worn it, along with the thigh-high nylons and skimpy blue satin bikini panties she wore underneath.

He looked down just then, saw them, and his eyes seemed to burn right through her. "You want to know how it feels when you make a man jealous?" He lifted her up on the fender and moved between her legs. She could hear the buzz of the zipper on his jeans sliding down. He released himself, his fingers found her softness, and he skillfully began to stroke her.

"You want to know how it feels?" He discovered how slick and wet she was and lifted her again, wrapping her legs around his waist. "It feels like this," he said, and plunged himself inside.

Kate whimpered and clung to his neck, absorbing the fullness, the hot, hard joining.

"I won't share you, Katie. Not with Ned Cummings or anyone else." Surging upward, he filled her again, slid out and then in, again and again. Hot hard kisses, his tongue plunging into her mouth with the same determined rhythm as his body, had her trembling, teetering on the edge of release. Sensation swamped her, battered her, slammed her into a powerful climax.

Chance didn't slow, just kept on pounding until she came again, her body shivering, tightening around him. Two more deep, driving thrusts and he followed her to release.

She was sobbing against his shoulder by the time they were through, shaking with the force of her emotions. She felt his hands sifting gently through her hair.

"I'm sorry, Katie." He pressed a kiss on her forehead. "I just got so turned on. I hope I didn't hurt you."

She dragged in a shaky breath, thinking of the intense pleasure he had brought her. "You didn't hurt me."

Chance shook his head as he lowered her back to her feet. "I don't know what there is about you, Kate. I can't seem to figure it out."

But Kate was beginning to know very clearly what it was about Chance McLain that made her behave as she never had before. Heaven help her, as much as she had tried to fight it, she knew she was falling in love with him.

It was nearly two in the morning by the time Chance pulled into his garage at the ranch. Conspiring a little with Jeremy, he had known Kate would be alone tonight, and he had planned to bring her home with him again. He wanted another night of leisurely love making.

Instead he had taken her home. After what had happened at the bar and later, up on Lookout Mountain, it was clear that getting more deeply involved with Kate was something he couldn't afford to do.

Damn, what the hell was the matter with him?

Sure he'd been jealous of women before. He wasn't a man who liked to share what belonged to him. In the beginning, he'd been jealous of Rachael, but he was younger then. Over the years, he'd outgrown his raging hormones, and they had settled into a fairly open relationship. She saw other men. He saw other women. By unspoken rule, neither of them ever got involved. It worked well for both of them.

Tonight was different. He hadn't been simply jealous, he'd been completely enraged. He didn't want Kate flirting with other men. He couldn't stand the thought of her being with Ned Cummings instead of him. By the time they had finished making wild, erotic love, he had realized just how much he cared for her, how badly he still wanted her — and how damned much trouble he was really in.

He was in way over his head and he wasn't exactly sure what to do about it.

Chance climbed the stairs to his room, trying to figure out where he'd gone wrong. With other women, he'd been honest from the start. He'd made it clear he wasn't interested in a permanent relationship. On a subconscious level, he must have known if he'd been completely honest with Kate, she would never have gotten involved with him.

Christ, if he just hadn't wanted her so damned badly.

He had to make things right with her, had to tell her the truth. Anything less wasn't fair to Kate.

And it wasn't fair to him.

Tomorrow he would talk to her, explain the way things were. The way they had to be. Maybe she would understand. Kate wasn't ready for a serious relationship either. Maybe she would even be relieved. God, he hoped so. He didn't want to stop seeing her. After last night, all he could think of was making love to her again.

Unfortunately, when the phone rang at eight o'clock the following morning, it was Rachael on the end of the line.

And she wasn't in New York City.

She had just arrived at her father's ranch.

Chapter Eighteen

Kate rose late on Sunday morning, a little stiff but smiling at memories of the night. She glanced at the clock on the bedside table, saw that David would soon be home from Chris Spotted Horse's house, showered and dressed in jeans and a dark green sweatshirt.

A little after ten, Jeremy's rattletrap pickup pulled up. One of the doors swung open and David hopped out. He smiled and waved goodbye to Chris. It was clear the two were becoming solid friends, and Kate said a silent thank you to Chance.

Thinking of him, she flicked a glance at the telephone, willing it to ring. She had been hoping he would call this morning. It was such a beautiful day, perfect for the three of them to go for a horseback ride. But he didn't call, so she and David took a picnic lunch and hiked up into the woods behind the house.

A can of pepper spray rode in Kate's green canvas backpack. Since they lived in grizzly country, Chance had been adamant about the spray, sending a can home with David the night he had taken him and Chris horseback riding.

"Personally, it's hard to imagine standing dead-still in the path of a charging grizzly," Chance had said seriously, "holding your breath and waiting for the damned thing to get close enough to hit in the face with a spray of pepper. But most woodsmen say it works and it's a whole lot better than nothing."

She wondered what he was doing today and whether he might be thinking of her. Last night, as they had stood on the porch outside the house, she had apologized for her behavior in the bar, assuring him that trying to make a man jealous wasn't part of her normal routine. By then his temper had cooled and in some odd way he seemed to find it amusing.

"It's all right," he'd said. "I don't normally behave like a bad-tempered bull, myself." A corner of his mouth curved up. "But I'm damned glad Ned Cummings didn't ask for another dance."

The new week began and the weather turned cool, but business at the cafe remained strong. The profits had grown steadily since the place had reopened, partly because of Aida Whittaker's longtime reputation for good food and service, which Kate had been careful to uphold; and partly because she was a very good money manager, able to keep food costs down and the overhead low.

She had a small, comfortable income from money she had invested during her years with Menger and Menger, but the extra earnings from the cafe certainly came in handy, and it was a point of pride that the business be a viable, profitable endeavor.

Still, from the start, she had scheduled her hours so she would have plenty of time for herself and her son. Lately, after the lunch shift while David was still working at the store, she usually worked for a while on the anti-mining campaign, then dug around on the Net or read books on forensics.

In the middle of the week, she returned upstairs to finish going through the boxes that Aida had stored in the attic. She had already gone through all of Nell's papers. It was time to start on the clothes, jewelry, and personal items. After she had taken a quick look at everything, David could carry the stuff down and they could donate it to the Salvation Army.

Sitting in the little maple rocker, Kate sighed as she dug through a pile of her grandmother's garments, mostly sweaters and heavy wool trousers. A little pink, heart-shaped sachet lay in the bottom of the box alongside a pair of worn knit slippers.

She had never felt anything but antipathy toward her grandmother. The enmity between Nell and her mother had left Kate with a bone-deep dislike of her. Still, as she went through the clothes, she couldn't help wondering what Nell had really been like, and how a woman could so completely abandon her only child.

A shutter banged outside the attic window and Kate glanced up. The wind had picked up and it whistled under the sill, making an eerie keening sound. It was September now, the temperature colder, the leaves turning yellow and red, beginning to fall off the trees. David would be starting school next week, a thought less painful to him now that he had been making friends. There would be others, he had begun to believe. Thanks to Chance, Jeremy, and Chief, the gap between the city boy from LA and the country boys in Montana wasn't as wide as it used to be.

David could fish and ride at least a little, and Chance had promised to get him enrolled in a hunter safety course.

"Are you insane?" Kate had argued at first. "I don't want my son shooting a gun. The last thing he needs is to be exposed to more violence."

"Hunting's a way of life up here, Kate. Every boy knows how to use a rifle. Even if David decides not to hunt, he needs to know how to take care of himself and his family. Every man ought to be capable of that."

Why it sounded so logical when Chance said it she couldn't begin to say, but if the day actually arrived and David wanted to learn, she knew that she would allow it.

Kate set another musty-smelling box next to the ones she'd already gone through and started on a third: long flannel nightgowns, long underwear, and thick woolen sox. The cotton bras were a size D cup, which made Kate smile. Nell was a small woman, yet it was obvious why Kate and her mother had both been born so well-endowed.

She dug through the box and found another, smaller box in the bottom. Kate lifted it out, took off the lid, and saw that it contained old letters. They were yellowed and faded, some of them water-spotted, the edges chewed by mice and bugs.

A funny, tingling sensation slipped through her, anticipation mixed with hesitation. The letters were private. They belonged to Nell. Yet Kate knew without the least amount of doubt that she wouldn't rest until she had read every one.

Two hours later, she was less than halfway through the stack. There were letters from old high school friends, correspondence from couples who were friends of the Harts, letters from business acquaintances. Reading them was like opening a window into Nell's life, seeing the sort of people she had been drawn to, discovering some of the reasons they had been drawn to her.

As always, she appeared to be a decent, kind sort of person. At least that was the way her friends saw her. Kate and her mother alone seemed to know the woman she truly was.

Kate finished the bundle and picked up another, turning it over in her hand. There were maybe a dozen letters in the bunch, the envelopes and handwriting all the same. The wide blue scroll looked masculine instead of feminine, and her pulse picked up a little. They were postmarked Walnut Creek, California, but as Nell drew out the first letter, she realized they were the work of someone living in Lost Peak. His name appeared on the outside of the envelope. Inside they were signed, *With loving regards, Silas.*

Kate's hand trembled as she unfolded the first letter and began to read. At first, Silas talked about the weather and told her about his son, a man named Milton who apparently had remarried and was "doing really well this time."

The second letter contained more of the same, just small talk between two old friends, yet it was obvious how much Silas loved his son, and though he was enjoying his stay in California he would be glad to get back to Lost Peak.

He missed his friends, he said, and apparently Nell — Nellie, Silas called her — was among them. There was a definite hint of affection in his tone, and Kate thought it was certainly possible that in their younger years, the pair might once have been lovers.

She had just finished the last of the letters — slightly disappointed not to have discovered some sort of secret information — and had plucked up the final bundle when she heard David calling from downstairs. *Tomorrow,* she silently promised, setting aside the aging envelopes, these in a faded shade of rose with tiny pink flowers in the corner.

As she hurried downstairs to her son, Kate told herself that reading the letters was merely an opportunity to look for clues.

But the truth was, she was looking for a chance to find the real Nell Hart, the grandmother that she had never known.

The end of the week arrived. Chance never called. He didn't stop by the cafe or come over to the house. Kate began to worry. The last time they'd made love had been incredible for her, but maybe for Chance it was nothing out of the ordinary. Maybe she had read him wrong. Aside from a couple of hot nights in the sack, maybe he didn't give a hoot about her.

If that was so, Kate wished she could be equally cavalier. Instead, at night she dreamed about him, dreamed of them making love, and woke up in a hot, damp sweat. One night she actually awakened in the pleasurable throes of a climax, her dream replaying the night they had made love on Lookout Mountain.

Good Lord, it was embarrassing what just thinking about him could do.

David went off to school the first of the week and Kate went to work, hoping Chance would call with some sort of explanation for his absence, but she was beginning to think that maybe their brief affair was over. She told herself it didn't matter. Men had short, heated encounters all the time; there was no reason she couldn't have one, too. So she'd never done it before. So what? But the truth was, she missed him, and not just the hot sex they had shared. She missed the sound of his voice, the warmth of his smile, the solid strength that had somehow made her feel stronger, too.

The sad truth was, Kate missed the man she had begun to fall in love with, and it wasn't going to be all that easy to get over him.

Still, she was determined to do just that. There had never been any actual commitment between them. Neither of them had talked about their feelings, and in a way that was good. She had held herself back a little, protected her heart as best she could. Knowing the risk was high, she hadn't given him that last little piece of herself and now she was glad.

Or at least she told herself she was as she worked through the morning, trying to smile at the customers, trying *not* to wonder where he was or what he was doing. She was fighting so hard not to think about him, she almost convinced herself the tall cowboy shoving through the door of the cafe wasn't Chance.

Then she realized it was, and the relief washing through her turned her legs to rubber bands.

Kate Rollins, you are in very serious trouble here.

The cafe was full. Chance waited for the first available seat and sat down in a booth at the window. Kate went over and filled his coffee mug, trying for an air of nonchalance, pretending she hadn't thought about him every day for more than a week.

"David started school today," she said matter-of-factly. "He was nervous, but I think this time he'll do okay."

Chance looked up, but she couldn't read his face. "I don't think he'll feel like such an outsider now," he said.

She pulled her pad and pencil out of the pocket of her uniform. "Ready to order?" she asked, her pasted-on smile still in place.

Chance hadn't even picked up the menu. "To tell you the truth I didn't come here to eat. I was hoping . . . after it slows down a little . . . we might have a chance to talk."

There was something in his voice, something regretful and gruff, that didn't bode well. Her stomach squeezed into a knot the size of a marble. "Sure. Probably another half an hour and I can get away."

Chance just nodded. He wasn't smiling. In fact he looked unbelievably grim. "I'll just have coffee, then."

Her mouth went dry. She began to steel herself against whatever he might be going to say. The bell above the door chimed again, admitting another customer, and she quickly made her escape. Two men walked in, Jake Dillon, the fifty-year-old widower who owned the mercantile, and a bald-headed man named Harvey Michaelson, a local who lived a few miles up Silver Fox Creek. Both of them had been doing volunteer work for the anti-mining coalition.

They sat down at a table and turned over their coffee cups.

"How's it going, guys?" Kate poured the steaming brew up to the rim.

Jake wrapped his big, weathered hands around the cup. "Pretty good, I guess, considering. We got that postcard-writing campaign off to a darned good start."

"Yeah," Harvey grumbled, "a little too good."

The coffeepot she held hung suspended above the table. "What do you mean?"

"He means we both got anonymous letters last week, warning us in no uncertain terms to butt out of mining affairs."

"You're kidding."

"I wish we were," Jake said darkly. "That's the reason we stopped by today. We figured you'd want to know."

Kate shoved down a thread of worry. "Well, we knew this kind of thing might happen. Have you talked to Ed Fontaine?"

"We took the letters over to his place yesterday."

"What about Chance?"

"Not yet."

"Well, he's sitting in that booth across the way. I'm sure he'd want to know."

The men turned their heads in that direction and shoved back their chairs. While they made their way over to where he sat, Kate served an order of hamburgers and fries to one of the customers, a big piece of pie to another, and collected money from some who were departing. She had just walked over to Chance, Jake, and Harvey when the window exploded in a shower of broken glass and a heavy object sailed into the room.

Customers screamed. Jake Dillon jumped out of the way just in time to keep from getting hit.

"Son of a bitch!" Chance was on his feet and running for the door before the big rock stopped rolling beneath one of the tables. He raced outside in time to see a big black pickup roaring off down the street. He followed it a ways, trying to get a look at the license plate, but the truck was already swerving around the corner, disappearing out of sight.

The door slammed behind him as he walked back inside and over to where Kate knelt in search of the rock.

"I didn't get the plate number, unfortunately, but it was a late-model, extended-cab Ford."

Lifting away a few jagged shards of glass, Kate picked up the rock, saw it was wrapped in a piece of brown paper like something torn from a grocery bag, pulled the rubber band away, unfolded and read the note.

GO HOME BITCH. WE DON'T WANT YOU HERE IN LOST PEAK.

Her hands shook. Twice she reread the words, an icy chill running up and down her spine. She had worked so hard to be accepted in Lost Peak. She wanted to make a home here for herself and David. She didn't want trouble with her neighbors.

Chance reached out and gripped her shoulders. "It's all right, Kate. They're just trying to scare you into quitting the campaign."

She thought of the newspaper articles in LA, the problems that had forced her to leave, and started shaking harder, the note still frozen in her hand.

"Dammit!" Chance pulled her into his arms. "It's all right, darlin'. They probably don't even live around here. They're probably just some guys who work for Barton."

She clung to him a moment, absorbing his solid strength, the warmth of his body driving away some of the fear. "Do you really think so?"

He eased her gently from his arms and took the note from her hand. "You heard what Jake and Harvey said. They both got letters like this last week."

She looked over at the men, feeling foolish for letting Barton and his goons get the best of her. "You're right. We knew this could happen. It just came as such a surprise, and . . ."

"And . . . ?"

"And I really like it here. I don't want to have to leave."

Jake Dillon's mouth flattened into a thin, white line. "No one's forcing anyone to leave. You've made a place for yourself here in Lost Peak, and Barton and his troublemakers haven't got a thing to say about it."

Kate gave him a grateful smile. "Thanks, Jake." She turned to the handful of customers who remained in the cafe, most of them now on their feet. "Sorry for the trouble, everyone. As most of you know, we've been trying to stop Consolidated Metals from opening a mine on Silver Fox Creek." She tilted her head toward the broken window. "Apparently, we're doing a pretty good job of it."

Faint laughter arose, breaking the tension. The customers sat back down in their seats and began to finish their meals.

Kate looked back at the window, now sporting a big jagged hole where the restaurant name used to be. "I can't believe they'd be willing to go this far."

"Believe it," Chance said. "Barton wants that mine to go in. He wants the cyanide ban over-turned and he doesn't like the fact that our efforts just might stop him."

Kate didn't say anything more, just turned and went into the kitchen. Pulling a broom and dustpan out of the closet, she went back into the dining room.

"We ought to call the sheriff before you clean that up," Chance said.

He was right, of course, but the idea of facing Mr. Politically Correct Sheriff Barney Conrad made her slightly sick to her stomach. "I suppose we should, but I've got a business to run. I'll call him later."

"Kate . . ."

"Please, Chance." He didn't say anything more and as soon as the last of the customers had left, she dragged out the vacuum and plugged it in.

"Why don't you let me do that?" Chance offered gently, reaching for the handle.

"No, thanks." It was obvious she was still upset and she wasn't surprised to look up and find him pulling his wide-brimmed hat down over his forehead and reaching for the door.

"You've got enough on your mind right now. We can talk another time."

"All right."

"And don't forget to call the sheriff."

Kate watched him leave with mixed emotions. Her woman's intuition was kicking in — big-time — telling her whatever Chance had to say wasn't going to be good. Another time, she could handle it.

Not today.

Not with the place in a shambles and threats being made against her.

Kate reached down and picked up the note scratched crudely on the piece of brown paper. "Go to hell, Lon Barton," she said out loud. "You're not going to scare me away."

Chance skimmed his fingers over the long, mahogany dining table, polished to such a glossy sheen he could see his own reflection. A crystal chandelier hung above it, each tiny prism alive with colored light. Fontaine House resembled a French chateau, slightly out of place on a Montana ranch, but Ed's wife, Gloria, had insisted on it. Whatever Glory Fontaine wanted, Ed made certain she got.

She'd been ten years younger than Ed, a beautiful blond grad student he met on a cattle-buying trip to Denver. Ed had fallen madly in love with her on sight and after an extravagant courtship, she had agreed to marry him. Glory moved to the ranch, gave him a daughter that same year, and became the center of Ed's world.

The sun shone each day for Glory, as far as Ed was concerned. When she died of breast cancer sixteen years later, Ed wanted to die along with her. But he had Rachael to think of. She was only fifteen, more beautiful even than her mother. Ed lavished her with attention, and it was Rachael who became the sun, the moon, and the center of his world.

"So what do you children think?" Ed's voice pulled him back from musings. Or perhaps he had simply been trying to escape.

"I think it's a lovely idea." Rachael turned the full force of her smile on him. Perfect pink lips. Perfectly even white teeth. She was tall and elegantly thin, her skin as pale and smooth as alabaster. Short blond hair, done in soft waves around her face, shone like twenty-four-karat gold in the candlelight. "What do you think, Chance?"

What did he think? He hadn't had time to

think. Rachael had flown in unexpectedly a week ago and his life had been in turmoil ever since. Now Ed wanted him to announce their engagement at the party Ed was throwing in Rachael's honor the end of the week.

What did he think? Until the last few minutes, he'd expected to remain single for years. Now in a matter of days, he would be making a lifetime commitment.

"That doesn't leave us much time. I won't have a chance to buy you a ring." Lame excuse. Damn, what was the matter with him? He should be glad Ed was trying to set things in motion. He wanted a family, didn't he? Rachael was twenty-seven, her biological clock ticking away. It was time they both settled down and got on with the future they had planned.

"The ring won't be a problem," Ed said. "There's some nice stores in Missoula. Get one of them to lend you something until whatever Rachael picks out comes in."

She'd want something big and flashy, he knew. Not that they'd ever talked about it. But everything about Rachael spoke of money and class. Nothing but a very expensive diamond would do. Then again, what did he care? He could afford it. He rarely spent money on anything but the ranch.

"I think we should do it." Rachael flashed those big baby blues and smiled so wide a dimple formed in her cheek.

"What about setting the date?" Ed pressed. It

was obvious he really wanted this. Chance's eyes drifted down to the heavy chrome wheelchair Ed sat in, and his insides slowly drew into a knot. For more than twenty years, he had tried to make amends for the accident that had put Ed in that chair. For more than twenty years, his guilt had festered, gnawing at his insides like a gangrenous wound, but there was no medicine he could take to make it heal.

He took a fortifying breath. There was only one thing he could do, and this was it. "I think it's a great idea. I only wish I'd been the one to suggest it."

Shoving back his chair he came to his feet and rounded the table to where Rachael sat. When she turned her face up and smiled, he bent his head and lightly kissed her mouth. "If this is what you want, too, then tomorrow we'll go look for that ring."

"Oh, Chance!" Rachael jumped to her feet and flung her arms around his neck. He couldn't help noticing how fragile she felt, all sharp edges and frail little bones, like holding a captured bird. "I don't know why we waited so long. We should have done this sooner."

He forced himself to smile. "If I remember correctly, I tried to get you to marry me years ago. You were the one who wanted a career as a model."

"True, but now I'm ready to give all of that up."

"Are you?" Chance asked, suddenly serious.

"Well, I'll still want to take a few modeling jobs, now and again. I'd get pretty bored if I just sat around the ranch all the time with nothing to do."

"But you do want to have a family?"

"Of course she does," Ed answered for her.

"Of course I do," Rachael agreed. "I've seen the world. I've modeled for every fashion magazine in the country. I've proven whatever I needed to prove." She flashed him another gorgeous smile. "But I've never been a wife. I've never been a mother. I'm finally ready for that now."

Chance gently slid her arms from where they rested on his shoulders. "When do you want to get married?"

"The sooner the better," Ed said.

"Don't be a pill, Daddy. Chance might need a little time to get used to the idea."

"He's had time. Too damned much time, if you ask me. What do you say, boy?"

"What about the wedding, Rachael? Do you want a big one?"

She smiled, rolled her big blue eyes. "Well . . ."

"Of course she does," Ed said. "And my little girl's gonna have it — the biggest damned wedding in the history of Silver County."

"It'll take a while to plan," Rachael continued, bubbling with enthusiasm. "How about six months from now? I'll need that much time to get organized."

Six months. In just six months he would be a

married man. When had the thought turned so grim?

"I'm going back to the city week after next," she was saying. "I've got a couple of modeling jobs to finish. I'll have to pack everything and sublet my apartment. Then I'll come back and help with the wedding."

Chance just nodded. He couldn't help wondering what had motivated her sudden change of heart. For the past few years, Rachael's career had been all-important. Odds were, like a number of her other adventures, she had simply gotten bored. He said a silent prayer she wouldn't get tired of being a wife and mother.

"All right, then, it's settled," he said. "Tomorrow we find a ring. Saturday night we make the announcement." He kissed her very briefly on the lips. "Six months from now you'll be Mrs. Rachael McLain."

The name sounded funny on his lips. He supposed he would get used to it.

"I think a toast is in order." Ed called into the kitchen for a bottle of champagne, and one of the servants returned with a bottle of Dom Perignon in an ornate silver bucket. Ed popped the cork and poured it into chilled Waterford crystal flutes.

"To my daughter, the most beautiful woman in the world — except for her mother. And my future son-in-law, a man who is and always will be, the son I never had."

Chance felt a lump rise in his throat. Ed had

been like a father to him, and he had always known the feeling was returned, but until tonight he had never heard Ed say it.

"To the future," Chance said gruffly, and all of them took a drink of their champagne.

The evening wore on for a little while longer, plans being made and discarded, talk of the party Ed was throwing at the house on Saturday night, now officially an engagement party.

By the time he was able to leave, Chance's stomach felt tied in knots and a heavy cloud of gloom seemed to have settled over his head. In the past few days, his life had taken one bizarre turn after another and now seemed out of his control. He was marrying Rachael but he couldn't stop thinking of Kate.

He never should have started seeing her, should have stayed away from the damned cafe, as Jeremy had warned him more than once. Instead, he'd pursued her relentlessly, until he managed to get her into his bed. The only trouble was, he wanted her to stay there.

It was impossible, he knew. He was committed now. It was over between them. He simply had to find a way to tell her.

An image of Kate arose in his mind, her glorious red hair spread out across his pillow. He remembered her laughter, as sweet and rich as cream, remembered the feel of her arms around his neck as they moved in rhythm around the dance floor, her soft breasts pillowed against his chest. He had never taken Rachael to the Antlers. Rachael hated country music. She thought it was too low class.

Still, she was a beautiful, desirable woman, and any man would be lucky to marry her.

"Chance?" He turned at the sound of her voice. "You look like you're a thousand miles away."

Not that far, less than twenty miles, he figured. "Sorry."

"Randy's taking Daddy up to bed. Maybe we could go for a walk . . . or something?"

He knew what she was offering. They hadn't been alone for more than a couple of hours since her arrival at the ranch. They hadn't found time to make love, and though Rachael wasn't the passionate woman Kate was, she expected him to want her. Sex was her way of feeling desirable — and there wasn't much doubt she was that.

Still, tonight, with so much on his mind, making love to her was the last thing he wanted. "We aren't kids anymore, Rachael. I'm not about to take you out in the barn on some damned pile of hay. And I don't think your father would appreciate finding me in your bed — engagement or no."

She sighed, smoothed a hand over her short golden hair. "I guess you're right. Why don't I tell Daddy I'm staying with Sarah Davis after the party on Saturday night? He'll know it's a lie, but it lets us all save face."

He just nodded.

Rachael kissed him full on the mouth and Chance kissed her back. Her lips felt smooth and cool and he thought of another pair, fuller, hotter, softer.

"Good night, Rach."

"Good night, Chance."

I'm lucky to have her, he thought. And he told himself that over and over, all the way back to the ranch.

Chapter Nineteen

On Thursday morning, Kate got a call from KGET-TV, the local television station in Missoula. It was from a woman named Diana Stevens, one of the anchors from the news department, who wanted to do an interview about the efforts of the anti-mining coalition.

"Is it possible you'd be available sometime this afternoon?"

"Absolutely," Kate said. The media was key to any successful campaign. The more people knew what was happening, the better chance they would have of stopping Consolidated's efforts.

"We should be there around three," the anchorwoman said. As soon as she hung up, Kate phoned Ed Fontaine. The interview would go better with at least two people to talk to, and Ed was well-known in both Silver and Missoula counties. Unfortunately, he wasn't in. His housekeeper said that his daughter was there for a visit and they had gone off somewhere together.

Kate hadn't known Ed had a daughter, but she thought it was nice for Ed that she was there. Chance was next on her list. He and Ed knew the most about Consolidated Metals, the history of their abuses, and what the consequences would be if they succeeded in overturning the cyanide ban. She picked up the phone to dial his number, but something held her back. She hadn't heard from him since he had come into the cafe. He might think this was just an excuse to talk to him and she didn't want that.

Jeremy was working at the mill, she knew. That left Jake Dillon, who was handy, over at the mercantile right across the street. She had always liked Jake, more so after he had come to her defense that day in the cafe. And once he'd gotten onboard the campaign, he'd been tireless in his efforts.

As soon as the lunch crowd was gone, Kate went into the house, gathered color brochures, T-shirts, and some of the photographs Jeremy had taken of the spill, blown up into disgusting eight-by-ten glossies. One showed a hundred dead fish, floating on Beaver Creek, another showed brown, dying foliage along a scenic stretch of Big Pine River. Others showed the efforts of the Salish-Kootenai to remove the huge sludge pile dumped on their reservation that had infiltrated the water above Chance's property and killed six of his steers.

Carrying the information into the back room of the cafe, she set them down on a table they had placed in front of the storyboard they had made. A quick trip across the street to enlist the aid of Jake Dillon and she was ready.

Diana Stevens appeared exactly on time at

three o'clock that afternoon, a thirtyish young woman, well groomed in a short navy-blue skirt, matching jacket, and a pair of four-inch-heeled navy pumps. She looked so out of place in Lost Peak, Kate almost smiled.

She led the woman and her cameraman, a tall, lanky, man with long hair and a beard, into the back room where Jake was waiting. Introductions were made and the crew went to work.

"Today we're interviewing Kaitlin Rollins, the woman who has been working so tirelessly behind the scenes of the Silver Fox Creek Anti-mining Coalition, and one of her volunteers, Jacob Dillon, a longtime resident of Lost Peak."

She went on to list Kate's credentials, which were lengthy. It was obvious Diane Stevens had done her homework.

"Some of our viewers have been asking why you and your people are working so hard on this effort when there is already a law in place that bans any new cyanide mining in the area."

"The fact is, Diane, the mining industry, backed in most part by Consolidated Metals, is currently in the process of filing a challenge to the ban that was passed last year. They've made no secret of it. As you may have read, Consolidated claims the ban was illegal. They cite the 1872 mining law that gives anyone who wishes to mine, an absolute right to do so on federal public lands. Since the proposed Silver Fox mine falls within those parameters, they believe they can defeat the ban and go forward with the mine as planned. Which means, all of the work that was done by groups like the Montana Wilderness Association, the Sierra Club, the Clark Fork Coalition, and others, is in jeopardy of having been done in vain."

"Consolidated already owns the land and water rights they need," Jake Dillon put in. "If they succeed in their efforts, we'll have a brand new heap-leach mine on Silver Fox Creek."

"And more desecration like what you see in these pictures." Kate turned toward the table and the camera focused on the photos laid out on top, panning from one horrendous sight to the next.

"We don't want the sort of environmental problems that have plagued Beaver Creek and dozens of other mountain streams," Jake said. "We want to maintain the wild beauty of Silver Fox Creek."

The interview ended with Kate's summation of the efforts currently being made by the anti-mining coalition as well as plans being formulated for the future. Apparently pleased by the way things had gone, Diane Stevens left with a promise to return in a couple of weeks for an interview that included Ed Fontaine and Chance McLain.

"All in all," Jake said, smiling after the woman had departed, "it was a damned successful afternoon."

Kate smiled, too. "Thanks for helping, Jake."

"No problem. A little TV coverage now and then is good for business."

Kate's smile slipped a little at the thought. She had come to Lost Peak to escape her notoriety. God forbid, it should surface all over again.

"What do you think, Rachael?" Chance stood next to her at the counter of Bookman's Jewelers on Higgins Street in Missoula.

Rachael held up a slender hand and turned it one way and then another, making the diamond flash beneath the bright white lights above the counter. "I don't know for sure. It's hard to imagine what it's going to look like with a bigger diamond in the center."

The jeweler leaned over, turned her hand to examine the ring. "Not just bigger in the center. Each stone will be larger, Ms. Fontaine. The ring is going to be spectacular — I can definitely promise you that." It was their second trip to Missoula, the first effort having resulted in a very long day at several local stores, then thumbing through catalogs and still coming up empty-handed.

At last Rachael smiled. "I think he's right. With a four-carat diamond in the center and two-carat baguettes on each side, it should be magnificent."

For eighty thousand dollars, it ought to be, Chance thought. He wondered if Kate would have wanted a big, expensive ring, and knew with a flash of certainty she wouldn't have been caught dead in a ring the size of the one Rachael had chosen. He almost smiled, might have, if the thought hadn't made him feel so bad.

"You're happy with this one, then?" He picked up the ring she had laid back down on the counter.

"Of course I am — what girl wouldn't be? It's gorgeous — or at least the one Mr. Bookman's going to order will be." She flashed him a radiant smile, slipped her arms around his neck. "Thank you, Chance. Daddy always said you'd take good care of me."

Mr. Bookman gave them a winning smile. "In the meantime, you can wear this one until yours gets here. We have insurance, so you don't have to worry about that."

"Thank you," Chance said. Taking the ring, he slid it on Rachael's third left finger. "I guess it's official, then."

Her mouth curved into a sexy smile. "Yes, I guess it is." She leaned over and kissed him, running her tongue inside his mouth. A year ago, it would have made him want her, now all he could think of was getting her back to her father's ranch. God, he hoped his mood would be better by the time he took her to bed on Saturday night.

Rachael beamed up at him. "We're going to be so happy, darling. Everything's going to be perfect."

But nothing was ever perfect. Except maybe Rachael's perfect lips. Life was hard. Times got tough. He hoped she'd turn out to be the sort of wife who would stand by him in the bad times as well as the good.

But he didn't dwell on the notion. Whatever sort of wife Rachael turned out to be, his decision was made, his course set, fixed by the winds of fate when he was twelve years old.

For better, for worse. For richer, for poorer. For as long as we both shall live.

That's what marriage meant.

And that was the way it was going to be for him.

Friday came. The rodeo in Polson was this weekend, but Chance hadn't mentioned it again. Kate hadn't seen him all week and he hadn't bothered to call, so apparently they weren't going. Early in the afternoon, worried and missing him, she returned to the last bundle of letters in the box upstairs.

It was crisp and clear outside, the sun beating down through the trees, a perfect fall day in the mountains, yet she felt moody and out of sorts. With David not yet home from school, the house was oddly silent, just the creak of the stairs as she climbed up to the dusty attic, and the rhythmic moan of the little maple rocker she sat in, unconsciously moving to and fro.

The door of the attic remained open. She kept an ear cocked toward the phone, just in case Chance called. Reaching into the box, she lifted out the last bundle of letters. They were yellowed and brittle with age, the pale rose stationery faded to a pink-tinged ivory hue. But the faint scent of roses drifted up to mingle with the musty odors in the attic.

She settled the letters in her lap and pulled the narrow pink satin ribbon that held them together. They spread out haphazardly across her knees, and for an instant, she simply sat there staring at them.

It was obvious the correspondence spanned a number of years and, once again, all of it was written in the same hand. The handwriting in the oldest, most faded letters was finely etched; beautiful, graceful strokes of the pen when the author was younger. The script became more erratic, less legible as the years slipped past.

Kate lifted the first letters in the stack and her hand began to tremble. Though the envelope carried a stamp, it had never been mailed. And it wasn't addressed to Nell.

Every letter in the stack was addressed to Kate's mother.

Hesitant now in a way she wasn't before, Kate withdrew the first letter in the stack, the oldest it appeared, and for a moment she just held it, afraid of what she would find when she opened it. Eventually, she worked up her courage, used the edge of the silver-handled letter opener that lay in the box, and very carefully sliced open the seal.

The page was so stiff it cracked at the seams when she unfolded it. For an instant, her heart seemed to stop. She wasn't sure exactly how she knew, but she didn't have to look at the signature to know the letters were written by Nell.

Something painful squeezed inside her. Though the envelopes had never been mailed, Nell had written to her daughter, over and over again, in a vain attempt to reach her.

Kate stared down at the tiny flowered border across the top of the page and started to read.

My dearest Mary Beth,

I know this letter cannot possibly reach you, since I have no idea where you are. You've slipped away from me like sand beneath the tide; like smoke rising up through the chimney. You're gone and perhaps nothing will ever bring you back to me. But I do so long for your presence, and I find, as I write these words, that it brings me a little comfort, a feeling that in some way you are still here.

My dearest child, how I wish that we could start over, that I had never said the terrible words that drove you away, that I could wrap you in my arms and keep you and the child you carry safe. But now it is too late.

You will never know how much I regret the things I said, lashing out at you as I did, though in truth it was more in anger at Jack Lambert for what he did to my precious child than at you for falling prey to his wicked charm. But of course you couldn't know that. Where are you, my Mary, my dear little girl? Are you well? Are you safe? Does the child still grow inside you? I agonize in fear for you, as any mother would. I beg you, please, wherever you are, come home.

It was signed simply, *Love always, Mother.*

Kate stared down at the paper, the words blurry through the tears that had collected in her eyes. She swallowed past the thick lump in her throat, thinking of the pain in Nell's words, the fierce emotion scrawled on the page.

She opened letter after letter.

My dear Mary Beth,

Still no word of you after all these years. How I grieve at the loss. I agonize with worry over what has become of you. Are you well and safe? Are you happy wherever you are? And what of your child? I often try to imagine was it a daughter or a son? A little boy with hints of his tall, handsome grandfather, or a little girl as pretty as you always were. How I wish I could see her, hold her just once. How I miss you, Mary. If only you could find it in your heart to forgive me.

Kate's hand shook as she replaced the letter. Dear God, how wrong she had been, how dreadfully, painfully wrong. She thought of her mother and she couldn't help feeling a shot of anger. Why had her mother never tried to mend the rift? Why had she never returned to her home?

But deep down, Kate knew. Celeste Heart, the woman Mary Beth had become, was far too proud for that, too stubborn to ever admit she had made a mistake. Because of her stiff, unbending pride, both of them had suffered a loss that could never be regained.

It tortured her to think of the family she had never known, the grandmother whose love she might have had when she was such a desperately lonely child. Kate gently slid the letter back into its weathered, faded envelope, and opened the next.

By the time she had finished, two hours later, she knew that she'd been wrong about Nell Hart and so had her mother.

She had also discovered it was only in the last few years, after Celeste was already dead, that Nell had been able to track down her granddaughter's whereabouts, and then only by a stroke of fortune. Nell had been watching an old movie on TV and recognized her daughter in the minor role she was playing. When the movie was over, Nell had written down the name she had found on the credits.

Mary Beth Hart Lambert was now Celeste Heart.

According to the letters, Nell had hired a detective to track her down. The man discovered her death in a car wreck eight years earlier, but went on to find the daughter she had borne,

Kaitlin Lambert Rollins. Unfortunately Nell had been afraid to call or propose any sort of meeting. Too many years had passed. Too much water under the bridge.

She had simply left everything to Kate, which in the end had brought her to Lost Peak.

"At least I know the truth, Grandmother," Kate said into the silence of the attic, but she felt anguished and heartsick, angry and disturbed. "Maybe the letters were the secret you were trying to tell me. Maybe they were what you wanted me to find."

If that was the case, then the mystery was solved. There was nothing left to discover, no murder involved. By the time she left the attic, Kate was more than halfway convinced it was true.

For now, she didn't want to think about anything but the letters. Passages kept popping into her mind: *Where are you, Mary? Please forgive me. Please come home.*

At last she knew the truth about the woman who was Nell Hart, but with the truth came anger over all those wasted years.

The more she thought about it, the more upset and disturbed she became. Nell had made a mistake, spoken harsh words she regretted for the rest of her life. We all made mistakes. Why couldn't her mother have tried to understand? But Celeste never even tried to reach her. Kate felt a terrible grief for Nell.

And a piece of her heart blossomed with love for her.

The cafe was about to close. He had timed it that way on purpose. Chance pulled the pickup to a stop out in front and turned off the ignition, then sat there for a moment, trying to work up his courage.

He had to see Kate, had to tell her the truth. He couldn't put it off any longer. With a sigh of resignation, he left the truck, jerked open the cafe door and walked in, pausing next to where Kate stood totaling out the register. Her hair was pulled back in the tidy little bun she wore when she was working, but he knew how silky it felt when the pins were gone, how it fell in a riot of curls around her shoulders.

Her breasts swayed a little as she worked, two perfect globes, tipped by big, dark rose circles, he remembered. Her waist looked tiny above her gently flaring hips, and even in her simple pink uniform, he thought she was the sexiest woman he'd ever seen.

She looked up and saw him and warm color rose in her cheeks. "Chance . . ."

"We need to talk, Kate. I thought we might take a drive."

She glanced over at the clock on the wall. "David will be waiting for me at home."

"It's important."

She bit down on her lip, then nodded. "I'll ask Myra to stay with him until we get back. I don't think she'll mind."

Apparently she didn't. Kate returned a few minutes later, grabbed her navy wool jacket off the coat tree beside the door, and Chance led her out to his truck. He hesitated a moment before encircling her waist with his hands to help her climb in, a little afraid to touch her.

In two short weeks, he had almost forgotten how soft and feminine she was, how attracted he was to her, how responsive she had been when he kissed her.

Almost, but not quite.

Even the hours he'd spent with Rachael couldn't erase Kate from his mind completely.

"Where are we going?" she asked, her eyes on the road ahead.

"A place I know down the way a piece." They should have stayed right there in the cafe. He should have made it short and sweet and gotten the hell out of there. But one look at the uncertainty on her face, and he knew he couldn't do it that way. She wasn't just a quick, meaningless screw, and he didn't want her to think she was. He wanted her to understand why he was ending their relationship. More than anything, when this was all over, he still wanted them to be friends.

He pulled off the road down a short gravel lane. He'd thought about going back up to Lookout Mountain, but the memories were still too hot and fresh. He didn't dare take the chance.

He pulled the car to a stop on the side of the road, dragged a blanket from behind the seat for them to sit on, went around and helped Kate out of the truck. She seemed edgy, distracted in some way. He wondered if he was the cause or if something else was bothering her.

"I saw you on TV last night," he said, just to make conversation, "with that anchor woman, Diana Stevens, on the six o'clock news."

She nodded, looked a little uncertain. "I hope I did all right."

"You were terrific."

"They're coming back in a couple of weeks. They want to interview you and Ed."

"Yeah, well, I'm sure we'll have a few more things to say." He spread the blanket beneath a pine tree and they both sat down.

It was quiet here, incredibly peaceful. A full moon rose above the trees so they could see across the little meadow stretching out in front of them. Water bubbled over the rocks in a nearby stream.

"Anything new on Nell?" He didn't know why he was asking. It wasn't what he'd come for. He just wasn't ready to say the words that would end it between them.

Kate sighed. "Actually, there is. I think I've figured out what she was trying to tell me."

He turned to look at her, saw something dark and painful in her eyes. "What was it?"

"I found her letters, Chance. They were upstairs in the attic. Letters she had written to my mother. I always thought that Nell had abandoned her. I hated her for it. I never told you that, but it's true. I hated her for not being there when we needed her, and for treating my mother so badly. But that isn't the way it was."

She told him about her mother, how she had run away to Hollywood and changed her name. How, in her own way, Celeste had loved her, but she was so caught up in her career, so dazzled by the thought of being a star, she was rarely around and not much of a mother. She had never been more than a small bit player, but that hadn't mattered to Celeste.

Kate told him how Nell had tried to find them, how she had written letters year after year. Painful, grief-filled letters, begging her daughter to come home.

"It wasn't her fault, Chance. She made a mistake, but she was sorry. She wanted to make things right. She grieved for my mother till the day she died. All this time, I blamed her, but it wasn't her fault. It's just . . . so unfair."

She was crying by the time she finished. He eased her into his arms and she curled against his chest.

"It's all right, darlin'. At least now you know. If that was what she wanted to tell you, maybe now she can find some peace."

She looked up at him, her cheeks streaked with tears, her eyes luminous in the silvery moonlight. He wiped away the wetness with the end of his finger, felt the cool dampness of her cheek against his hand. He didn't mean to kiss her. It wasn't the reason he was here. He knew it was wrong, but he couldn't seem to help himself. He barely brushed his lips over hers and it was as if a fire had started.

"Katie . . ." he whispered, kissing her softly again. He felt her fingers sliding into his hair, trembling a little, making him tremble, too.

"Make love to me, Chance."

He shook his head. He couldn't make love to her. Not tonight. Not ever again. "We need to talk. There's something I have to —"

Her soft lips cut him off. They shaped perfectly to his, melted into them, pressed deeper. Her tongue touched the corner of his mouth, slid over his bottom lip, and he was lost.

He couldn't stop kissing her, couldn't stop touching her. Her breasts rubbed against him, round, soft, tantalizing. Her coat was open. He unbuttoned the front of her pink nylon uniform and reached inside, pulled her lacy white bra down, and her breasts spilled forward. They were pale and full, with the sexiest nipples he'd ever seen. He sucked each one, kissed them, caressed them.

He told himself to stop, promised himself he would, but Kate was leaning over him, urging him down on the blanket, tearing open the snaps on the front of his shirt. Her coat was gone. She slid her small hands over his bare chest, ran her tongue around a nipple, reached down and unzipped his jeans.

His shaft sprang free. She touched him there, stroked him, wrapped her fingers around him. He was hard, so incredibly hard.

"God, Katie . . ."

"Please, Chance, I need you. I don't want to think anymore, not tonight. I just want to feel."

"Katie . . ." Her small hands moved over him, exploring him, making his shaft ache and throb. He wanted to be inside her, wanted to drive into her until the aching stopped. He knew he couldn't. He was going to marry Rachael. Kate deserved better treatment. Hell, she would have been better off if she had never met him.

She leaned over and kissed him, pressed those magnificent breasts into his chest. His hand slid behind her neck, and he deepened the kiss, plundered her mouth, took her again and again with his tongue. Her glorious auburn hair came loose from its tidy bun. He pulled out the last of the pins and it swung down around her shoulders.

His body shuddered, tightened. He felt like he was on fire.

Just this one last time, he told himself. Just this one last time he would have her, and carry the memory with him for all of the years he would spend without her.

He framed her face between his hands and kissed her eyes, her nose, her beautiful, sensuous mouth.

"I'm crazy about you, Katie." It was the wrong thing to say, the very worst thing he could say, and he meant every word.

"Chance . . ." she whispered, bending down to kiss him again. Then she raised her slim pink nylon skirt, peeled off her panties and stockings, and straddled him there on the blanket, sinking down on him and making him groan.

God, she was incredible. So much woman, the sort he had dreamed of, once upon a time. She started to move, riding him like a stallion, all of that beautiful hair curling wildly around her face. He could feel her gripping him, teasing him, warm and wet all around him. Her head fell back. Her breasts swayed tantalizingly in front of his face. He cupped one in each of his hands.

He was close to climax, hot and so hard he hurt, but he held himself back, letting her take her pleasure, watching the expression on her face as she reached her release, then gripping her hips and driving into her, making her come again.

His own release came hard and fast, jackknifing into him, slicing through him in gut-wrenching waves. It was unlike anything he had ever experienced or probably ever would.

He pulled Kate down on top of him and waited for their heartbeats to slow. She was so small she fit neatly against his side, making him want to curl himself around her. Making him want her again.

He still hadn't talked to her. How could he do that now? Damn, he hated himself, yet he wouldn't change what had happened. Not for anything in the world.

He would wait until he got her home and they were sitting on her sofa. It would be tougher now. Kate had given him something special tonight, some part of herself she had held back from him before. He felt like a thief, but he still wasn't sorry, not when it was such a beautiful gift.

They drove home in silence and his nervousness returned. What could he possibly say that wouldn't hurt her? How could he make her understand?

Unfortunately, by the time they reached the house, Kate had fallen asleep on his shoulder. She looked like a small, soft kitten nestled there, and he steeled himself against the notion of making love to her again.

Christ, I can't tell her now.

Tomorrow he would be busy at Ed's getting ready for the party. *Sunday.* On Sunday he would come over early and explain, tell her everything, make her see that he had no choice. There was no way she could find out before then. And the timing would surely be better.

Wrapping her navy wool jacket more snugly around her, he carried her past Myra, who held open the door, into the house and up the stairs. Resisting an urge to undress her, he left her sleeping on top of the covers and returned downstairs.

"You two have a good time?" Myra eyed the

row of snaps he had forgotten to fasten on his shirt and the bare chest that peeked through the opening.

Chance felt the heat rising at the back of his neck. "Yeah. Thanks for watching David."

"No problem. He went to bed about an hour ago."

Chance said nothing more, just walked out and climbed into his truck. For a moment he just sat there, wondering how the evening had gone so far afield from what he had planned. How was it that every time he was with Kate, things got so out of hand?

He dragged in a long, shuddering breath and fired up the truck. On Sunday, he'd make things right with her. He'd tell her the truth about everything, find a way to make her see why it had to be this way.

Until then, he would try not to think about how right it had felt to make love to her.

He would try. But Chance was fairly certain that he was going to fail.

Chapter Twenty

The cafe was busy that Saturday morning. After lunch it thinned to a crawl, giving Kate time to think. Too much time. Every time she thought of her behavior the night before, her face turned a flaming shade of pink.

How could I? she silently groaned. She had practically attacked Chance last night. She remembered tearing open his shirt, remembered the burning kisses, and riding him to climax. Dear God, she had never behaved so outrageously in her life!

Kate sighed as she cleared the last of the dishes off the tables. God, what had driven her to such insane behavior?

She knew the letters were the root of it. Her emotions had been in turmoil ever since she'd read them. They still were. For a few sweet moments last night, she had wanted to forget the past, forget her mother, forget Nell Hart.

She knew Chance could make her forget.

I'm crazy about you, Katie. The words were more precious than gold. She had lost herself in those words, been undone by them. She was in love with him. There was no question in her mind, not the slightest doubt. And she had shown him that love last night.

She was standing there, holding a greasy

platter of half-finished eggs and wondering if he might be thinking about her, when the bell chimed over the door and Jake Dillon walked in.

"Mornin' Kate." Maybe five-foot-ten, with iron-gray hair and a slight paunch that hung over his Western buckle, Jake showed up at the cafe for lunch at least three days a week.

"Hi, Jake. I'll be with you in a minute."

He was still standing when she returned from the kitchen to take his order. Today, he obviously wasn't there to eat.

"What's up? Not more trouble with Consolidated Metals, I hope."

"No, no. It's nothing like that. I was just wondering if I might ask you a favor."

"Sure. What is it?"

"There's a big doin's over at Ed Fontaine's tonight — are you going?"

"To tell you the truth, I didn't know anything about it. I didn't get invited."

"Damn near everyone's going. I'm sure it was just an oversight, you being new to the area and all. I told Ed I'd be there, but I really hate to go by myself. Do you think you might go with me — just as a friend, I mean. Like I said, I sure do hate going alone."

Kate hesitated. She and Ed had spent hours together, working on the campaign. Why hadn't he mentioned it? She wondered why Chance hadn't asked her to go, and an uncomfortable shiver slipped down her spine. Maybe he was helping Ed with the preparations and just assumed she would be there. As Jake had said, it was probably just an oversight. Surely Chance wouldn't have invited someone else.

I'm crazy about you, Katie. He wouldn't have said that if he hadn't meant it. Chance wasn't the kind of man who lied.

"All right, Jake, I'd love to go. I can't stay late, though. David will be home alone." His birthday was coming up next week. He'd be thirteen, old enough not to have a sitter . . . as long as Kate was home early and Myra was a phone call away if he needed her.

"We'll come back whenever you say. Thanks, Kate."

Jake left. Kate finished her lunch duties and made arrangements for Bonnie to work the evening shift. Unfortunately, Bonnie couldn't come till six, which meant she and Jake would be arriving at the party a little late.

Wearing a short black Escada cocktail dress she had bought back in her fashion-conscious days in LA, a string of pearls she had saved months to buy, and black high heels, she was ready when he banged on the door.

"Damn. Lady, you look gorgeous. If this old cowboy was ten years younger, he might give Chance McLain a little competition."

It was the first time anyone had even hinted at her relationship with Chance and Kate found herself smiling, liking the idea.

"I think you could still give him competition,

318

Jake." He did look good, in a dark brown, Western-cut suit, beige cowboy shirt, and brown string tie. He'd shined his boots till they gleamed, and he carefully stepped around the mud-puddles in the driveway as he helped her into his freshly washed Chevy Blazer.

"I've never been to Ed's," Kate told him as they drove toward the ranch.

"It's *some* place, I can tell you. His late wife had it built. You'll be surprised when you see it."

She was definitely that. The French chateau looked as out of place up on the side of the hill as a prostitute in church.

Still, it was done in good taste and immaculately tended. The party was in full swing by the time they got there, the house so crowded they could barely get in. Waiters seemed to be everywhere, imported from Missoula, no doubt, the nearest town of any size. They carried silver trays of hors d'oeuvres and champagne, which seemed to be flowing like water.

"Ed certainly knows how to throw a party," Kate said, accepting a glass of champagne.

Jake took a canape off a silver tray and popped it into his mouth. "Sure does."

They said hello to Maddie and Tom Webster, stopped a moment to talk to Harvey Michaelson, then made their way downstairs to the massive entertainment room. There was a pool table, a twelve-foot bar, and the biggest

TV she had ever seen — and the room wasn't the least bit crowded. The rest of the furniture had been moved out and a dance floor set up in the middle. A makeshift stage had been erected at the opposite end.

She still hadn't seen Ed, or any sign of Chance. Her nerves began to kick up and she took another fortifying sip of champagne. *Maybe I shouldn't have come.* When Jake spotted a friend and began moving farther into the room, she lagged back, standing in the shadows of the doorway. The room began to fill up, people making their way toward the stage. A few minutes later, Ed and Chance appeared and the crowd that had gathered in front of them began to fall silent.

"Welcome, everyone," Ed said. "I hope you're all enjoying yourselves."

They all applauded. Somebody whistled.

"As some of you know, this shindig is being thrown in honor of my daughter, Rachael. She doesn't get home all that much anymore, and well, we just wanted her to know how glad we are she's here. Rachael — honey, come on up with your dad."

The crowd parted as she walked out a side door with perfect grace and made her way up the wooden stairs. She was dressed in a wispy, knee-length designer silk dress, a filmy print in shades of blue and green that had to have cost a fortune. Short blond hair gleamed like a cap of gold above a face any sculptor would love.

She was stunning, quite possibly the most beautiful woman Kate had ever seen.

Her father took her hand and kissed it, then reached over and linked it with Chance's. Rachael smiled up at him. When Chance smiled back and entwined his fingers with hers, Kate's stomach seemed to turn upside down.

They were the perfect couple. Chance dark and handsome as the devil, Rachael a tall, golden angel. Kate felt sick to her stomach.

"I asked you here tonight for more than just a party," Ed said. "Tonight, I'm proud to announce there's going to be a wedding. It's official. My daughter Rachael — after too damned long in the city — is finally coming home to marry Chance McLain."

In the single instant of silence that fell, the champagne glass slipped through Kate's numb fingers and shattered on the polished hardwood floor. Chance must have heard it. The crowd gave up a cheer, but above their heads, his eyes locked with hers and the blood seemed to drain from his face. He silently whispered her name the instant before she turned and fled back up the stairs.

Oh dear God, dear God. Her heart was squeezing, her chest aching. Her eyes filled with tears, blurring her vision until she couldn't see where to go. She ran into a short-coated waiter and his tray went flying.

"I — I'm sorry," she sputtered and kept up her rapid pace. French doors led out to the terrace. She hurried toward them, turned the brass handles, and raced out into the night. Tears rolled down her cheeks. She ran down a winding brick path, tripped on a loose brick, winced at the pain that shot into her ankle, and kept on running.

Her legs were shaking. She was trembling all over, sick and numb, and aching. She thought she heard someone calling her name, and veered off the path into the darkness, making her way across the grass, out toward the stables. Her ankle throbbed. A cold breeze rustled through the trees and her bare skin dimpled with the chill, but she didn't really feel it.

She reached the fence around the corral and clung to the rail, her body shaking with the sobs she had held back until now. Great waves of pain broke over her. Dear God, if only she could wake up, banish this terrible nightmare that she had stumbled into, but she knew in her heart it was real.

She heard his voice, soft, gruff, distorted by something that sounded oddly like pain. "Katie . . . God, I'm so sorry."

She whirled toward him and her hand cracked hard across his cheek. "Get away from me. Don't ever come near me again." She started walking away from him, heading toward the side of the house.

Chance came up beside her. "I know I should have told you. I wanted to . . . I tried to, but something always seemed to get in the way."

"Something seemed to get in the way?" She stopped and turned to face him. "Like what? Having sex? I thought at the very least we were friends. I thought no matter what happened between us, you would treat me with a certain amount of respect."

"We are friends, Kate. More then friends."

"Then how could you let me humiliate myself like I did last night? How could you let me make such a fool of myself?"

"It wasn't that way and you know it."

"How was it, then? Why didn't you tell me, Chance?"

In the light of the moon, his features looked harsh and grim, his jaw so hard it appeared carved in stone. "I know I've hurt you. I was coming to see you tomorrow. I was going to explain everything. I thought, hoped, maybe I could make you understand."

"Understand what? That you were tired of your latest plaything?" Her voice broke. "God, how could I have been such a fool?" She started walking, but he caught her arm.

"You've got to listen to me, Kate. There are things you don't know, things I need to explain. I wish I had. God, you'll never know how much I wish I had."

"That's enough! I don't want to hear another word. Go back inside, Chance — get out of my life and on with your own." She gave him a cool, bitter smile. "Your fiancée is waiting."

For the third time she started walking and

this time he didn't try to stop her. As she headed into the shadowy darkness at the side of the house, a squat, silver-haired man appeared by her side, an old man, slightly stoop-shouldered, his skin ancient and weathered.

"I will tell Jake Dillon you are not feeling well and that I am taking you home."

Kate swallowed, summoned a faint, almost imperceptible nod. "Thank you, Chief."

"Wait here." He sat her down on a wrought-iron bench she hadn't even seen, and she sat there gratefully. She was freezing now and still shaking. She couldn't seem to stop the tears.

God, she hated him.

Just hours ago, she had loved him.

She thought she had known him, but she had been wrong.

And she never would have guessed how much losing him would hurt.

The weekend passed and Kate returned to work. Her eyes were still a little gritty, her skin overly pale. She knew she looked like hell warmed over.

She was standing in the kitchen, getting ready for the first of the customers to arrive, when Myra walked up beside her. "I imagine I'm ratin' pretty low on your list of friends right now."

Kate's heart sank. "Obviously, you heard about Chance's engagement. Please don't tell me you knew he was involved with someone else and didn't tell me."

"Lord no. I never would have encouraged you if I'd had the slightest notion of anything like that. I knew he used to see her a lot. I thought it was over between them. She hasn't been back in town for months, and she was never the right girl for him, anyhow."

Kate bit down on the inside of her jaw, fighting the urge to cry. "Apparently Chance doesn't see it that way."

Myra sighed. She ran a pencil into the brassy blond curls piled up beneath her hairnet and used it to scratch her head. "Somethin' just ain't right. He ain't in love with Rachael — never has been. Anytime they were together, that was as plain as the nose on your face."

"Then why is he marrying her?"

"I don't know for sure. But he and Ed are powerful close, have been since Chance was a boy. His father never gave him the time of day. Hollis McLain was always too busy building his empire. Ed was their closest neighbor and he never had a son. He sort of adopted Chance."

"Well, whatever the reason, in six months he's getting married. And he didn't even have the decency to tell me." Kate blinked back tears. She wasn't going to cry, not again. She had cried enough for Chance McLain.

"It ain't like him to do somethin' like this. Chance has always gone out of his way to treat a woman fairly. That boy musta had a powerful itch for you, Kate."

She swallowed back the lump that kept trying to form in her throat. "Well, now that I've scratched it, he can go back to his beauty queen and live happily ever after."

"Maybe he will, but I got a pretty fair suspicion his life with Rachael Fontaine is purely gonna be hell."

Kate said nothing to that. She didn't want to talk about Chance. She never wanted to think of him ever again. It wasn't going to happen. Chance was stuck in her heart like a painful thorn she couldn't get rid of. If he was unhappy with Rachael, she couldn't care less. She wanted him to be miserable — didn't she? After the way he had treated her, of course she did.

But even as she worked taking orders and carrying plates, she couldn't help remembering the pain in those brilliant blue eyes when Chance had come after her at Ed's house that night.

Kate sighed as she picked up a bowl of broccoli soup. Perhaps in some small way, he actually had cared about her. It didn't really matter. Whatever his intentions, he had hurt her very badly.

And Kate would never forgive him.

A week dragged past. Still sleeping poorly, by the end of her shift, Kate was exhausted. Still, she knew once she got home she would start to think about Chance and she was determined not to do that.

"I think I'll go over and have a beer," she told Myra. "You want to come?"

Myra's blond eyebrow arched up. "You're goin' over to the Antlers?"

She had never gone into a bar by herself in her life. Maybe it was time she did. "Why not? I like Tom and Maddie and tonight I could really use a drink."

Myra grinned. "Now you're talkin', gal."

They finished closing up and walked catty-corner across the street. The bar was practically deserted, just a couple of locals Kate didn't know but had seen once or twice in town, and plump, good-natured Maddie Webster, working behind the bar.

"Well, hello there, ladies."

"You got one of them Moose Drools back there?" Myra asked.

"Sure do. How 'bout you, Kate?"

"A Bud Light would be great."

"You got it." Maddie brought their beers, set them on the top of the bar, and Kate took a drink. It was cold and refreshing and she could feel the slight relaxation after only a couple of sips.

Maddie wiped an imaginary spot on the bar in front of them, looking a little uncomfortable. "What happened out at Ed's . . . I guess that came as kind of a surprise."

Kate toyed with her beer mug. "You might say that."

"I can't believe he didn't tell you."

"Yeah, well if you think it's hard to believe, you ought to see how it looks from my shoes."

"You ask me, it was a pretty darned rotten thing to do."

Kate shrugged her shoulders, wishing they could talk about something else, wishing just the mention of his name didn't make her heart start to ache. "Maybe he saw her again and realized how much he loved her."

Maddie made a grunting sound in her throat. "You ever met Rachael Fontaine?"

"No."

Whatever point Maddie was making, Myra seemed to agree. "She might have a beautiful face, but there's lots of things more important than looks."

"You can say that again." Maddie wiped her wet towel in a circle on the bar. "Chance is a fool to marry a featherhead like Rachael. Not when he had the chance to hook up with a woman like you."

Kate flushed, but her bruised heart felt a little better. "Thank you, Maddie."

The heavyset woman moved down to the other end of the bar to refill the other customers' drinks, then returned and resumed her conversation. "I heard a couple days back you was asking questions about your grandma Nell."

"That's right." But she had given up that pursuit. She had found the letters, unlocked Nell's secret. Her search was at an end.

"What kind of questions?" Maddie asked.

"I wanted to know a little bit more about how she died. I wanted to know what happened the day of the accident."

Maddie made a sort of clucking sound and shook her head. "Your grandma was a doozie. We all still miss her. It was a sorry day for all of us when she died."

"How did you hear about it?"

"Aida Whittaker stopped by. She found her, you know. They'd been friends for years. It was real hard on Aida, I can tell you."

"I found some of Nell's letters up in the attic," Kate said softly. "After my mother left, Nell tried to find her. She must have searched for years."

"Nell loved Mary Beth," Maddie said. "It durn near killed her when the girl run off with that no-good Jack Lambert — meanin' no offense."

Kate's mouth inched up. "None taken." She took a sip of her beer. "I found some letters Silas wrote her. I guess they were pretty good friends."

"Better than that. Silas was in love with your grandma for years. He was real torn up when she died. He come in here drunker than a cowhand on payday, cryin' like a baby. Said he and Nell had a real bad fight that day. Said now he would never be able to tell her he was sorry."

The beer mug paused halfway to Kate's lips. "Nell and Silas had a fight the day she died?"

"That's what he said. Said he went over there to talk to her about sellin' that parcel they owned together and he and Nell started arguin'. A couple of hours later she was dead."

A feeling of uneasiness began to move through her. "I didn't see anything about that in the sheriff's report."

"Don't guess Silas mentioned it. You know how it is when you own a bar — you're everybody's confessor."

"I asked him about the accident, but he never mentioned he had seen Nell that day."

"I guess he still feels real bad about it."

Maybe he did. Maybe he felt worse than anyone knew. "You finished with your beer?" Kate asked Myra, suddenly eager to leave.

Myra deftly upended her mug. "Am now."

"Thanks for the drink, Maddie." Kate slid off the barstool, pulled her jacket on over her uniform, and waited while Myra did the same.

She had told herself this was over. She had convinced herself she was wrong, that Nell's message had nothing to do with murder. Now she wouldn't rest until she talked one more time to Silas Marshall. It wouldn't happen tonight, but sooner or later, the opportunity would arise.

She couldn't help wondering exactly what Silas would say when it did.

Chapter Twenty-one

The nights all seemed to run together. Kate tossed and turned, and Nell appeared in her dreams. She didn't remember much about them, just awakened in the morning with a vague sense that something was out of kilter. She felt tired and edgy as she watched David climb aboard the big yellow school bus and head down the road to the Ronan Middle School where he was enrolled.

Finishing the last of her coffee, she draped a sweater around her shoulders and set off for the cafe.

Twenty minutes before it was time to open, she was stunned to see a tall, lanky, dark-haired man walk through the back door into the kitchen.

Chance McLain.

Anger kept her back ramrod straight. It infuriated her to see how good he looked, freshly shaven, his wavy black hair carefully combed, sporting only the tiniest crease where his black felt hat had ridden on his forehead. He held it against his jeans in a callused hand, and she tried not to remember the intimate things those skillful dark fingers had done to her.

Country music played softly in the background, *"Easy on the eyes . . . hard on the heart."*

No truer words had ever been sung.

She finally walked over to where he stood. "The cafe opens in twenty minutes. Customers usually use the front door."

"I need to talk to you, Kate."

"There is nothing you have to say that I would possibly be interested in hearing. Now if you would please just leave."

"I know you're angry. Give me ten minutes. That's all I ask. Ten minutes and I'll be out of your life for good."

"You're already out of my life." Kate turned to Myra. "Would you tell Mr. McLain I'm too busy to talk to him right now. I've got to be ready to open in just a few minutes."

"Dammit, Kate —"

Myra stepped between them as Kate walked away. "Another time might be better, Chance. Give her a while to cool off. Maybe she'll be ready to listen then."

Chance cast a last look in her direction, swore softly, and stalked away, slamming the door a little too hard on his way out.

Myra eyed her from across the counter. "You ought to hear what he has to say."

"Why? He's getting married to someone else. I'm not interested in continuing a relationship whenever his girlfriend happens to be out of town."

Myra just sighed and turned away. Tying her apron on over her uniform, she set to work.

The cafe was busy. Kate left after the lunch

shift, went home and made some phone calls to a couple of environmental groups. She was working tonight, so she returned for the dinner shift. David wouldn't be waiting when she got home.

She smiled to think of Brian Holloway, the new friend that he had made at school. Tonight there was a Boy Scout meeting at Brian's house, and Brian and Chris Spotted Horse, who was also a scout, had convinced David to go.

Since it was a thirty-minute bus ride each way to Ronan, and the Holloways lived only a few blocks from the school, Mr. Holloway, who was also the scoutmaster, had called and asked if David could spend the night at his son's house.

Kate had been thrilled to agree. When David had asked if he could join the Scouts, Kate felt as if her prayers had finally been answered. He was becoming part of the community, making friends with children who came from good, wholesome families.

When the supper shift was over, Kate closed the cafe and made the short walk up the hill to the house. She frowned at the darkness surrounding it. She thought she had left a lamp on in the living room, but apparently she had forgotten. Digging out the key to her front door as she climbed the wooden stairs to the porch, she opened the door, went into the darkened hallway, and reached for the light switch.

Kate gasped as a hand shot out of the darkness and clamped hard over her mouth. A thick arm locked around her waist, dragging her back against a man's big body. She forced out a scream, but his gloved hand muffled the sound.

"You'd better keep quiet if you know what's good for you."

She clawed at the silencing hand and tried to twist free as he dragged her into the living room, but the man was at least a foot taller and probably a hundred pounds heavier than she was. *Oh dear God!* She'd always been afraid of something like this happening in the city, but not out here. Certainly not out here.

Frantically, she groped behind her, trying to scratch his face, grabbed a handful of soft knit fabric and realized he was wearing a ski mask. Her breath caught and the blood froze in her veins.

Oh God, oh God. Dragging in a steadying breath, she mentally ran over her options, which didn't take long, since she really didn't have any. There was no one around and she was too far away from the restaurant for anyone to hear her scream. She couldn't reach the phone, not even to knock it off the hook. With no one to help her, she had no choice but to try to help herself.

Kate kicked backward as hard as she could, twisted at the same time, and suddenly she was free. She unleashed a scream that would have wakened the dead, if anyone had been near enough to hear it, and started to run, but the man was on her in an instant, knocking her down before she could reach the front door, landing hard on top of her, knocking the air from her lungs.

She ignored the aching in her ribs, fought for breath, tried to drag off his ski mask, and succeeded in digging a long scratch along the side of his thick neck.

He rolled her over and slapped her hard across the face. "You little bitch. You wanna play rough?" Another hard slap and she moaned.

"I came to give you a message. You bow out of the anti-mining coalition. You don't, you're gonna get hurt real bad." Through the opening in the ski mask, she could see his lips pull up in a leer. "And just in case you might forget, I'm gonna give you a little something to help you remember."

Kate screamed as he caught the neck of her uniform blouse and ripped it open to the waist. Massive hands tore her bra in two, then he started to shove up her skirt. She tried to scream, got another vicious slap for the effort, and a wave of nausea washed over her, making her head spin. She tried to twist away from him, tried to shove him off her, but the more she fought, the more it seemed to excite him.

She heard the sound of his zipper sliding down, then another sound intruded, and his big hard body went tense. Kate started struggling again. She swallowed and tried to scream, but her mouth was so dry it came out more like a whimper.

Then the door flew open and Chance stormed in. "Son of a bitch!"

Her attacker flew off her as if he weighed less than a feather instead of over two hundred pounds. Curling herself into a protective ball, she managed to roll to her knees and shove down her skirt. Her stockings were torn. Her blouse gaped open.

In the darkness of the living room, she could hear the sound of furniture crashing against the walls. A lamp went flying. In the moonlight streaming in through the windows, she saw Chance throw a punch that sent the heavier man sliding across the floor. He was up and running in a heartbeat, slamming through the door leading into the kitchen. Running after him in the darkness, Chance didn't see the chair the man had dragged into his path. He hit it hard and went sprawling, cursed, tried to get back on his feet. By the time he did, her attacker was out the door and heading for the woods.

Chance didn't follow. Instead he whirled toward the living room, flipped the light on beside the sofa, and ran over to where she sagged against the wall, still crouched in a ball, holding the tattered remnants of her ruined blouse together.

Chance helped her to her feet, but she was

shaking so hard, she wasn't sure she could stay upright. He must have realized how close she was to collapse because he swore a violent oath and swept her up in his arms.

He carried her over to the sofa and sat down with her in his lap, his arms wrapped protectively around her. She thought of his betrayal and knew she should pull away, but she didn't have the strength.

"How badly are you hurt?" he asked.

She swallowed, fought to stop shaking. "Not . . . not too bad. He hit me a couple of times. He tried to . . . If you hadn't come when you did, he would have . . . he would have . . ."

"Sssh, I know. It's all right. He can't hurt you now." He glanced around, the muscles still tense across his shoulders. "Where's David?"

"At a scout meeting. He's spending the night with a friend." Another shiver ran through her to think what might have happened if her son had been in the house.

Unconsciously Chance tightened his hold. "I wonder how the bastard knew you'd be alone."

"I'm not . . . not sure he did."

"What do you mean?"

"I don't know, exactly. He seemed to be playing this thing minute by minute as he went along. He wanted me to stop . . . stop working on the campaign."

Chance's face turned grim. "God, Kate. When I asked you to help, I never thought it would come to this."

Her eyes slid closed. She had to get up, get away from him, give up the warmth and safety she felt in his arms. As if he sensed her thoughts, he settled her onto the sofa beside him, pulled the afghan off the back and wrapped it carefully around her.

"I'm calling the sheriff." Heading for the phone, he dialed 911 and briefly told the dispatcher what had happened.

"There's a deputy on his way. It'll take a while — it always does — but he'll be here as soon as he can."

Kate said nothing. Her jaw ached and her lip was beginning to swell. Chance went into the bathroom and came out with a washcloth dampened with cold water. Kate took it gratefully and held it against her jaw.

"Where's your aspirin?"

"Upstairs bathroom."

He came down carrying the bottle a few minutes later, fetched her a glass of water, and waited while she swallowed the pills.

Kate set the glass down on the coffee table and turned to look at him. "What are you doing here, Chance? How did you happen to come along when you did?"

"I wanted to talk to you. I still do. But now is hardly the time."

Never was the time as far as Kate was concerned. She lay back against the sofa trying to ignore her throbbing jaw and the pounding in her head. Eventually headlights flashed through the glass in the front door and Chance got up to let the deputy, an officer named Winston, into the house. Half an hour later, a report had been filed, and at Chance's insistence, Myra had been summoned to spend the night.

"I don't need Myra to stay with me," Kate argued. "I'm sure he won't be back again tonight."

"If I had my way, I'd be the one who was staying. I know what you'd say about that, so Myra will have to do. It isn't negotiable, Kate."

She opened her mouth to argue, but she was simply too exhausted. And the truth was she didn't really want to be alone. Myra arrived a few minutes later and instantly started fussing.

"Poor little thing. Just ain't right. A woman oughta be safe in her own home."

Chance paused beside the door. "Tomorrow I'll stop by to make sure you're okay."

"No! I mean . . . thank you, but there's no need for you to be concerned." The last thing she wanted was to see Chance again, though she had to admit she was grateful for his timely arrival tonight. "The sheriff said they'd be keeping a close watch on the house."

"Yeah, well, that isn't good enough. Tomorrow I'm bringing you a gun."

"A gun!" She tried to sit up, but the motion made her dizzy so she eased herself back down. "I don't have the slightest idea how to use a gun."

"Then it's about time you learned." He

didn't wait for her reply, just shoved open the door and stepped out into the night.

"Good thing he stopped by," Myra said, parroting her earlier thoughts.

"I don't want to talk to him. Can't you tell him that?"

"You know what he's like. Hardheaded as a mule and determined as a pit bull. He wants to talk to you. Sooner or later, you'll have to listen."

But Kate was equally determined. She was finished with Chance McLain and though she would always be grateful for his rescue tonight, she wasn't interested in hearing anything he had to say.

"Dammit, I told you to scare her, shake her up a little! That's all I told you to do!" Lon Barton paced in front of the small rock fireplace in his office.

"Yeah, well, you weren't there. That little bitch fought like a wildcat. She was asking for it." His lips curled up. "And if McLain hadn't shown up when he did, I'd have given it to her good."

Lon spun to face him. "Listen to me, Mullens. We're getting closer and closer to our goal. We don't need any more trouble with Kaitlin Rollins."

"Are you kidding? The woman was scared shitless. She won't give you any more trouble. She knows what'll happen if she sticks her nose into mining business again."

"I hope you're right . . . for all our sakes." Lon picked up an antique flintlock pistol from the collection on the wall above the fireplace. He loved old weapons, the older the better, but they didn't come cheap. Maybe that was one of the reasons he liked them so much. "At any rate, it's time to let things cool down a little." He turned, aimed the gun, peered through the sight, then put it back in the rack. "You're sure nobody knew it was you."

"I told you I wore a mask. Even if McLain guessed it was me, he's got no way to prove it."

Lon nodded. "All right, then for now we won't worry about it. For the next few days, just lay low and stay out of trouble. Take a few days off. Make a trip to Missoula. Find yourself a woman, if that's what you want."

Duke Mullens grinned. "Sounds like a good idea to me."

Lon watched him leave and returned to his desk. Duke had gone further than he should have with the girl, but at least she was off the coalition and out of his hair. Without her, the group would be floundering in no time, far less a threat than they were before.

Lon smiled. Duke might be a bit overzealous at times, but he always got the job done. And considering what a tempting little piece Kate Rollins was, in a way Lon didn't blame him for trying to screw her.

Standing next to Ed Fontaine's wheelchair in

the passenger terminal of the Missoula Airport, Chance watched the silver Delta 727 winging its way toward Salt Lake City on the way to New York. The plane disappeared into the clouds, and Chance turned away from the window, hiding a sharp sense of relief. He felt guilty for it. Dammit, in six months, Rachael would be his wife. He wanted to watch that plane depart and feel overwhelmed by a stinging sense of loss.

The way he had last night.

But Rachael was Rachael, not Kate. He and Rachael responded to each other as they had for most of their lives, with a comfortable acceptance, Rachael resigned to returning to Montana and beginning a life with him, Chance resigned to making her his wife. He cared about her. He always had. He had known her since she was a little girl and in a lot of ways she still was. It wasn't her fault he had finally discovered he wanted more from a marriage than that.

"Well, son, I guess we're on our own for a while."

Chance just nodded. Pushing the wheelchair in front of him, he made his way out of the terminal to the passenger loading zone in front of the airport and waited while Randy pulled the van up to the curb. The electric gate lifted Ed and the wheelchair into the back, and Randy and Chance climbed into their seats in the front.

Randy was the one who brought up the subject that had been hammering away at his mind all morning.

"I heard you ran into some trouble in Lost Peak last night."

A thread of tension filtered through him as an image arose of Kate struggling beneath her attacker. Unconsciously his hand tightened into a fist. "Some."

"What kind of trouble?" Ed asked.

"Some guy broke into Kate Rollins' place," Randy supplied. "I guess he roughed her up pretty good. Might have done more than that if Chance hadn't happened along when he did."

"You scared him away?" Ed asked.

Chance nodded. "They must have seen the television interview Kate did last week. Consolidated's running scared. They want her off the campaign."

"Is she all right?"

"She was pretty shook up. I got a hunch the guy was Duke Mullens, but he was wearing a ski mask, so there's no way to know for sure."

"Then you don't think the sheriff will come up with anything."

"He had on leather gloves. There won't be any fingerprints. Unless someone happened to see him — which is damned unlikely — there isn't much hope of that." Ed didn't ask him what he was doing at Kate's house and Chance didn't offer to tell him. Nothing was going on between them — not anymore. He just wanted a chance to explain.

Since the plane left at 6:50 A.M., it was early when Randy dropped him off back at his truck. Chance drove over to Kate's house to check on her and was amazed to find no one at home. Worried that something else might have happened to her, he hurried down to the cafe.

Breakfast was pretty much over by the time he got there and lunch hadn't yet rolled around. Looking through the recently repaired front window, he saw Kate, dressed in jeans and a dark green T-shirt with the cafe logo on the front, standing behind the cash register.

Why it made him so damned mad he couldn't say. He just knew he was furious. Storming through the doors like a madman, he slammed to a halt directly in front of her.

"What the hell do you think you're doing?"

"Adding up breakfast tickets. What does it look like I'm doing?"

"Last night someone beat the crap out of you and today you're adding up tickets? You ought to be home resting, taking care of yourself."

"Well, I happen to have a restaurant to run. And for your information, I feel perfectly fine."

He caught her chin between his fingers and examined the purplish bruise, her slightly puffy lip. "You don't look fine. You look like you ought to be in bed." The minute he said the words, he wished he hadn't. Images flashed through his head: Kate's glorious red hair sliding through his fingers, her magnificent breasts spilling into his hands.

The color was high in her cheeks when he looked down at her, and he wondered if she had been remembering, too.

"I have to be getting back to work," she said, trying to shove past him.

"You aren't dressed for work. Where's your uniform?"

"Change of policy, starting today. Jeans and T-shirts from now on." She gave him a sarcastic smile — "When in Rome . . ." — and headed for the kitchen.

Chance let her go. He felt guilty for even thinking about Kate when he was committed to Rachael, but there didn't seem to be a damned thing he could do to stop it. Still, whether Kate belonged to him or not, he was determined to keep her safe.

He caught her wrist as she sailed back into the dining room.

"Come on. There's something we need to do." He started tugging her toward the door at the rear of the cafe, but Kate jerked away.

"Are you crazy? I'm not going anywhere with you. I made that mistake before."

With a sigh, he pulled the gun from the waistband at the back of his jeans. "You're through with the campaign, but you still might need this." He showed her the .38 caliber automatic he figured would be the easiest thing for her to shoot.

"First of all, I'm not through with the campaign until we're sure that mine isn't going to go in. Second, I don't need a gun."

"First — you *are* through. I don't want you hurt any more than you already have been. Second — you may not need a gun, but it can't hurt to know how to shoot one."

"If I did, I might just consider shooting you!"

"Dammit, Kate. What you think of me has nothing to do with this. You need to be able to defend yourself."

Her mouth tightened. She might not want to admit it, but she knew he was right. She eyed the gun warily, then stiffened her spine. "All right. At least if the guy comes back, I won't be completely at his mercy."

Chance's stomach tightened at the thought of the bastard hurting her again. "If he does, you don't hesitate. You aim and pull the trigger — understand? Come on. I'll show you what I mean."

It was obvious she didn't want to go with him, and equally obvious she wanted to able to take care of herself. They went out behind the cafe to a spot on the opposite side of Little Sandy Creek where a mountainside formed a natural barrier that was a safe place to fire the gun. Chance set up targets, then showed her how to load the pistol. He made her load it a couple of times herself, then they were ready to shoot.

"Just remember — there's no such thing as an unloaded weapon. That's the reason you never point it at anyone — unless you intend to shoot."

He fired the pistol a couple of times, then handed it to Kate. "Hold your arms out straight, just the way I did, one hand wrapped around the other. Now brace your feet apart. Aim and fire."

She missed, but not by much. He set up another few targets and she fired a couple more rounds. Still not satisfied, he moved behind her. He felt her body stiffen, straining not to touch him, but her drive to master the weapon won out and she didn't move again.

"Ready?"

She held out the gun and Chance braced his arms around hers. He could feel her bottom pressing into his groin and bit back a silent curse. Kate fired again, hit the target dead-center, and Chance stepped away.

He cleared his throat, turned a little so she wouldn't see his erection. "Keep it handy. You probably won't need it, but I'll feel better knowing you've got it."

Kate just nodded. Chance said nothing more, and they walked in silence back to the cafe.

For the next full week, he stayed away. Fall was a busy time at the ranch, getting ready for winter, moving the cattle down from the high pastures to the lower ones out of the coming snows. But worry for Kate nagged at him, and his conscience nagged even more.

He had treated her badly and he knew it. She

347

thought he wanted Rachael, that he had simply grown tired of her. Chance didn't think he would ever grow tired of Kate, and even though he couldn't have her, he wanted her to know the truth.

It wouldn't change things. Nothing could do that. But at least if she understood, in time she might forgive him.

Chance set his jaw. One way or another, he vowed, this time she was going to hear what he had to say.

Chapter Twenty-two

Kate finished the Friday lunch shift feeling better than she had all week. Her bruises had faded and no other incidents had occurred. Sheriff Conrad himself had stopped by to express his concern and assure her the department would be keeping a close eye on things. They hadn't found any trace of the man who attacked her, and it didn't look like they would, but they were going to keep trying.

Her life was almost back to normal.

Almost.

She was still a little edgy whenever she was in the house. A man had nearly raped her. It wasn't something she would soon forget. Fortunately, she had other business to occupy her mind, namely the matter of Silas Marshall, and this afternoon she had made up her mind to go see him.

Kate felt an odd tug of anticipation. Whenever she looked into Nell's death, Silas's name seemed to surface. She wanted to know the truth about what happened that day, and she was more and more certain Silas Marshall held the answers to her questions.

She was sitting in one of the booths in the nearly empty cafe, drinking a cup of coffee and planning what she was going to say when a familiar deep voice spoke up from beside her.

"It's time for us to talk."

She hadn't heard him come in. Kate carefully set her cup down in its saucer and slowly came to her feet, tipping her head back so she could look him squarely in the face.

"I told you — I'm not interested."

"Fine. Now I'm telling you — you're going to hear what I've got to say."

Kate's temper cranked up a notch. She whirled toward the last few patrons still eating their lunch, all eyes now fixed in their direction. She gave him a sarcastic smile and planted her hands on her hips. "All right. You want to talk. Go ahead and talk."

Chance glanced around, saw the inquisitive faces staring in their direction, and fury blazed in his eyes. "I'm going to say this one more time. We're going to talk, Kate. Somewhere private. After that, I'll leave you alone." He reached out and took hold of her wrist, started tugging her toward the door.

Kate dug her heels into the carpet and caught hold of the back of a chair. "I told you, I'm not going." His face darkened, his scowl so black it gave her a moment of pause.

Chance glared at her and set his jaw. "All right, fine. I've tried to be patient. I've done everything I can think of to convince you. I can see it isn't going to work."

Kate yelped as he bent and tossed her over his shoulder, one long arm clamped around her knees, the other resting familiarly over her bottom.

"Are you insane? Put me down!"

"I intend to." He jerked open the door and walked out onto the wooden boardwalk. "As soon as we get to my truck."

Kate stopped struggling. It wasn't going to do a lick of good, and it only made her look more ridiculous. Thank God for her recent change of policy that allowed them all to work in jeans. Chance closed the distance to his pickup, opened the door, and dumped her in, then rounded the front of the truck, climbed in, and fired up the engine.

"This won't take long," he said. "But dammit you're going to hear what I have to say."

Kate said nothing, just let him drive away, recognizing the direction he was heading as the road to Lookout Mountain. They pulled into the overlook on the Flathead Valley, spread out below them in the distinctive red, orange, and yellows of fall.

"All right," Kate said. "You've dragged me up here. What do you have to say that's so important?"

Chance sighed. He took off his black felt hat and set it on the dashboard, raked a hand through his hair. "First of all, I didn't plan any of the things that happened. I didn't even know Rachael was going to be here until she called me from her father's ranch."

"But you were involved with her. You should

351

have told me that from the start."

"I hadn't seen Rachael in months. We led separate lives. We had for years. Even when she got here, I wasn't thinking about marriage. Her father thought it was time. That's how it happened."

"Her father? What does Ed have to do with it?"

Chance released another sigh, seemed to be struggling for words. "It's kind of hard to explain. Ed is more than just a friend. He's been like a father to me since I was a boy. His ranch borders a portion of the Running Moon. From the time Rachael was just a girl, her father expected the two of us to marry. We never talked about it, not really. We just assumed some day we would."

"This isn't the Dark Ages, Chance. People don't have to accept arranged marriages."

"Maybe not in most cases. My case is different."

"Why is that?"

"Because I'm the guy who put Ed Fontaine in a wheelchair."

There were a lot of things he might have said. This was one she hadn't expected. Her mouth felt suddenly dry. "Are you . . . are you saying it was somehow your fault that he's paralyzed?"

Chance stared out through the windshield. The blue of his eyes seemed to have faded, making them look like the sky on a too-hot day. "I was twelve years old when it happened. My father told me not to go riding that day. A lightning storm was coming in, he said. He told me to stay near the house."

"But you didn't," Kate said softly.

"No. I did what I wanted. That was pretty much the way it was. My father was never around. There was no one to tell me what to do. When he did say something, I rarely listened. I didn't listen that day."

Oh God. "What happened?"

"The storm came in, just like my father said. I was riding Sunny, this little buckskin gelding I liked. He was kind of skittery, hard to handle, but he was full of fire and he could run like the wind. We were in some pretty rugged country when the storm swept in, lots of gulleys and rocky ravines. It hit without much warning, a real bad one, raining like hell, wind blowing so hard you couldn't see. The buckskin stepped in a hole and went down. I lost my stirrups and went over his head. I landed on the edge of a steep ravine and rolled over the edge. I must have grabbed hold of a bush as I fell, but I really don't remember. I hung there for hours in the rain, yelling my head off, knowing it wouldn't do a lick of good. Then I heard the sound of voices, someone shouting my name."

"Your father came after you?"

Chance shook his head. "Ed came. I guess he stopped by my dad's place and realized I was out in the storm. The buckskin showed up about then, but my dad figured I'd just been thrown. He said a long walk home in the rain would serve me right for not doing what he said."

Kate bit down on her lip and discovered it was trembling. "So Ed was the one who found you."

"Unfortunately for him, yeah. He took one of his Indian cowhands along. Three Bulls could track a hayseed in a cloudburst. He found a spot where the ground was torn up, the place where the buckskin went down, then they heard me yelling. Ed tried to throw me a rope, but my hands were so numb by then I couldn't catch it."

Kate listened to the despair in his voice and a sweep of pity rolled through her. She could imagine how terrified David would have been, out there alone in a terrible storm, thinking no one cared enough to come after him.

"Ed told me not to worry, said he'd come down and get me. He took the rope from Three Bulls's saddle horn, tied it to a rock, and lowered himself over the cliff. He helped me get a noose around my waist and Three Bulls hauled me up."

Chance's throat worked, but for a moment, no more words came out. "Before he could climb back up himself, the rock he had tied his rope around gave way and Ed fell into the bottom of the ravine."

"Oh, Chance." Her throat was so tight she was surprised he could hear her. Maybe he didn't.

"Ed came after me," he said. "And because he did, he never walked again."

Tears burned her eyes. Kate reached over and caught his hand. It felt stiff and icy against the warmth of her own. "You were only a boy, Chance. It wasn't your fault."

Those piercing blue eyes swung to her face. "It was my fault. That's why I have to marry Rachael. Because I owe it to Ed. He wants his daughter close to him and married to a man who'll take care of her. He wants his land to go to sons who'll appreciate what they've been given and know how to take care of it. He knows I can give him those things."

The tears in Kate's eyes began to trickle down her cheeks. "What about you, Chance? You want to make Ed happy. Don't you deserve to be happy yourself?"

"Maybe I did. Once. Not anymore. Not since I was twelve years old."

Her throat ached. "And Rachael? Does she know how you feel?"

"Rachael's tired of life in the city. She wants to come home. She wants to marry a man who will give her whatever she wants."

"Maybe . . . maybe she'll make you happy."

He made no reply. He clamped his jaw and a muscle leapt in his cheek. When he looked at her, there was so much pain in his eyes, her own eyes filled with tears.

Kate leaned against him, slid her arms around his neck, felt his arms come around her.

She held him tightly and he held her.

"I'm sorry I didn't tell you sooner. I guess I just wasn't ready to let you go."

"Chance . . ." She tightened her hold around his neck and the tears in her eyes began to roll down her cheeks. She was in love with him. The feeling was lodged in her heart and it wasn't going to go away.

Her throat closed up. It was over between them, but at least now she knew she hadn't been wrong about the kind of man he was.

And after what he'd told her, she loved him more than ever.

"I'm glad you made me listen," she said, pulling away from him, dashing the tears from her cheeks.

"I never meant to hurt you. I'm sorry, Kate, for everything."

She nodded, accepting the sincerity of his words. She dragged in a shaky breath of air. "It's all right. Sometimes things just happen."

"Yeah, I guess so." They sat there in silence for a few minutes more, as if neither of them wanted the moment to end. Then Chance reached for the key and started the engine. "I'll take you back now."

They didn't talk on their way down the hill. There was nothing for either of them to say.

Chance helped her out of the truck in front of the cafe and walked her to the door. "I wish things could be different," he said.

"So do I." But they couldn't be, and both of

them knew it. Chance's mind was set and he wasn't going to change it. His strong sense of duty was one of the things she liked best about him. She watched him climb back in the truck and slowly drive away.

As he had promised she would, at least now she understood. She should have felt better.

Instead she felt ten times worse.

The weekend slipped past. She thought of Chance only a few times a day, resigned as she was to burying her feelings for him as deeply as she could. Instead she renewed her resolve to gather the final pieces of the puzzle of Nell's death and speak to Silas Marshall. As soon as lunch was over, she marched across the street to Marshall's Grocery.

Kate shoved through the door, listening to a bell that rang a little louder than the one in the cafe, and glanced around looking for Silas. Until she came to Lost Peak, she had never been in a market quite like this one, with its sagging plank floor, tiny vegetable counter, and frozen meat section. There wasn't a heck of a lot to choose from, but when you ran out of eggs in the middle of baking a cake or found the last quart of milk sitting empty in the fridge, you were darned glad it was there. It was a long way to the supermarket and though this was the only game in town when it came to buying groceries, Silas's prices were surprisingly fair.

She glanced around again, spotted him stacking Campbell's soup cans on one of the shelves, and started in that direction. There were a couple of customers up in front, but Carol Simmons, Silas's cashier, was handling them without any problem.

"Hello, Silas."

He glanced up, got a funny look on his face. "Hi, Kate. You need some help finding something?" He stood up, stretching his pale, thin body what seemed like several feet above her head.

"Actually, there was something I wanted to ask you about."

His expression turned slightly wary. "What is it?"

"I was wondering . . . the last time we talked about my grandmother, you didn't mention you had seen her the day she died."

He blinked owlishly, as if he couldn't figure out how she could possibly have known. "I didn't?"

"No, you didn't. I don't think you mentioned it to Sheriff Conrad, either."

He cleared his throat. "I guess . . . I guess it didn't seem important at the time."

"How about the fight you two had? Did that also not seem important?"

He wet his thin lips, glanced around as if he was looking for a path of escape. "I . . . I guess it didn't . . . at the time."

"What was the fight about?"

"The property we owned."

"You wanted Nell to sell it . . . isn't that right?"

"Yes . . ."

"But she refused."

He nodded. "She didn't want the mine going in. I told you that before."

"Yes, you did. But that day you were determined to convince her. Isn't that the reason you went to see her?"

His pale face turned paper white, his eyes squinting, deep lines forming at the corners. "Yes."

"But she still wouldn't sell."

Silas swallowed. His body started to tremble. He ran a shaking hand over his lips. "We argued something awful. I don't think we ever had such a row. My boy, Milton . . . he wanted to borrow some money. He'd married again, said the third time was the charm. He begged me to help him make a fresh start." He was no longer looking at her, just staring at the row of red and white cans on the shelf. "I didn't want to disappoint him. I pleaded with Nell to sell. She said she wouldn't do it — not for my no-account son or anyone else. That's what she said." He blinked and his eyes slowly filled with tears. "I never meant to hurt her. I swear it. I loved her. I can't remember a time I didn't love her."

Kate went suddenly numb. She had prodded him, goaded him to tell her the truth about that day, yet she had never believed he would actually admit he had killed her.

But it certainly sounded that way.

"Go on," she softly urged. "You argued, but you never meant to hurt her."

He shook his head and the tears in his eyes slid into the hollows of his cheeks. "I couldn't believe she wouldn't agree. Not when she knew how much it meant to me. I grabbed her and I shook her. I guess I must have shoved her backwards a little when I let go. The rug caught between her feet and she fell." His eyes slid closed, but tears leaked from under his sparse gray lashes. "There was so much blood. So much blood." He began to sob then, deep, wrenching sobs, and a surge of pity washed over her.

She shouldn't have felt it, not after what he had done, but somehow she did. Gently, she took his arm and led him through the door leading into his office, sat him down in the old oak chair behind his battered desk.

"I knew she was dead. I turned and ran to my car," he said, his face distorted with pain. "I never meant to hurt her. I loved her. I always loved her."

Kate just stood there, a thousand different emotions rolling around inside her head. Anger. Pity. Relief that she finally knew the truth.

Silas dragged in a ragged breath. "Go on. Call the sheriff. Let's get this over with, once and for all."

She reached for the phone, but something held her back. Silas had killed Nell, but he hadn't meant to. He had loved her, and Nell had cared about him, too. He was an old man. Would her grandmother want him to go to prison?

"I don't know if . . . I just . . ."

"You wanted to know the truth and now you do." Silas picked up the phone with long, bony fingers that trembled. He dialed 911. "Get me Sheriff Conrad. Tell him it's Silas Marshall calling. I got something important to tell him."

Kate didn't stay to hear the rest. Silas was doing what he should have done in the first place and yet, instead of feeling triumphant, she felt heartsick about it.

Half an hour later, once more back at the cafe, she saw the sheriff's Chevy SUV roll up in front of the grocery store, and tall, blond Sheriff Conrad get out. A short time later, he led Silas back to the car and helped him into the rear seat, pressing his head down so he wouldn't bump it on the door. Kate was glad to see the old man wasn't handcuffed.

Myra walked up beside her. "Darned shame, is what it is."

Kate had told her what happened. She wished she could have talked to Chance. "I wonder what they'll do to him."

Myra just shook her head.

Kate turned away from the window, dragged in a slow breath of air. *It's over*, she thought. *It's over at last and now Nell can rest in peace.*

It wasn't exactly murder. Involuntary manslaughter, they called it. Still, an old woman's death had been the result of Silas's actions.

Kate released a weary breath. At least her own personal search was at an end. What happened to her that night in LA must have been real. Surely all of this couldn't simply have been a coincidence.

That knowledge alone should have cheered her. Instead that night, she dreamed of Nell and awakened in the middle of the night feeling more disturbed than she was before. Eventually, she was able to go back to sleep but this time she dreamed of Chance. In the dream she held his tiny black-haired infant son. They were happy. So happy.

She awakened with a smile that slowly faded as she realized none of it was real, would never be real. Chance was lost to her forever. Kate cursed her bad luck in finally finding a man she could love but never have.

At least in moving to Lost Peak she had found a home for herself and her son. She could thank Nell for that, and be content that the mystery of her death was solved at last.

Unfortunately, a few days later when an unexpected photo arrived in the mail, her doubts arose once more.

Chance sat on his porch talking to Ed Fontaine, absorbing the afternoon sun and an oddly warm first week of October. Ed had come with news of Consolidated Metals and the news wasn't good. It put a damper on what should have been a gorgeous day.

"So they've finally done it." He read the document Ed had brought, a copy of the lawsuit filed by Consolidated against the State of Montana.

"We knew they were going to, sooner or later. It was only a matter of time."

"We've got to step up the campaign," Chance said, "make sure the public is informed. Consolidated will be bearing down, using every ounce of pressure they can muster. We need to do the same."

"Kate's already on it. She's been working —"

"Kate? Kate's off the project. You and I already talked about that."

"Yes, we did. Fortunately for us, Kate had other ideas. She says she's not going to let Lon Barton and his thugs stop her from doing what's right for Lost Peak."

Chance said nothing. He was torn between fury that Kate was still willing to put herself in danger and a grudging respect for her.

"She's an amazing woman," Ed said softly.

Chance felt a sharp stab of pain. "Yes, she is."

"You heard what happened with her and Silas Marshall?"

Chance snapped to attention once more. "No. What the hell happened with Silas?"

"Apparently Kate was convinced Silas had

something to do with her grandmother's death. She went to see him and believe it or not, Silas confessed."

Chance came to his feet. "You mean he actually killed Nell Hart?"

"Apparently not on purpose. They had an argument over that little piece of property they owned, the one with the artesian well on it. Silas accidentally shoved her. Nell tripped and hit her head."

Chance sat back down, knowing how Ed hated having to look up at him. "I can't believe it. Kate was right."

"How'd she know?"

"It's a long story, I'm afraid. Suffice it to say, her instincts were right all along."

"She's no fool, that girl."

Only when it came to him, Chance thought morosely. But that was a mistake on both their parts.

"I know you've got work to do," Ed said. "I got plenty to do myself. I just wanted to let you know what Lon Barton was up to." Ed motioned to Randy, who stood over by the corral, talking to a group of cowhands. Randy waved and began walking back in their direction. He took hold of the wheelchair and started pushing it toward the van.

"Keep me posted," Chance called after them.

"I'll do that," Ed called back.

"And tell the sheriff to keep a close eye on Kate."

"Already done," Ed said.

Chance watched the van pull away, then headed out to the corral. Thinking of Kate made his chest feel tight. He wanted to see her. He couldn't, of course. He had made a commitment and he didn't take it lightly. Still, staying away from Kate was the hardest thing he'd ever done.

It'll get easier, once you're married.

But Chance wasn't convinced it would ever be easy to stay away from Kate.

Chapter Twenty-three

A warm afternoon sun shone in through the kitchen windows, forming patterns on the old oak table in the breakfast room. Down near the stream, Kate could see a doe standing beneath one of the pines on the hill. Seated across from her, Willow Spotted Horse sipped a cup of steaming black coffee.

Like David, Kate had needed a friend near her age, someone she could talk to, and in Willow she seemed to have found one.

"Chris said David joined his Boy Scout troop," Willow said, taking a drink from her mug. With the cafe running so smoothly, Kate now took both Saturdays and Sundays off. She had come to Lost Peak to spend time with her son and she had been able to do that more and more. "I hope he enjoys it." At present, the boys were upstairs in David's room, getting ready for an afternoon hike.

"He's really excited about it," Kate said. "And I might add I'm delighted myself."

Willow smiled. She was incredibly pretty with her big dark eyes, sculpted cheeks, and olive complexion. "They're really a nice bunch of kids, and Mr. Holloway does a great job of keeping them interested in the various projects."

Kate heard the two boys thundering down the stairs. "We're all set," David said.

"So I see," said Kate. "Now tell me again where you're going."

"Up the Little Sandy trail. We're taking our rods along in case we want to fish."

"And Chief is going with you?"

"He's meeting us up the creek a little ways, a spot he showed us before."

"Okay, but you'll have to be home by five."

"That's right," Willow agreed. "I'll be back to pick Chris up and he had better be here when I arrive."

"I'll be here," Chris promised. They tore out the back door, David the taller of the two and finally beginning to fill out a little.

"They're quite a pair," Willow said.

"David thinks the world of Chris."

Willow smiled softly and both of them sipped their coffee. Outside the dining room window, the local postal carrier drove up in front of the mailbox at the bottom of the lane.

"Mail's here," Willow said as his battered Buick sedan — the Lost Peak version of a mail truck — pulled back onto the road. "I'll walk down with you. I always look forward to getting the mail. I imagine, with so many friends still living in LA, it's even more so for you."

Kate smiled. Though there was never much of anything important, she always looked forward to the mail. "I have a friend named Sally. We usually stay in touch by e-mail, but she sends me cards now and then. Mostly it's a holdover from when I was a little girl. I was always hoping a letter would come from my father. It never did, of course."

"My father wasn't much of a dad, either, but at least he was there. Come on. I need the exercise."

Willow didn't need much of anything that Kate could see. She was intelligent and beautiful, and terribly in love with her husband.

"Jeremy is taking us camping this weekend," Willow said with a smile, linking her arm with Kate's. "We always pitch two tents, one for the kids and a separate one for us." A faint blush rose beneath her high, carved cheekbones. "Even with children, Jeremy insists on having our privacy."

Her soft look spoke of the love she felt for the man she had married, and an unexpected lump formed in Kate's throat.

"You're lucky to have found each other."

Willow nodded. "I know. I'm sorry about you and Chance. I know he felt differently about you than any other woman he ever dated. I thought it might work out."

Kate swallowed past the ache in her throat. "So did I."

"He's always cared for Rachael, but I never thought he would marry her."

They had reached the big black mailbox that sat on a post at the beginning of the gravel drive. Kate opened it as an excuse not to have to make a reply. She began to sift through the envelopes: a couple of utility bills, a credit card bill, a coupon flyer from the supermarket in Ronan, and a Bloomingdale's catalog, one of her few remaining attachments to life in the city. The last envelope slipped out of her grasp. Willow picked it up and handed it over.

"It's from Aida Whittaker," Kate said. "I've never met her, but I've talked to her a couple of times on the phone. She seems really nice. I wonder what it says." As they walked back up the drive, Kate carefully tore open the envelope. There was a letter inside, accompanied by a Polaroid picture.

"Good Lord." Willow paused at the top of the front porch stairs. "That's a photo of your grandmother in her coffin." She shivered. "I know a lot of people do that, but I think it's gruesome."

"To tell you the truth, so do I." As they went back into the house, Kate skimmed the letter, then read it aloud, knowing Aida and Willow were friends. It said that Aida was well and happy, that she had forgotten about the photo her daughter had taken the day of the funeral, and thought that Kate might want it. She asked how things were going in Lost Peak and if Consolidated Metals was still trying to open a mine on Silver Fox Creek.

"She and Nell were both real opposed to that mine," Willow said.

"I'll have to drop her a note, give her an update, and thank her for the photo." For the first time, Kate took a long look at the picture. The mortician had done Nell's hair and makeup, which seemed oddly wrong, a little too much blush on her cheeks, a little too dark a lipstick.

And there was something else, something she couldn't quite put her finger on.

"You knew Nell. Take a look at this picture and see if you notice anything wrong with it."

Willow studied the photo. "She never wore that much makeup."

"Anything else?"

Willow squinted down at the photo. "Her nose looks funny. Wider, and kind of puffy or something."

"That's what I thought." Back in the kitchen again, Kate left Willow at the table, ran upstairs, and got the file she had made on Nell Hart. The photos she had borrowed from the mortuary were still inside. She had made a note to herself just that morning to return them.

"Her face looks different in these," Kate said, handing Willow a photo of Nell lying on her back in the embalming room. There was another, closer shot, showing only her head and shoulders. Her nose looked perfectly normal.

Willow studied the picture. "They must have done something to her at the mortuary."

"I wonder what happened. In the pictures taken the day of the accident, her nose looks normal. In the ones taken the day of the funeral, it almost looks like it's broken. You don't think they dropped her or something?"

"Not a pleasant thought," Willow said.

"No, I don't guess it is." It isn't important, she told herself. You know how she died. But every time she looked at the photo, something nagged at her.

"I never talked to the undertaker, not the one who actually worked on Nell. His name was Hobbs. I called him, but he was never home."

"Maybe you ought to. You've gone this far, you might as well finish." Willow knew about Silas and about Kate's search to discover the truth of how she died. Everyone in town did by now. Silas was back at work, charged with involuntary manslaughter, but out on bail. No one seemed to know exactly what would happen now.

"Maybe I should go see Hobbs."

Her mind made up, for the next two days she phoned Walter Hobbs. When she finally reached him, he sounded impatient and slightly distracted, and she thought he might be pleasantly drunk.

Willow went with her to Polson, the day Kate finally convinced the man to talk to her. It was raining, a harsh October wind whistling through the trees.

"I love your car," Willow said, sitting in the plush leather passenger seat of the Lexus. "But once it starts to snow, you're going to need something more practical."

"I know it. I've been thinking about making a

371

trade. I just haven't gotten around to it."

Though the roads were wet and slick, and the traffic slowed them down, they reached Polson on time for their one o'clock appointment. Hobbs's address on Sixth Avenue turned out to be an old gray wood-frame house with a sagging porch and a lawn that hadn't been cut all year. They walked up a broken, uneven sidewalk, trying to avoid the weeds protruding through the cracks in the cement, and climbed the wooden stairs onto the porch out of the rain.

Kate knocked and Hobbs answered, opening the door so they could come in.

"Thanks for taking the time to see us, Mr. Hobbs." She and Willow crossed a dreary living room with old-fashioned brown shag carpeting to sit on a worn brown velvet sofa with the stuffing coming out.

Hobbs fit right in, a short, overweight, unshaven man in an undershirt and baggy jeans. Though he wasn't drunk, she could clearly smell alcohol on his breath and understood why Mr. Dorfman, the mortician, had said they only rarely called him in, as they had done the day of the accident.

She cast Willow a grateful glance for coming along.

"You wanted to see me," Hobbs said. "What can I do for you?"

"Mr. Dorfman told me you were the person who worked on Nell Hart the day she died."

When he didn't seem to remember, Kate handed him the photos.

"Yeah. Now, I remember."

"Was there anything out of the ordinary you noticed about her?"

"Out of the ordinary how?"

She could see this wasn't going to be easy. "For instance, if you look at those photos, you can see they look different. One was taken when Nell was first brought in, the other was taken the day of the funeral. If you look at the face, you can see she looks different in one than in the other."

"I don't see any difference."

Kate moved closer, tried to ignore his stale alcohol breath. "Look at her nose."

"What about it?"

Kate pushed past her frustration. "Why does it look like it's been broken or something?"

"Because it was. I remember noticing it after the embalming."

"I'm afraid I don't understand. If her nose was broken, why doesn't it show up in the first picture?"

"Because there wasn't any blood. The heart wasn't pumping any. The nose couldn't swell because there wasn't any blood in the veins. The embalming solution acts like a substitute. The tissues puff up just like they would have if she had been alive."

A cold chill snaked down Kate's spine.

Willow spoke the question that was hovering

on her lips. "Are you saying that Mrs. Hart's nose was broken when she was brought into the mortuary?"

"That's the way I remember it, yes."

"Why didn't you report it to the authorities?" Kate asked.

"The woman took a fall. Wouldn't be unlikely she might have broken her nose."

"My grandmother fell backward. She hit the back of her head." She handed him the other photos, those taken with Nell on her stomach. "There is no way a fall backward could have been responsible for breaking her nose."

Walter Hobbs just shrugged. "Don't know what to tell you. Must have happened some other way."

Some other way? Had Silas hit her, knocked her into that sideboard? If he had, any sympathy she felt for him, any effort she might have made to help him, would be finished. She needed to talk to him.

And she intended to do just that.

"Was there anything else you remember?"

He scratched his unshaven chin. "Not that I can think of."

Kate got up from the sofa and Willow stood up, too. "Thank you, Mr. Hobbs." He didn't answer, just walked them to the door and held it open so they could go out.

"Charming fellow," Willow said when they got back into the car.

"Not very competent, I'm afraid. He should

have reported that injury, but I guess, since the deputy wasn't there to explain how it happened, it's possible he simply misunderstood."

"Do you think Silas hit her? God, I can't imagine it. He's always been such a kind, gentle old man."

"He shoved her. He must have hit her, too. I can't figure out any other way it could have happened." She started the car and pulled onto the street. "I'll tell you one thing. I darn well intend to find out."

Kate was so intent on speaking to Silas, she didn't see the silver Dodge pickup parked off to the side of the market when she crossed the street and went into the store. Instead, she shoved through the glass front door, took a quick glance around, spotted Silas's long, bony frame, and marched in that direction.

"Hello, Silas."

He glanced away, up then down at the floor. "Hello, Kate."

"I need to talk to you. We should probably go into your office."

He nodded, looked resigned. "All right."

A deep male voice cut in just then. "I'm sorry to intrude, but I couldn't help overhearing." Chance stepped into the aisle from behind a tall stack of Coca-Cola twelve packs. He fixed those penetrating blue eyes on Kate and she could feel their warmth clear into her bones. "Is everything all right, Kate?"

"To tell you the truth, I'm not sure." He must have heard the anxiety in her voice. She was certain Silas had. "Maybe Silas will be able to help me figure it out."

"Mind if I come along?"

Of course she minded. She was trying her best to forget the man ever existed, but his worry was apparent, and she could use a little support in this. She turned to Silas, who started shuffling toward his office like a man being led to the gallows.

As soon as the door was closed, he turned and looked at her down his crooked, bony nose. "What is it, Kate?"

"I'm sorry to bother you, Silas, but yesterday I spoke to a man named Hobbs. Mr. Hobbs works part time at Dorfman's mortuary. After the accident, when my grandmother was taken there, Mr. Hobbs was the man who worked on her."

Silas looked utterly grim.

"I showed him a couple of photos I had and he told me Nell had arrived that day with a broken nose. Since you claim that when you *accidentally* pushed her, she fell backward, I want to know how that could have happened."

Silas looked confused. "I don't know."

"Did you hit her, Silas? Is that how she fell?"

"Hit her? I didn't hit her."

"You were angry. Nell wouldn't agree to sell. Are you certain you didn't strike her, maybe just once? One good hard punch and that poor old lady fell, hit her head, and died?"

Silas looked stricken. "No! I never hit a woman in my life!" He was shaking his head, looking at her with eyes that were bleak and filled with pain. "I swear it, Kate. I loved Nell. I deserve whatever I get for what I did to her that day, but I swear it was an accident. I never hit her." His voice cracked. "I would die before I'd ever have hurt her on purpose."

Why she believed him she couldn't really say. She only knew that she did.

"I loved Nell Hart," Silas was saying. "I loved her." He sank down in the old oak chair and buried his head in his hands. Kate felt the unwanted sting of tears.

She felt Chance's hold on her arm. "Let's go, Kate."

She nodded, let him guide her out of the office and close the door.

"How did you happen to find out Nell had a broken nose?"

"Aida Whittaker sent me a photo. I compared it to the ones we got from Dorfman at the mortuary. Then I went to see Walter Hobbs."

Chance sighed. "I don't think Silas hit her."

"Neither do I."

"Then again, I didn't think he killed her, either."

Kate thought about that and the same thought that had been nagging her since yesterday rose at the back of her mind. "Maybe he didn't."

Chance froze. "What do you mean?"

Kate shook her head. "I'm not sure yet." They passed a stack of flour sacks, sitting at the end of an aisle, and walked on past the cash register. Chance shoved open the door, and they walked out under the overhanging eaves.

"I don't get it, Kate. You believed Silas killed Nell. You got him to admit it. Now you're saying he didn't?"

"I'm not saying anything, yet. But when you look at the whole picture you have to wonder. Silas says he didn't hit her. If he didn't, who did? Which brings us back to the question — who had the most to gain? Silas, yes, but ultimately it was Consolidated Metals. With Nell out of the way, they got the well they needed and a shot at a valuable gold mine. They — or someone who wants that mine to go in — was serious enough about all of this to send a man to my house. That man tried to rape me. It doesn't seem like much of a stretch to think that same someone would go as far as murder."

Chance's expression turned grim. "I don't like this, Kate. Not one little bit. So far your instincts have been dead-on. If you're right about Consolidated and you keep digging for answers, you could be in for some very big trouble."

Kate shuddered, knowing he was right.

"Is finding out if Nell was murdered worth risking your life?"

A shiver ran through her. Was it worth it?

"There was a time I might have said no. But even then I was determined to find out if what happened to me the night of the shooting was real. Now I've read Nell's letters. I know what she was really like and how much she loved my mother and me. Now it's even more important for me to know the truth."

"What are you going to do?"

"I'm not sure yet."

Chance caught her arm. Even through her heavy wool sweater, she could feel the contact like a hot brand on her skin. "Whatever we once were, we're still friends. Friends help each other. Let me help you, Kate."

She dragged in a shaky breath. She didn't want his help; she didn't want to be near him. But she trusted him and she might very well need him.

"If I stumble onto anything important I'll let you know."

His grip only tightened. "Promise me, Kate. Promise you'll call before you do anything that might get you into trouble."

She looked up at him, thought how handsome he was, thought how much she still loved him. "I promise."

Chance let her go. "Be careful, Katie."

Kate just nodded. With a last worried glance, Chance turned and walked away.

A cold October wind whistled down through the pines surrounding the town. A dark platinum sky washed the landscape in dismal gray. At the bar in the Antlers Saloon, Chance sat next to Jeremy Spotted Horse. It was late in the afternoon. They had run into each other at the mercantile and stopped in for a beer before heading home for the night.

"I guess you heard the latest on Silas and Nell," Chance said to his friend.

"You mean Nell's broken nose? Willow's been keeping me posted. She and Kate are becoming real good friends. Willow went with her to see that guy in Polson, Walter Hobbs."

"Kate's always believed Nell was murdered. Unless Silas went crazy and punched Nell in the face, she just might be right."

"I've tried to imagine it. I can see how he might have accidentally caused her to fall, but I can't imagine him hitting her. They'd been friends for too many years. Nell would never have put up with him if he'd been the sort who would ever have hurt her."

"That's what I think, too."

"Which means Kate could be involving herself in something she can't handle."

"Yeah."

"And you're worried about her."

"Damned right I'm worried. If Kate's right and Consolidated Metals is involved, she could be asking for serious trouble." On the surface it seemed crazy. Silas wanted Nell to sell the parcel of land they jointly owned. They argued. Silas hit her. Nell had fallen and died when her head hit the sideboard.

Silas had made his deal on the land and that was the end of it.

But Consolidated Metals was also mixed up in that particular deal. As far as Chance was concerned, he wouldn't put anything past them. And now that Kate had put the notion of murder into his head, he couldn't seem to get it out.

Jeremy took a sip of his beer, set it back down on the bar. "Willow thinks you're in love with Kate."

The words came out of nowhere. Chance glanced up from his mug. "Oh yeah?"

"Know what?"

"What?"

"So do I."

Chance looked away, raked a hand through his hair. "Yeah, well, then all three of us have figured it out. Unfortunately, it doesn't make a lick of difference."

"Maybe you should talk to Rachael, tell her the truth."

"What truth? The truth is I have to marry Rachael. I owe it to her father. The truth is I'll make her a damned good husband. I'll take care of her, see she gets anything she wants — which is all that matters to Rachael. She'll be close to her dad, which both of them want; and she'll give him the grandkids he and I both want. That's the only truth that matters."

"You sure it's fair to Rachael?"

"If I didn't think so, I wouldn't do it." He sighed. "We both know Rachael isn't in love with me. Hell, neither of us were ever in love. That isn't important — at least not to Rachael. Until I met Kate, it wasn't important to me."

Jeremy said nothing, just took a long drink of his beer. One of the stools down at the end of the bar scraped against the wooden floor and Ned Cummings strode toward them.

"Hey, Chance! I didn't see you come in." He stuck out his hand. "Congratulations, man."

Chance shook. "Thanks, Ned."

"You and Rachael." He grinned. "I guess I should have figured the two of you would finally get together, but somehow I just never did."

"I'm lucky she said yes."

"You can say that again. That is one gorgeous female. And speaking of gorgeous women, since you're no longer in the market, I don't suppose you'd mind if I asked Kate Rollins out."

His body tightened like a five-pound line hooked onto a ten-pound fish. Ned didn't suppose he'd mind? The thought made him sick to his stomach. Ned Cummings was handsome and smart. He owned one of the nicest little ranches in the county. He'd be a good man for Kate. It was the last thing he wanted. "No . . . of course I don't mind."

Ned slapped him hard on the back. "Thanks, Chance." He grinned and winked at Jeremy.

"I'll see you boys later. I'm going over to the cafe, see if I can manage to convince that little gal to go out with me on Saturday night."

As Ned strolled out of the bar, Chance's stomach clenched into a knot. It was all he could do to stay in his seat.

"Easy, man." He felt Jeremy's hand on his shoulder, and the tension eased a little.

"Sorry. I know I don't have any right, but . . ."

"But that doesn't make it any easier."

"No."

"Maybe she won't go."

"She'd be a fool if she didn't."

"Yeah, well that goes without saying. She fell for you, didn't she?"

A corner of his mouth edged up. "God, I miss her. She was really something special, you know."

Jeremy squeezed his shoulder. "Come on. I'll buy you another beer."

Chance nodded, but his mind was on Ned Cummings and what was going on across the street.

"By the way," Jeremy's voice pulled him back to the bar. "Chief says that tail pond up on Beaver Creek has started leaking again."

"You're kidding."

"He thinks there's a tear in the plastic liner. He says he's gonna try to get some pictures."

"He'd have to go onto Consolidated property to do that. I don't think it's a good idea, especially not now, with tempers running so high."

"Yeah, well you know Chief."

"First time I see him, I'll talk to him about it."

"Good idea."

They finished their beer and headed for the door. Chance walked outside just in time to see Ned Cummings walking out of the Lost Peak Cafe.

Chance bit back a curse when he saw the grin on Ned's face.

Chapter Twenty-four

Kate sat facing the computer in her office upstairs. An icy wind blew leaves against the window, and a branch scratched persistently against the outside wall. A shutter banged loudly and she jumped.

Ever since the rape attempt, she'd been more nervous, less comfortable being alone in the house. But she loved the old place and she told herself she was far safer here than she would have been in the city.

She focused her attention on the computer screen and scrolled down the page, having accessed this particular website, *www.forensicsciencejournals.com*, several times before. She had read this section, but among the voluminous material she had perused, had only retained a foggy memory of it. That memory had nagged her, building bit by bit, until finally it returned full-blown, driving her upstairs to the computer.

She pressed the print button, making a copy of the pages, picked them up, and scanned them more closely. It was a criminal case, one of several dozen she had read, a death by asphyxiation where the assailant had used a pillow to commit the murder. During the autopsy, the medical examiner had discovered that the victim's nose had been broken. It hadn't been spotted by the officers on the scene because there wasn't any blood pumping, and therefore no swelling of the tissues.

Kate read the information one last time, how the forensic experts, once they established the means, were able to track down the killer.

She studied the printed pages, her mind going over what she'd learned. "Is that what happened, Nell?" she muttered out loud. Maybe after Silas had shoved her and Nell hit her head, she hadn't died. Maybe Silas had decided to finish the job. Maybe he'd pressed a pillow over her face until she had finally stopped breathing.

But she had talked to Silas on two separate occasions and she simply wasn't convinced the man could willfully murder anyone.

Kate stared at the computer screen, her fingers tapping lightly on the keys. *What if Silas only thought Nell was dead?* He was frightened. It was obvious he had run away in terror. *What if someone came along a few minutes later, saw Nell lying there injured, realized Silas would take the blame, and killed her?*

It was possible. Not probable, but then nothing about this entire bizarre affair had been anything but wild conjecture from the start. Since that was the case, she might as well forge ahead as she had before.

Assuming someone had killed Nell by suffocating her with a pillow, thereby breaking her nose, then the dining room wasn't the scene of an accident, it was the scene of a murder. The entire house was a crime scene.

Kate resisted a shudder. She thought about the wonderful old house she had come to love. The place had been repainted before she moved in, but the lovely antique sideboard in the dining room had only been cleaned and protected with a coating of lemon oil. The carpet had been pulled up and the floors refinished, but a number of Nell's antiques remained.

Including the pillows on the sofa.

The shudder surfaced full-force. Kate shook her head. There was no way it could possibly be that simple. No way Nell's murderer — if there was such a person — could have simply picked up one of the pillows on the sofa and pressed it over a severely injured Nell's face.

She turned back to the computer screen, read on down the page.

Mechanical asphyxia is often marked by the appearance of petechial hemorrhages in the eye, but such a finding is not specific to the condition, and may be caused in a number of other ways.

A petechial hemorrhage was broken blood vessels in the eye and though suffocation often caused it, apparently an injury to the head could also be the cause. There was no mention of such a hemorrhage in Nell's case, but even if it had happened, it wouldn't have been reason enough for the officer or mortician to suspect any sort of foul play.

It might, however, help substantiate the actual cause of death, should other factors arise. Still thinking of the pillows, Kate made her way downstairs.

There were three throw pillows on the sofa, little fringed affairs that Nell had sewn in petit point and Kate couldn't bear to throw away. She had never noticed anything unusual about them, no spots or stains that she could recall. She picked up the first one and examined it closely. Nothing. At least nothing she could see.

A search of the second pillow proved equally fruitless. The third appeared clean as well, except for a tiny, rust-colored smudge near a corner in the back.

It was probably nothing. The pillows were old. The slight discoloration could be anything.

Still, there had been a lot of blood on the floor that day, from the injury to the back of Nell's head. If the killer had used the pillow to end Nell's life and hadn't noticed the single smear of blood, he might have returned it to its place on the sofa.

Hurrying back up the stairs, she sat down once more at the computer. Backing up several pages, she punched up a section of the website that talked about blood detection and skimmed the page.

Blood spatters can help a great deal in recon-

structing a crime scene. Drops falling from a low height, for example, will leave a small cohesive circle. At greater heights, the circle will be larger. Blood hitting a surface at an angle will bulge in one direction, indicating the travel of the droplet.

Interesting, but not what she was looking for. She knew it was here, somewhere. If not on the Internet, then maybe in one of the books she had purchased. She searched the Net a little longer, then reached for the stack of books, digging through one after another, flipping open to the pages she had marked with yellow stickers.

Yes! There it was, in *The Casebook of Forensic Detection.* She reread the section on blood and the word she'd been searching for jumped out at her.

Luminol.

A very useful test for searching large areas for blood, it said, *especially if the area has been cleaned up. Invisible bloodstains react with the Luminol by luminescing. Darkness is essential.*

Kate whirled back to the computer, punched in the key word, *Luminol,* and there it was. *Luminol-16 Invisible Blood Reagent with Spray Head.* She clicked on price, ordered a bottle, typed in her credit card number, paid extra for two-day shipping, and the stuff was on its way.

Kate leaned back in her chair with a grin. City girl she might be, but there were definitely some advantages to having lived in the fast lane. She would test the pillow — and everything else in the dining room — as soon as the Luminol arrived. If the spot on the pillow turned out to be blood, she was going to go to the sheriff, find out if the blood was Nell's.

If it was, she was going to ask him to exhume the body.

She could image what smiling Barney Conrad would have to say about that.

Saturday night came and went. Kate was supposed to go to the dance at the Antlers with Ned Cummings, but she just couldn't bring herself to go. Ned was an attractive man and she liked him. She had accepted the date in the hope that going out with him might help her forget about Chance.

She was tired of remembering, thinking of Chance and wishing things could be different. She had known from the start an affair with him would probably end in disaster. She had to accept that he belonged to someone else and get on with her life.

Going out with Ned Cummings should have been a start. Ned was a big, warm, teddy bear of a man, jovial and fun-loving. Unfortunately, Kate felt not the least attraction to him. He was kind and considerate, but every time he walked into the cafe in his cowboy hat, she thought of Chance and her heart squeezed painfully.

In the end, she came up with the old standby

headache excuse, cancelled her date, and stayed home.

One Wednesday, the Luminol arrived UPS. Kate carefully read the directions on the spray bottle. As soon as it was dark, she went into the dining room and set to work.

Chance heard Hannah's voice ringing across the back yard all the way to the stables. She hung out the back door, an apron tied around her considerable girth, a dishrag clutched in one plump hand. "Sheriff's on the phone! He says it's important!"

The sheriff. A fist of anxiety tightened in Chance's stomach. "I'll pick up in the barn!" he called back, walking rapidly in that direction and grabbing the receiver off the wall.

"It's Chance, Barney. What's up?"

"Kate Rollins came to see me today."

"She's all right, isn't she? I mean nothing's happened to her?" He could feel his heart, pounding hard against his ribs.

"Well now, that all depends on your definition. If you mean is she physically all right, then yes. Mentally, I'm not so sure."

"What's that supposed to mean?"

"It means she was in here spouting a bunch of nonsense about Nell Hart's death. She says the old lady might not have died in the fall — she might have been suffocated by somebody afterward. Apparently she went to see the undertaker, found out the old woman had a broken nose. I guess she found a pillow with some blood on it. She wants me to test it, see if it matches Nell's blood type."

Chance mulled that over, thinking how right Kate had been so far. "Maybe that's not such a bad idea."

"Yeah, well, if the blood type matches, she wants me to exhume the body. I'm not about to do that — not under any circumstances."

"Why not?"

"Because we already know how Nell died. Silas Marshall's confessed to killing her."

"Maybe he didn't do it. Maybe he just thought she was dead."

"And maybe it was an accident, just like he said."

"I realize Kate's theory might not be the easiest to swallow, but it just might be true."

"Forget it."

"I don't suppose your refusal has anything to do with this being an election year? If it turns out Nell's death was murder, not manslaughter, it might make the department look bad. Like maybe they should have been more careful."

"I'm telling you, Chance. This is not going to happen. You need to talk some sense into that woman, make her understand. The old lady is dead and buried. Silas will probably get a suspended sentence and that'll be the end of it. She'll listen to you. Convince her to let the matter drop."

Chance swore softly. As sheriff of Silver Fox

County, Barney Conrad wielded a lot of influence. It wasn't smart to get on his bad side. On the other hand, murder wasn't a matter the man should ignore. "Do me a favor. Run the blood test. Let me know how it comes out. In the meantime, I'll talk to Kate."

"All right, I'll go that far."

Barney signed off and Chance hung up the phone. Kate had promised to call him if anything came up. Obviously, she didn't consider going to see the sheriff important enough to bother. Or she simply didn't want to talk to him.

He couldn't really blame her.

On the other hand, she was getting into this mess deeper and deeper. One way or another it was going to lead to trouble.

In the morning he would talk to her. Like Barney said, maybe he could convince her to let the matter drop.

He told himself it wasn't just a convenient excuse to see her. Chance hoped to hell he was right.

They were busy at the ranch, getting ready for the fall roundup, collecting the remuda, putting the corrals in shape for the branding. To make matters worse, three days ago one of the outbuildings near the barn had been set on fire. Orange spray paint on the ground in front of it warned, WE NEED JOBS. STAY OUT OF MINING AFFAIRS.

Fortunately the fire hadn't caused much damage, but the point had certainly been made. It wasn't just Consolidated Metals who wanted that mine to go in. There were people who needed the jobs the mine could offer.

Damn, he knew the hardship miners faced in trying to support their families, but the fact remained — the environment was more important. Once the land and streams were gone, there wouldn't be any more. The destruction had to stop.

By the time Chance left the ranch and made the drive to the cafe, it was late afternoon, the roads muddy and slick from two days of non-stop rain. As he passed the driveway leading up to Kate's house, his foot hit the brakes.

A sheriff's car sat out in front. Chance shoved the pickup in reverse, backed up, and turned down the gravel lane.

By the time he got out of the truck, his pulse was hammering away. He leapt a couple of mud puddles, took the porch stairs two at a time, and pounded on the door.

David pulled it open. "Chance! Boy, I'm glad to see you. Mom had an accident."

"An accident?" With a hand on David's shoulder, he urged the boy into the living room and saw Kate lying on the sofa, a bandage wrapped around her head. A trace of red seeped through, and worry hit him like a fist in the stomach.

"What the hell happened?"

Kate smiled weakly. "My brakes went out. The road was slick and I slid into a ditch."

Standing a few feet away, notepad in hand, Deputy Winston turned to face him, the officer who had come out to the house before. "She's got a mild concussion and a gash on the side of her head that took half a dozen stitches, but it could have been a lot worse. The road's real steep right through there. She could have slid off down the side of the mountain. Fortunately, she was wearing her seatbelt or likely she would have gone through the windshield."

Chance peeled off his sheepskin coat, took off his hat and tossed them over the back of a chair. Sitting carefully down next to Kate, he reached out and took hold of her hand. It felt small and soft in his, and colder than it should have been. He wanted to press it against his cheek, but settled for warming it between his palms. "Where were you going when this happened?"

"Up to Ronan. I needed a load of groceries. I thought I'd pick David up at school and take him along to help me. I never got that far."

"And the brakes just suddenly failed? That seems odd for such a new car."

"Unfortunately, that's what happened. I pushed on the pedal. Nothing. Even the parking brake wouldn't work." She gave him a halfhearted smile. "I needed a new car anyway, something good for driving in snow. I guess it's time I started looking around."

"Where's the car now?"

Deputy Winston answered. "They towed it to Trumper's Auto in Ronan."

Chance squeezed Kate's hand. "Can I get you something? A glass of water or maybe a cup of tea?"

"Tea would be great, if you wouldn't mind going to that much trouble."

"No trouble. I'll be right back." He went in and put the teakettle on, grateful for a chance to use the phone. Dialing information for Trumper's Auto, he jotted down the number and punched it in.

"Trumper's Auto, Pete Trumper here."

"You've got a car there, just towed in, a white Lexus, maybe a year or two old, belongs to Kaitlin Rollins."

"Yeah, what about it?"

"I'm a friend of Kate's. Chance McLain."

"You the guy with the silver Dodge?"

"Yeah."

"I know who you are. You had your truck in for service not long ago."

"That's right. Have you had a chance to look at the Lexus yet?"

"Sure have. Funny thing, that."

"What do you mean?"

"Looks to me like those brake lines were cut."

Dread moved down Chance's spine. "I was afraid you were going to say that."

"I gotta call the sheriff about it. I'm sure he'll want to know."

"I'm sure he will." But Barney wouldn't be happy about it, and neither was he. "Thanks, Pete."

He signed off the phone, wondering if the brakes had been cut because of Kate's work on the campaign, or if it might have something to do with Nell Hart's death.

He returned to the living room and set the mug of tea down on the coffee table in front of her. Deputy Winston had already gone.

"Good thing I had my cell phone," Kate said. "Out here, those things are worth their weight in gold."

"You can say that again."

David came over and sat on the chair beside her. "Are you feeling better, Mom?"

Kate smiled at him softly. "A lot better. I'll be fine by tomorrow."

Chance draped an arm around David's shoulder. "Come on, Davy. Let's let your mom rest a minute while we get something to drink." He had missed seeing the boy. He couldn't help wondering what Kate had told him about why he no longer came around.

They went into the kitchen. David popped open a can of Coke and Chance made himself a cup of instant coffee.

"I want you to keep an eye on your mom," he said as they sat down at the kitchen table. "Make sure she gets completely well before she tries to go back to work."

"I will."

"Good boy. It's been a while since I've seen you. I was thinking . . . you ever been to a roundup?"

David shook his head.

"We do it every spring and fall. This time of year, we'll be branding the calves we missed earlier, and cutting the yearlings out for sale. Chris and his dad will be working. I thought maybe you might like to work, too."

David grinned, obviously pleased. "That'd be great, Chance."

"In the meantime, why don't you and Chris come over some weekend? You can borrow a couple of horses and we'll go fishing like we did before."

David nodded. He looked like there was something he wanted to say, and Chance was afraid he knew what it was.

"Go on, boy, spit it out."

"I was wondering about what happened between you and my mom. Mom says you're getting married to Mr. Fontaine's daughter. I thought you liked my mom."

"I do like her, Davy. I like her a lot. Your mom and I are friends, just like you and me. Nothing's ever gonna change that."

"I was kind of hoping . . . maybe you could be more than just friends."

Chance's chest squeezed hard. "I guess, for a while, I kinda let myself hope that, too. Sometimes things don't work out the way we want them to."

"Yeah, I guess so."

Chance finished his coffee; David finished his Coke, and they went back into the living room to check on Kate.

"You still working at the grocery store?" Chance asked David.

"Yeah. I'm supposed to be working a couple of hours today, but —"

"Why don't you go ahead and go? I'll sit with your mother till you get back."

David glanced at Kate, whose eyes were about half closed. "Mom?"

She slowly opened them and her gaze swung to Chance's. "You don't need to stay. I'll be fine for a couple of hours."

"Go on, Davy. There's a couple of things I need to talk to your mom about. I'll be here when you get home."

"Thanks, Chance." He headed upstairs to get his jacket, came back down a few minutes later, and pulled open the front door. "I'll be home as soon as I can." Then he was gone.

"Myra working this afternoon?" Chance asked once the boy was gone.

"Uh-huh," she answered groggily."

"What did the doctor say about you staying here alone?"

Her eyes cracked open. "I'm not alone. You're here and David will back in a couple of hours."

His mouth edged up. He was there, but he didn't think Kate was all that pleased about it.

He started to say something else but the phone rang, cutting off his words.

Kate's eyes slowly closed. "Would you mind?"

Chance strode into the entry and picked up the phone that was sitting on a marble-topped table. "Rollins residence."

A man's voice replied. "Who the hell are you?"

He ignored a shot of irritation. "My name's McLain. I'm a friend of Kate's."

"I'll just bet you are."

"You want to tell me who this is before I hang up the phone?"

"Just tell Kate I hope she's happy now. Tell her someday she's gonna regret it." The phone clicked in his ear. Chance hung up the receiver, wondering at Kate's obnoxious caller, and walked back into the living room.

"Who was it?"

"I don't know. Said he hoped you were happy now. Said to tell you someday you'd regret it."

Her pretty lips curved up. He could remember the way they melted under his and desire slid into his groin.

"That was Tommy," she said. "My divorce is final today."

He should have been happy for her and in a way he was. He forced himself to smile. "Congratulations."

Kate's smile deepened. "I can't tell you how good it feels."

From his single brief conversation with her ex, he could pretty well guess. "Does he ever talk to David?"

"Once in a great while. David is supposed to go down to LA for Thanksgiving. A few months back, he would have been looking forward to it. I don't think he is any more."

"Every boy needs a father. In time, you'll find someone —"

"Don't, Chance, please." Her glance slid away to the back of the sofa. "Can't we talk about something besides the men in my life?"

She was right. What he was going to say was bullshit anyway. He didn't want her to find someone else. He wanted her to belong to him. He wanted to hold her, protect her, make love to her. He couldn't help wondering how her date had gone with Ned Cummings and if she planned to see him again. He knew better than to ask.

"Actually, there is something I need to talk to you about. It's one of the reasons I wanted to stay."

Her gaze swung back to his. "What is it?"

"Your brakes didn't just go out, Kate. I talked to the man at Trumper's Auto. Someone cut them."

"Oh my God." She tried to sit up, a soft moan escaped, and Chance eased her back down.

"Take it easy. You've got a concussion, remember?"

"If I didn't, I do now." She settled back against the pillow and Chance replaced the damp cloth over her forehead.

"The auto repair guy is going to call the sheriff. I'm gonna call him, too. Whoever did this is serious, Kate."

"Do you think they did it because I'm still working on the campaign?"

"I don't know. Three nights ago, someone burned one of my outbuildings. There are people who want that mine to go in. Whether they'd be willing to kill to accomplish the job, I don't know."

"There's another possibility, Chance."

He sat there stiffly. "I know. Barney Conrad called me."

A sigh slowly seeped past her lips. "It was awful, Chance. I used this stuff I found on the Internet. It's called Luminol. You can't see the blood unless it's good and dark, but when I sprayed it in the dining room, I could see splotches of it on the sideboard and down in the crack beneath the baseboard. I found it on the back of one of the sofa pillows."

She went on to tell him how she had read a murder case where a woman was suffocated with a pillow and how her nose had been broken.

"I'm convinced that's what happened to Nell. She didn't die when she fell. Someone came along and murdered her afterward."

"Then you don't think Silas did it."

"No, I don't. The man simply hasn't got it in him."

"I don't think so, either."

"We need more evidence. We have to find out who the real murderer is."

Chance sat down on the edge of the chair beside the sofa. "It isn't worth it, Kate. Someone tried to rape you. Today you could have been killed. If you keep digging —"

"The two things may not be related."

"True, but there's no way to know for sure. The first thing you have to do is resign from the committee."

She hesitated longer than he would have liked. "All right," she finally agreed. "I'll make a public announcement as soon as I can arrange it. We've got things well underway. You and Ed can keep the campaign rolling. At this point, whether I'm involved or not won't make much difference."

"And what if you're right about Nell? What if someone murdered her, just the way you said. That man wouldn't have the slightest qualms about killing you, too."

Her face paled to an even whiter shade than it was already.

"Let this drop, Kate. If you won't think of yourself, think of your son. He doesn't have much of a father. What the hell would he do if he wound up losing his mother, too?"

Kate closed her eyes and the air seemed to sigh from her lungs. "I guess I never thought of it that way."

"Well, it's damn well time you started."

She swallowed. Beneath her thick dark lashes, he could see the faint glitter of tears. "You're right. I have to think of David. I'm sure even Nell would want that."

He reached over and took her hand, wrapping it in both of his. "I know she would. Your grandmother wouldn't want anything to happen to either one of you because of her."

And neither would he, Chance thought, more worried than ever. There very well might be a killer loose in Lost Peak. Kate wouldn't be safe until someone discovered who it was. It was too dangerous for her to keep searching, but there was nothing stopping Chance.

He squeezed her hand, wishing he could lean down and kiss her, knowing that time was past.

He was determined to do whatever he had to in order to keep her safe.

Chapter Twenty-five

The phone rang in the family room. Ed Fontaine wheeled himself over to where it rested on an antique William and Mary table and picked up the receiver.

"Ed Fontaine."

"Hi, Daddy."

He brightened at the sound of Rachael's voice. "Hi, little girl. How are things going in the big city? You 'bout ready to hightail it back home? I thought you'd be here by now."

"That's what I called about, Daddy. Everything's taking longer than I expected. On top of that, yesterday I got a call from the Ford Agency. They want me for a *Vogue* cover. It's a big shoot, Daddy, very prestigious and the money's great. It would only take a couple more weeks and I'd really like to do it."

Ed frowned. "Have you talked to Chance about it?"

"I'm going to. I wanted to talk to you first. And I've also been thinking that as long as I'm here in New York, I ought to go ahead and pick out my wedding dress. I certainly won't find anything suitable in Montana. I was thinking maybe Fendi or Dior. What do you think?"

"You know I don't know squat about women's clothes. You just pick out whatever you want and have them send me the bill."

He could almost see her beautiful face smiling into the receiver. "Thank you, Daddy. You're the sweetest man on earth."

He grumbled, always a little embarrassed when she said things like that. "Chance isn't gonna be happy about this, you know. He expects you to start acting like a woman with marriage and family on her mind, instead of a career."

"I know. It'll just be this one last time, I promise. Then I'll be there to help. Which reminds me, I called Vincent St. Claire in Seattle. I got his name from André Duvallier. The weddings André does are simply the most scrumptious, most spectacular in New York. André won't come all the way to Montana, but he says M'sieur St. Claire will be happy to do it. He'll take care of everything, Daddy, and it'll turn out just perfect . . . if that's all right with you."

"You know it is. I just want my little girl to be happy."

"All right, then. I'll call Chance and tell him I'll be there a little later than we planned. I'm sure he'll understand."

But Ed wasn't so sure. Chance expected Rachael to settle down and start thinking about having a couple of kids. Dammit, so did he.

"You best not wait too long, little girl, if you want that man of yours to be waitin' when you get here."

Rachael just laughed. "Chance's been waiting

for me for years. I don't imagine another few weeks will make any difference."

Maybe it wouldn't. Still, Ed didn't want to take any chances. He mentally smiled at the pun. "You just get that job done, buy that dress, and get yourself back home."

"I will, Daddy. I love you."

"I love you, too, little girl."

They hung up and Ed realized the tapping he could hear was the unconscious drumming of his fingers on the arm of the chair. There was nothing to worry about, he told himself. Once Rachael got back, everything would work out just the way they'd planned. All she needed was a man who could handle her, and he had no doubt that Chance could do that. The boy was a wonder when it came to women.

Ed rolled himself back into position in front of the TV. A game show was on and he liked to play at answering the questions. There was no need to worry, he repeated. All he had to do was leave things to Chance. Chance could handle just about anything.

Even his beautiful, self-indulgent daughter.

The first thing Monday morning, Chance pulled up in front of the Silver County Courthouse on his way to the sheriff's office. A thick gray mist hung over the Mission Mountains and lay like a blanket in the Flathead Valley, and the drive up to Polson had been slow.

He had called ahead and Barney was expecting him, but the sheriff hadn't arrived at the office just yet. The secretary, a woman named Barbara Murdock he had seen a couple of times before, poured him a cup of coffee while he waited.

"He called in just a minute ago," Barbara reassured him. "Said to tell you he's on his way." She was pretty, a woman in her late twenties — and single, Barney had told him — with thick black hair, pale skin, and a trim, sexy figure. Funny, six months ago, he would have asked her out, been looking forward to the challenge of maybe taking her to bed.

Now he looked at her and saw an attractive, desirable woman, but the thought of making love to her held none of the usual appeal. There was only one woman he wanted in his bed. Kate Rollins had brains and grit, and the sweetest little body he'd ever seen.

Unfortunately, making love to Kate was out of the question.

Chance glanced up, realized Barbara had been talking, smiling at him sweetly, and he hadn't heard a single word she'd said. "I'm sorry, I guess my mind was somewhere else." Yeah, like making love to Kate. "What did you say?" He could feel the heat of embarrassment burning at the back of his neck.

"I said the sheriff came in through the back. He's ready to see you now."

"Thanks." He walked past Barbara into Barney's private office and closed the door.

"I figured you'd show up here, sooner or later," Barney said from behind his desk.

Chance sat down in a chair across from him. "Did Pete Trumper call you?"

"Yes, unfortunately, he did."

"What do you think?"

"Someone probably wanted to scare her off the anti-mining campaign."

"Well, it worked. Kate's making the announcement today on KGET-TV. She's going to say that pressing business matters have forced her resignation. The coalition will now be run by executive committee."

"Smart move. Doesn't give them any real target. Maybe things will cool down a little."

"And maybe they won't. If Kate's right about Nell Hart being murdered, someone might have cut her brake lines to keep her quiet."

"It's possible, I suppose."

"Maybe someone's been watching her house. They could have followed her the day she came to see you. Speaking of which, how did that blood sample she brought you turn out?"

"O-negative. Same type as Nell's."

"And not very common at that."

"That blood could have splattered onto the pillow when Nell fell and hit her head."

"Kate said it wasn't a spot, more of a smudge, and it was on the back. The pillow would most likely have been sitting faceup on the sofa."

Barney tossed the pen he'd been holding

down on his desk. "Dammit, Chance, what do you want me to do?"

"Exhume the body. If Nell was murdered, maybe you can find some DNA evidence or something. Maybe it'll help prove who it was."

"And maybe this is all a load of crap."

"Maybe. But until we find out for sure, Kate and her son could be in danger."

Barney still seemed uncertain. "I'll give it some thought. If we do exhume, maybe I can make it sound like the sheriff's department is willing to go the extra mile to solve a possible murder and protect its citizens."

Leave it to Barney to find a political advantage.

"On the other hand," he said. "Silver County is far from rich. If I go to the expense of digging up that old woman's body and we don't find anything, the taxpayers are going to have a fit."

"I don't care what the taxpayers say and neither should you." Chance just wanted to find a way to protect David and Kate. Those brake lines could have broken just as easily when David was in the car. It was a miracle neither of them had been seriously injured or even killed. "I want to find out if Nell Hart was murdered."

"Like I said, I'll give it some thought."

Chance silently cursed. "In the meantime, how about assigning a deputy to look after Kate?"

Barney picked up his pen and began to tap it

on the top of his desk. "I can't do that. We don't have that many extra men. I'll put an extra car in the area. That's the best I can do."

Chance sighed, accepting what he had already figured the sheriff would say. "Keep me posted, will you, Barney?"

"Of course."

Chance just nodded. If he did exhume the body, Barney would expect a major contribution to his reelection campaign.

It would be money well spent if what he found helped put an end to the threat against Kate.

"You seen the news?" Duke Mullens sauntered into Lon Barton's Beavertail office a little after the five o'clock shift change. "Kate Rollins resigned from the anti-mining campaign."

"I saw it."

"Looks like your troubles are over. She's quit the coalition and holed up like a scared rabbit. I told you I'd take care of things, just like I always do."

Lon walked over to the small refrigerator beneath his built-in bar, opened the door, and dragged out a can of beer. "You could have killed her with that broken brake line stunt."

Mullens just shrugged. "Well, I didn't, did I?"

Lon popped the top on his beer. "You want a Bud?"

Mullens straightened up his big body as it

411

leaned against the door. "Sounds good to me."

Lon tossed him a can, walked back over to his desk. "Kate's off the campaign, but I heard she's still nosing around, trying to prove Nell Hart was murdered. If she proves it wasn't an accident, that Silas Marshall killed her with calculated premeditation, the court might just set aside the deal he made with us."

"What do you mean? They can't do that — can they?"

"They might. If Kate could prove Silas directly benefited by causing his partner's death. If that happened, Kate Rollins, being Nell's sole heir, could end up owning that well, and we'd be right back where we started."

"What about the money you paid?"

"Silas would have to pay it back. The court would probably award us a judgement, but that is hardly what we want."

Mullens took several swallows of beer, his neck muscles working up and down. He wiped the foam from his mouth with the back of a big, weathered hand. "That woman's a royal pain in the ass."

"True, though from what I've seen, she has a rather nice one."

Mullens grinned. "Maybe I should deliver another message, give her a little taste of what she almost got the first time. I bet that'd convince her to quit snooping into other people's business."

"Let's give it a little time, see how it all shakes out."

"I think we ought to take care of her now, before this goes any farther."

"You're awfully eager, Duke. Any particular reason?"

Duke upended his beer, drained the contents, and tossed the empty can in the trashcan, a good six feet away. "Maybe I just wanna even the score with McLain. He might be marrying Rachael Fontaine, but he's still got the hots for the redhead. Nothing I'd like better than to plow that fertile field, show Kate Rollins what it's like to be humped by a real man."

Lon stiffened. When he spoke, his voice rang with authority. "I said we're going to wait. You go near Kate Rollins right now, the sheriff'll be all over you. You get caught, he'll be thinking you have something to do with Nell Hart's murder."

Mullens grumbled a dirty word Lon couldn't quite hear. "Whatever you say, boss."

Lon nodded, satisfied Duke would do whatever he was told. "Why don't you have another beer?" Without waiting for a response, he returned to the fridge, took out another Bud, and tossed it to Mullens.

"Thanks," Duke replied a bit sullenly. There was something in his eyes Lon didn't like, but for now he would ignore it. Duke might be a little hard to control, but pit bulls had their uses.

Lon watched as Duke polished off his second beer in a matter of seconds. If things heated up any more than they were already, he might need his prize bulldog again.

The heavy white layers of cloud that had hovered over the mountains all day settled thickly around the ranch house, encompassing the log structure in a damp, misty fog. Sitting at his desk, a fire crackling in the stone fireplace in the corner, Chance pressed the telephone receiver against his ear.

"I don't like it, Rachael. You said you'd be back home by now."

"I know, Chance, but a couple of things have come up." She told him about some fancy modeling job she'd been offered, said how important it was, and that it would give her the time she needed to pick out a wedding dress.

"As soon as I'm done, I'll be back. Please say yes, Chance, just this one more time."

Just this one more time. Chance had a feeling his life would be nothing but a series of *just one more times.* "Your daddy spoiled you something fierce, Rachael."

"I know."

He sighed. Ed should have put her over his knee years ago. Chance wondered if he would be able to resist the temptation, once they were married.

"All right, go ahead. We both know you would, anyway."

"Oh, thank you, Chance." She made kissing

sounds into the receiver. "Love you. See you soon."

Chance said goodbye and hung up the phone, disgusted, irritated — and wildly relieved. Dammit, he wasn't supposed to feel that way. He was marrying Rachael. Now that he'd made up his mind, he wanted to get it over and done with. He cared for Rachael, more than cared. He had known her for years, had always been attracted to her, at least he had been until he'd met Kate. There was a time he'd wanted desperately to marry her.

Things will fall into place, once she's my wife, he told himself again.

He wished to hell they could simply elope, go off somewhere and make it official. Instead, he would have to wait, to hear that little voice inside his head whispering, *Maybe you won't have to go through with it. Maybe you'll find some other way.*

There was no other way. Not for him. He was marrying Rachael and he intended to do everything in his power to make her happy. Once they were together, he would stop thinking about Kate.

Maybe he would even stop worrying about her.

Chance sighed. That wasn't going to happen anytime soon. At least not until he could be sure she and David were safe. The sooner Nell's body was exhumed and the problem resting securely in the sheriff's hands, the better for all of them.

He needed to speak to Kate, see how she was feeling, and if the sheriff had brought the papers she would need to sign to exhume the body. He hoped to hell he had. And he hoped, for her sake, the mystery she had been trying so hard to solve would come to an end very soon.

Harold "Chief" Ironstone slowly turned his head, searching the shadows of the deep pine forest, listening for the sound of human voices, hearing nothing but the sweet whisper of the wind sighing through the trees, the occasional cry of the white-tailed hawk that circled above his head.

Moving silently forward, he paused at the fence line that stretched along the mountain, disappeared into a ravine, then came up on the opposite side. He scanned the hillsides once more, but saw no one. Jamming his rubber-soled hiking boot on the lowest strand of barbed wire, he grabbed hold of another strand, and stretched the two as far apart as he could. He grunted as he bent and eased his stooped shoulders between them, careful not to release the wires until he was completely in the clear.

As a boy, there had been no fences here, nothing but mountains that climbed straight up to the sky and forests so thick and dark a man could disappear in them forever. The ground wore a carpet of moss and lichen, the earth, spongy beneath his feet, smelled of pine needles and musky decaying wood, a pleasant odor that filled his nostrils and beckoned him deeper into the forest.

Today he smelled something new. As he neared the banks of a narrow stream, he could see the bodies of a dozen dead fish, beautiful rainbow trout whose flashing silver bodies had faded to a dull pewter gray.

A few feet away, a dead raccoon lay on its side, its limbs stiff and twisted, the once-soft fur now coated by a layer of reddish, muddy earth.

Harold slung his canvas back pack down on the ground beneath a bush and pulled out the small Kodak camera he had purchased at the mercantile, a cheap one that only cost fifteen dollars and ninety-nine cents.

He had asked Jeremy Spotted Horse to lend him one, but as soon as Jeremy found out what he planned to do with it, he'd refused. It didn't matter. This one would take good enough pictures to accomplish what needed to be done.

He took several shots of the stream, then started up the hill, making his way farther onto Consolidated Metals property. The Beavertail Mine sat on the knoll up ahead. Off to one side and slightly below the main building, the tail pond sprawled in deadly proximity to the little trickling stream that fed into Beaver Creek. The only thing preventing the pond's lethal seepage was a thin plastic liner at the bottom.

Harold swore a white man's curse, the thought like bile in his mouth. Leaning over, he spat on the ground at his feet. Did no one care what happened to the land? Did no one care about the animals, the birds, or the fish?

But he knew that there were people who did care. More every day. They were beginning to see, beginning to understand all that they would lose if they continued to destroy the beauty around them.

Harold kept walking, making silent progress toward his destination. He moved among the shadows of the forest, skirting the tail pond, keeping himself out of sight.

As he drew closer, he began to hear the hum of engines, the faint sound of voices, men working at the mine. The days were growing shorter and soon the sun would drop out of sight behind the hills. He would have to hurry, make his move when the men changed shifts. Harold just hoped there would be enough light left to get a clear picture of the leaks in the pond.

Hidden in the depths of the forest, he waited as the minutes crept past. He wasn't in a hurry. He enjoyed being there in the woods, watching the way the wind moved a single blade of grass, hearing the rat-tat-tat of a woodpecker working to find its supper in the trunk of a heavy-barked tree.

Eventually, the hum of machinery slowed, marking the end of the shift. Harold waited patiently for the men to file out to their cars and drive away while others arrived to take their places. In the orderly chaos of car engines starting and doors being opened and closed, he quietly moved toward the tail pond.

Here and there, he could see fresh rips in the plastic, see contaminated water oozing sluggishly into the ground. Worried about the light, he took photos of the leaks as quickly as he could, and several photos showing the pond in proximity to the narrow little stream.

He finished the first roll of film, returned to the bush and stuck it into his backpack, loaded another roll, and returned to the pond. A few more shots and he would leave. In a couple more minutes, the light would be gone and it would be so dark it wouldn't matter.

His flash went off. Just one more shot of the stuff oozing out between those two rocks near the stream and he could disappear back into the forest. He lifted the camera, pressed it against his eye, then pain shot into his stomach and the breath burst out of his lungs. As he doubled over fighting for air, someone wrenched the camera away from his numb, shaking fingers. He saw it crash against a rock, shattering the lens, mangling the gray plastic casing. It slipped beneath the water of the gently meandering stream.

Ignoring the pain and the trembling in his limbs, Harold straightened, turned to face three of Consolidated's men.

"You're trespassing on mine property, old man." One of them, a bulky miner with thick shoulders and a dark red beard, poked a finger into his chest. "You know what happens to trespassers?"

Harold didn't answer. He wasn't sure but whatever it was, it wasn't good.

"Go get Mullens," the miner ordered, and the second man, the youngest of the group, turned and raced away.

The third man jerked him around by the shoulder. "You heard what Joe said. You're trespassin'. We don't cotton to trespassers 'round here."

Hauling back a fist, the man threw a punch that must have broken a bone in his face and slammed him into the dirt. Pain rolled over him in waves. Through a blinding haze, he saw that the man was tall and gaunt, grinning beneath a bright green John Deere baseball cap. His hands still balled into fists, he grabbed the front of Harold's jacket, hauled him to his feet, and hit him again.

"You need a lesson, Indian," the bearded man said.

"Yeah — we're gonna teach you it doesn't pay to stick your nose into other people's business."

Harold tried to climb to his feet, but his legs felt rubbery and refused to do what he told them. The gaunt man kicked him in the ribs. He heard a snapping sound, and the searing pain that screamed through his body nearly knocked him out. The bearded man dragged him up and punched him again. He could feel the blood running down the back of his throat and a knifing agony that spread outward through his chest and down his legs.

The taller man laughed, dragged him upright, and hit him again. He heard the sound of boots, shuffling through the forest as the second man returned, bringing a fourth. He recognized the sound of Duke Mullens's laughter.

The toe of Mullens's heavy boot slamming into his stomach was the last thing he remembered.

Chapter Twenty-six

David sat next to Chris Spotted Horse on a rock in the clearing next to Little Sandy Creek. They were waiting for Chief, fishing in the spot he had shown them, one of his favorites. Waiting and waiting, but Chief didn't come.

"Do you think he forgot?" Chris asked, having just returned from fishing a little way upstream.

"I don't think so. We talked about it yesterday after school." He looked up at Chris, an awful thought striking. "You don't suppose something's happened to him, do you? When we talked, he said he was going to take some pictures up at the Beavertail Mine. He said the tail pond was leaking arsenic into the little feeder stream that ran into Beaver Creek."

Chris's dark skin looked suddenly pale. "My dad told him not to go. Chief wanted to borrow a camera but my dad wouldn't loan it to him. He said it was too dangerous. He said he'd have to sneak onto Consolidated property and if they caught him, there would be hell to pay."

For all of two seconds, David stood immobile, his hand wrapped tightly around the fly fishing rod, a brand-new Orvis he had just purchased with the money he had earned over the summer. "We gotta tell someone. We gotta do something. I got a real bad feeling about this."

"Me, too," Chris said, and both of them bolted toward the trail that ran along Little Sandy Creek. They didn't slow down till they reached the clearing where David's house sat on the gently rising knoll above the cafe.

"Come on. My mom's working today. She'll know what to do."

They made their way down the hill and burst through the back door into the kitchen of the cafe.

"Well, for heaven's sake." Myra jumped out of the way, spatula in hand. "Where's the fire, you two?"

"Chief's missing," David panted, trying to catch his breath. "He was supposed to meet us up at the fishing hole, but he never showed up. Where's Mom?"

"I'm right here." She smiled as she set down a tray of dirty dishes. "Are you sure Chief didn't just forget?"

David told her the story, Chris chiming in about Chief wanting to borrow a camera from his dad.

"I know something's happened, Mom. We've got to go find him."

Kate looked down at her son, unconsciously biting her lip. Chief had never once disappointed the boys. His word was as reliable as the sun coming up. If he said he would be there, he would be there — unless he wasn't physically able.

She glanced up at the clock, saw it was nearly ten A.M., and untied the apron she wore over her jeans. "Call Bonnie," she said to Myra. "Ask her to work the lunch shift."

"You ain't plannin' to go off lookin' for Chief by yourself?"

Kate paused. "I thought I'd call Jeremy, see if he would go with me."

"I think we ought to call Chance," David said, and Kate's stomach instantly knotted. "He's got horses. We might need to borrow them. There's lots of mountains and forest up there."

"I don't think that's a very good —"

"David's right," Myra agreed. "With Chance and Jeremy's help, you might just be able to find him. And Jeremy would probably call him anyway."

The knot in her stomach tightened even more. She didn't want to call Chance. She was doing everything in her power to stay away from him.

"I'll call him," David said before she could argue. "I know his number."

It was only a few minutes later that Chance's big silver Dodge pulled up in front of the cafe. He took off his black felt hat as he strode through the door. His eyes swung to hers, and a sweet, warm frisson rippled up her spine. She hadn't seen him since the day her brakes had failed. Watching him stride toward her, her heart pattering as if she had run a race, she could imagine how hard it was going to be to see him with another woman.

He stopped a few feet in front of her, so tall she had to tip her head back to look into his face. "David told me what happened."

She nodded, tried in vain to pull her gaze away. God it felt good just to look at him. "He thinks Chief may have gone onto Consolidated property."

"If he did, and they happened to see him, he could be in serious trouble."

"That's what I was afraid of. We've got to find him, Chance, but I'm not sure where to start looking."

"I talked to Jeremy. Chief doesn't have a phone, so Jeremy's going to stop by his trailer." Like a number of other Salish, Chief lived in a single-wide trailer on the reservation. "He'll talk to Chief's neighbor, see if he might know something. He ought to be calling any minute."

A few more minutes passed then the phone rang, and Kate picked it up. Hearing the deep, familiar roll of Jeremy's voice, she handed the phone to Chance.

"What'd you turn up?" he asked. She couldn't hear the answer, but Chance frowned. "Okay, so that's it, then. I'll meet you there."

"What is it?" Kate asked worriedly.

"Joe Three Bulls is Chief's closest neighbor on the rez. He says Chief mentioned getting pictures of the tail pond last night and Joe hasn't seen him since."

"Oh no."

"If that's where he went, I know where we can start looking." He reached out and took hold of her shoulders. "Don't worry, Kate. We'll find him. We won't give up until we do." He turned to leave.

"Wait a minute — I'm going with you."

He stopped before he had gone two paces. "No way."

"Chief is my friend," David put in. "Me and Chris are going, too." The boys moved closer, their determination clear.

Chance set his jaw. "You can't go — none of you. We'll have to go onto Consolidated land. That means we'll be trespassing. I don't want any of you involved in something like that."

Kate squared her shoulders. "I said I'm going, Chance, and that's all there is to it."

"Me, too," David said stubbornly.

"If Dad's going, I'm going," said Chris.

Chance sighed. "All right. You can go as far as the fence line. Jeremy is meeting me there. We're going to walk the rest of the way in. If we can't find Chief, we'll have to call the sheriff, round up some men, and go in on horseback. For now, let's just hope we find him."

Kate changed out of the tennis shoes she had been wearing into a pair of Hi-Tec leather and canvas boots she had recently purchased and already fallen in love with. She grabbed her jacket, and they all trooped out to the truck, the boys climbing into the bed behind the cab, Kate climbing into the passenger seat next to Chance.

She hadn't been in the Dodge for weeks, but the familiar smell of gun oil, rope, and leather reminded her instantly of the man sitting beside her. Memories returned: the first time he had kissed her, dancing together at the Antlers, the night they'd made love on Lookout Mountain.

Chance must have been remembering, too. She could feel those piercing blue eyes on her, but when she looked at him, he glanced away. Kate forced the memories to the back of her mind and vowed not to think of them again.

They drove in silence along the road that followed Beaver Creek up into the Mission Mountains, Chance's jaw tight and grim, his hands gripping tightly the steering wheel. At a bend in the road, they turned down a gravel lane that led onto reservation land and soon deteriorated into a rutted dirt track.

Chance shifted into four-wheel drive and kept on going. "This winds its way up to the northern border of Consolidated's property," he told her as the big truck dipped and swayed in the deep, hard-crusted ruts. "If Chief wanted to get to the tail pond without being seen, this is likely the way he would come."

Kate said nothing, just clung precariously to the seat, each bump in the road jarring her teeth. She looked back through the window to be sure the boys were okay and gave up a sigh of relief when the truck finally pulled over to the side of the road, stopping next to Jeremy's battered blue Chevy pickup.

The boys jumped out of the truck bed and Kate used the running board Chance had installed to lever herself to the ground.

Jeremy walked toward them, a black look on his face. "What the devil are they doing here?" he said to Chance, jerking his thumb toward Kate and the boys.

"They were determined to come along. I told them I'd bring them this far, but they'd have to wait here."

Kate ignored the comment, just hauled her jacket out of the truck, slid her arms into the sleeves, and zipped it partway up. "The boys are staying here until we get back. I'm going with you."

"No way," Chance said. "This is tough terrain. You'll stay here with David and Chris."

Kate just smiled. "I walk a million miles a day in that cafe. I'm going with you." Little by little, she was becoming more and more of a mountain person and today she was glad. Ignoring the hard set to the two men's features, she marched toward the barbed-wire fence, propped one of her boots on the bottom wire, spread it open as she had learned to do, and ducked through to the opposite side.

"Coming?" she prodded, flashing them a confident smile. Chance just sighed and started walking toward the fence.

"We'll be back in a couple of hours," Jeremy called to the boys. "Keep an eye out for Chief and stay close to the trucks."

The boys nodded their understanding, and the three of them started climbing up the steep mountain trail leading into the forest.

"The Beavertail Mine is about two miles from here," Chance said. "We'll head in that direction and keep our eyes open along the way. Once we get there, we'll search the area around the tail pond. If we don't see any sign Chief's been there, we'll head back to the trucks, drive down the hill into cell phone range, and get on the horn to the sheriff."

Kate nodded and fell in line between Chance, who led the way, and Jeremy, who followed behind. The going was steep, and a cold, blustery wind swept down through the mountains, whistling eerily through the trees. It was nearly November. At this altitude, it was clear that winter was on its way.

The trail continued, a narrow winding path that penetrated more deeply into the forest. Chance settled into a brisk but bearable pace, probably slower than he would have traveled if Kate hadn't been along, but covering a lot of ground just the same. Kate managed to keep up with less effort than she had expected. Chance looked back a couple of times, seemed satisfied that she was able to stand the pace, and continued up the trail.

She watched his broad back ahead of her, shoulders stretching well beyond his canvas backpack, his lean frame moving with a comfortable stride that could only come from years of living in this beautiful, rugged country.

Her breath came hard by the time the trail leveled off at the top of the hill. Chance stopped for a moment to give them a breather, for which she and Jeremy both seemed grateful. When he turned in her direction, she couldn't miss the warm approval on his face.

"You're making this look far too easy," he teased. "You're supposed to be huffing and puffing by now."

Kate smiled, her breathing already back to normal. "Maybe I'm turning into a mountain girl."

His expression softened, lingered a moment on her face. "Maybe you are."

His eyes held hers, seemed to reach inside her. She wanted to touch him, run her finger over the hard planes of his face, the strong, lean sinews of his body.

"Anybody need a drink of water?" Jeremy held out his canteen, ending the moment, and both of them turned away. Kate accepted the metal flask just to have something to do, cranked off the cap, and took a welcome drink. She passed it to Chance, who must have tasted a hint of her lipstick on the rim, for when he looked at her again, his eyes seemed darker, more intense.

He put the cap back on with brisk efficiency and returned the canteen to Jeremy, careful to keep his eyes focused off toward the distant ridge. "Time's wasting. We'd better get back on the trail."

They set out again, heading inward, across the top of the mountain, then beginning a steep, short descent down the opposite side of the hill. When they reached the far edge of the forest, Chance lifted his hand, calling a silent halt to their progress.

"You can see the tail pond from here," he said softly, careful to stay back in the cover of the trees. "Jeremy — you circle left and I'll go right. I'll take Kate with me."

Jeremy nodded, the wind whipping the ends of his long black braid. He set out slowly, his footsteps nearly silent as he disappeared into the shadowy forest.

"Stay close," Chance said. "And try to be as quiet as you can. There'll be men working not far away."

She followed along behind him, walking as soundlessly as she could. She noticed him looking back several times to make sure that she was still there.

A little stream trickled out of the woods, swirling around mossy rocks and boulders as it ran off down the hill. Chance stepped over, took her hand, and helped her across, and they kept on going, traveling along the muddy bank on the opposite side. His nearly soundless footsteps, muffled by the moist, dark earth, turned toward the tail pond. That was the moment she spotted it — a small, bright flash of yellow at the bottom of the stream.

"Chance . . ." she whispered, halting him and bringing him back down the trail. Crouching beside the creek, she reached into the icy water and pulled out a small torn piece of yellow cardboard. It was the top off a box of film. She searched along the bank of the stream until she spotted several pieces of mangled gray plastic. She pulled them from where they lay half hidden in the rocks.

"It's a camera," Chance said darkly, recognizing the crushed and broken pieces as one of the inexpensive kind tourists bought at Dillon's Mercantile. "Chief must have been here."

"Yes, and after coming this far, he wouldn't have left without it."

"Let's fan out, see what we can find. Just don't get too far away."

She nodded and began to search the ground, looking for tracks or marks of any kind that might indicate where Chief had gone. They searched for at least twenty minutes before she heard Chance's urgent whisper, "Over here!"

Kate hurried in that direction, heading for the shallow ravine where he had disappeared. She found him down on one knee behind a thick stand of brush in the gully.

"What is it?" Before he could answer, she spotted the thin, jean-clad legs sticking out of the brush. "Oh God, no."

Chief was covered in dirt and blood, his face so swollen he was barely recognizable. Her hands shook as she quickly knelt beside him, her heart thumping at an agonizing rate.

"Is he . . . ?"

"He's still breathing, but barely." Chance slung his backpack off his shoulder, unzipped the center pouch, and hauled out a blanket and first aid kit. "It looks like they dragged him here. Probably figured the weather or the animals would finish him off." He carefully opened the old man's jacket to find the front of his plaid flannel shirt covered in blood. Chance unbuttoned and eased it open. Frothy blood leaked out a small ragged hole in his thin, gray-haired chest, and a sob welled up in Kate's throat. She bit hard on her lip to keep it firm.

"His cheekbone is broken. He's got a couple of busted ribs. One of them must have punctured a lung." He draped the blanket over the unconscious man on the ground in an effort to get him warm. "He probably has internal injuries as well. It's amazing he's still breathing."

Her throat closed up. She swallowed past the thick lump swelling there. "We have to get help. We have to get him out of here."

She gasped at the strength of the gnarled old hand that reached out and gripped her wrist. Chief's ancient eyes slowly opened and came to rest on her face.

"Pictures . . ." he whispered. "Pack. Under the bush."

"Take it easy, *say-laht*," Chance said, speaking to the old man in Salish as Kate hadn't even known he could. He said a lot of words she didn't understand, but the gist of it seemed to be that they had come to help him. *"Yo lu hom-kanu-le-hu,"* Chance said to him gently. "We'll take you to a place where it's safe."

Chief gave the faintest shake of his head. *"Chiks imsh lu ch'en-ku dtu-leewh."* His eyes slowly closed. For a moment Kate thought he had slipped away. Then his frail chest rose on another shallow breath of air.

Chance's face looked grim. "He says today is the day he journeys to the other world."

"No!" She caught hold of Chief's weathered hand. "You aren't going to die. We won't let you!"

At the edge of her vision, she saw Jeremy standing like a statue in the brush. She hadn't even noticed his arrival.

"I'll go down to the mine and get help."

"He'll need a chopper," Chance said. "It's the only chance he has."

Jeremy nodded. "I'll be back as quick as I can." He disappeared as quietly as he had arrived and Kate's worried gaze swung to Chance.

"Isn't it dangerous for him to go down there? Look what they did to Chief."

"Chief was a harmless old man. Jeremy is

well known in the community. Besides, he'll go directly into the main office, tell them we're here and what we've found. They'll be forced to help — they won't have any other choice."

Her hand trembled as she laced it with Chief's. "Just hold on," she whispered, looking down into his swollen, battered face. The tears she had been fighting welled in her eyes and began to slide down her cheeks.

"Do not cry, *I-huk-spu-us*. Friends are here. It is good to die with friends."

The lump in her throat grew so large she could barely speak. She squeezed his icy fingers, then looked up at Chance, whose own eyes looked suspiciously moist. "What did he call me?"

"The nearest translation is 'pure heart'."

Kate bit down on her lip. *Pure heart.* He had once said something like that to her, that she had a very good heart. She had come to love this old man who had befriended her and her son and now lingered on the very edge of death. He had lost so much blood and he was so weak. Beneath her fingers, she could barely feel his feeble, erratic pulse. She said a silent prayer but she thought that God's will might very well be to carry him on his journey homeward, just as he had said.

Chief's icy, brittle fingers tightened faintly around her hand. "I have . . . heard . . . that you have been there . . . that you have seen . . . *Schi-mas-ket.*"

She didn't need Chance to translate what he said or the question that was clear in his pain-filled eyes. She brushed at the tears on her cheeks. "Yes, I've been there. It's the most beautiful place. Greener even than the mountains here. The sky is so blue it hurts your eyes, and the light . . . the light is like a fine mist of gold that shimmers all around you. It warms you from inside, fills you with a joy unlike anything you've known on earth. All of your friends will be there. And your family, Chief. Your mother and your father. They'll be there to welcome you home. They'll be so happy to see you after all of these years."

She looked down at his face, barely able to see for the thick film of tears. "It's everything you ever believed it would be and more."

She felt a faint squeezing of her hand. The edges of his mouth lifted up in the faintest, briefest of smiles, then his eyes slowly closed. The hand that held hers went limp and slack, and she knew that he was gone.

Oh dear God! Part of her wanted to call him back, to beseech him to stay, to let the doctors have a chance to heal him. But another part knew the peace he had already found, knew the pain was now gone and joy replaced it, and she could not summon the words.

She felt Chance's hand on her shoulder, just the gentlest of touches, and yet she could feel his strength. It began to flow into her even as the tears rained down and she clung to the old man's ancient, weathered hand.

"He's gone, Katie. There's nothing more we can do."

She shook with silent sobs but still she did not move. She felt Chance's hand on her elbow, helping her to her feet, then he pulled her into his arms.

"Oh, Chance," she sobbed, unable to stop the tears.

"It's all right, darlin'. He heard your words and it gave him peace."

She looked up at him through the wetness. "Do you think he believed me?"

The edge of his thumb brushed over her trembling lips. "I know he did."

She buried her face against his chest and cried until her tears soaked the front of his jacket. Chance just held her, whispering soothing words, telling her how glad he was that she had been there, how much of a comfort she had been to Chief.

"How could someone do this?" she asked between ragged breaths. "How could they hurt that dear, sweet old man?"

She felt his hand gently smoothing over her back. "I don't know what drives people to do something like this. I don't know who it was, but I promise you, Kate, I'll find out."

Chance didn't say anymore and Kate just stood there, grateful for his comforting presence. In what seemed like hours, but must have been less than thirty minutes, the whop, whop,

whop of a chopper pressed down from over-head.

The helicopter landed in a clearing not far from the ravine and two men in white uniforms leaped out. They pulled out a stretcher, ducked beneath the whirling blades, and ran toward where she and Chance stood at the top of the ravine.

Kate stood forlornly, the wind whipping her hair, as Chance led them over to where Chief lay beneath the blanket and they loaded his body onto the stretcher. The helicopter hadn't yet lifted off when Jeremy arrived, a worried look on his face.

Chance just shook his head.

They made one final stop before they left — to retrieve the pack and the roll of film that had been important enough for Chief to die for. Then they started back toward the trucks.

It was a grim trio who arrived at the base of the mountain. One look at Kate's tear-stained face and David knew the worst had happened.

"They killed him, didn't they? Those dirty bastards murdered him!"

Jeremy led Chris a little way away and Chance clamped a steadying hand on David's shoulder. "We'll find out who did it, son. We'll make them pay for what they did."

David tried not to cry, but his eyes were wet and his hands were shaking. Chance drew him hard against his chest and wrapped his arms around the boy's shoulders.

"It's all right to cry, Davy. Sometimes that's what it takes to get rid of the pain."

David clung to him for several long seconds, then he stepped away. When they drove up in front of the house, he jumped out of the truck and ran inside, letting the screen door slam behind him.

Kate started to climb down from the pickup and go after him, but Chance caught her arm. "Let him go, Kate. He needs a little time to sort things out."

He was right and she knew it. She sighed and leaned back against the seat. Chance bent over her, caught her chin between his fingers, and turned her to face him.

"I want you to know how proud I am of you, Kate. I'm glad you were there today. I've never known another woman like you."

Kate blinked and fresh tears rolled down her cheeks. "Thank you."

"There's something else. Something I'll say just this once and never again." She saw the emotion in his face he didn't try to hide. "I love you, Katie. It doesn't change anything. Nothing can change what I have to do. I just wanted you to know."

She wanted to tell him she loved him too, wanted to say it so badly she ached. But he was marrying someone else. He would never be hers, and she just couldn't say the words. She swallowed past the thick lump in her throat.

"I have to go in," she said.

Chance nodded, looked away. "I know."

With a last painful glance at his dear, beloved face, Kate jumped down from the pickup and raced up the front porch steps. She was sick inside, sick with pain and grief for Chief.

And aching with a bitter, agonizing despair for herself, she knew it would not go away anytime soon.

Chapter Twenty-seven

Lon Barton hung up the telephone in his office and leaned back in his chair. His hands were shaking. He was thirty-seven years old and when his father called, he trembled like a kid.

He slammed a fist down on the top of the desk, sending a paper clip flying into the air. Sonofabitch! Forcing himself to take a calming breath, he reached over and pressed the intercom button.

His secretary answered immediately. "Yes, Mr. Barton?"

"Find Mullens. Get him in here ASAP."

"Yes, sir. Right away."

Twenty minutes later, Duke knocked lightly on the door and sauntered in. "What's up, boss?"

Lon leaned back in his expensive black-leather swivel chair. "My father called from his place up in Whitefish." It was just one of the houses he owned from Beverly Hills to West Palm Beach. "He got word today from that lady friend of his in the sheriff's office. You know the one — Barbara what's-her-name." An attractive woman Lon had asked out a few times himself. Barbara had said no to him, but not to his father. At fifty-seven, William Barton was lean, fit and handsome, one of the wealthiest and most powerful men in the country. Women had always found him attractive and he never took no for an answer. Though he was married to his fourth and presumably final wife, he'd been seeing Barbara in secret for nearly a year.

Lon looked over at Duke, whose big body lounged against the closed door, his arms crossed over his chest.

"Barbara says the sheriff's being pressured to exhume Nell Hart's body."

"Shit."

"If that happens, and it turns out her death wasn't an accident like Silas Marshall claims, if the sonofabitch actually murdered her, that property we bought could wind up in court, just like I said. My father doesn't want that to happen. He wants this matter settled, once and for all."

I'm tired of your incompetence, his father had said in his usual disapproving tone. *I want this over and done with — you hear me? I don't care how it happens.*

Duke straightened, came away from the door. "You want me to handle it?"

Lon nodded, feeling slightly sick. "That ought to make your day."

"Let me make sure I got this right. You want Kate Rollins out of the picture. You figure, once she's gone, the whole thing will eventually blow over."

"That's about it."

"When do you want it done?"

"I figured maybe Halloween. That's tomorrow night. Her kid will probably be out trick-or-treating. There are always troublemakers out and about, and the cops will be busy."

"Sounds like a good idea to me." Duke turned toward the door.

"One more thing. This has to look like an accident. If it appears to be anything else, we'll be stirring up more trouble than we've got already."

Duke seemed to mull that over, then he nodded. "I'll take care of it. It's amazing what happens to a house when someone accidentally leaves the propane on."

Lon grimaced. He didn't want to hear the gory details, but this time he needed to know. He needed to be sure the matter was handled correctly. Too much was at stake if anything went wrong. "All right, if that's what it takes. Do it."

Duke flashed him a look he couldn't quite read and turned to leave. Maybe he wasn't as happy about the job as Lon would have guessed. Cruelty was one thing, murder was another. Still, whatever it took, Lon could count on him to get the job done.

Swearing silently at his father, who always seemed to demand more than his son could possibly give, Lon returned to the paperwork piling up on his desk.

"Have a good time!" Standing on the front

porch, Kate smiled and waved goodbye to David, who jumped into the back seat of Willow's minivan next to Chris.

"I'll have him home no later than eleven," Willow promised. She and Jeremy were taking the boys to the Halloween carnival at Chris's school, then to visit the "haunted house" in Ronan put on by the local 4-H Club.

"Are you sure you don't want to come with us?" Willow asked.

Kate shook her head. "Sounds like you're going to have fun, but tonight's the coalition's weekly online chat group. Since I'm not running things anymore, I try to be there to answer questions and help them come up with new ideas."

"That's important stuff." Willow jerked open the passenger door and slid into the seat next to her husband, who sat behind the wheel. All of them waved as Jeremy turned the minivan around, headed down the driveway, and turned onto the road, disappearing seconds later into the thickening darkness.

The wind was blowing tonight, whining through the branches of the pine trees, stirring up grass and dead leaves. A dense layer of heavy black clouds smothered the moon and stars and warned of a coming storm.

As she walked back into the house, Kate ignored a faint uneasiness and remembered instead the smile on David's face when he climbed in the car, the first she had seen since the day Chief had died. The funeral had been just yesterday. A simple graveside service at the little cemetery on the reservation, but most of the townspeople were there, as well as those from the surrounding area, including Ed and Chance. Chief would surely be missed.

Kate and David had gone with Willow and Jeremy. Knowing the grief David suffered, Kate had spent every spare moment with him, which was why she hadn't gone tonight. She thought it might be good for him to go without her.

With a last look into the darkness outside the house, Kate checked to be sure the front door was locked — a habit she had acquired living in the city — went into the kitchen, made herself a cup of tea, and carried it upstairs to her office.

She could hear the wind whistling, rattling the windows, an eerie sound in the creaky old wooden house, a perfect night for Halloween. Sitting behind her desk, she flipped on the computer and it started humming away, dispelling some of the Halloween chill.

She typed in the proper commands and pulled up her e-mail, read a message from Sally, an update on life in LA and what was happening at Menger and Menger. She answered with the latest on the anti-mining campaign, telling Sally she had resigned her position and wishing her a happy Halloween. She replied to an e-mail from a friend in Chicago she had met on a business trip and still kept in touch with. Then, at eight o'clock, it was time to go into the AOL chat room where members of the coalition met once a week.

Usually no more than five or six people attended. Ed Fontaine was the moderator, great at keeping everyone on track. Jake Dillon typically made at least a brief appearance. Kate had mentioned the meeting once to Aida Whittaker and, using her son-in-law's PC, she had dropped in for a visit last week. Diane Stevens, the television anchor, had joined the group once, and that lawyer up in Polson, Frank Mills, who had represented the Salish in their bid for an injunction, was a guest at one of the group's recent meetings. Sometimes, Chance dropped in.

Kate put that thought out of her mind as she tuned in to the group, reading comments from Ed as to what had occurred since the previous meeting.

Half an hour into the chat, her thoughts began to wander. Something tugged at the back of her mind, drawing her attention away. Sliding her chair back from the screen, she listened to the rattle of the wind, the scrape of the branches against the windowpanes, and another, indistinct sound that seemed to be coming from downstairs.

Her heart kicked up a little. Kate left the computer running, went across the room, eased open the door, and leaned out into the hallway.

Nothing but silence greeted her. She shook

her head at her runaway imagination. *What did you expect — it's Halloween.*

She started to close the door when she heard a faint scraping sound in the kitchen, as if one of the breakfast table chairs was being moved.

This is silly, she told herself, but she couldn't go back to work until she knew. Better to face the unknown than to let it grow into phantoms inside her head. She pulled open the door and headed downstairs. She reached the bottom step, flipped on another light switch, marched through the dining room and into the kitchen. Terror streaked through her. A scream erupted at the unexpected sight of the man in the ski mask standing in front of the stove.

Kate turned and started running.

"Oh no you don't!" He was behind her in a heartbeat, catching her before she could reach the front door, his arm snaking around her waist, slamming her up against his chest. "I think we've done this little dance before, haven't we, sweetheart?"

"Let me go!"

"Sorry. Not this time." Dragging her away from the door, he pulled a roll of duct tape out from inside his shirt, jerked her wrists in front of her, and wrapped them with the tape. "I warned you, but no — you wouldn't listen. Now you'll have to pay."

"I did what you asked," she told him desperately. "I resigned from the campaign."

"But you couldn't quit stirring up trouble,

447

could you? You just couldn't let things alone."

"I don't . . . I don't know what you mean."

"Yeah, well it doesn't matter whether you know or not."

Kate tried to twist her hands free but the tape wouldn't budge. All she succeeded in doing was hurting her wrist. She looked up, saw him standing with his feet splayed, a big brawny man that somehow looked familiar. An image arose of that same bulky frame brawling with Chance in the parking lot. Good Lord, it was Duke Mullens! She should have figured it out the first time he was there. Not that it would have mattered, since she didn't have even a shred of proof.

"What are you going to do?"

Through the opening of the ski mask, she could see his big teeth flash and his thick lips move. "If you mean am I going to get between those pretty little legs of yours — sorry, sweetheart, I don't have time." Gripping her arm, he started dragging her toward the closet, and fear bloomed inside her.

Kate had no idea what he meant to do, but she wasn't going to let him do it without a fight. She could scream, but she was too far from the cafe for anyone to hear her. Instead, as they neared the closet, she twisted, kicked him hard in the shin with her sturdy Hi-Tec boot, and started running.

Duke grunted and swore. "Sonofabitch!"

The front door was locked. She would never

have time to get it open. Whirling to the left, she raced up the stairs, her heart pounding as hard as her feet. There was a phone in her office. She slammed the door, wedged a stout oak chair beneath the knob, and raced for the phone on her desk.

Her bound hands were shaking as she jerked up the receiver, jammed it against her ear, and punched in 911. She could hear Duke Mullens outside the door, turning the knob, swearing when it didn't open, ramming his shoulder against the thick slab of wood.

"Come on," she whispered, dialing the number again. Nothing. It took a moment for her to realize the wires had been cut. The phone line was dead.

Oh, dear God. A wave of fear rolled through her and her mind went numb. For a moment, she couldn't seem to think. Kate whirled toward the computer, the screen glowing with its usual warmth. When she had accepted the job heading up the anti-mining campaign, she'd had a separate phone line installed for the computer. It came into the house from a different location than the older telephone lines Nell had installed years earlier. She was still hooked into the chat room!

With her wrists bound tightly in front of her, her hands were beginning to go to numb. Her fingers felt stiff and unresponsive as she twisted her arm a little and was finally able to rest one hand on the keyboard. Forcing herself to go slow, she typed in: *Man in the house. Trying to kill me. Dial 911. Kate.*

Wood cracked. Any second Mullens would burst through the door. "You're dead, you hear me, you little bitch? First I'm gonna fuck you, then I'm gonna turn the gas on and blow you to kingdom come!"

Oh, God! She was shaking now, terrified of what would happen once he got into the room. She needed a weapon, something that — For God's sake — the gun Chance had lent her! It was lying right there on the credenza behind her desk. She'd been using it as a paperweight to glue some photos into an album she was making.

She whirled in that direction, fumbled for a moment, fighting to pick it up with the duct tape so tight around her wrists, jerked open the top drawer of her desk, and fumbled for the box of shells. The cardboard cut one of her fingers. Her hands were shaking so badly she nearly dropped the box. Eventually, she shoved two bullets in, closed the cylinder, and aimed it toward the door.

"Get away from the door! I've got a gun in here and it's pointed right at you! Get away or I swear I'll pull the trigger!"

"No one fucks with the Duke — you hear me? I'm gonna kill you! And I'm gonna do it real slow!" He threw his heavy weight against the door one last time, splintering the wood, and Kate fired the pistol.

The shot was deafening in the small, closed up room. Her ears rang as she pulled the trigger a second time, heard it rip through the wood, then the door gave completely away and crashed forward into the office.

Duke Mullens sprawled on top of it, arms and legs bent in unnatural positions, blood pooling beneath him, a bright red puddle that spread like a growing tide all over the door, pumping out of Mullens's chest with every heartbeat. He was breathing hard, sucking in great gulps of air.

"I should have . . . killed you the first time."

Kate pointed the empty revolver in his direction as he clumsily levered himself to his feet. She was shaking so hard she could barely hold onto her useless weapon. Instead of coming toward her, Mullens turned and staggered back toward the stairs, smearing blood on the wall as he leaned against it for support. He made it to the top of the landing, took the first step, and pitched forward, rolling headlong, then crashing in a bloody heap at the bottom of the staircase.

Kate let go of the gun and it hit the floor with a clatter. Racing down the stairs, she stopped a few feet from Mullens's body.

"Why?" she asked, desperate to know. "Why did you want to kill me?" But Mullens didn't answer. His chest no longer moved. Duke Mullens was dead.

Kate slumped against the wall, trembling all

over, her stomach rolling with nausea. She didn't understand what had happened. Why had Duke Mullens wanted her dead?

She had to get up, go back to her computer, make sure her message was received and the sheriff was on his way, but her legs felt like cotton and her lungs burned like fire with each breath.

"Why?" she whispered, wondering if she would ever find out. "Are you the one who murdered Nell?"

"Duke didn't kill her. I did."

Kate jerked toward the sound of the voice coming from below the stairs. Lon Barton, dressed in black from head to foot, stood with an automatic pistol in a black-gloved hand. It was obvious he had been watching through the window and equally obvious he wasn't pleased that Duke's mission had failed.

"You . . . you were the one?"

"I didn't intend to. I only came to the house that day to convince her to sell the well."

"But . . . but surely —"

"My father was adamant about owning it. Nell refused to see reason. I had to do something."

"Silas Marshall said that he was the one who killed her."

Lon shook his head. The ends of his curly blond hair stuck out from beneath his black knit cap. "He must have shoved her, like he told the police. I guess he thought he killed her

— he drove out of here like a madman. When I went into the house, Nell was lying there in the dining room."

"But she was still alive."

"She was breathing, but just barely. When I realized how close she was to death, I figured — why not? I pressed a pillow over her face. I figured if anyone found out, Silas would get the blame."

Chills raced up and down Kate's arms. Lon Barton had killed Nell. That was the reason he had sent Duke Mullens to kill her. She had to keep him talking, give the sheriff time to get there. God knew how long that would take — especially since tonight was Halloween. And she wasn't even sure her message got through.

"Surely Nell fought you."

"Only a little; she was too weak. It only took a few seconds and she was dead." Barton raised the pistol, aimed it straight at her heart. "Just like you're going to be."

"The sheriff is coming," Kate said hastily, inching backward up the stairs. "Even if you kill me, they'll catch you."

Barton shook his head. "I don't think so. I think Duke Mullens killed you . . . just like you killed him." He moved closer. "He was always overzealous. That's why he killed Nell. He knew Consolidated wanted to buy that well and that Silas Marshall would sell it, once Nell was out of the way. Then you started digging and Duke got scared. He had to shut you up. Unfortunately, he died in the process." He slid the action back on the deadly-looking pistol.

"I'm sorry, Kate, I really am. I never wanted any of this to happen. Somehow it just did."

Kate turned and bolted up the stairs. Barton fired the pistol and the shot slammed into the wall behind her. A second shot splintered the handrail, but Kate kept running. She had almost reached the upstairs hall when she heard the back door crash open and the thunder of a man's heavy boots. Chance tackled Lon Barton like a champion bulldogger going for the rodeo record.

The pistol went flying, sailing across the hardwood floor and cracking against the wall. Kate raced after it, bolting down the stairs in time to see Chance roll on top of Barton and began to slam one hard punch after another into his face.

Someone started pounding on the door. Kate spotted Ed Fontaine's van out in front, the driver's door open, the tailgate down, Ed wheeling himself up the path toward the steps. Randy Wiggins stood on the porch, hammering madly away.

Kate hurried to let him in and he raced past her into the entry, stopping next to where Chance continued to batter an unconscious Lon Barton.

"He's had enough," Randy said. "You'll kill him, Chance."

Chance pulled his next punch but the effort

it took left his fist shaking. He climbed off Lon Barton, and walked straight toward her, stopping only long enough to pull a folding knife out of the pocket of his jeans and cut through the duct tape, then she was securely in his arms.

"God, Katie." He gathered her closer, buried his face in her hair, and she clung to him, her arms sliding up around his neck. "I've never been so scared in my life. Are you all right?"

She nodded against his shoulder, felt the tremors running through his lean frame. "I shot him, Chance. I killed Duke Mullens."

He looked over the top of her head to the body sprawled like a broken toy at the foot of the stairs. "I'm just glad I gave you that gun."

"How did . . . how did you know?"

"I was with you in the chat room. I knew you'd be uncomfortable if you knew I was there, so I just kept quiet. When I read what you wrote, I thought I was going to be sick."

"Barton killed Nell, Chance. He said his father wanted the well she and Silas owned."

Chance released a weary sigh. One of his hands slid over her hair to cup the back of her head and he cradled her cheek against his shoulder. "I suppose that makes sense. William Barton has been pulling Lon's string for years. Lon was completely dependent on him. His position with the company, his high-paying salary. All the wealth he had accumulated over the years was a direct result of his father's good will. If he lost it, he lost everything."

"I wonder how his father is going to feel now."

Ed Fontaine spoke up from the doorway, where Randy had managed to wheel his chair. "I know how I'd feel if I drove my son to do something like that." For an instant, his gaze flicked to Chance, who still held onto Kate. "But William Barton? I don't think we'll ever really know."

Colored lights flashed on the walls of the living room as the sheriff's car finally drove up. Halloween was a busy night, the perfect time to commit a murder. Another car arrived and Lon Barton was taken into custody. Ed and Chance both stayed until one of the deputies had taken Kate's statement, then she was finally done.

"You can't stay here." Chance cast a glance toward the body being photographed at the bottom of the stairs. "As soon as David gets home, I'll drive the two of you down to that little motel on the way to Ronan. In the meantime, we'll wait for David over in the cafe." He caught one of the deputies' eyes and he nodded, understanding where to send the boy when he got home.

"I — I have to pack a bag." She moistened her lips, wishing she didn't have to pass Mullens's body to get upstairs.

Reading her thoughts, Chance took her hand.

456

"Come on. I'll take you up."

"Be careful what you touch," one of the deputies called out. "Remember this is a crime scene."

Again. Kate shivered, thinking of Nell's murder and wondering how she would handle living in the house with so many bad memories.

They made their way up to her bedroom, being careful not to disturb anything along the way. Kate packed a bag for herself and one for David and they headed back downstairs. They were sitting in the cafe, drinking decaf coffee when a pale-faced David walked in with Jeremy, Willow, and Chris.

"Mom!" he raced toward her and she opened her arms, felt his thin frame shaking against her as she closed them around him. "Are you all right?" David asked. "The cop said a man tried to kill you and you shot him."

"I'm fine, honey. And it's all over now. We're going to stay in a motel for a couple of days, until they get the house cleaned up. Chance is going to drive us."

It would be easier if she just drove the rental car she had been using, but she was still so shaky she didn't trust herself behind the wheel.

"Why don't you stay with us?" Willow offered.

"Good idea," Jeremy agreed. "We might be a little bit crowded but —"

"I appreciate it, but I'd really rather not. You've both been wonderful friends. But to tell you the truth, I think David and I need a little time to ourselves."

"Are you sure you'll be all right?" Willow asked worriedly, while Myra hovered protectively a few feet away.

"I'll be fine. I'm just glad this whole thing is finally over."

At the Night's Rest Motel, a little row of faux-log cabins on the road down to Ronan, Chance checked them in and carried her bag inside. David carried his own in, turned on the TV, and flopped down in front of it as Kate walked Chance to the door.

"Thank you for coming when you did. You saved my life, Chance."

Chance ran a finger along her jaw and a thread of heat filtered through her. "Even if I hadn't gotten there, I think you would have outsmarted Barton, just the way you did Duke. You're an amazing woman, Kate."

Kate said nothing. She was looking at Chance and wishing he were staying there with her, wishing she could convince him not to marry a woman he didn't love.

Knowing that he wouldn't listen.

"I thought Rachael would be back by now," she said, just to put some distance between them. Chance stiffened, drew away, as she had known he would.

He sighed into the frosty darkness. "She'll be

back the end of the week."

Kate ignored a stab of pain. "I appreciate everything you've done, Chance. But after tonight, I don't want . . . I don't want to see you again. Not even as a friend."

"What about your car? At least let me take you back to get it in the morning."

"Myra can come and get me."

He looked away, off into the silent world around them. Somewhere in the night, an owl hooted, a forlorn, empty sound. Kate stared at Chance's hard, implacable features, thought how much she loved him, and a hollow ache rose in her chest.

"You're right," he said. "It's better if we stay away from each other. At least now I won't have to worry about you. With Duke Mullens dead and Nell's murder out in the open, you'll be safe."

Knowing she shouldn't, Kate laid a hand against his cheek. She could feel the roughness of his late-night beard and the warmth of his skin. For a moment his eyes slid closed and he leaned his face into her palm. Then her hand fell away. When he looked at her again, his features were dark with pain.

Kate swallowed past the lump in her throat. "I love you, Chance," she told him, her chest aching, fighting to hold back tears. "I had to tell you, just once."

"Katie . . ."

She only shook her head, unable to hear him

say more. Turning away, she left him standing on the porch in front of the little cabin. Her heart felt like it weighed a thousand pounds as she walked back into the room and quietly closed the door.

Chapter Twenty-eight

Sitting in his wheelchair behind the big mahogany desk in his study, Ed Fontaine waited while Chance walked in and closed the door.

"You wanted to see me?"

Ed wheeled his chair out from behind the desk and motioned Chance to take a seat in one of the leather chairs in front of it. He hated looking up to people, especially a man as tall as Chance.

"My daughter's flying in tomorrow night. I imagine she called to tell you."

Chance nodded. "She phoned a couple of days ago. Said she was finished with her job in the city." He jackknifed one long leg across the other then settled his dusty black Stetson on his knee, turning it absently with his hand. "She says she's got things pretty much all lined out for the wedding."

Ed didn't respond to that. "Tell me something, Chance. Are you in love with my daughter?"

Chance's wide shoulders went a little bit straighter. He sat up taller in his chair. "I love Rachael. You know that. I can hardly remember a time I didn't know her. The two us have been friends for years."

"I know you love her. You two were practi-

461

cally raised together. I want to know if you're *in* love with her."

For an instant, Chance looked away. Ed watched him fiddle with the crease in his hat, outlining the folds with his index finger. Then he looked Ed straight in the eye.

"I'll make her a damned good husband. I'll take care of her, see she gets anything she wants. She won't lack for a thing."

"But you aren't in love with her."

Fierce blue eyes fixed on his face. There was so much emotion there it made Ed's chest feel tight. "Rachael and I both know where we stand. She wants the same things I want. Neither of us is going into this marriage with our eyes closed."

"So you're saying she isn't in love with you, either."

Chance came to his feet. "Dammit, Ed, you're turning this all around. What do you want me to say? Rachael and I have been planning to marry for years. We've both agreed. Now that's just what we're gonna do."

"Even if it means losing the woman you're in love with?"

Chance stared over Ed's head, his gaze fixed on a spot on the wall. The muscles in his throat moved up and down, but no words came out.

"You do love her, don't you? I've known you for years, Chance, and you've never looked at a woman the way you look at Kaitlin Rollins."

When Chance finally spoke, his voice came

out deep and rusty. "It doesn't matter. My future is set. I'm marrying Rachael. I give you my word I'll make her happy."

"Sit down, son. You know how I hate looking up at you."

Chance sank like a stone in the chair, the muscles in his neck and shoulders rigid with tension.

"You're marrying Rachael because of me, aren't you, son? You think it's what I want. You think you owe it to me because of what happened that day on the mountain. Because you blame yourself for the accident that put me in this chair."

Chance's jaw looked rigid. "It was my fault. If I had listened to my father —"

"If you'd listened to half of what that hard-headed old SOB said, you wouldn't be the man you are today. What happened in that storm could have happened any time, any place, anywhere. Life's hard here. You know that. My luck just ran bad that day."

Chance said nothing. Twenty-one years of guilt wasn't that easy to wash away. Ed had hoped that by now it would have faded.

"Listen to me, son. I know you're doing this for me. There was a time I wanted you to marry Rachael more than anything on this earth. I wanted you to be the father of her children. I wanted that strong blood of yours to run through my grandchildren's veins. Now that I know you're in love with someone else, it isn't what I want anymore."

Chance swallowed, his fingers gripping the hat so hard he was putting a new crease in it. "What about the ranch? What about the legacy you wanted your grandchildren to have? You've talked about it for years."

"When the time comes, my grandkids will inherit the Circle Bar F. That's as fine a legacy as any man could ask."

"What about Rachael? I made her a promise. I can't just —"

"Yes, you can. We both know Rachael isn't any more in love with you than you are with her. Maybe I was doing as big a disservice to her as I was to you. We'll let Rachael save face and call the engagement off. That'll take some of the sting out of it. She's a beautiful girl. She'll find someone else, hopefully a man she can love the way I loved her mother. In the meantime, I'll leave it to you to give me those grandkids. After all, you're as close to me as any son I might have had. And more than anything in the world, I want you to be happy."

Chance sat forward in his chair. "Are you sure, Ed?"

"Last night I saw what happened when a man put his own selfish interests ahead of what was best for his son. I'm sure, Chance. More sure than I've ever been of anything in my life."

Chance came to his feet. Reaching out, he clasped Ed's hand in his, leaned over, and hugged him. He was smiling, but his eyes looked moist. "Thanks, Ed. You'll never know how much this means to me."

Ed just smiled. "I think I got a pretty good notion. You give Kate my best, will you?"

Chance grinned. Ed realized he hadn't seen the boy do that in weeks.

"I'll tell her." Long strides carried him out of the study and down the hall, and Ed's smile widened. He had done the right thing. Rachael would be fit to be tied, but in the long run, she would agree it was the right thing for both of them. She cared for Chance, the same way he cared for her, and she would want him to be happy.

Besides there were other good men in Silver County. Take that big, strappin' Ned Cummings. He was a damned fine rancher and he'd always had a secret yen for Rachael. Now that he thought of it, the two of them might just get along.

Ed chuckled to himself as he wheeled himself over to the desk. Maybe he'd throw a nice little dinner party on Saturday night to celebrate Rachael's return and her broken engagement.

He picked up the phone. And maybe he would just invite Ned Cummings.

Kate tied an apron on over her jeans and went to work. The best way to put the ugliness of the past few days behind her was to keep herself busy and get on with her life.

Since they were still living in the little motel

on the road to Ronan, she'd had to take David to school, so she had missed the morning shift. Lunch was in full swing by the time she got there. Bonnie was working, but she could always use a hand. Kate busied herself serving a platter of chicken-fried steak, country gravy, and mashed potatoes. Then the bell rang over the door and Chance walked in.

He looked so good in his butter-soft jeans and white Western shirt that for a moment she found herself staring, drinking in the sight of him. She quickly turned her eyes away and set the platter of chicken-fried steak down on the table. Harvey Michaelson thanked her and dug right in.

Chance took a seat in one of the booths in front of the window. He was studying the menu, his eyes carefully trained there, but there was something different about him, something she couldn't exactly pin down. His eyes looked different, less guarded, even bluer than they usually did, and his posture seemed more relaxed.

He was handsome as sin, and incredibly appealing — and he belonged to someone else. Dammit, he wasn't supposed to be there, Kate recalled with a shot of anger. He was supposed to leave her alone. Tomorrow night, his fiancée would be arriving, for heaven's sake.

She clamped her jaw. Maybe seeing Rachael was the reason he looked so damned pleased with himself.

Fighting to hold onto her temper, Kate walked briskly over to his booth. "Are you ready to order, cowboy?"

Chance looked up at her and smiled so sweetly her heart turned completely over. "Yeah. But first I was wondering . . . you know that coconut cake you served last week?"

"What about it?" Kate snapped.

"I was thinking . . . if you could make a coconut cake as good as that, maybe you could whip up a wedding cake."

For a minute she just stood there, her temper so hot she wondered if flames might be shooting out of her head. She clamped her hands on her hips and leaned toward him.

"If you think for one minute I'm gonna bake you and that anorexic blonde you're engaged to a wedding cake, you have gone completely —"

Chance actually grinned. She couldn't remember the last time she had seen him grin like that.

"It's not for Rachael and me," he said. "It's for you and me. How about it, Katie? Will you marry me?"

For a moment, the room seemed to spin. She had to grab hold of a chair to steady herself. When she looked around, she saw that everyone in the restaurant was staring at her, waiting for her to answer.

"What . . . what about Rachael?"

White teeth flashed. "Rachael threw me over. I'm a free man again. What do you say, Kate?"

Rachael threw him over? Kate didn't think that was anywhere near the truth. No woman — not even one who looked like Rachael Fontaine — would ever be that insane. "You'd better be serious, Chance McLain."

Chance slid out of the booth and took hold of her hand. "I'm dead serious, darlin'." The cocky grin slipped from his face. "Say yes, Katie. Put me out of my misery. I don't want to live another day without you."

Her heart expanded, felt as if it would burst through the walls of her chest. "Well, when you put it that way, I guess I've got no choice. I'll marry you, cowboy."

Everyone cheered as he wrapped her in his arms, lifted her off her feet, and whirled her around in the center of the room.

Kate hugged his neck, laughing and crying at the very same time. She didn't know how it had happened, but she was marrying Chance McLain. What had started out as a miserable day of trying to forget the past and get on with a very lonely future had turned into the happiest day of her life.

"Let's get out of here," Chance whispered. Sliding an arm beneath her knees, he hoisted her up and carried her out the door. She didn't know where he was taking her and she didn't care. She loved him and he loved her. At far as Kate was concerned, that was all that mattered.

She waved goodbye to Myra, who had followed them out of the cafe and now stood wiping away happy tears with the corner of her apron.

Smiling up at Chance, Kate slid her arms around his neck, pulled his mouth down to hers for a deep, sexy kiss. She didn't stop till she heard him groan.

Epilogue

Kate padded out of the bathroom and quietly returned to bed. Sliding beneath the covers, she rolled over on her stomach and plumped the soft down pillow, using it to prop herself up.

It was dark outside, not yet daylight, but the bedroom was cozy and warm. The big king-sized bed was rumpled, quilted comforter askew, the sheets in disarray and smelling pleasantly of last night's lovemaking.

Chance was busy getting dressed, preparing to go out and join his men. Today was the last day of spring roundup. There was still lots to do and Kate was planning to help, but she had always hated getting up early, and this morning Chance had insisted she sleep in.

"Hannah will have breakfast ready for the men," he'd argued when she had groggily, half-heartedly insisted. "You can come down and join us whenever you're ready."

Kate smiled to think of the way he pampered her. And Hannah watched out for her, too. To Kate's surprise, the two of them had bonded almost instantly. Hannah liked her job at the ranch and Kate had no intention of taking it away from her. Kate loved having someone to help her manage such a big place, especially since she still had a restaurant to run.

And David already loved her. Hannah had taken to the boy like a hen to a chick, mothering him the same way she had always mothered Chance. David, of course, basked in the older woman's attention, seeing her as the grandmother that he had never had.

Hannah had clearly accepted Kate as part of the family, mostly because she knew how much Kate loved Chance.

Watching him now, his back turned toward her, lean and muscled in the soft light of the lamp, as he pulled on his jeans and boots, she wished she had awakened earlier. Chance enjoyed making love in the mornings and so did she. This morning she had simply been too sleepy.

Fighting down an annoying jolt of lust, Kate shoved her curly red hair back over her shoulder. It was longer now, since Chance seemed to like it that way. He particularly loved her breasts, she knew, and thinking about the way he had kissed them last night made them feel swollen and achey.

She watched him pull his Western shirt on and pop the snaps closed on the front. He tucked in his shirttail and tightened his leather belt. Reaching for the chaps he wore when he was working, he buckled them around his waist, picked up his hat, and turned toward the bed, meaning to kiss her goodbye, the way he always did.

"I thought you were going back to sleep," he

said, striding toward her, making the wide leather at the bottom of his chaps flip out over his boots.

"I've been watching you get dressed."

He smiled, reached down and sifted a hand through her curly mop of hair. "Lady, you look good enough to eat."

Kate returned the smile. "So do you." Lord, did he. There was something about a man in chaps — particularly her man. The way they cradled his slim hips. The way the opening at the front neatly cupped his sex. As his hand ran over her bare shoulder and gently stroked a breast, the fit of his jeans grew snug and it was obvious she had aroused more than his interest.

Kate looked up at him from beneath her lashes. "Did you know I have a secret fantasy about making love to a man in chaps?"

Chance cocked a black eyebrow. "Is that so?"

"Too bad you have to leave."

"Isn't it, though?" But he didn't seem to be in all that much of a hurry. Instead he bent down and kissed her full on the mouth, running his tongue inside and making her heart set up a clatter. Long dark fingers teased her nipple and it tightened almost painfully.

"I don't have much time," he said softly, kissing the side of her neck, nibbling on an earlobe.

"Maybe we can improvise."

"Yeah . . . maybe we can." Reaching down, he unzipped his fly and Kate reached out to touch him. He was big and hard, pulsing as her fingers closed around him. Tossing back the covers, she came up on her knees and before he realized her intention, took him fully into her mouth.

Chance hissed in a breath and a shudder went through him. "God, Katie."

Ignoring the feel of his hands sliding into her hair, she teased him a while, enjoying the taste of him, enjoying the fantasy. She squeaked in surprise as he pulled her away, lifted her up, and wrapped her legs around his waist.

"All right, darlin' — now it's my turn." Stroking her gently, he kissed her hard, then drove himself fully inside. Pleasure tore through her like a bolt of white lightning, and she heard Chance groan.

Kate gasped at the feel of his smooth leather chaps against her bottom. She clung to his neck and closed her eyes, savoring the feel of him, thinking how much she loved him. Chance drove into her again and again, heightening the pleasure, sending little shafts of heat roaring into her stomach.

Her body throbbed, ached for release. Something hot and sweet burst open inside her. She reached a powerful climax that left her trembling from head to foot, and softly moaned his name. A few more driving thrusts and Chance came, too, his lean body shaking, the muscles across his shoulders as rigid as bands of steel.

He held her for several sweet moments, bent

his head and gently kissed her, then he settled her back down on the bed. Kate yawned as he adjusted himself, zipped his fly, and pulled the sheet up over her breasts.

"Go back to sleep, darlin'. I'll see you a little while later."

Kate just nodded, a drowsy smile on her face, her eyes already drifting closed. When she woke up two hours later, she felt pleasantly sated and deliciously content.

By the time she walked into the kitchen, David had left to join Chance out at the corral. Her son had finally adjusted to life on the ranch, though it hadn't been easy in the beginning. He didn't know the first thing about cattle or ranching, but the hands respected his determination and eagerness to learn and helped him any way they could. And Chance was always there for him, as his real father never had been.

David was a good rider now. He could fish like a native, and even shoot a rifle, though she wasn't sure he would ever want to hunt.

The deaths that had touched him so young, his grandmother and Chief, even Duke Mullens, had destroyed a portion of his youth. He often seemed more man than boy, and though she missed the child he once was, she was proud of the adult he was becoming.

Interest in Nell's murder had finally faded. The charges against Silas Marshall had been dropped the day after Lon Barton's arrest. William Barton had, of course, hired the country's most expensive attorneys. Lon had pled innocent at first, but the evidence continued to mount against him.

Along with his attempt on Kate's life, Nell's body was exhumed and traces of skin were found under her fingernails. The DNA perfectly matched Lon Barton's. Then an itinerant Indian named Bobby Red Elk showed up, claiming he had seen Barton's car parked near Nell's house the day of the murder.

Bobby had been headed south, to panhandle in a warmer climate, but on his return to the reservation, he had heard about Nell and Barton's upcoming trial. Apparently, Bobby had stopped by to see Nell on his way out of town, since she was always good for a handout. He'd seen Silas drive away and a white Jeep Cherokee pull up on the side of the road. Since Nell had visitors, he had decided not to stop.

Bobby wasn't much of a witness, as witnesses went, but the evidence was becoming harder and harder to refute. On his attorney's advice, Lon had accepted a deal. He'd pled guilty to manslaughter, accepted a fifteen-year sentence at a minimum-security prison, and hoped to be out in ten. It didn't seem like a high enough price for murder, but with the courts the way they were, they were lucky he hadn't walked away.

And to sweeten the deal, he had given up the men responsible for killing Harold Ironstone —

Joe Saugus, Ben Weeks, Fred Thompson, and Duke Mullens, all employees of the Beavertail mine.

Which meant there was even better news. Consolidated Metals had dropped their attempt to overthrow the cyanide ban and build a new heap-leach mine in Silver County. With all that had happened, the public was simply too solidly entrenched against them. The Beavertail mine was closing — thanks to Chief's photos of the leaks in the tail pond and the gigantic fines the court had finally imposed.

There would be no new mine on Silver Fox Creek.

Kate reached the big pine kitchen and shoved open the door.

Holding a cup of hot coffee, Hannah turned at her approach and padded toward her across the wood plank floor. "Here. This'll warm you up."

"Thanks, Hannah. Maybe now I'll finally be able to wake up. I don't know what's the matter with me this morning."

Hannah cast her a look that said she knew very well what the matter was, and what exactly had gone on upstairs. Fighting down her embarrassment, Kate shoved open the back door and stepped out into the brisk spring morning.

Dressed in jeans, the cowboy boots Chance had bought her, and a sweatshirt with a picture of a moose on the front, she walked down the gentle slope to the corral. A dozen cowboys, some horseback, others on foot, were busy branding calves.

She wrinkled her nose at the smell of burnt hair and tried to ignore the little calves' bawling as they were branded, vaccinated, and neutered, but she wasn't worried about them anymore. The first time she had watched the men working, she had been surprised and pleased to see the calves treated with so much care.

Chance spotted her walking toward him, jumped down from the fence, and strode toward her. Unconsciously, her glance strayed to the front of his chaps where the leather cupped his sex, and her face heated up again.

Chance grinned, reading her thoughts exactly. "You know what I love about you, Katie?"

Her blush deepened, sure he was going to say something embarrassing about how much she liked making love. "What?"

Chance leaned down and kissed her. "Everything." His expression turned serious. "Marrying you was the best thing I've ever done, Kate. You've made me the happiest man on earth."

Kate smiled, her eyes misting with tears. God, how she loved him. "How are things going?"

He looked back toward the corral. Little puffs of dust rose beneath the horses' hooves as the men lassoed each calf and brought it down. "We'll be done by the end of the day, just like we planned."

The customary steak barbecue was scheduled for late afternoon and a number of friends, and everyone who helped, was invited. Kate had been working with Hannah for the last two days, getting everything ready.

"Anything I can do to help?"

"How 'bout keeping me company for a while?"

She grinned. "My pleasure, cowboy." She walked with him back to the corral and he helped her climb up on the fence. On the opposite side, David sat on the little buckskin gelding Chance had given him as what he termed "a wedding present." Kate had her own horse, too, a pretty little palomino quarter horse that she had fallen instantly in love with.

Life on the Running Moon was good, had been since the day she and David moved in. They had never lived in Nell's old house again, not since the night she'd shot Duke Mullens. As soon as Chance had settled things with Rachael — which went better than either of them had expected, thanks to Ed, and perhaps Ned Cummings — Kate and Chance had been married.

It was a small church ceremony with only a few close friends, but it was what both of them wanted.

Chance cast her a teasing, slightly wicked glance. "You get any more sleep after I left?"

Kate just smiled. "Actually, I did. It was strange, though. I had a dream about Nell. She was thanking me for proving Silas wasn't to blame for her death." Kate stared up at him. "You don't suppose that was her real message, do you? That Silas wasn't the man who killed her and she didn't want him to go on blaming himself?"

Chance just shrugged. "Maybe. It would be just like her. She always used to worry about him. I guess you'll never know for sure."

But Kate thought that maybe she would know . . . someday in the far distant future. The day she left her earthly body and made the journey home. When she joined friends and family who had gone before.

And she saw her grandmother again.